STORM FRONT

King of the Roses

Blood Lies

STORM FRONT

VIRGINIA ANDERSON

A PERFECT CRIME BOOK

DOUBLEDAY

New York London Toronto Sydney Auckland

A PERFECT CRIME BOOK

PUBLISHED BY DOUBLEDAY
a division of Bantam Doubleday Dell
Publishing Group, Inc.

DOUBLEDAY is a trademark of Doubleday,
a division of Bantam Doubleday Dell
Publishing Group, Inc.

Library of Congress Cataloging-in-Publication Data

Anderson, V. S.
Storm front / by Virginia Anderson.
p.   cm.
"A Perfect Crime book"—T.p. verso.
I. Title.
PS3551.N395S76   1992
813'.54—dc20   91-26781
CIP

ISBN 0-385-42232-6
Copyright © 1992 by Virginia Anderson
All Rights Reserved
Printed in the United States of America
February 1992

1   3   5   7   9   1   0   8   6   4   2

FIRST EDITION

For Betty Lou, who read all those words.

I would like to thank Special Agent Alan "Lee" Strope of the Florida Department of Law Enforcement for his generous technical assistance in the writing of this book.

A NOTE ON THE MAPS

Those familiar with south Florida will notice that I have taken some liberties with physical geography, in particular the liberty of building, demolishing, or renaming certain lesser-used roads where it seemed helpful in establishing a functional geography for my tale. Most major landmarks, however, I have left in place, and I hope that the topography of the landscape, both mental and physical, strikes a chord of recognition in anyone who has had the good fortune to go there and marvel, and the bad fortune to wonder if all we can do now is cry.

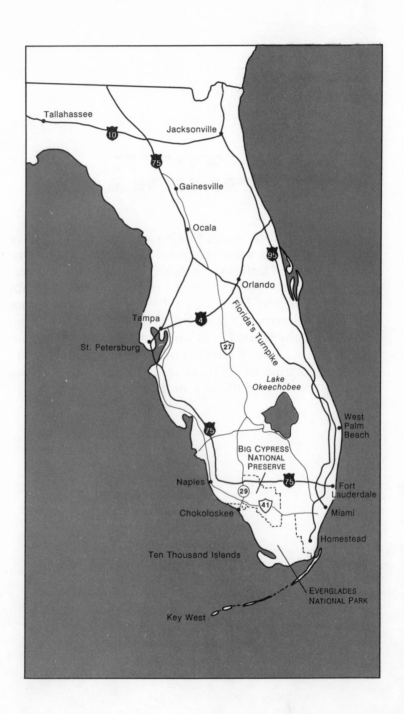

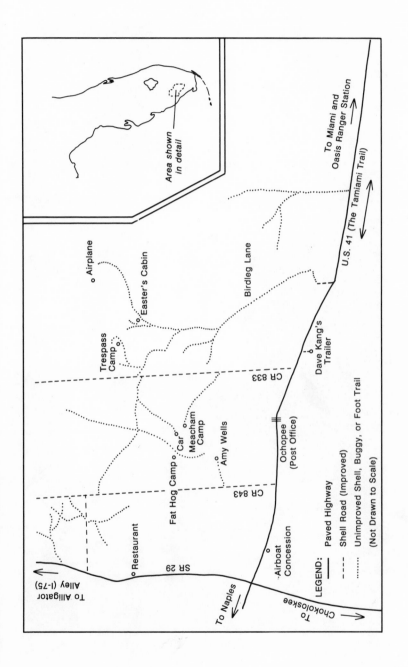

1

ON HIS BELT, A GUN: A 9MM BERETTA semiautomatic. A weapon for heroes or killers. He was neither. Against his heart, inside his limp suit coat, his ID: Special Agent Joe Hope, Florida Department of Law Enforcement. It wasn't enough. Nothing ever was.

He had just spent eight tedious hours getting nowhere. Now he was driving west, across Tampa Bay toward St. Petersburg, into a sultry falling-off-by-stages sunset, into the end of a long June day. Out there somewhere lay the ocean, beyond the strip malls and the subdivisions and the fortress line of condos. The air was so steeped in gasoline he could have set it off with a Bic lighter; cars piled up in the intersections like trash in a dammed stream.

He came upon the restaurant where the causeway from the mainland began, where the languid tides had packed mud up under the seawall. The restaurant had been built of weathered wood and rusted hardware, artfully tacked together to impersonate a crabbing shack. The kind of place, Terry Bessel insisted, where even the Florida grouper was flown in from Chicago in little frozen packs. At the rear, where the bay lapped up underneath it, the place smelled not like mud or seaweed, but like its dumpster. A brassy pair of gulls perched on the seawall, clacking their yellow beaks.

Joe pushed open the wood-framed screen door. The women clustered around the long plank table were all black, their translucent surgical gloves rolled into cuffs; they seemed to be hunkered together over some kind of medical experiment, their fingers ripping the embryonic slivers of shrimp bodies from their clear, thin shells. A big white man in an apron stood wielding a knife with a blade like an airplane wing. The lobsters, at least, didn't come in frozen; between the man's feet a liver-colored jumble of them squirmed in a crate. "Help you, bub?"

"I'm looking for Mrs. Sarah Gibbons."

The man tossed a lobster onto a board in front of him, whacked the knife down, and with a twist of his wrists snapped the shell open so the clean, still-twitching flesh extruded. The smallest of the women, never stopping the jerk and tear of her gloved hands, said, "I'm Sarah Gibbons. Who're you?"

It was then he saw the sleeping child curled around her shins in their tight, new-looking jeans. It was a little girl, as gracefully and improbably comfortable as a dozing cat. "*He* send you here?" the woman asked.

"You mean your husband?"

"Ain't got no husband," she said.

In his shirt pocket was the list of assignments Kaplan, the special agent supervisor of D-squad in Tampa, had given him that morning. Next to Sarah Gibbons's name the computer had smartly printed: *Informant states that he observed his common-law wife, Mrs. Sarah Gibbons, 115 14th Ave S., place of employment Cousin Andy's Seafood Shanty, with man who resembled suspect on evening of May 23rd departing House of Cards Lounge, 2203 W. 25th Street, St. Pete. Witness may be hostile.* She was staring stolidly now, still peeling. He got out his ID. Her hands slowed, then stopped. "What that son of a bitch say I did?"

He took out and unfolded a print of the crude police composite all the agents on Kaplan's special task force carried. "You know this man?"

One of the other women, still peeling, let out a yowl like a cat out night hunting. "Sarah, honey, you tell that bastard he just wish you couldn't catch no one better looking than that!"

"Get up," Mrs. Gibbons said suddenly, kicking with her foot. The girl sleeping against her shin wakened, jerking herself up her mother's leg. "Get up and go ask Miss Laura to give you a Coke. Go on." The child wandered off docilely, scratching her small, tight butt. Her mother snapped off the plastic gloves and circled the table. "You gonna talk to me, you talk outside."

Joe Hope followed her. She was thinner than the other women; the skin of her bare arms was a deep solid shining brown, and the rough wedge of her hair, burnt yellow at the ends, had been forked up in a bright orange comb. As they stepped out into the sunset, gulls condensed out of the streaked sky above them. The woman looked up at them as if their cries were obscenities, and wheeled. "You gonna arrest me? You got something that man said I did?"

"No one's going to arrest you unless there's a reason, Mrs. Gibbons. I just want to talk."

The gulls dived lower, and over Joe's head and over hers hung the whole shrieking troop of them, down-breasted and coal-eyed, quivering in the air currents like white shapes on a mobile, each cry a twisting stab of sound.

The woman advanced on Joe, a fist unconsciously clenched at him. "The fucker done got all my money! Now what's he want?"

"This man in the picture, did you ever—"

"Now my name's down, isn't it?" The lower lids of her dark eyes were rolled up over them, and he had a feeling that if he could have read what she was thinking, it would have come back in the night to trouble him.

"That's what he wanted; he didn't see me with nobody in no picture. He turned my name in, and now they got it. *They* gone be watching me!"

"Not unless you—"

"Motherfucker! You tell him I'll kill him!" She plunged forward in a frenzy of helplessness, squalling. "You tell him when he don't know it I'll be behind him! You—"

He wasn't sure where he thought she was going, but suddenly it seemed really important she not go there. He caught the fist she was shaking at him, and when she raised the other to fend him off he caught that, too. Suddenly she was in the lee of his body, and he was holding her wrists like the stems of two hard blooms he had gathered. She wasn't struggling, but he knew he had not contained her. "You're going to get in real bad trouble," he said.

"You don't know trouble. But before long, somebody will."

He let go. For a moment he thought the preying gulls would grab her, but they just increased their hectic chatter. She pulled her arms in against her chest like a flower closing up for the night.

"You hurt anybody, I will be back," he said.

He turned and walked away from her. From the front seat of the department car he was driving he picked up his clipboard. While she watched—though she couldn't have known what he was writing—he scrawled furiously, *Subject uncooperative. Denies any knowledge of suspect. Follow-up later if warranted.* He flung the clipboard back into the car hard so she could hear it clatter. Sarah Gibbons turned and went back inside, while the gulls bawled at being shut out.

THE CASE HAD BEEN LIKE AN OPTICAL trick. They had been staring right at it for months but hadn't noticed it. Now that they knew what to look for, it was obvious. It was like a prehistoric breastwork in a field: so enormous that from the middle of it you couldn't make it out at all.

Now it had a name and a location and a topography; now it was fourteen red pins on a map in the D-squad bay, following, as was at last abundantly clear, the gently kinked Atlanta-to-Tampa spine of Interstate 75. If you let yourself, you could imagine it as an underground presence that for the last two years—and maybe longer— had lain in its lair watching and waiting; each red pin marked an entrance to its burrow, a space in time and misfortune where a young woman, alone on the highway, had turned her back for just one second, just long enough for it to reach out of the ground and draw her in.

Throughout those two years, in the offices of the FBI, the statewide agency called the Florida Department of Law Enforcement, and the Georgia Bureau of Investigation, information had been obediently threading its way into the terminals of sophisticated computers. By an accident of organization, which a hapless intelligence analyst would soon find himself called upon to explain, the computers had ingested the information but had merely brooded it in their complicated innards, hatching nothing. No one had noticed the pattern; no one, as Special Agent Supervisor Kaplan of the Tampa Regional Operations Bureau had lambasted his hand-picked task force at its first meeting, had had sense enough to stick a few pins in a map. In the end it had been neither the convoluted electronic wizardry of the computer nor the professional perspicacity of trained and talented detectives that had tied those fourteen disappearances together. It had been pure chance.

It had been a dry spring. Winter had ended early; March had swept in right on the heels of January, ominously clear and cool. Lake levels dropped; starved rivers burrowed into the sandy bottoms of their channels; the sky continued a pitiless blue. Tourists and kids on spring break loved it; Fort Lauderdale reported the highest April arrest rate in its history as an adolescent mecca, and twice Disney World, overrun by seekers after its particular brand of rapture, had to hold lines of would-be paying customers at its gates. It was said that toward the end of May, Tampa residents could wade up the shrinking Hillsborough River and pluck fish out of the water, where they clustered by the dozens, fighting over the scant oxygen in the disappearing pools.

Other things were happening, not entirely unnoticed: the kinds of oddities you read with extra interest when you chanced across them in the paper, never dreaming they might one day reach out of the realm of the unlikely and take a bite of you.

Tampa, as had many cities before it, was growing like a fungus, sending out subdivisions ahead of its heart to pull its bulk along. To the east, for a hundred years, there had been only cattle range and grove land, a mosaic of low prairie and sand hill roamed by half-wild Brahmin cattle and armadillos and gopher turtles, bounded on the north by the Green Swamp, on the east by the Peace River, and on the west by the swelling gulf coast towns. But now the wide, flat plains of Hillsborough County had been reduced to helpless substrate for the concrete scourge. In its growth, Tampa was obsessed by water: whatever lakes, springs, swamps, or rivers it found in its path, it made haste to control and conscript. So in the walled community of Cloud Lake Acres, where David Berkman's parents, both lawyers, had bought themselves a three-bedroom, two-bath pool home advertised as "waterfront," people clustered on artificial sand banks bordering artificial channels; creek banks had been breached, spring runs diverted, so that into these channels every drop of available water for miles around could be artificially drained.

Young David, who was only eight, was for a brief and electrifying stretch of his life to become famous—not for anything he did, but, in fact, for his ignorance. He was to become famous, in effect, because he did not know, and his parents didn't know to warn him, not to ride his bike down to play in the newly dried-out streambed at the end of Needy Lane. Didn't know not to climb in the huge bowed oak tree beside old Mrs. Needy's deserted cabin. Didn't know to watch out for holes opening up in the ground.

He was to tell his story many times, swearing to his terror over and over but finally, in his excitement, forgetting what it had been like, nearly getting killed. Yes, he told his parents, the police, reporters, he had noticed how the sand seemed to be shrinking away from the grip of the old tree roots, but when he poked a stick down into the crumbling cavities, no snakes or monsters had rushed out at him, and he had lost interest. He had been more intrigued by a torn place in the roof of the old cabin, and he had climbed up in the oak, thinking no one would mind if he managed to peek in. What had he been looking for? He didn't know. Not dead bodies, no.

When the gaunt old tree began to shiver under him, raining leaves and acorns and scattering hidden birds skyward, he thought someone was playing a joke on him, though he admitted he couldn't imagine who could manage such a thing. Then the tree began to tilt and the sand to pour through its roots in a sibilant torrent, and the cabin to lean and crack and break up like a boat caught in a rapids, convincing David utterly that the end of the world had come. The tree limb he clung to carried him downward and sand and shattered brick showered around him and there had been groaning and thundering as loud and gross as ghosts would have made dying, and suddenly he was being sucked down, down, until the blue sky seemed to be traveling forever out of his reach.

It had been cold, the boy said, in the throat of the vortex; it had smelled wet, and he had been sure he would be smothered or carried away by an underground river and drowned. As well he might have, had the tree not relented and saved him, bridging the widening pit at last with its broken branches; a last shiver of sand had sighed down from the surface and the splintered cabin walls had settled and the tree had moaned one last time and stopped shaking, and little David, scratched and whimpering, had poked his head out of the leaves timidly like an abandoned hatchling, desperately struggling to work his half-buried body free. The sun had been blinding, he had insisted, and his eyes had been full of tears. No! He hadn't been crying! There had been sand in them, and the more he wiped them the more he ground the grit in. So he had been halfway up the steep slope in his panicked scramble for safety before he began to notice the queer feel of the soil under him, before he pushed up on hands and knees and looked about him, before he discovered that he had been clawing his way blindly through a rattling gray scree of human skulls and bones.

If you pick up a shell on the beach and find that it is home to a sea creature, and you want to expunge all trace of life from your treasure so that it will not stink later, do this with it: bury it in dry sand. Unseen and indifferent, the ants will work for you, and soon you can reclaim your clean, eviscerated, calcium prize.

Thus it had happened with the buried bodies eight-year-old David Berkman discovered. The unknown monster who came to be called the Sinkhole Killer had surrendered his victims to the ants and the sand. Now, in the Tallahassee office of the Florida Department of Law Enforcement's Division of Criminal Investigation, there were fourteen photographs, of fourteen dry gray clusters, reassembled and laid out like anonymous archaeological finds. It is often a surprise to visitors to learn that the bones of homicide victims are catalogued according to markings stroked on with ordinary nail polish; on the May weekend of the Sinkhole findings the color at hand had been a deep red called Heartstorm, by Maybelline. The arm and leg fragments had been arranged end to end, as if, Joe had thought on seeing them, they might grow back together; the jawbones with their telltale fillings had been photographed spread open so the numbered points of identification could be seen. Joe knew about the numbered crowns and fillings; still, he had found himself thinking, on thumbing through the pictures on one of his routine pilgrimages to Tallahassee, that surely all the jaws were cocked open because they had been found open; all the women, it seemed to him, must surely have died screaming their lungs out, and now they shared in this chorus of silent, tuneless cries.

In Joe's drawer, in his corner of the squad bay in Tampa, and in the desks and filing cabinets and dossiers

of state agents and policemen and deputies throughout
Georgia and Florida, there was another collection of photographs, a collection that was supposed to stir something besides clinical interest: the photos of the victims'
faces, testaments to their unblemished youth, their flaw-
less smiles. But try as he might, Joe could not help finding his examination of his set of those pictures a little
like idling through someone else's college yearbook.
Even after he had interviewed people who could stroke
memories on over the faces, he still had the feeling that
the same girl—cheerful, bright, warm, loving—had died
the same unfathomable death fourteen times.

He kept the fourteen photographs in a manilla folder
and had used up his need to look at them. Rick Portman,
however, tacked his set up on a corkboard on the wall in
his corner of the squad bay, each girl's name and home-
town and date of disappearance hand-lettered on the
white border alongside her smile. One lunch hour when
no one was around, Hube Habin, who was the case agent
for the sinkhole killings, had sidled over and pried loose
the pictures, mistakenly thinking, he told Joe, that he
might find each girl's measurements from the bios
logged on the backs of the images. It was the sort of in-
discretion Hube very much hoped to catch Portman in,
though so far he had failed.

To the other five of them on the special squad, giving
Portman any part at all of the Tampa D-squad bay had
come to seem like a deliberate rake of nails across chalk-
board. Portman really belonged to the Lakeland squad
and was nominally into local narcotics investigation.
Special Agent Supervisor Kaplan, charged with opening
up the sinkhole case out of the Tampa Regional Operations Bureau, had commandeered him, planting him
among them like an unwelcome changeling. "We're the
heart of a team," Kaplan had said, "and I want us together, wrapped in the same muscle, breathing to the
same beat." After their first week together, Natalie
Pranthoff observed that any heart with Portman in it

would have valve trouble. Maybe that was it—that lack of flow to the center—maybe that was what had kept the six of them, Portman and the pick of D-squad, from doing anything but scratching up bad tips and other people's heartaches, from gathering anything more substantial than a seineful of sand.

BUT NATALIE, TOO, KEPT HER SET OF
the girls' pictures close at hand. That Friday morning, as
the six agents on the task force gathered upstairs in the
undistinguished little building on Fifty-sixth Street in
north Tampa for that unusually early meeting, Joe came
upon Natalie warming herself over a Styrofoam cup of
black coffee, going through the images as carefully as if
they had been illuminated leaves in a very old, frail book.
She looked up, yellow earrings the size of catamaran
sails bobbing. "Jeez, Joe, I thought it was that dick
Portman. Not that he ever walked into a room with his
mouth shut in his life."

He poured himself coffee, coming over to let the steam
from the two cups mingle. "What are you doing, counting
their teeth?"

"No, that's on file in the computer already. Their
freckles. Their eyelashes." Her own eyelashes, as always,
were hard and black and separate, so that her big dark
eyes seemed to be rimmed with a little row of claws.
"Hube told me about Stacey, Joe. I'm sorry."

He didn't say anything. After a minute he wiggled his
finger for her coffee cup and took it over and refilled it.

She breathed on it, sucking in the heat before drinking. "You're not hung over, are you?"

"So he told you about that, too?"

"No harm intended." Natalie was far from soft-hearted, but she often gave off a kind of flinty empathy that was absurdly convincing. "You don't look *too* bad. Maybe Kaplan won't notice. By the way, is he pissed over something? I mean, what are we doing here at fucking seven o'clock?"

Normally each agent dropped in around nine, checking in with Kaplan to unload the previous day's failures and submit to a new burden of improbability. But now daylight was just edging in at the windows; outside in the still, hot morning, the U.S. and Florida flags, newly hoisted, flapped drowsily against their pole. "Isn't that when they shoot people? At dawn?"

"I have a feeling you may be right. You realize it's been a month? And none of us has done a damn thing?"

Terry Bessel and Juan Pressa came in. Terry was so black it was sometimes hard to make out his features, but you couldn't miss his smiles. He was fiddling nervously with the cuffs of his favorite suit, the old-fashioned suit like the ones Howard Rollins wore in *Ragtime*. Juan, too, always dressed carefully, but in bright colors and skewed folds that halfway did justice to his rich curly hair and quick gypsy eyes. Terry had caught Natalie's remark. "None of us been *let* to do anything."

"You guys didn't hear the grapevine?" Juan asked cheerfully. He drank Cuban coffee, and brought it himself.

"You don't *hear* a grapevine," Natalie corrected.

"Well, I heard this one. Heard it rattle."

"That was the damn snake under it," Terry rumbled, holding his cup far away so he wouldn't stain the suit if he spilled it.

"Kaplan's been trying to get kicked upstairs. To assistant director of executive investigations. He's driving upstate to meet Win Haggertie at noon."

"Shit." Terry grimaced. "Kaplan, with his temper, in fucking internal affairs?"

"At least he'd have to move to Tallahassee," Natalie said.

Hube came in, toting what was left of a box of doughnuts. He counted, shaking his square gray head. "Only five left. Too bad. None for Portman."

Natalie scored the biggest, biting down happily into the cream-filled center. "Portman won't want one anyway. He only eats things that make your turds hard. He told me so himself."

Joe took a jelly doughnut, though he wasn't sure he could stomach it. The purple jelly dripped on his shirt cuff. "Go rinse it," said Natalie, "so it doesn't stain."

So he was in the washroom running cold water over the smear when Rick Portman came in, carrying, as always, an armload of papers, although whatever was in them he seldom shared. Portman stowed the papers on the metal shelf but saw Joe and stopped midway to the urinal, leaning against the wall with his arms crossed. He was younger than the rest of them and wore his hair brushed straight up in stiff bristles; Hube said he looked like a bottle brush. "Oh, you still work here, Hope?"

Joe straightened. The spikes of Portman's hair looked particularly stiff and dangerous this morning, like sea urchin spines. "Is that supposed to mean something?"

"I guess not, if you don't know already."

"So how early did you have to get up this morning to have your private conference with Kaplan?"

"I didn't have any private conference. Anybody could have talked to him."

"Yes," said Joe, drying his hands. "But no one else did."

He started out the door, letting it swing, but Portman caught it. "Sorry I tried to do you a goddamn favor."

"So do it."

"Well, if I were you, Hope, this is one morning I'd try to look alert for a change."

He was conscious of Portman following him back to the meeting room. Conscious, too, that there was something Portman wanted him to be afraid of. Portman often tried to unsettle him before meetings by bluffing: everyone, especially Portman, knew that for years Kaplan had craved an excuse to dump Joe. He had been thwarted by Joe's friends, and Joe's reputation. And by the fact that what Joe was afraid of couldn't fire him. Probably couldn't even kill him. What Joe was afraid of already had hold of him and knew how to take its cut of him in other ways.

Kaplan had just arrived for the meeting when he and Portman entered. Their boss went straight to the window and snapped the blinds shut. Portman, without being told, clicked on the fluorescents. Time in the cluttered room seemed to have been turned backward, to a darker, colder hour of the dawn.

On the surface, there was not much to Norman Kaplan. From the yellow pie of his face and his puffy round belly to his tiny feet that turned out when he walked, he reminded Joe of an unwashed penguin. Yet over the years many of the people who had worked for Kaplan had feared him. Now he waddled comically to the end of the table, the pin-riddled Florida map behind him, and bent forward, his palms down on the polished surface, the square black mat of his mustache quivering. And suddenly, irrationally obedient, his agents fell silent and slid hurriedly into their waiting chairs.

Portman, as always, asserted his status by letting his avalanche of papers sprawl across the narrow table into everyone else's space. Then he put his feet up and yawned. As always, Juan and Natalie, on either side of him, restacked his debris on his side of the imaginary boundary he had crossed. He did not notice. Today he was looking at Joe. Ordinarily Joe's confrontations with Portman were as surreptitious as everyone else's, but today he could almost feel Portman straining against the bounds of his better judgment. Deliberately, Joe took out a sheet of scratch paper and began to doodle. He drew, as he often did, a sailboat. Slowly it became one of his best sailboats, striking off over the horizon, its sail so bold and full you could almost see the carrying wind.

"What a team," Kaplan said.

Natalie sucked her breath in softly. Hube, on Joe's left, drew his feet under him. Joe drew a man on the sailboat, but of course the boat was too far away for the man to have any features. Kaplan went on grimly. "I'd have done better with a bunch of Girl Scouts," he said.

Terry Bessel cleared his throat; the shadow line of his tough beard darkened. "I admit," he said with slow dignity, folding his muscled arms and staring back at his boss stolidly, "that we haven't come up with much. But if you ask me, this is one of those cases where we're not going to. Whoever this guy is, he's no boozed-up bum. He's slick and he's smart."

"So what are you suggesting?" Kaplan challenged him nastily. He often used his nastiness as a ploy, but today it seemed bitter, personal. "That this *exclusive*, hand-picked team of world-class agents sit around with its thumb up its ass until the guy gets religion and turns himself in?"

Hube took out his glasses. Hube seldom got really riled, but when he did, out came those glasses, the slow ritual of polishing them deliberate and intense.

"We're not exactly getting much support from the department," he said. "They lump us together and throw us at it, and tell the papers they've done something. Weren't we supposed to get some psychological profiles? What happened to those?"

"Psychological profiles?" Kaplan snorted. "I trashed them. They said they had to know whether he raped them before he killed them or after. They say you can't tell things like that from bones."

Portman suddenly took his feet off his desk and pivoted, knocking against Natalie's chair. "Gee, boss," he yelped in his squeeze-toy tenor, "I don't think you're being a hundred percent fair to the guys. They're working hard. They're not perfect." Natalie hitched herself out from under him. Unaware of her, Portman snatched a photocopy of the rough police composite from his stack of papers and skimmed it onto the table. "Personally, I think we've all been doing a bang-up job on this!"

The sketch landed by Terry Bessel's elbow. He wrinkled his nose distastefully, as if not certain Portman's Pet, as he called the sketch in private, was housebroken. "Sure," said Terry. "Too bad it hasn't done us any good."

"But it's a lead, isn't it?" Portman looked around for confirmation. "I mean, what else have we got?"

"Fine," Terry retorted. "You spotted the file and you went up and interviewed her. Congratulations. But you led her like a prosecuting attorney. By the time you got done she didn't know what had happened. She was yes-siring everything you said."

"Besides," interjected Hube, "we've had other leads. But we've dropped them cold for this sketch. All we've had time to do is check out these five hundred and something half-baked tips we've gotten in the week since the papers ran it." He tried the glasses, grimaced, but left them. "Speaking for myself, I hope you guys don't expect anything for Christmas, because at this rate I'll still be too busy knocking on doors to shop."

Portman suddenly scooped up the composite and tore it into four pieces. He dropped them back onto his pile, winding his arms across his chest in hurt splendor. "Okay. So forget it. Pretend we don't have it. I'm for anything everybody else is."

"Nobody said anything about forgetting it," said Hube patiently.

"So somebody suggest *something.*" Portman waved his hands in a gesture of concession. "Anything anybody else can come up with is terrific. Hey, Joe! You're the idea man. What about you?"

There was a tiny eruption of silence. Even Kaplan, who had been listening with grim expectation as his agents wrangled, seemed to let his breath out, as if somewhere in the distance he had heard a snare snap. But before he could do more than tilt his head toward Joe, Natalie jumped into the gap, brandishing one of the thin brown cigarettes she was always trying to stop smoking. "Excuse me, boys, but for the fourth time in two weeks, *I* will make a suggestion—that somebody get in a car and drive to Macon, Georgia, and explain the facts of life to some local yokels and extradite that newspaper with that note."

"But, Natalie!" admonished Portman tolerantly. "Talk about a gamble! So far it's pure guesswork that that scribbling on that paper has anything to do with our man!"

In their files they all had a picture of the newspaper. The Drummond girl's car had not been found, as the other girls' cars had, in the interstate rest area from which she had presumably been abducted. It had been found abandoned down a dirt lane off a middle Georgia exit. The newspaper, with its cryptic scratching in the margin, had been found shoved under the front seat, the only clue of any sort any of the girls' cars had given up. The Georgia Bureau of Investigation, which had been granted the sole right of inspection, had expressed the guarded judgment that the note had been written in the Drummond girl's hand.

For the FDLE team, getting a look at the note itself had shown signs of becoming a sort of crusade, not, Joe thought, because any of them really hoped to see something the GBI had missed, but because otherwise there wasn't much else to do but what they had been doing, knocking on doors.

Grudgingly, Terry opened his manilla envelope on the case and took out his photo. Hube looked over at it while Joe drew a sea gull. Joe had memorized the photo: The Atlanta morning paper, bought from a box, crumpled from being wadded under the seat. *If* she had written the note at all, clearly she had written desperately, perhaps even with her hands bound, with a felt-tip marker that skipped and bled on the page. There was a number: *1124.* A shaky hieroglyph some said was *B-a-r-m,* others *B-a-l-m.* A blotch after the *B* that could have been either a period or a slip of the marker. And an angular, one-legged something the GBI claimed was a capital *A.* Hube snorted grumpily, his sentiments self-evident. Fourteen counties, two state crime labs: this.

There was the factor, though it still seemed to be meaningless, that southeast of Tampa there was a cross-roads hamlet called Balm. Terry Bessel said what he had not been called to this meeting to say, because he had already said it, with emphasis, half a dozen times. "Look, once and for all, the Drummond girl wasn't setting up an appointment with anybody in Balm because nobody in Balm has the faintest idea who she was."

"Nobody in Balm *admits* knowing her," said Natalie. The cigarettes always made Joe think of stick candy.

"Terry's right," said Portman, swinging around on her. "You've been prowling around down there so long your questions are about to need carbon dating. He didn't give her his address in Balm because he wanted to try and have a real relationship with her and only de-cided to murder her afterwards. Balm or Barm is the name of some place she was going to buy herself a collie pup—" He sat forward suddenly. "In fact, that's one hell of an idea." He flipped open a pad and made himself an expansive note. "I'm going to get the want-ad section out of that paper and start checking the ads and see if any of them—pets, used dishwashers, houses, what have you—was filed by somebody who's named or who lives on an Atlanta street named Balm or Barm."

"Great." Natalie sighed. "Then what will we know? One more thing the guy isn't or didn't. What we need are the answers to 'is' and 'did.' "

Joe had started drawing the sun behind the sailboat. But it had looked strange, the big empty circle hanging in the sky. So he fenced it off from the sailboat and began hatching it, giving it contour. It began to look like Kaplan's body, so he turned it into an apple. He sketched a stem, but that looked like Kaplan's stiff little neck with his bald torpedo head set on it, so Joe hastily started a glassy highlight.

He felt Portman shift, and looked up at him. Portman had pushed out of his chair, ostensibly to corral more wayward papers, and had paused, twisting to look down at Joe's drawing. "Gee, Joe, no wonder you're so quiet," he said with a light chuckle. "But aren't you a little old for cartoons?"

The storm of emphatic voices died out like gusts in hurricane weather. For an instant Kaplan stood rigidly at the head of the table. When he moved, he moved slowly, almost strolling, as if what he had captured could not get away. It seemed a long, sad time before his shadow fell over Joe's shoulder. He positioned the paper with his fingertips, contorting his round body to study it. Then suddenly he crumpled the sheet, wheeling around on his small feet like a top and slamming the wadded paper across the room toward a wastebasket in the corner, where the paper bounced off the wall and dropped neatly through the basket rim.

Then he tipped forward and brought his fist down on the table by Joe's elbow. It whapped rather than banged, but everyone stiffened anyway. "Hand picked! Crack agents! A half hour I've been sitting here listening to you argue, and what have you accomplished? Not a thing! Next time I want a case solved I'll hire a bunch of Ybor City faggots. At least then I'll get some gossip. I'd just as soon read the *National Enquirer* as listen to the six of you!"

No one spoke. Kaplan shoved himself upright and cut his eyes at Hube. Hube caught a sigh midway out and sorted a handful of papers from the collection before him. He leaned across the table, dealing out the lists to the silent agents. Nobody picked the sheets up. Before Joe's list settled, Kaplan grabbed it, and when he straightened, he held Joe in the chair, weighting his shoulder with a damp hand.

"Crack agents," he repeated. "Especially Hope here, our bureau genius. Personally, I think it's time to say *fuck* genius. Maybe we need some old-fashioned police work for a change."

Suddenly Natalie picked up her sheet, using the sharp points of her nails. "Eight names," she said. "Could be worse. Maybe for once I'll get lucky."

Juan, too, whipped up his list. Then Terry, less obligingly.

"Get on out of here, all of you," said Kaplan. His voice had lost its abrasive timbre, but when Joe, too, moved, the hand that held him tightened. "I don't care what you bring me. Just for God's sake, bring me something!" He jerked his solid head one last time. "Go on."

So they all went, all but Joe, slowly. Portman went last, pausing at the door, but Kaplan just glared. When he and Joe were alone, Kaplan made his way to the window. He jerked the blinds open. The sun, climbing fast, hung watchfully in the blue rectangle of sky.

"For twenty years people have been telling me you had talent, Hope," said Kaplan, "but I didn't know it was caricature they meant."

Joe drew his feet back to get up, but Kaplan didn't see him. He was talking up to the sun, diddling his fingers behind him. "Let me tell you a little story," he said.

"I think I know it."

"But you haven't heard it from my side. And you probably haven't heard *quite* all of it." He turned back, solicitous now. "So don't be in such a hurry, Joe."

Joe let himself back down in the chair. He could see, among the stacked papers Kaplan had left on the table, a dense memo that ended with Portman's pinched signature. He couldn't quite read it, or tell if Portman had dared list names.

Kaplan was proceeding grimly, knuckles on the table. "Once upon a time in Jacksonville, there were two cops who got on each other's nerves. One was a captain and one was a sergeant. And when the sergeant transferred to the FDLE and got assigned to the Tampa bureau, all of a sudden the captain followed him." His grating voice tensed. "Some people say it was on purpose, but they don't know what they're talking about. They're nuts."

"So get to the part I don't know," Joe said.

Kaplan threw his head back theatrically. "Two cops. One of them thought he was God, and the other one knew he wasn't. One of them flopped around on his butt and acted bored and drew pictures in briefings, and the other one paid attention and took notes and made sure all the shit got done. One of them drove around all day and played Sonny Crockett, and the other one stayed up late and did paperwork. Only one of them was lucky. The other one wasn't. And one of them had a friend who was a goddamn newspaper reporter." Again his voice thickened, old, bitter hurt coming out sarcastic. " 'The Cop with ESP.' " Suddenly, from deep in the sheaf of papers before him, he pulled out a folded newspaper, that morning's *Miami Herald*. He spun it down the table. "I intended to give you the benefit of the doubt about this. I assume you didn't know."

The paper flumped to the floor so that Joe had to bend over to pick it up. He skimmed the front page article silently, then skidded the paper back to Kaplan. "No. I didn't know."

Kaplan picked up the paper and read. " 'Will FDLE fetters stop the ex-Wunderkind of Jacksonville from solving the Sinkhole Case?' " The paper smacking down on the table made a much more satisfactory noise than Kaplan's fist had. "You all know I'm in line for promotion. I was going up to Tallahassee today to see Win Haggertie and discuss it. What do I tell him when he asks how I've *fettered* you, Hope?"

Joe thought, not for the first time, that sunlight as dense as that outside ought to make a noise falling. Once in a while he had thought he could hear it, but it had always turned out to be the wind or a distant plane engine humming. Now it was the air-conditioning, wrenching into a new gear somewhere deep in the workings of the building, a grinding, ill-tuned sound.

"You can tell them," he said, surrendering each fatal word slowly, "how you've stuck all six of us for a solid week on that damn composite of Portman's. How you've shot down every idea anyone else has offered."

"No," said Kaplan mildly, "Portman doesn't like you, either."

Joe started to stand up, thought about it, did it anyway. "Portman's not the problem. You are. You're sold on Portman's idea just because it's Portman's. Because you know whatever he comes up with, you'll get the credit. In the meantime, you've wasted what little talent I do have —and the good bit some of the others have—sending us day in and day out to do mental blow jobs on paranoid glory seekers who wouldn't know Jesus Christ himself if he stepped out of the picture on the wall."

He did not know Kaplan as well as he thought he did. All Kaplan did was pivot slowly and frown at the window, as if the scene beyond—the sunshine, the flapping flags, the Fifty-sixth Street traffic—was some kind of blemish the cleaning crew should have wiped away. "You know, Joe," Kaplan said, still not turning back, "I really think this time I can get you fired."

No, there had never really been any chance of compromise. Too many years, too many not quite finished confrontations. "And you can get it past Win Haggertie and the state attorney?"

"But, Joe!" said Kaplan, wheeling, almost whispering. "Win Haggertie's worried sick about you! That mess in Lakeland! Two reprimands in six months! He thinks you're cracking up!"

He made a little lunge from the waist, then smiled to himself as if Joe had flinched when Joe was sure he hadn't.

"So, yes, Joe, when I get to Tallahassee, your future

might just come up for discussion. Maybe this time I'll win."

Joe did not confess that the only thing running through his head was the conviction that Kaplan had somehow grown shorter, the only thing stirring in him a sad and wordless sense that it wouldn't matter if Kaplan fired him, that nothing would change, in him or in Kaplan either. Kaplan had dropped the list of the day's assignments Hube had dealt Joe back on the table. Joe turned it toward him. After a minute, he picked it up.

But his boss had turned away again.

"Survival," he murmured. "A decent retirement. You know, I don't have any grandchildren. Most people have grandchildren."

Yes, Joe was thinking, definitely shorter. Maybe it was happening to him, too. Maybe as you grew older, your body became victim to a weeding out of molecules, so you collapsed inward, and maybe those molecules in leaching out took something with them. Joe pocketed the sheet. "I'm not lucky," he said. "I don't call it being lucky."

"No?" Kaplan responded dully. "Genius? Don't shit me."

"People make their luck," Joe said.

Kaplan looked around. The only expression on his face was annoyance, as if he had been about to doze off standing.

"Yeah, that's your list of names for today," he said indifferently. "Now get out of here. I'm tired."

4

SOMETIMES THEY WENT TO LESS PRE-
tentious places than Club Sydney, but Friday nights
there was a seafood buffet. For the cost of the cover, you
could pile a plate with snow crab legs and rub hips, as
Hube liked to do, with all the twenty-one-year-olds who
had just gotten off work from the mall. The roar of unre-
strained, mostly young, slightly drunken voices was part
of the bargain. Hube was ten years older than Joe, gray-
headed, divorced, built like a jar of pickles. He was com-
monsensical, efficient and, unlike Kaplan, could even
move fast enough on occasion to run a suspect down. He
was there at Sydney's first, waiting for the others, having
dispensed with his list of interviews with his usual brisk
and decisive calm. He had also been cultivating a grudge
since Joe had told him about the talk with Kaplan that
morning. "Goddamn him, Joe. I'm the case agent. If he's
finally decided he's got to hang you after all these years,
he should have let me know."

Joe had stacked his plate because he didn't want to
start drinking. Last night had been enough to hold him
for a lifetime. "What would you have done about it if he
had warned you?"

"Told you to act more like Portman until things blew over."

"Somebody showed him Zack's article in the Miami paper."

"Great!" Hube chased his boiled shrimp with a slug from his Heineken. "The last thing we need is old sores open. Call that dippy friend of yours and tell him hands off."

"Zack's harmless."

"He would be if somebody threw him down a hole somewhere."

Terry, materializing out of the crowd, which, as usual, responded to his size and presence by making way for him, overheard Joe. "Maybe if people like Zack would quit reminding him, Kaplan would forget about what you did to him back in Jax."

Hube contemplated some girls who had fought their way through the labyrinth of people but couldn't find a vacant table. They looked sixteen, though at the door they must have been carded. Two of them snuck speculative glances at Joe.

"Don't do it, Habin," Terry warned. "My wife will find out and see the judge for certain." A pair of young men who looked like lawyers but probably sold TVs at Sears waved the girls over, and Hube sat back, resigned. Terry returned to their perennial grouse, Kaplan. "Not that he didn't deserve anything you handed him. From what I hear, he was doing the same thing he's doing now. He gets tired of being a desk jockey and he wants some credit for something. So he takes off on a tangent like that damn picture."

"As desk jockeys go, he's good," reasoned Hube. "And Tallahassee knows it."

"But he wants articles about him in the paper. He wants to be Joe."

"Who wants to be Joe?" said Natalie, coming up and looking around for a vacant chair she could steal. "What a fool!"

"Win Haggertie won't pay him any attention," said Terry. "Win'll just do what he should have done in the first place, transfer Joe down to Miami to work for Orren." He stole one of Joe's shrimp. "You and Orren always got along."

Natalie commandeered a chair and expertly caught the eye of a waitress. "My theory is that Kaplan figures the only reason he hasn't gotten the promotions he thinks he has coming is because the state attorney is still down on him for that mess in Jax."

"You would be, too," said Terry, "if it had been your little daughter."

"But now," said Natalie unsympathetically, "he wants this promotion or else. He's got to discredit Joe."

"The worst thing," mused Terry, still reliving the sensational fifteen-year-old case which none of them but Joe had been involved in but which they all knew all about, "would have been knowing that if Kaplan had listened to Joe instead of stonewalling him, the kid would probably still have been alive when they found her. That a couple of hours could make that much difference."

"Will you please change the fucking subject?" Joe said.

The waitress finally appeared and Hube took her hand. "How's the cop business?" she asked him.

"For the tenth time, we're not cops," said Hube. "We are to cops as the director of NASA is to mechanics."

Natalie snorted. She was fixing her lipstick.

"I hear your field is libation," interrupted Terry. "What do you know about beer?"

"How to pour it and how to drink it," said the waitress.

"An expert," muttered Natalie.

"You pour a Bud, then," said Terry. "I need practice drinking."

"I want white wine," said Natalie. "But bring a couple of twists on the side."

Joe got up to go back to the buffet and found Hube shadowing him. "Joe," said Hube, "he *could* get you this time."

"He hasn't made any progress on this case," said Joe. "Mostly because he's spent so much time trying to make sure it looks like Portman who solves it."

"I just wish you acted like you cared a little."

"I do care."

"What did you break up with Stacey about?"

Joe turned away and began putting food on his plate, a great deal more than he really thought he would eat.

"I am the case agent," Hube reminded him. "It is my business."

"Not if I do my job."

"Well, if you want to do it on this case, I'd better not find you with any more half-empty Jack Daniel's bottles between your knees at six in the morning."

"She wanted to get married," Joe said wearily.

"I thought you were planning to."

"I wasn't that certain."

Hube's flat, square face grew earnest. "I'm just telling you—I need you. I want you to stay on board."

There was so much food on Joe's plate, it was starting to slide off onto the floor. He started to turn back to the table, but Hube stopped him. "Suppose you were in charge, Joe? What would you do?"

For one thing, he thought, he would not let the damn case hound him like this. It was hounding Hube, too. Hube looked as if what he needed most was a fast game of tennis. "Hube, I'm as dry as everybody else. Probably drier."

"But why not the composite? We dislike it that much, we ought to have a reason."

People were having a hard time getting past them, getting up to the steam table. "I told Kaplan what I thought two weeks ago when he first planned on running the sketch in the paper. Our guy seems to have a fairly rigid pattern. A regular timetable. Maybe he works by lunar cycles or something. Whoever abducted that girl Portman interviewed is probably a public menace, and if we catch him we'll be doing a service. But the MO is wrong, the timing is wrong. I'd give a hundred to one he's not our guy."

"So we ditch the composite and what do we do then? Consult a medium?"

"Juan had a good idea." Joe raised the plate overhead so a young couple could thread between the two of them. "In fact, it was good enough Kaplan promptly squelched it."

"More advertising in the paper," said Hube glumly.

"In the paper, on TV, anyway we can get people to listen. True, we don't know how many women this guy has killed, and we don't know how many different tricks he used to get close enough to grab them. But we do know that he killed at least fourteen women, and out of those fourteen, nine were driving cars with hoods that could be opened from the outside. Juan thought that meant something, and so do I."

Hube's gray eyes narrowed. When Juan had first proposed the alternative, Hube had gone along with Kaplan, seduced by Portman's composite, thinking it a better gamble. Since then he, like Joe, had had plenty of chance to replay Juan's imaginary scenario: the lone woman stopping at an interstate rest area to use the bathroom; the stranger whose face they could only vaguely envision creeping out of the darkness while she was inside, doing something to her car to disable it; the stranger's offer of help; the woman turning unsuspecting to thank him. . . . And time to think, as Juan had asked them to do, about the times when the plot failed, when the killer got cold feet, or when someone came along and interrupted. And now, somewhere, there might be a woman who had not sensed the touch of death when it brushed her, had shared smiles with the Sinkhole Killer, and who carried an image of his face in her head.

But Hube only frowned. "Kaplan won't give up on that composite."

"I didn't say he had to."

"If we split up like that, we would need more agents. Six wouldn't do it."

"Kaplan is too stubborn," said Joe impatiently. "You're too damn careful. I'm going back to the table."

Hube followed him grumpily. Before they reached the others, he said, "Maybe some other people around here ought to be careful, too."

Juan had finally arrived and was using Natalie's mirror to comb his hair. Terry was recounting one of his day's adventures. "The guy is fifty-five years old, twenty years in an accounting firm up north, and then, boom, he decides he's got to come down here and train racehorses. So before I set eyes on him I know he's a squirrel."

"Would you say that about me if I quit the department to be a rock star?" Juan asked.

"I'll say worse if I find a damn hair in my food," Natalie told him.

"So the guy is hot for this young chick," Terry continued. "Then she runs off to the Everglades with this photographer. The trainer's so burned he can't see straight. Now he's decided the photographer's the guy in the sketch!"

"Any corroboration?" Hube asked seriously.

"Oh, his wife met the guy, too," Terry said. "But I couldn't interview her. Oh, no. *She* might get worried."

"You mean," put in Juan, "she'd look him right in the eye and tell him he was blowing it out his ass."

"Well, I had a guy answer the door naked," said Natalie.

"He saw you coming," said Terry.

"To tell the truth, he wasn't that bad. Except he didn't even remember calling in on the damn composite. You working tomorrow, Terry?"

"Is anybody at this table *not* working tomorrow?" scowled Terry. *"And* Sunday?"

"Sundays forever," retorted Natalie bitterly. "Well, you guys better have it wrapped up by August, because I *am* going to Bermuda. Are you really leaving all that food, Joe? Pass me his plate, Juan."

The eyes of the four agents followed Joe, who was tall enough that he towered over the heads of the milling people.

"He just wants to get it over with," judged Natalie with brittle sympathy.

"Get what over with?" Juan stole a mussel from the plate as he passed it.

"Going home, you dope."

THE CONDO, HE HAD BEEN TOLD WHEN
he bought it, "made good use of the light." Now he knew
the salesman had been referring to the flat illumination
radiating down into the great room from the upstairs
skylights. Stacey had claimed the diffuse anemic glow
was ideal for ferns and philodendrons. But during the
day while he was out running Kaplan's inane errands,
she had come in and carried all the plants away.

Now he found himself facing an immense wintry wall
like the face of an iceberg, rising out of the steel-blue
carpet where her eighteenth-century Spanish chest had
stood. He bent to pick up a few sad brown leaves that
littered the carpet like the shriveled spawn of a ship-
wreck, and for an unreasonable moment felt a kick
of anger, as if thinking to himself that she should not
have left this trash behind her; she should have taken
it, too.

But when he went into the kitchen to throw the leaves
away, he saw that she had cleaned up the dishes they
had left standing when they had started arguing; she
had thrown away the liquor bottle; everything gleamed
from her attention. There was even a new plastic liner in

the trash can. And on the counter, like a little crafted talisman from one wanderer to another, her key.

For a moment he made the mistake of wondering how she had felt as she worked here, but both images made him flinch in his stomach: the image of her struggling in tears through every action, or that of her moving briskly, hateful and cold.

Upstairs he saw that she had been scrupulous. She had taken nothing she had not brought with her, or that she had not bought in the interim with her own money. He sat down on the waterbed he had agreed on because she wanted one, amazed at the bareness, and thought, *And I didn't even love her.* He had simply not realized, until he saw it uncovered like this, how little he had.

He changed into jogging shorts and a torn T-shirt and hurried back downstairs. He had not locked the door because he planned to go right out again, but as he realized who sat in the lush bare carpet with his back propped against the wall, he decided he damn well should have. The greasy little figure in the ancient army fatigues and dingy sneakers was trying to position a tiny pinch of marijuana roach in the thin jaws of a surgical clamp, and barely glanced up as Joe reared over him sternly. "I wish to hell you wouldn't smoke that in here."

But the greasy figure only grinned from under a black felt beret that looked as if it had been fished out of a car wreck; the brown unkempt hair that always made Joe think of a nest of pine needles had been twisted into a stringy braided tail. "Joe the Boy Scout."

"No, Zack. Joe the suburbanite who has neighbors."

"Yeah, I see." Zack peered around appreciatively. "For an ex-street cop, very nice." He worked his butt down into the rich nap of the carpet. "Except that when I heard you had a condo, I expected, like, furniture. What happened? One half of a duo split?"

Zack looked like a forlorn plant Stacey had decided

not to take with her. The trouble was, in the nearly twenty years they had known each other, Joe had always talked to Zack, maybe in the same spirit people sometimes talk to pets. It was hard to believe that something that looked like leaf mold would talk back or humiliate you. But the trouble also was, when you talked about things, especially to Zack, they had a way of becoming a lot more real. "You've got a hell of a nerve. Breaking into people's homes and asking personal questions."

"Why, Joe! Upset? Not about the story?"

"I'm calm. You should have seen Kaplan."

"Didn't take it well, did he?"

"Since you made him look like the dim bulb of the century, I guess not."

Zack shook his head philosophically. "Is that why he's gone to Tallahassee to talk Haggertie into letting him fire you?"

"How did you find out about that so fast, anyway? A bug in Haggertie's office? Or is Portman really your mole?"

Zack pressed extended forefingers to his temple. "No, emanations. Why are you evading my question about the girl?"

Joe threw up his hands, defeated. "We had a fight."

Zack nodded sagely. "Eloquently put. You were with her a while, weren't you?"

"Two years."

Zack whistled, searching in the ill-fitting pants for his Bic. "It wouldn't have done to break up with her before somebody could get hurt by it. Nope, not for the Joe I know."

"You're gonna smoke that thing anyway, aren't you?"

"Aren't the walls insulated? You *did* check the insulation? Want some?"

Joe didn't bother to shake his head. Zack lit the roach with the delicacy of an artist, and then puffed, coughing painfully. Joe dragged a chair out of the breakfast nook and straddled it resignedly. "Just what are you up to, Zack?"

Zack's slow grin under his wire-framed glasses made him look like a cheerful hedgehog. "I plan to be here if and when you get a phone call from Tallahassee."

"Well, you won't."

"Oh, come on, Joe. How can you turn your back on twenty years of friendship?"

"Try twenty years of exploitation."

"Is it my fault you make such good copy? 'The Cop with ESP.' "

"A story like that won't win you another Pulitzer."

"The first one about you didn't either."

"Indirectly. It got you the job with UPI. Which got you to Bangladesh, which got you—"

"Point taken. But this is a story with promise. Last week, would you believe, my editor at the *Herald* actually wanted me to go out and interview people who had been *Miami Vice* extras?"

He took a deep swig from the roach, this time holding the breath expertly, without choking, then reluctantly letting go. The sweet, unmistakable smell flooded the room. Much sweeter, really, than Joe remembered. Sweet times, maybe. Nights when there was something to want and you could almost get your hands on it.

"I'm doing it for you," said Zack, as if he were the mind reader. "You need some inspiration. You need to get out of this yuppie cold storage and prowl around in a cruiser, like we used to. Trying to figure out which of the winos was really Jesus in disguise."

"Or had been talking to him."

"You used to really listen to those guys, didn't you? You really paid attention."

"Yeah, but I didn't hear any more than you did."

Zack settled down deeper. He blinked dreamily at the skylights, then abruptly flipped the clamp with the still smoking roach in it to Joe. Joe swept it up just as it touched the carpet. "Don't be so hard on yourself." Zack leaned forward with evangelical energy. "You and I could solve this case, Joe."

"How?" said Joe dryly. "Magic?"

"You used to think it was magic."

There was too much truth to that. He had.

"So what do you say?"

"Fuck off."

Zack inchwormed to his feet unsteadily and crossed to where Joe had set the charred morsel of leaf and paper on the back of the chair. He picked it up sympathetically, folding it into an old leather wallet he fished out of his pants. "Speaking of girlfriends, I ran into Janet a couple of weeks ago."

Joe's ex-wife had been so far from his mind it took him a second to react. "Oh?"

"She looks like a million bucks."

"She's still not remarried?"

"Get serious. She was a one-man woman. The kid—Hunter—he's fucking eighteen."

"What's he look like?"

"You've never seen him?"

"When he was a baby."

"He doesn't look like you, if that's what you're wondering."

"Once in a while I think I'm allowed to wonder."

"Don't be so damned defensive," Zack complained. "It looks like guilt."

Joe stood up abruptly, kicking the chair back so hard it teetered. "I'm going jogging. So if the phone rings, I won't be here anyway."

"I could wait around for it."

But Joe opened the front door. "Sure. Outside."

Amiably Zack preceded Joe out onto the breezeway. The showy June evening splashed pink light on his up-turned glasses. There was no sign of his '75 Z in the lot below them, so he had flown up to Tampa from Miami. And was serious about turning Joe's part in the sinkhole case into a major story. Following him downstairs, Joe thought how innocent he looked for someone who could be such a virulent force when he wanted to. They passed the pool with the fountains. A stylishly dressed foursome —the women with sweatbands propping up their hairdos, the men all in white like cricket players—still chased tennis balls in the fading light. Zack stopped by a rental car, a sedate Corolla. And Joe almost got him into the car, almost got rid of him, without having to hear anything else he couldn't quite deny.

But then, with the car door open, Zack wheeled on him scornfully. "Your trouble is you've always hedged. You've always half believed sanity was the answer. Like marrying Janet. If I hadn't been in Bolivia at the time, I'd have shot both of you before I let it happen." He was waving his short arms now. "You thought being married to Janet would give you a nice civilized little armchair to come back to when you got tired of being extraordinary. Only it doesn't work that way. Look at me. Do you think I could have married Janet?"

"Janet is a nice girl."

"My point exactly." He began fishing in his voluminous pockets. Cars driving past them through the parking lot were beginning to turn on headlights, and repeatedly the unkind glare passed over Zack as he nonchalantly fished out a fresh reefer. Joe could not help sighing. "See? They've turned you into a big chicken. Better start running, chicken."

"Blow a smoke ring when you've finished abusing me."

Zack frowned up at him sadly. "Haven't I made any impression?"

"You've made me cough. When does your plane leave?"

"It doesn't. Not yet, anyway. I'm staying at that fancy new hotel down by Harbour Island."

"They let you in?"

"Now who's abusive?" Zack wriggled into the little car

at last, parking the messy, smoking fag on the dashboard. "Don't look so smug. I'm not through with you,
Joe."

"You'd better be."

"You'll thank me one day," Zack told him.

"When I'm through crying," Joe said.

He had not jogged far before he broke out sweating, and
he wished he had a rag to wipe off the oily summer
moon.

Of all the mistakes he had made in his early years on
the Jacksonville police force, making friends with Zack
was probably one of the gravest. Zack had never been
good for him. Zack had led him out into the back streets,
downwind of the bus station. Had played to his delusion
that he was indeed something special, sitting with him in
the shadows, watching the bums and winos wander in
and out of the neon stagelight like Scorsese extras, muttering in Beckett gibberish that would mean something
to you if you had done your penance, only he later realized neither of them had.

Of course he had been a good cop. Too good. He
learned the routines so easily he disdained them. It was
his disdain that ultimately saved him. It was out of his
ugly audacity that the things that made his reputation
happened, out of that conviction which Zack helped feed,
that the sky hung heavy with manna waiting to drop on
him.

There was, for example, the gun he had walked into.
They said afterward he had looked into the kid's eyes
and read his mind, had known it was not loaded, that
tiny silver trinket that looked as if it would fire rhine-
stones. He had known no such thing. He knew, of
course, he had been scared, but it was the pride of his
courage more than the terror he remembered now.

Anyway, the kid had not shot him, he had stabbed
him, a blow to the groin that had felt not like a violation

but more like the dull punch Ricky Zywickie down the block had given him twelve years before over whose baseball was whose. He had bled enough to go to the hospital. There his frightened partner had whispered his belief that the kid had meant to castrate him. For just a moment, hearing that, Joe had felt something touch him, a clutch at the back of the neck that managed to score the linings of his organs before it let go of him and was gone.

Janet had been the ER nurse whose job it was to bathe and shave him for the stitches, and assist, with a blank calm, while the doctor manipulated him with an indignity that didn't become a hero. Joe had thought her rather cold; her uniform, white hat and stockings, and the abnormally scrubbed smell of her hair as she bent over him made him wonder drunkenly through the medication if she had bloomed full grown in a patch of tiny babies, out of a talcum powder storm.

"Will I be all right?" he had asked the doctor.

"I'm sure you will," the doctor had answered, which somehow wasn't quite the response he wanted.

But when the doctor had gone Janet bent forward with perfect seriousness. "That's all right," she had whispered. "If it doesn't work when he finishes I know a great room downstairs where I can get you another one. Lots of terrific bargains."

"Don't worry," he told her. "I have a feeling it's going to work just fine."

He had taken her to bed the first time she went out with him. He knew right away she was in love with him. And he had known from the start that what he was doing with Janet was something he would regret later. But she made it easy, and he did it. It was a lot like walking into the gun, a feeling that this was something that ought to happen, part of his education. A little suffering seemed meet, part of the bargain, and what guilt he took away with him later looked like the best thing he had done.

And for just a short time, just a few years, he had

thought he *was* going to be somebody special: He was the Cop Who Could Read Minds. For a while it had seemed as if that was going to be enough. But it turned out Kaplan had called it right, at that: luck, beginner's luck, playing dirty. Then for a while he had thought that just being good was going to be enough, too, but it wasn't. Just being good sustained him until he realized it was habit, something he couldn't help doing, like crying around cut onions, and being tall.

He wished he could put his finger on what had gone wrong. What woke him up sometimes, left him staring long hours at the stars spying down through the skylights, was the thought that he might in fact be like Kaplan. That he was not different, better, blessed, but in fact condemned to the same dirty little rounds Kaplan ploughed through so mindlessly, condemned to the same grubbing, unimaginative future where nothing ever happened, nothing ever changed. Grabbing at half-baked ideas, defying orders to pursue them, as he had when he got in trouble last month in Lakeland, had been acts of desperation. There had been a few short heady moments when Joe thought his faith in himself was going to redeem him, but for some reason it had lost the power to carry him. He had lost heart, that was the trouble; an attrition he had not noticed had demoralized him, used him up.

Maybe Zack was right, and he had lived too long in the lee of comfort. Maybe he had not been afraid of anything but himself for too long. Sometimes he felt that if the knife the kid had stuck in him had really hurt, if he had been felled with an instant and debilitating anguish, a lot of pain might have been avoided. But there was no agony, and he was not forewarned.

HE HAD NOT REALLY EXPECTED WIN Haggertie to call him. He had thought he would find out his fate brutally, the next time he saw Kaplan. But Haggertie, the director at Executive Investigations, called late that night, perhaps after he got in from dinner, his conversation, very much off the record, firm and to the point.

"I've stood up for you the best I could, Joe," he said. "But if he's really made up his mind he can't work with you, the best I can do is a transfer. Except that the word's going around all of a sudden that you're hard to handle. If that's the case—well, I just don't know what kind of a transfer it will be."

The night before, the Jack Daniel's would have told Haggertie not to bother with transfers. But now Joe was sober, aware that he was tired, and that there were less gentle ways Haggertie could have conveyed what he meant. So he simply said, "Thanks for sticking up for me, Win."

"I've talked him into a reprieve," said Haggertie. "For a couple of weeks, anyway. At least until we see which way this damn case is headed."

Joe wished he had not been able to interpret that message. "I'm not any closer to cracking it than he is."

"I'm not trying to start a contest," protested Haggertie. "That's counterproductive. But it might make a difference in a lot of quarters if *somebody* could produce *something*. The press is tearing us to shreds. Maybe you're using up your resources on the wrong thing, Joe."

So there it was, he thought, standing in the dark by the phone. Delicate, but still an ultimatum: *We have faith in you. Now justify it.* He tried to empty his mind, tried to hear: Somewhere out there, he thought, was this thing of unimaginable evil he was supposed to be pursuing. Surely it had a voice, and surely if he was as good as they thought he was, he should be able to hear it. He listened, but nothing came.

He used up some of those resources Saturday looking for a Snell Isle address that didn't exist. He drove back across the bay from St. Petersburg as afternoon ended, under the glowers of long-necked black birds—the girl he dated before Stacey had told him they were cormorants, birds that fished by diving—who oversaw the unending traffic as indifferently as creatures of stone.

In the parking lot outside the Temple Terrace building, the streetlights were kicking on. Mole crickets swarmed around him, smacking against his windshield and popping under his tires. He parked in darkness to avoid them, and circled to the southside stairwell, intending to drop off his unused notebook and pick up the paper he had bought that morning; he put his foot on the first step and saw with dismay that someone had dumped an ominous dark shape in the shadows halfway up.

He inched stealthily upward, barely able to resist digging at the shape with the toe of his shoe as he passed it; it didn't move. He unlocked the side door noisily, opened and then slammed it. The shape stirred unwillingly, pivoting its white face toward him and blinking.

"This isn't exactly the bus station," Joe snapped. "You waiting for someone?"

"Jeez." The kid dropped the lumpy backpack he had guarded in the curl of his body and pushed himself up the stair rail defensively. "Fell asleep. I hitched all the way from Miami. Homestead." He passed both hands over his face; it was too haggard and beaten for a kid's face. "You're him. You're Joe."

In the clearest memory Joe had of the face this one resembled, it had been looking back at him out of the mirror he had been dressing in front of. Angry tears had been streaming down it, and for just a second his own image had seemed two-headed, and it seemed as if half of him had been crying. "Hunter, please don't tell me your mother sent you here."

"She doesn't know I came."

The kid wore sweatpants with tube socks pulled high up his ankles, stained running shoes, and a truncated denim jacket that at one time had probably cost a lot. His hair, though, was as tidily cut and shining as if he had just come from a church supper. Joe opened the door again, and the kid hoisted the pack and went in. The dispatcher, on duty twenty-four hours, put her head around the corner, saw who it was, and disappeared with a wave. "If your mom doesn't know you're here," Joe said, "where does she think you are?"

"At school. In the dorm, naturally. I'm taking some classes." The kid surveyed the dimly lit squad bay, dropping the knapsack gratefully into a chair. "Not bad . . . roomy. Is this your PC?"

"The department's, links up with a national database. So what does this shit mean? Are you running away?"

"I came to see you."

In his days in uniform, Joe had thought he knew enough about kids to recognize some of the things they had in common, in particular a shared distance, a withdrawal and rebuff, in their eyes. This kid had that air of retreat, but it didn't look as if it belonged to him; it seemed he must have mugged some youngster and stolen the look off him. His bland charm could not cover the bite of his mirthless stare.

"You're not in some kind of trouble, are you?" Joe asked.

"Trouble? Shit, no, man. I got something. Wait." The boy bent busily over the backpack. "Yesterday I saw that. That's why I decided to come."

This copy of the *Miami Herald*, from being crammed in the pack, seemed mildewed and dusty, like something dug out of a tomb. There was his own face smirking at him from Zack's article. The two *o*'s of his name, many times repeated, seemed to punch holes in the flat gray page.

"Good article, isn't it?" prompted Hunter.

"It must be if it made you hitch up here from Homestead."

"Well, it made me think of you," the kid said. "Because of something else that happened. Here."

This time the articles he produced had been clipped. One of them, dated six days earlier, the thirteenth of June, had a long, thin tail, a column of print with a picture at the bottom of a young woman whose yearbook grin and blond curls did not go with her stark, mannish uniform. The caption underneath said she was a wildlife officer, and she was dead.

He doubled the leggy clipping back on itself and let it settle on top of the folded *Herald*. "Aren't you even interested?" Hunter demanded.

"I'm interested in your mother's feelings. She'd be upset if she knew you came up here."

"Hey. I'm eighteen. Mom doesn't worry about me. I've got my own car, my own money—"

"So where's your car? Why're you hitchhiking?"

"Well, it's sort of getting fixed. I sort of wrecked it. But I pay my own insurance." He frowned suspiciously, reaching irritably for the clipping. "I just thought you'd be interested. This doesn't have anything to do with Mom. This is between you and me."

Joe caught the clipping before the kid could fold it. The kid watched, strangely braced; as Joe read, he could hear him breathing. Janet, when she slept, had had a way of ending every third breath or so on a rising whimper too plaintive to be called snoring; Joe could not decide whether or not it was his imagination that Janet's son, who looked so much like her, breathed with that troubled whine, too. "The police down there know about this. Don't you think it's their job to call us?"

"But the papers say you can't find out anything. Maybe the guy who's been operating up here has picked up and moved."

For some reason, he did not want to confess to this kid, this invader, the tingle of anticipation he felt, the tingle of possibility. He kept his face bland instead, indifferent, as if the kid was just taking up time, not making sense.

"Well, anyway," said Hunter accusingly, "if you're not interested—"

"I didn't say I wasn't interested." He crossed to his own desk; there were no ashtrays or picture frames on the desk, nothing solid; he anchored the clipping under the edge of his notebook. The office suddenly seemed minuscule, filled with the kid, who seemed to be occupying space that up to now Joe had not known he had set aside for something. He sighed. "Where exactly did you plan to sleep?"

"I have friends. Believe it or not."

"You'll spend the night with me. In the morning I'll get you a bus ticket."

"I might get in the way of your girlfriend or something."

"As it happens, right at the moment I don't have one."

"Mom said you did."

"Mom doesn't know."

Outside, the mole crickets were still looping randomly through the lamplight. "What happened?" Hunter asked as Joe unlocked the car door. "She walk out?"

"We had a fight."

"I'm not going to tell Mom anything, if that's what you're worried about."

"We were together more than two years," he said, though he didn't know why or to whom he was saying it.

"Gee, that's a long time, isn't it?" Hunter said.

Stacey had always come home before he had, and when she didn't bring supper with her, she cooked it. Tonight all he could smell in the condo was the latex tang of the almost new carpet—no dope, thank God—and faintly, seeping in from somewhere far away, a smell that always made him feel left out when he smelled it, the soft, half-gassy stench of someone who had not asked him over starting coals in an outdoor grill.

Hunter put his backpack down right beside the front door. "Nice place."

"Thank you."

"Say . . . I don't do this all the time, but you wouldn't have anything to drink or anything? I'm wired and I might not sleep or something—"

"There's beer in the fridge and bourbon over the sink. Help yourself."

Hunter chose the beer, leaning over the Formica-topped kitchen island and skating the can around in its own puddle. In the half light from the stove hood his eyes were bagged, his unshaved jaws drooping. The furtive wariness seemed to be retreating, a screen of reckless-ness replacing it. Joe had talked to Janet last year, but how long had it been since he saw her? four years? five?

"What if my case *did* turn out to be connected?" Hunter persisted. "You'd have to come down to Miami and investigate, wouldn't you?"

"I don't know who they'd send."

"But it would be your case!"

"It would be my boss's case. Why are you so interested, anyway?"

"Just asking. Can't I ask?"

Joe went into the denuded living room. Stacey's table had left four punch marks in the carpet. He tried to rub them out with his foot. "Hunter, level. You're sure this doesn't have anything to do with your mom?"

Behind him the beer can smacked down on the counter. "Just what is it between you and my mom, anyway?"

"There's nothing between us. I told you, we don't see—"

"But why do you hate each other?"

"We don't, we just don't have anything in—"

"Well, she acts like she hates you and she thinks you hate her."

"Hunter," he protested tiredly, "Janet has got to have told you, I'm not your father."

Hunter hoisted the beer can, taking a headlong swallow. Then he flung the half-full can down onto the blue carpet. "I know, and it's a damn good thing you're not, you're so damn fucked up."

Joe picked up the can and set it on the counter. Hunter backed away but Joe kept coming. Hunter bent backward over the sink, his white face obdurate. "Go on, hit me," he said.

Joe wished he could just throw him out, like bagged-up, cornered garbage, for somebody else to deal with. But he took a breath, and stopped. Hunter straightened slowly. "If I *was* your kid, you'd hit me, wouldn't you?"

"No."

The boy twisted away and bent over the counter, mutilating his own slick hair, his fingers rampaging through it.

"You're tired," Joe told him.

"I was just goddamn trying to *help*."

"You'll feel better tomorrow."

"I'll sleep on the floor. I won't bother you. You don't have to worry."

"You can sleep on the couch in the den. I'll get you a blanket."

Hunter raised his head, his eyelids raw. He looked much older, chastened. "You won't tell my mom I was such an idiot?"

"I probably won't see your mom unless she calls me."

"She won't do that, don't worry. You're really an okay guy, Joe."

He didn't sleep well, though. He kept going downstairs to look into the den where the kid lay as good as unconscious. It was as if he had left an unbanked fire burning; the damage it might cause, if not watched, appalled him. At six on Sunday morning they drove together to the Trailways station, and Joe bought him a seat among the pregnant black women and unwashed, ragged drifters, who, to be fair, did not look one iota worse than he felt. The bus pulled away and the breeze it stirred died and the still, everyday, morning heat descended. Joe walked back to his car, almost unconsciously hoping that the kid would turn out to have left behind something he could not do without.

HE WAS THE ONLY ONE TO DROP BY THE office Sunday, and when he opened the door, there before the computer terminal sat Zack. The green mask of the VDT blinked peevishly, wakened by Zack's punch.

Joe didn't fight back a surge of irritability. "What the hell are you still doing in town?"

"You disappointed me," said Zack. "You didn't get fired."

"So you thought you'd come back and give me another shove, is that right?"

"Joe! So suspicious!"

"How'd you get in here, anyway?"

"Dispatcher let me in. She seems to have the mistaken notion I'm a friend of yours."

"You sure won't be if you've screwed up my CRT."

Zack grinned, looking as deceptively benign as one of the less tractable Muppets. "Look. I've taught it a trick."

He played an array of keys. The green light rolled itself out in an obedient pattern. *Shut up, Joe,* it said.

"So now it'll do that every time anybody asks it something?"

Zack disciplined his frail glasses with a thump of his fingers. "Depends on what they ask it."

"How did you access it in the first place?"

"I've known how to do that for eons. I've got my own modem. I can interface with the whole NCIC system."

Joe crossed his arms and leaned on Portman's desk, rubbing his jaw wearily. Zack smirked. The clippings Hunter had brought still poked out from under Joe's notebook. He sat down in his own chair and reached for them, letting the clipping about the wildlife officer unfurl from his fingers. "Did you help yourself to a look at this?"

"Didn't have to," said Zack innocently. "I already knew all about it."

"So what're the insiders saying?"

"That's Collier County, not Dade."

"But I know how you like a sensation."

For a minute, behind the white light patterns, Zack's button eyes were hidden. "I don't have that many friends in Collier. Nobody wanted to chat."

Someone had bent a corner of the clipping. Joe worked at it, trying to fix it. "They don't know, or they won't say?"

"Well, a couple of days ago they asked all the people in the choir she sang in to list everybody she could have been dating."

"Oh. The scientific method."

"Unlike the psychological method you've been practicing on me."

"This is not a tip," said Joe.

"I hope not. The pattern's not even ballpark."

"Hunter—Janet's kid, of all people—brought the clipping last night, God knows what for."

"Maybe he just wanted to get a look at you. After all, you're probably as close as the poor kid's got to a father. Were you nice to him?"

"I told him I'd look into it. But that's all there is to it."

Zack sat up suddenly and swung back to the computer. "Watch this." He pounced on the keys energetically. *Shove it, Joe,* the green lights said.

"They still arrest people for subverting government property." Joe got up and punched off the computer.

"Don't do that! We were just getting friendly!"

"Zack . . ."

"Yeah, I know." Zack pushed out of the chair, grunting. "You want me to leave you alone. Leave you in your little slot."

"I want some peace and quiet." Ungraciously he rebooted the program. "I hope to God I can get into the machine and undo the damage."

Zack opened the door, showing his teeth quickly. "You wouldn't obstruct justice in your own interests, would you?"

"Zack, Jesus! No more articles!"

"Conscience calls," Zack said, with the door open. Joe took a step toward him, but he winked and was gone.

When he finally found the place, what Terry had called a horse farm looked, at first, like a blank tongue of sparse grass and thistles sandwiched between two trailer parks, enclosed in rusty barbed wire and split by a dry sand lane that grabbed his tires as he slewed his inexpert way along.

Damn Hunter, he thought, sweating in spite of the a.c.; and goddamn Zack. Without quite saying so, Zack had managed to give the impression in his latest unwelcome column—a blurb that had appeared in Monday's *Miami Herald* and that had been excerpted Tuesday by the *Tampa Trib*—that the department was burying crucial evidence that would link the murder of the wildlife officer in Collier County with the sinkhole killings. Vehemently denying the implication promised to do neither Kaplan nor Tallahassee any good. "Hey," Terry had said scornfully, "that racehorse trainer I wrote off Friday calls back all stressed out because that's where this photographer took this girl he's so hot for, down to Collier County, and they want you to go talk to him? Hey, go talk to him. What do I know?"

The lane turned a corner, and the weedy pastures grew up even thicker, and ahead, like the wild fields' triumph, reared a thick copse of live oaks. The air changed and squirrels dashed past him and small birds flushed up before him in the shade. He passed a barn so gnarled it might have been hewn from tree roots, and bogged down in a small unkempt lawn splashed with swamp lilies. In the middle of it all had been strewn the inevitable, dirty oblong box of the trailer, a piece of litter that would take lifetimes to rot.

By the trailer steps was parked what had once been an orange Corolla, oxidized to brown. As he turned off his car engine, Joe heard, for just a second before it ceased, the indelicate hacking of a poorly tuned lawn mower. Turning to look, he saw a woman in shapeless bermuda shorts standing ankle deep in the swatch she had been cutting. She was petite, with short, brown curls, just at that age where her freckles were beginning to turn liver-colored. Her frown was wary, and he realized she was alone.

This was surely the wife Terry had not been allowed to interview. Chances were good she didn't know what her husband had been up to. She waded a hesitant step forward, the look on her face asserting quite clearly that, no, she didn't want her property reassessed. He flipped the ID out as always, and as always, in spite of himself, had to suppress an unkind twinge of anticipation as he waited for her to react.

And that rare thing happened: her face changed. Into the resistance crept a slow, sad knowledge, an acceptance that the worst had either happened or, unavoidably, soon would. "You're Mrs. Ray Shorter?" he asked.

People often didn't answer directly. "Is there some problem, Officer?"

He would have felt less like a predator over a cup of coffee, but she didn't oblige him. "Do you know a Miss Cherry Miller?"

"Of course. She's a friend of the family. She's . . . my husband trains racehorses and she rides for him. She's not—" For a moment, improbably, he thought her frown had lightened. "Nothing's happened, has it? Cherry . . . I know she—"

"You know she what?"

She cupped her palms distractedly over her hair. "But why ask us about Cherry? She rides for lots of people, not just Ray."

"I understood she had a friend—apparently she had just met him. A Sal Sapia . . . ?"

"Oh. Oh, yes." Again, unmistakably this time, the frown unscrewed itself a half-turn. "But you still haven't told me exactly what the problem is."

Slowly he extracted and unfolded the sheet with the sketch on it. They watched each other over it, until slowly she took it, and he let go. "I understand your husband came into a sheriff's department substation the day the *Tribune* ran that."

She concentrated on the drawing perplexedly. "Oh," she said suddenly. "Ray thinks—but that's utterly ridiculous. I suppose this does look a little like him, like that fellow Cherry brought by here, but—" This time she shook her head with vehement certainty. "Is that what my husband told you? Well, he's wrong, it's not the same man."

She pushed the sketch back at him. He didn't take it immediately. After a second she pushed it forward again. "Exactly what *did* my husband say?"

"Just that Miss Miller had gone off to someplace in south Florida with this man and that there was some resemblance to the man we're looking for."

She bent and began brusquely knocking grass cuttings from her bony shins. "What did you say your name was?"

"Hope. Special Agent Hope."

"Oh. Not *Officer.*"

"Most people don't know the difference."

"I imagine there's not much difference, is there? Well, Agent—in fact, it sounds silly—Ray will be home in a matter of minutes. I agree, you ought to talk to him." She marched past him. "You might as well come inside."

The furniture inside the flimsy metal box looked as if it had been handed down from somewhere much grander; the walls had been plastered with photos, as if familiar faces, so fiercely smiling, could turn the masonite-sided cubicle into a corner of dreams. He sat in a chair backed with worn velvet. Mrs. Shorter had not lied about the racehorses; their pictures were scattered among the others, and the burly, pleased-looking man at the heads of all the horses must have been her husband, Ray.

The coffee she did offer was instant, but she was generous, and it came out rich and black. She didn't sit, but went back into the kitchen. He could just see what she was doing over the narrow bar that set the halves of the room apart from each other: taking dishes out of a drain, stacking them, then storing them on shelves. She worked quickly, a thousand tiny gestures. "I take it you're not from Florida," he said.

When she spoke she had her back turned, reaching for a high cabinet. "We had a paid-for home in Albany. I was an insurance rater and he had five years to go on a good pension. But no. This is what he had to be doing. This is where we had to be."

He looked around the trailer, counting the racing pictures. "Aren't all these winners?" She didn't answer. "It doesn't look like he's done so bad."

"Over five years? No, that's not many winners at all."

She mixed herself coffee, her features so small she could almost hide in her mug, like a little dun mouse. He started to set his own cup down but hesitated. "It's all right," she said quickly. "It won't leave a ring."

"Do you happen to have a picture of this Miss Miller?"

She came out from behind the barrier, drying her hands on her shorts. She took down a picture. "There. Right by my husband. The girl in red."

He reached for the picture, and as she let go of it, they both heard the car engine. He thought for a minute she was going to take the picture back. But he persisted, and was holding it when they felt the trailer shake from Shorter's footsteps on the metal stoop. The door opened, and he came in.

Shorter was tall, and at first, in his T-shirt under his open-necked sport shirt, he looked muscular, but in profile his body broadened in the wrong places. He looked as if he ate a lot and probably drank some, but hard work saved him. He was rough-shaven, as if he had little time to spare for appearances, and his gray eyes would have been attractive had they not been so belligerent, red-streaked, and grieved. He did not even seem to look at his wife, but he instantly saw Joe. "It's about time," he growled.

Joe had pushed halfway to his feet, letting Mrs. Shorter have the photo. "Don't bother," Shorter told him. "Lyssa, get the man some more coffee. He's dry."

"I'm—"

"Let her, she'll be looking for something to do anyway." His wife came in, with the pot of hot water and a cup for her husband; she filled it and he took it. But Joe shook his head when she turned to him; she shrugged philosophically and went back into the kitchen. Shorter took a big, loud gulp of the coffee. "So what have you got to tell me, pal?"

"I thought you had something to tell us."

"What happened to the other guy, the black guy?"

"They consider me the south Florida specialist now, I guess."

Shorter raised his brows skeptically. "I don't have anything I haven't already told you. It just seems that now that you've got that other case, that girl in Collier County, you ought to take a new look at mine."

Joe sat back carefully in Mrs. Shorter's good chair. "Are you sure you've got a case, Mr. Shorter?"

Shorter dashed his cup down onto the end table behind him, splashing a stack of magazines with hot coffee. "You sound just like that other bastard! Corroboration! You could wait a lifetime for corroboration, and in the meantime an innocent girl's dead!"

"It would just help," said Joe soothingly, "if you could come up with somebody else who met the guy."

Shorter crossed the small room in two swift strides. He jerked open a drawer and took a folded newspaper from it. The familiar ads told Joe it was the now two-week-old issue that had carried the sketch. Shorter wheeled, but his wife was already facing him over the short bar. They stared at each other for a minute. "I'm sorry," she told him. "I've already told Agent Hope I don't think it's the same man."

Shorter turned away. He did not look disgusted as Joe had expected him to look. He looked ill.

"So you're not going to do anything," he asserted stupidly. The blood that had risen into his jowls seemed to have pooled there. "You're going to wait for a damn hurricane to float the body out."

Joe tilted his head back. "According to Agent Bessel's report, you had a postcard from Ms. Miller on the thirteenth, just over a week ago."

"That was the first I knew they'd actually gone off—I mean, I tried to talk her out of it, and I thought I had." He thumped the composite. "Otherwise, believe me, I'd have called you guys a lot sooner, the day I saw this, except from the way you people act, I don't guess it would have done me any good."

"The point is," explained Joe tolerantly, "apparently

she was all right then. Meanwhile you haven't produced anybody else who even saw the guy."

"Well, goddamn it, I will."

"You didn't like him, did you?" demanded Joe suddenly.

"What's that mean?"

"You didn't like her going off with him."

The wife had put down her rag. She was standing in the kitchen entrance, wrists cocked on her hips, her small stomach pouched out, her pert face pensive.

"No," sneered Shorter, bending over Joe heavily. "I didn't like him. He was an overdressed bum."

Suddenly the wife pushed between them. She craned her neck at her husband like a sparrow scolding a bull. "Ray, are you out of your mind?"

Shorter flinched. His ears reddened. "They won't even go and look for her!"

"When they can see perfectly well exactly what this officer's saying? That you did not like that man?"

"You!" spat Shorter suddenly. "As far as *you're* concerned, Cherry can just stay gone!"

Joe would have called her eyes dull green, like the color of pellets you buy to feed rabbits. But when they widened he saw he was wrong.

She wheeled. "I'm sorry, Officer. Agent." She spun again and marched past her husband, out the front door. It banged tinnily behind her. "Damn you," Shorter said.

Joe unfolded himself from the chair slowly. The two of them were almost the same height, and he felt Shorter assess him. Suspects, witnesses, especially men, often did it. As most often happened, Shorter took a step backward. After a moment, Joe turned and let himself down into the velvet-backed chair again. "Did he drive her here?"

Shorter frowned, licking his lips. Then, gingerly, he sat, too. "No, they came in her car."

"You said Sapia said he was a photographer. Did he have any equipment with him, lenses, flashes—?"

Shorter's jowls flushed. "No, he didn't, and to tell you the truth, I thought it was damn suspicious."

"Did she mention anywhere he'd sold his work?"

"All *he* said was that he freelanced. *She* said he'd sold to *Audubon.* He didn't deny it." Shorter screwed up his face vehemently. "Another thing I thought was suspicious—he claimed he was from south Georgia. I mean—south Georgia's a big mess of nothing. Pine trees. Why would a bigtime photographer set up shop there?"

Joe said nothing, scratching his jaw. "One thing I did," Shorter blurted suddenly, "I didn't tell Lyssa—I went by Cherry's trailer. I couldn't get in, it's all locked up, but Cherry's car is still there."

Terry had taken down the girl's address, but hadn't gone looking for her. "Did she have any credit cards?"

"No. She didn't believe in them. Him, I'm not sure. That's right, you can trace him that way."

Joe took one of the embossed cardboard squares the department provided him from his shirt pocket. "Your best bet is still finding somebody else who met him. That's me, Special Agent Hope. And my number. Call me there."

"In the meantime—"

"In the meantime I can't promise. It's too messy."

"What's messy about it?"

Joe rose, shaking down his pants legs. "You."

Shorter stood and moved quickly as if to get between Joe and the door. But all he did was raise a hand and then drop it. "Mountain lions," he said suddenly. "He told her they were going to photograph mountain lions. Doesn't that sound screwy to you?"

"I presume he meant Florida panthers."

"So where do they have Florida panthers? Couldn't you just drive down there?"

"You looked at a map recently?" Shorter frowned at him. "One thing my bureau chief won't authorize is a blind foot search of Collier County." He pointed out the card, already limp with sweat, in Shorter's fingers. "Get me that witness. And in the meantime, don't do anything dumb."

With a flick of his thick wrist, Shorter ditched the card in a nearby ashtray, a small, losing gesture of defiance. Joe shrugged and stepped out the door.

Mrs. Shorter was raking grass cuttings. She froze, wary again, and watched him come. The raw grass smelled like leaking acid. Joe took out his sunglasses. "There's no chance," he asked her steadily, "despite what you told your husband—that you could be letting your feelings influence your judgment?"

"No," she said, tight-lipped.

"I would keep an eye on him, if I were you. He could buy himself a whole lot of trouble."

Impatiently she brushed the limp hair back again, smearing grass stains on her forehead. "He'll come to his senses," she said.

He drove back down the sand lane, thinking not about where he was going but about what he had left behind. Dark was falling, and he didn't stop to consult his written directions, and somewhere on his way back toward Brandon he took a wrong turn. He stopped at a crossroads where the street names meant nothing to him. His left was surely still east, though, because that was where the moon was just edging over the horizon, red and blotched like a big bruised peach.

He turned on the inside light. From over the visor he took a map of Florida. He bent over the jutting spar of the peninsula, the narrow white thumb against the blue ocean with the keys trailing off its tip like a back-curving claw. Up and down both coasts to the south was the busy fuzz of the cities, Miami to the east, and to the west, Naples, but between them, as he had hinted to Shorter, was an emptiness he could fit his fist into, a hole where the roads made but a sparse red web and the towns were just motes. Collier County. Mountain lions.

He looked up at the moon. It was fast losing its blush and turning cold and hardbitten. He rolled up the window quickly and started the car engine, but it was too late. He had lied to Zack. What Zack had urged was exactly what he had been wishing for: a touch of the old magic, the old faith. Now here it was, oozing in and taking form beside him, a hunch, unfounded but irresistible, and inexplicably alive. He turned tight corners at random, emerging at last on a road he recognized with no idea how he had gotten there, while the hunch slathered itself up against him, grappling his privates, until all he could do was lie back and let it, telling himself to give up, surrender logic; only then would his need be answered, and certainty come.

THEY ALL FELT LIKE HELL THURSDAY
morning. The thunder in the distance had bothered
Hube and he hadn't slept. Terry had been out of coffee
and needed a fix bad. Juan had almost had an accident
on the way from his beach house. Natalie alone looked
comfortable, in white cotton with a wide red belt.

The sun coming in the window lurked at Kaplan's
shoulder like a tame yellow bear. He was fingering the
two sheets of the report, grunting at the contents. "So
this is it, Joe? This your big score?"

To Joe the two sheets of paper were like a gun he had
brought into the room and aimed at Kaplan, knowing he
could not have made a dumber move. But the time had
come to use it or die by it. "All that is, is my weekend off
in Miami," he said.

Kaplan flattened a hand over the sheets before him,
glaring around at his dreary company. Terry was rubbing his eyes, turning their red rims outward. Hube was
yawning. "This isn't in Miami," Kaplan said.

"To get to Miami I have to go by there."

"There's nothing there to stop for. Unless you're deliberately looking for trouble."

Joe frowned at the papers under Kaplan's crouching fingers. "Maybe I'll have a flat tire."

Kaplan threw the papers at him. But they were too light and only fluttered pointlessly down into his lap. Kaplan was breathing heavily. "You can't seriously believe this is it?"

Joe smoothed the sheets, folding them. When he had made Kaplan wait longer than he had really intended, he shrugged.

"What can it hurt?" Natalie said boldly from the end of the table.

Kaplan glared at her distractedly. He spun in his chair. Portman felt the move and turned to face him. Kaplan stalked over and jerked the folded papers from between Joe's fingers. He sailed them to Portman. "Get your butt down there."

Portman's face contorted. "But it's bullshit! The wife didn't recognize the picture! The husband was a flake!"

"Yeah, the world is full of them," Kaplan said. "Don't fart around. If it's bullshit, come back in two days and prove it. Don't come back and tell me it is if it's not."

"But I can't go tomorrow! I've got important interviews scheduled!"

"So go tomorrow night, then."

"What's Hope going to be doing?"

Kaplan looked at Joe. Portman didn't.

"I don't know," said Kaplan. "Tomorrow he's got lots to do here, too. But he does have some time off coming, maybe more than he thinks. Maybe Saturday he'll go to Miami."

Portman considered for a moment, his gaze ranging toward Joe and back again. Suddenly he jammed the square of paper into his shirt pocket with a barely concealed air of triumph. "I'll watch for him," he sneered. "I'll wave."

.   .   .

Hube brought copies of the computer printouts Portman had spent the morning working up to Espo's on Thirtieth Street. Sapia's VISA had been issued out of the First National Bank of Atlanta, fifteen years ago, credit rating A-1; his personal bank was the First Union, in Brunswick, Georgia. Joe knew where Brunswick was, just north of Jacksonville, on the coast, inward from the lush sea islands. There was a federal law-enforcement training center there. There was no criminal history on Sapia in the NCIC system. The post office in Brunswick had no record of a forwarding address.

Espo's had vinyl-topped cafeteria-style tables and served roast pork and yellow rice, plantains, yucca, and boliche on plastic trays. Inexplicably the motif was penguins. Hube just picked up a cup of coffee. "Kaplan *wants* you to do this, Joe," he said urgently. "He and Portman *want* you to get down there and waste a lot of money and time."

The last entry posted on Sapia's credit card record was a week old: a hotel entry in Naples, far down on the west coast of Florida: a double room.

"Two days ago you didn't believe in the picture," Hube pressed. "You go to the trouble to shoot the damn thing full of holes, and now you try to raft across the Everglades on it."

"I wish these credit card charges went back further."

"Damn it, Joe, are you listening?"

"No, I'm thinking."

"Like hell you are."

Joe ignored him. "According to what Shorter told Terry, he met Sapia on June seventh. Sapia and the Miller girl left Tampa on the ninth. This wildlife officer, this Amy Wells, was found dead on the twelfth, killed sometime on the night of the eleventh. According to these sheets, we've got Sapia and Miller back in Naples, in a hotel, on the fifteenth."

"Doesn't give him much time to set up the Wells murder, does it?" Hube argued smugly. "Or pull it off, with the Miller chick hanging on his neck."

"Another month's worth of records might tell us if Sapia had been down there before. He might have met her then, and made his plans. Killing her might have just been a matter of getting the Miller girl off his hands for a couple of hours." He raised his brows at Hube. "You know, you could do that for me."

"Get you more records? And not give them to Portman?"

"I don't care if you give them to Portman."

Hube snatched up a sheet and brooded over it. "The guy drives a 1960 Karmann Ghia. Red." He tossed the sheet down again. "In Collier County? Birthplace of the swamp buggy? Portman'll find that car before you get your toothbrush packed."

Portman had also pulled up stats on the Miller girl. Cherry Miller had a raft of tickets, mostly for speeding. At eighteen, five years ago, she had been booked for misdemeanor possession and had spent six months on probation. There was a copy of her prints on file. According to her Social Security records, she had once worked for the telephone company and delivered the newspaper, but for three years, presumably her racetrack years, she'd been self-employed. "What do you know about Collier County?" he asked Hube.

"You've never been there?"

"I've been to Naples."

Hube snorted. "You'll hate it. Grass and bugs."

There were no pictures of either Sapia or the girl among the printouts, though surely Portman had had driver's license photos faxed. The picture Mrs. Shorter had shown Joe had been too small to help much: just a lot of dark hair topping what looked like a wiry body, a pink smear of a face undefined by makeup. He did remember her white, full smile.

"I get the impression Shorter spends his days in Oldsmar, with his horses. All I have to do is find a way to get in ahead of Portman."

"He's got the inside track. The sheriff down there'll have to cooperate with him."

Joe stood, shaking down his jacket sleeves. "Then I'll have to think of something he doesn't."

"Joe, if you get in trouble . . . you could end up. . . . God knows."

For a moment, the worried look on his friend's up-turned face made Joe feel as if someone had slapped him. "Please don't worry. I won't give Portman anything to use against me."

"The whole damn case is what you ought to give him," Hube grunted. "Wrapped up in ribbons and bows."

The farm near the racetrack where Shorter kept his horses seemed deserted. Weeds sprang up between the ramshackle stables; last spring's compost cooked slowly in big concrete bins. Shorter's barn was set back off the main drive, fronting a field full of black, squawking birds. The tops of five of the stall doors were open, and between the dark dens, brightly painted tubs hung like crimson shields.

Joe got out into the pungent heat slowly. There was no one in sight, but something stirred in one of the caverns beyond the Dutch doors. Before he could dodge, a brown horse with a white blotch on its forehead lunged out of the darkness, a sneering curl of wrinkles ringing its damp nostril. Its yellow teeth caught his sleeve as he jumped back. An old man in limp green work pants appeared around the corner of the barn, pushing a squashed brown hat off his lined forehead. "Well, I woulda said watch out, if you'd given me the chance."

"These things don't get rabies, do they?" Joe asked, inspecting the tear in his sleeve grimly.

"Nah, it's what we feed 'em makes 'em so mean," the

old man chortled. "Raw meat and gristle. Keeps their guts churned up good."

"I'm looking for Ray Shorter."

"He's over at the training track." He gestured vaguely.

"You by any chance know a young woman named Cherry Miller?"

"Yeah, but don't give me no medal. Everybody does."

They both turned at the sound of raised voices. Across the field Shorter had emerged from a tumbledown shed with a struggling little man in his grip. The little man was muscular through the shoulders with strong short legs and loose graying hair that curled low on his cheekbones. He was squirming and kicking at Shorter, who shouted, "Now damn it, Phillie, it's Cherry's life!"

"Damn it your goddamn self, Ray," the little man retorted, struggling ineffectually. "I told you, I ain't talking about nobody or nothing to no cops!"

Joe started through the rising black cloud of birds toward them. Shorter, catching sight of him, thrust his captive forward. "Here's your *corroboration,* Hope! Phillie met that bastard! Tell him he's got to look at that thing!"

But the sight of Joe seemed to feed Phillie's fury. Suddenly he leapt up on Shorter with a speedy, vicious pummeling that staggered the bigger man. Freed, the little man bolted. Shorter recovered and bounded after him. He caught the dirty T-shirt and lifted Phillie off the ground, spinning him, then pulled his fist back and landed it hard. Phillie's eyes rolled and he grunted. Again Shorter drew an arm back, his lips curled and his teeth bared. By then Joe had reached them. He forced himself between them, deflecting Shorter's blow with a chop of his own so that the trainer's thrust landed dully below his collarbone. Phillie scrambled backward, and though Joe turned, he was too late to catch him. Scuttling in panic, the little man disappeared into the shed and slammed the door.

Shorter was gasping, writhing, trying to bowl Joe

aside. "Damn it, Hope, let me get at that little prick! Getting Cherry killed! I'll make him talk!"

But Joe shook him hard, shoving him backward. "Listen to me. Calm down. No more fighting." Shorter tried again to push past him. "You ever been in the county jail?" Joe asked.

"What the hell does that have to do with anything?"

"You'll find out if you don't back off this shit."

Shorter panted, almost babbling. "But he . . . saw that . . . he said he . . . God!"

"Beat it out of him," said Joe, "and it won't be worth the breath he wastes on it. Now use your head."

"Jesus!" Joe saw tears flash, blinked back quickly. "Everybody's so goddamn sensible! And I'm crazy! Look at you—you just stand there, like we're talking about a stray cat!"

"I'm here, aren't I?"

Shorter scrubbed at his face passionately. "Shit. Maybe the guy'll keel over dead or something before he can hurt her. Maybe he'll run out of his pills or something—"

"What pills?"

"The pills he was popping. Cherry said it was for blood pressure, but hey, maybe it was speed or something. Maybe he'll OD."

Joe took his arm, urging him back toward his barn and Joe's car. The old man was still standing there watching them. "Why didn't you tell me about this?" Joe asked.

"I told that first guy. The black guy."

"Was it a prescription? in a bottle with a label?"

"I didn't see the label. But it was a pill bottle—plastic, with one of those lids where you line up the arrows. Why? Is that important?"

"Possibly." They reached the car. Back across the field, the shed door opened and Phillie poked his head out defiantly. "So he saw Sapia?"

"Yeah! And he thought the same thing I did, that he was a—"

"If he comes to you on his own and wants to talk, fine," said Joe. "If I need him, I'll come after him. When he's calmed down a little. In the meantime, *you* don't hurt anybody. Do you understand?"

"Yeah, yeah," Shorter grunted impatiently.

"Somebody else from the department might be around asking questions. Whatever they ask, tell them."

"Where'll you be?"

"I'll be off this weekend."

"What's with you, anyway?" the trainer demanded. "This is just a job to you, isn't it? You don't care about her. She wasn't your friend."

"They usually aren't," Joe said.

He stopped at the condo for his own car. It was one of the little black Isuzus, sort of a sports car, but not really. Stacey had considered it an affectation, and he had almost let her talk him out of buying it. But sometimes when he drove it, he felt as if he were eighteen again, flying low to the ground in his old Cougar, when getting places fast still mattered. When he reached the community of Ruskin, on the southeastern edge of Tampa, the sky was pus-yellow, coated with a layer of acrid phosphate plant smog.

The subdivision he was seeking was a new one, a maze of cul-de-sacs clogged with small concrete-block houses, chopped from a freeze-burned tomato field and hedged by a blank brown wall. By the time he found Pelican Circle, the sun had come melting down out of the haze, its flat eye pale and baleful. As he turned onto Pelican, he found the narrow lane between the cars parked at both curbs blocked by a familiar blue Caprice with a radio antenna jutting from the trunk: a department car.

He sighed, and got out. The door of the other car opened. Portman squirmed out and started toward him, fussily adjusting the arms of his expensive sunglasses. Alone with Joe, he had no need to cap his animosity. "Looking for a Mrs. Sally Miller Bryson? Forget it, the bitch is a dope."

"Maybe you asked her dopey questions," Joe said.

"You know, Hope, this could get old in a hurry, following each other around. Especially since you're practically defying orders."

"Except that like Hube pointed out, Kaplan was careful not to give me any."

"Well, you're wasting your time here. Mrs. Bryson thinks her stupid twat of a sister's probably getting what she deserves. Says she's been bucking to end up in a ditch somewhere with a Coke bottle shoved up her cunt since she was twelve years old. Says if she's run off with some racetrack loser it won't be the first time. Says she personally never set eyes on the guy or heard of him, and hasn't seen her sister for more than two years."

"Thank you. That was very visual."

Portman's pursed mouth worked. He shouldered up to Joe, but he was too short to make the threat very effective. "You know, Hope, I'm going to get you."

Joe had always wondered if the bristles of Portman's hair were hard and sharp or soft. They were standing so close together it was all he could do to keep from reaching over and patting Portman's head to find out.

"You can laugh at me all you want," Portman challenged. "You'll screw yourself sooner or later."

"I'm not laughing."

"Back your car up."

Joe looked up and down the street. One of them would have to move. After a minute he turned and climbed into the Isuzu and put it in reverse. Portman waited until he had actually backed out into the main road before he got in the Chevy. He took a long time about it. He burned rubber leaving Joe behind.

Joe negotiated the clogged street and then the turnaround. One-thirteen was a blank-looking little cubicle, with heavily curtained windows and a sad eucalyptus with just a few thirsty yellow leaves clinging to its branches. He got out and went to the door.

Mrs. Bryson was prettier, but older, than he had expected. She said, "What is this? You two guys trying to beat each other out?"

"No, just follow-up."

"Look," said the woman. "I saw you talking through the window, so I know he told you what I said. I got dinner cooking and a kid in the bathtub. I haven't seen Cherry, I don't know where she is, and she don't send me postcards." A timer went off somewhere in the house behind her. "So that's it. Excuse me, I got to go."

Joe let her. If he could build a case, she, like the reluctant little man at Shorter's stable, might be surprised by what she remembered. But for now, he had something better. Grilling hostile witnesses could wait.

He went home to the condo. He popped open a beer, moved a dining table chair in by the kitchen phone, and dialed long distance. "Bernie? This is Joe."

"Joe! Long time no see."

"Business, Bernie."

"Shit. I should have known you wouldn't spend money being social. How's my gal Stacey?"

"She's fine."

"Let me guess, you're going to call in that marker. Please, guy, Beth and I were going to a movie!"

"It's five-thirty now. This'll take you an hour, you can do it on your way. Beth can help."

Bernie sighed. Joe could almost see him smashing his palm into his bald spot, the way he always did when he was cornered.

"Public library ought to be open," Joe told him. "Or a college library. That close to the state line, they ought to have either a phone book or a Polk's for Brunswick, Georgia."

"Maybe," said Bernie grudgingly.

"I need a list of all the pharmacies and drugstores in

Brunswick. If you can get hold of a street map, I especially need any that might be in the neighborhood of a street where a suspect I'm after lives—a place called Angel Lane."

"Maps, I don't know. This can't wait till morning?"

"Kaplan's got me hunting snipes in the morning. *All* morning."

Bernie sighed. "You sitting down?"

"Yeah, why?"

"Don't lean back, don't put your feet up, don't turn on the TV, don't open a beer, until I call back."

"I've already opened a beer. Take one in the car with you. As a law enforcement officer, I give you permission."

"Never take favors off hard-hearted bastards," said Bernie as he hung up.

I-75 WAS A BEAUTIFUL ROAD, ALL RIGHT, sometimes six lanes, long curves sailing southward. Where the narrow country roads came winging out of the woods to meet it, there were no gas stations, no Burger Kings, just the straight, watchful spires of pine and cypress. But as he neared Naples, three hours south of Tampa, the scenery changed: broken ground here, the fresh new facade of a Circle K there, a scarred and cratered battle zone where the side that couldn't kill was losing. At some interchanges, acres of trees had been bulldozed; in the noon sun, on the bare plains, the stacked limbs burned.

He'd been to Miami often, of course, but he'd always taken what on the map looked like the sanest route: across the state on U.S. 60, then south on the turnpike. This other way, the back way through the Everglades, had seemed like a big loop through nowhere for no reason. Stacey, eager for novelty, had wanted to go down there camping, but he hadn't; the whole idea of tents and sweaty sleeping bags and smelly bug spray had seemed more like aggravation than fun. As for alligators, he could see dozens of them at Busch Gardens in Tampa whenever he wanted, piled up on each other in rubbery, brain-dead jumbles; he couldn't for the life of him imagine anyone walking a hundred yards, let alone driving two hundred miles, to see more.

But now, setting out at eight that Saturday morning, he had looked hard at the map again. Grass, Hube had said. By the legend on the map margin, square mile after square mile of it. The national park, south of the red weal U.S. 41 made across the blankness, was a boxy discoloration like a smacked nail at the end of the Florida thumb. North of 41 was a second irregular stain called the Big Cypress. Looking at the map, he couldn't tell what the difference was.

But he felt closer to the case and surer, and for the moment, at least, his journey did not seem quite so blind. For one thing, he had persuaded a girl he knew at the *Miami Herald* to fax him photos of the murdered wildlife officer, Amy Wells. His friend had sent him two: the one in the clipping Hunter had shown him, of the murdered girl in uniform, and another that looked distressingly as if it had been made at a photography studio —for her mother, no doubt. She was, he discovered from the copy that had come with the pictures, a National Park Service employee, a park ranger, rather than a warden for the state game and fish agency. She had held a bachelor's degree in biology and had been progressing steadily toward her master's as her job allowed.

The Olan Mills picture, though clear, had been touched up too much, the character prettied out of it. The photo of Amy in uniform, now that he took time to study it, was the one that made her look alive. In that shot, she was not just a long-haired blonde with a smile and a gold locket; she was looking *at* him, with eyes that in life had clearly measured what she saw.

He had been moved by Portman's driver's license photo of the Miller girl, true. Even that typically unflattering pose had breathed with the audacious coquetry that must have drawn Shorter. But Joe, more used to looking at disassociated shots of girls' faces, had read a blindness in her insolence; she was the kind of girl who did not think. Promise her a good time, and you had her. He had often sensed the sadness attending that kind of girl even when he was the one who was kissing her. He had to protect Cherry Miller because he knew what she was heading for—maybe what her sister had predicted—when clearly she did not.

This Amy was different. She lacked the blue-eyed come-on; she would not have been the kind to smooth a working partnership by flirting. Instead she stared out from under the homely ranger's hat with a directness that dared him to judge her more keenly than she could judge herself, and an unashamed self-awareness that made him wonder what he was going to find out she had done.

What was more, despite his grousing, Hube had pirated the two more months' worth of credit card charges Joe had requested. And there on the new printouts had been exactly what Joe had hoped for, a whole string of purchases from Naples, Miami, and a place called Everglades City. So Sapia had been there before. Sapia knew the country and could easily have built up dozens of ties with Amy Wells. Joe had celebrated last night by driving down to Albertson's and buying a shiny red folder. He set off with the map and the folder and an overnight bag on the seat beside him, turning on the air and radio, feeling as if he were a spy going underground.

He had considered leaving the department Beretta behind. He had a gun of his own, a Smith and Wesson .38 airweight with a two-inch barrel he wore against his stomach. But he had not been without the Beretta since it had been issued to him, and he had never shot anyone with it before. Why worry about starting now? So finally he took it along.

Halfway through the journey, he found himself thinking that Hube's worries had been misplaced: he hadn't set out on this trip because of Kaplan or Portman. Despite his strengthened sense of mission, he was really going just to be going, because one foot had to keep falling in front of the other, because there was an expanse to be crossed and some blind need to cross it—and an unconfessed part of him that hoped the Miller girl was dead. He could see, then, the man's face fleeing for a long bearable time before him, glowing in the dark of the future, lurid but alluring, dragging him through nights into mornings like a star drowning itself in the sun.

He had talked, at six-thirty A.M., to the pharmacist on duty in an all-night Eckerd's off the main drag into Naples. With the help of the map, he found the store easily; the day pharmacist, a trim black woman with big earrings and close-cropped hair, handed him the photocopied sheet he had been promised. The charges on the sheet included the long distance call to Brunswick to get the prescription. As Shorter had said, the pills were for blood pressure. "Would he have filled in this handwritten part here? Oystercatcher Motel, Chok . . . Choko . . . ?"

"Chokoloskee. Probably."

"What's Chokoloskee?"

She sealed a vial she had been counting tablets into. "Fishing town. In the Ten Thousand Islands."

"Resort?"

She spared a second to wink at him. "I've never been there. People have told me, if you're into fish and mud, it is."

There it was on the map, stuck on the end of the only road south in an infinity of jigsaw-cut islands. But first he had a long stretch of U.S. 41 to contend with, a bouncy, claustrophobic road along which everyone else wanted to go ninety. There was no scenery, just trash weeds growing up in green walls on both sides.

He did come to grass, finally, a tedious vastness: a buff wall of stalks rising out of a dark canal and stretching off to hazy smears of trees. Against the blank horizon protruded ragged palm pinwheels. To the south the grass was gray-green and patchy, with dollops of unidentifiable plants spotted here and there as if dribbled out of a spoon. The hot white sky arched overhead like a dome of milky tin.

He turned south at a neat little Gulf station. The traffic thinned out. Insects the size of bullets sprayed his windshield. Vibrantly colored billboards began to scream at him: boat rides, alligator wrestling, captive panthers, trained birds. Everglades City was the first place he came to. He slowed to a crawl. Suddenly on both sides there was water, on his right broad and sunlit, on his left washing into a lowering mass of stilt-rooted mangroves, stinking, as the pharmacist had promised, of stagnant mudflat and fish.

The Oystercatcher was a sort of combination motel and camper park at the end of a tangle of rundown trailers, weed-bordered little houses, abandoned cars, and uprooted trees. He parked before a white-painted camper, under a sign with a black-and-white bird and the word *Office,* and got out stiffly. A breeze like the blow of a fist struck off the lead-blue water, corrosive with salt.

The door of the camper rattled when he knocked on it, but no one answered. He heard a splash behind him and turned. On a seawall above the nasty brown mudflats stood a rickety wooden table where a red-bearded kid in a work shirt and billed cap, ruddy and well-fed as a lumberjack, leaned over a chewed-up Styrofoam cooler. "Did you call ahead," the kid asked contentiously, "or did you just come?"

"Full up for the season?" Joe asked idly.

"Ain't the season," said the kid. "But we're full up anyway. Still got a few mullet running."

"I'm not here for the mullet. I'm looking for a couple of people."

The kid's mouth, flower-pink in the red beard, puckered. "What're they into? Got to be marijuana or cocaine."

Hands in his pockets, Joe ambled closer. "Sounds like you know a little about it."

The kid reached into the ice chest, let loose a choking fish reek, and pulled out a ten-inch mullet, which he flopped onto the table. He reached behind him and produced a gleaming knife. In one stroke he slit the fish open, spilling its dark guts out onto the table. He gathered them barehanded and hurled them into the water. "There, that's what I know about. You want to confiscate 'em, go right ahead."

"I'm not DEA," said Joe.

The kid took him in critically. "You're something."

"I'm with the state Department of Law Enforcement."

The kid chewed his lip. "If it ain't drugs, you must think these people killed someone."

Joe eased back his coat lapel and took out a set of Portman's pictures. The one of Sapia did look a little like the composite. The kid held them by the edges so he wouldn't get dirty prints on them. His red tongue shot out of the fiery growth of his beard, then disappeared. "These folks know you're after them?"

"I don't think so."

"I reckon you'll find them sooner or later, won't you?"

"Hopefully, sooner."

The kid handed back the pictures. "No use getting a hemorrhage over it. They were here. I took them out."

"Fishing?"

"Hell, no. Taking photographs. But they weren't no murderers."

"How do you know? Did you ask?"

The abrupt pink-lipped grin fitted the boy better than wariness. "No, but if that guy ever took up anything where they let him near a firearm, I'd have to move to another continent. Dang." He flicked shiny bits of fish scale out of the russet hair on his forearms, arching his chestnut brows passionately. "That guy didn't want to hear nothing! He'd argue the stripes off a coon's tail! Lord! He'd be the kind to wander into a drug dealer's powwow and get his brains blowed out, not the kind to set one up."

"You think he *was* a photographer? He had cameras, equipment, with him?"

"A whole four-wheel-drive full. Hell of a lot more than he could carry. Big brand-new blue Cherokee."

"That was what he was driving? Not an old Karmann Ghia?" The kid shook his head emphatically, digging out a second fish. "And the girl—she seem to like him all right?"

The candy-colored mouth suddenly opened wide in a soundless guffaw. "Like him? She didn't have to like him. That one'd fuck a snake head first if she could get it to hold stiff long enough."

Joe turned away from him, waiting for an image. The one that came at last was bothersome: Sal and Cherry in a little boat, bobbing in the shallows, Sal comic and clumsy. The low, dark islands, overlapping each other in the receding distance, lay along the surface of the water like a dense herd of belly-traveling creatures browsing on the sparkle. "When they left here, where did they go?"

In one stroke the kid scored the fish open and eviscerated it, then set it aside with the other one. "Well," he grunted, "they might have gone to this old place in the Cypress I told them about. Trespass camp called Fat Hog Pond."

"Trespass camp?"

"Illegal squatters' hideout. The rangers burn them out when they find them, but the Cypress is still full of them."

"Are there panthers?"

"Matter of fact, he said he wanted to see panthers, and I figured he might get in a little less trouble where there was less water. In fact, he told me he'd been up that way taking pictures already, thought he knew about where it was."

"Which is where?"

"Got something I can make a map with?" On scratch paper Joe gave him, he sketched a smeared diagram. "Here's Chokoloskee, here's Forty-one, here's a dirt road, county Eight forty-three." He ran the line of the dirt road up the sheet of paper, then marked a turning off it. "This trestle over the canal here, it's rotted out, you have to cross on foot. That's why only a few of the old-timers use Fat Hog anymore. The new breed can't navigate without a clear trail, and this one's overgrown because you can't get a swamp buggy in from this side."

"So he'd have had to walk in?"

"Unless he knew his way in from the backside." He grimaced. " 'Course, not knowing probably wouldn't have stopped him trying. He was like that."

"Would he have had to get permission from anybody to go there?"

"Well, he should, from the rangers, but he probably didn't. If he was driving, anyway. They won't let you drive in the Cypress without permits. Which means maybe they run him out already." He watched Joe stick the map back in his pocket. "But I really don't want to get nobody in no trouble."

"Any trouble they're in, you didn't get them there."

"They just didn't strike me as murderers."

"They probably aren't."

He left the kid working his way emphatically through the pile of dead fish. Back in the car, he realized he had brought the fish smell with him, on his hands, his clothes, his breath. He didn't want to open his windows, but he had to. Halfway back down the little highway, a dragonfly the size of a slingshot hit his side mirror, ricocheted off the car frame, and crashed in his lap. It was iridescent green, stunned, probably dead. He picked it up gingerly by a long amber wing and dumped it out onto the pavement. It made him shiver, as if something out there had gone to the trouble to mark him and take aim.

10

BY THE TIME HE PULLED OUT ONCE MORE onto 41, the Tamiami Trail, the sun had turned dusty red behind him, piecing out of the sky faint, ominously pendant, pink-tinted blooms of cloud. He came to a stretch of dense forest, where signs told him he was in the Big Cypress, and promised him he would see panthers crossing, though he didn't. Then he burst out again into open country, a plain of wiry scrub trees stealing up like a starved army playing red light, freezing in its tracks whenever he turned to look. The day began to dim so he could no longer see the black canal beside him, but he could smell it; darkness itself seemed to boil up out of the land like a flood rising, the few unexplained lights he passed like pinpoints of memory, the last to glow brightly while all else died.

Then the moon came up, and his windshield swept up bugs, pale spreading splats of them, and the road widened and began to glitter with the phosphorescence of Miami. His fingers ached; he found he had been clawing the wheel, fighting his way eastward; he struggled to remember, to extract from the darkness, some sense of where he was going, how to get there, to the sane calm he planned on finding at Orren Cruse's house.

Orren's house was packed in among its neighbors like a border piece in a puzzle, its front yard gravel, its backyard a walled concrete courtyard with a pool. When Joe knocked on the door he had to wait long minutes before the racks of locks began to click free. Orren stepped out onto the small stoop beside him without turning any lights on. Joe put out his hand and Orren took it, mashing, his palm as cool and rough as a cat's tongue. But he didn't speak until he had done up all the front door locks behind them, and they stood facing each other in the scant light that reached them from the kitchen.

Orren was husky, black-haired, and monumental. He had been D-squad SAS in Tampa before Kaplan, and now was assistant special agent in charge for the Miami Operations Bureau. He had remarkable eyebrows, rampant black growths with exuberant curling tendrils, and a mustache that quivered with a life of its own when he was pleased or angry. Now the look on his face was a shaggy glower. "Today I got a dispatch about some agent up there in Tampa, Portman. It said he was the only official liaison on this case and I wasn't to pass information to anyone but him."

"I told you I wasn't official."

Orren turned away, the mustache quaking. "I just wish you woulda told me it was war."

Anita Cruse was propped among satin pillows on the couch in the family room, watching a Joan Crawford movie. She stood up when Orren came in and set Joe's bag on the coffee table among the *Good Housekeeping*s and *Crime Control Digest*s. Anita wore tight black pants with straps around the insteps and a pullover that hid her little nut of a stomach. She had always shown their age more than Orren, with his full red cheeks and thick unstreaked hair. She tilted her head back so Joe could peck her cheek. She felt frailer than he remembered her, as if time had been drinking her up while he wasn't watching. "So you finally came back to Miami. I shoulda known it would take a body to bring you. You got poor taste, Joe."

"We're going out by the pool, Nita." Orren looked at his watch. "Hey, it's ten o'clock. Where the hell's Cindy? How the hell late she going to be?"

"She said eleven, it'll be eleven." Nita was worming her feet into slippers. "Go sit down. I'll get beers."

The walls of Orren's yard were also the walls of the three yards adjoining it. Orren settled into one cushioned lounge chair and hooked another over for Joe; the pool lights shivered, slightly refracted in the still green water, and faint jangles from three different radio stations competed with not-so-distant road noise and the burp and spin of the dishwasher changing cycles in the kitchen. The beer was St. Pauli Girl; Orren thought Mexican beer tasted like carbonated piss. Nita set a bowl of cassava chips between them. "You remember my brother Jaime?" Orren asked, taking a handful. "Cindy's his daughter by his first marriage. Her mother's in Paris; she hangs pictures for art museums. Crazy job if you ask me, but they say it pays good. Cindy was staying with Jaime, but he's in Texas, something with the Department of Agriculture, so Cindy's staying with us so she can take summer classes at school."

"And Orren thinks he's inherited a daughter," said Nita.

"She's not in Boca now. This is Dade County. Nine o'clock is too late in Dade County."

"Your boys used to stay out until two in the morning."

"Boys are different."

"Men are different," said Nita, winking at Joe as if he were some third sex with no stake and bound to agree with her. "They got popsicles for brains."

She turned for the glass doors and her movie. Orren made a defiant gesture, just in time for her to miss it.

"Well, I win on the big stuff." A faint chop at the ends of his words was all that was left of his accent. "Cindy's okay. She's not like these kids you see around. She's going to be a scientist." The eyebrows capered: it was Anita who, years ago, had persuaded him to stop trimming them and let them run riot. "So what do you really think you're going to get out of this shit, Joe? Kaplan's balls? After all these years, what for?"

"What's wrong with wanting to solve the case?"

"Which case? Your case? The Sinkhole Case? So what are you doing down here digging up Amy Wells?"

"Because there could be a connection. I've got another girl who could be missing—"

" 'Could be'? I bet *that* looked good in your proposal."

"Nobody knows where this Cherry Miller is right now. She's down here with a potential suspect."

"Well, ten to one, you'll find her, but I'll be damned surprised if you find out anything else." Dissatisfied, he grunted. "If you screw up, Kaplan will hang you. If you solve it, you really think he'll call out a parade?"

Vapor rising off the pool made the still air heavy and humid. A couple of years back Orren had stretched a screen from the eaves of the house to the top of the wall opposite, to keep out the pigeons; the mesh of the screen sectioned the thin rim of the moon, as if it had been mapped and platted and would any day be thrown open to settlers. "Well, I didn't want to stay home."

"What's that nice girl you were seeing the last time I was up there think of this project? What's her name? Stacey?"

"We broke up."

Orren settled back heavily, even more ruffled. "Well, I can't be there to point out the shit piles."

"Meaning I should steer clear of the sheriff?"

"Amy Wells is their case, their jurisdiction, and they haven't asked for help. They're not gonna thank me when I show up dragging this Mr. Official Portman. You they'll feed to the moccasins."

"Not being official means I'm not your worry."

"Not worry?" snorted Orren. "In this part of the world? With you running around in that stinking grass desert?" He worked his fingers between the taut buttons of his shirt and scratched. "I wouldn't be one of those wildlife officers for a million bucks. Riding around alone, back in those swamps, everybody you drive up to at least armed with a deer rifle, and sometimes a lot more. And with all this drug business, every time the damn water goes down, the canals are full of bodies. On top of that, ten miles west of here, you're in backwoods Florida. Maybe the local crackers—rednecks—maybe some of them do drugs and maybe they don't, but one thing that's sure is that they've been shooting and killing things all their lives."

"So they do have an idea who killed Amy, then?" Joe prompted.

"Like we 'have an idea' who murdered John Kennedy." That was a hobby horse of Orren's, that the CIA had murdered Kennedy.

"Sex crime?"

Orren moved his shoulders ambivalently. "More like a grudge killing."

Joe saw again the unforgiving stare in the Park Service picture. "So what made Amy Wells so special she got herself murdered?"

"I never met her," said Orren. "But then, I wouldn't've. We don't get much call to get mixed up in Park business. But I know what a lot of people think." Still lying back, he swigged the last of his beer precariously. "You know the Park Service, they've made a religion out of those damn panthers. They say there's only thirty left, but they don't know that. People all over claim to have seen 'em. Just the other day, they found two of 'em living the life of Riley all the way up in Highlands County, fat as ticks."

"Well, that's thirty-two," Joe said.

Orren's black eyes glistened. "Thirty-two. But you

know how when people've been living out in the country all their lives and they hear stories from their grandparents that make it sound like fifty years ago cats and snakes were just dripping out of the trees, they get it in their heads the government's got things backwards. Animals are for getting rid of. It's people that count."

"So Amy had religion?"

"Did she ever!" Orren's eyes narrowed. "Well, we got two boys, their old man runs a machine shop just off Forty-one outside of Sweetwater, the boys been mud bogging and gator poaching since they were old enough to load a cylinder, they claimed a panther came up on them in camp one night and jumped them, so they shot it. That little girl, Amy Wells, proved the panther got killed two miles from their camp and got dragged back. That's a federal offense. Maximum twenty grand, and a year in jail."

"So the boys went to prison?"

"The oldest one mouthed off in court. Called Judge Bentham a communist, if you can believe it."

"Paul Bentham?"

"Yeah. One way not to get what you want for Christmas, huh? But there's an appeal pending. They're free on bond. They were free when somebody started hounding Amy, following her around at night. They were free, and supposedly in their old man's shop with him, the night she was killed."

"And there's no evidence to charge them? like guns?"

"Those kids got guns like most people got hemorrhoids—only there's no gunshot wound to connect up with any of them. At least none the coroner could find."

Joe pivoted to face him, raising his brows.

"I understand the circumstances were such he could have missed it," Orren said mildly. "I haven't seen the pictures."

"And the murder weapon?"

"Inside money says a machete."

"Was she armed?"

"No, she wasn't certified for law enforcement. She was

what they call an interpretive ranger, with a degree in biology. But she had applied for law enforcement—she had a tendency anyway to take things in her own hands when she saw infractions that made her mad."

So that was what had gotten her killed, Joe thought. Caring too much. Courage. He leaned forward. "We've got cuts on our bones that look like a machete."

"That's hardly a link."

"It's more than I was expecting."

"Come on, Joe, don't lie to yourself, the cases are a hundred and eighty out."

Joe let it lie a minute. Then he said, "Any chance if I read the papers I could find out where the site is?"

"Oh, I'll tell you where the site is. Getting to it's the problem."

"Roped off still?"

"Maybe, but this time of year they don't need ropes; they can count on the deer flies. I wouldn't do that hike unless they issued me a spacesuit."

Something unseen, maybe a breeze so faint they couldn't feel it, breathed across the aqua inset of the pool. "Where would you go if you wanted to photograph those panthers?"

"What do the panthers have to do with it?"

"The guy who came down here with the Miller girl claims to be a nature photographer."

"That's even thinner."

"Thin or not, *I* came down here to bump into him."

"In seven hundred thousand acres of wilderness?" Orren shrugged. "Maybe Cindy'll know. She knows something about the panthers. She's been out on— speaking of Cindy, what time do you have?"

"Ten after eleven."

"Shit." Orren sat up abruptly. "Nita? Nita! Babe!"

A figure much too slim to be Nita's appeared beyond the glass doors and slid them open. "She's gone to bed, Uncle Orren. Can I get you anything?"

"How long you been home, baby?"

The girl came out on the patio. "Fifteen, twenty minutes." She sat on the foot of Orren's chair and swamped his prickly impatience in an unabashed hug. "Clock watching again?"

"You should be damn glad somebody bothers. Let me smell your breath."

"We went to Funnies. They don't even sell liquor there."

The only lights that fell on her were the pool lights, shining up through the green water. Her eyes looked dark and sunken, her skin tinged the shade of the water, like an image on a TV screen that is supposed to be in color but needs a flick of a knob. She wore a plain white clinging dress, and had long black hair, whipped up and fretted into directionless tangles; she was thin, like a very young tree that will dance in any direction. It was hard to tell how old she was; she could not have been quite twenty, but the depth of her eyes made her look older. "So, sweetheart," said Orren, "this is my old pal Joe Hope from Tampa. If Joe wanted to take a few pictures, how would he find out where those panthers of yours are?"

She turned. She had Orren's brows: dark and positive. She hiked them up reproachfully. "You don't just take a few snapshots. It's not a zoo. You walk and you wait and you pray."

"Actually, I'm not here to take pictures. I'm looking for a guy who is."

"You're with the department, too, then?"

"Joe's with the Tampa bureau."

"And you're looking for somebody out in the Cypress?"

"A guy and a girl. At least they're supposed to be out in the swamp somewhere."

"There's not just 'the swamp.' There's either the national park or the national preserve. There's a considerable difference. The park's all regulated, but the preserve is still open to hunting and camping."

"How should Joe know all that, Cin?" Orren asked diplomatically. "He don't live in South Florida."

The girl directed Orren a grimace that said plainly she still thought Joe's ignorance inexcusable. "There's panthers in the preserve?" Joe asked her. She nodded. "That sounds like where they'd be, then."

"Have they been murdered or something?"

"Not officially."

"That means you *hope* they've been murdered," said Cindy, "because otherwise it wouldn't be nearly as exciting. But if they're in the preserve, and they haven't been murdered, the rangers or inholders would have seen them or heard about them."

"That's just what he's thinking," put in Orren, his tone ever so slightly apologetic. "You know some of those park people, don't you? Who should Joe talk to over there?"

She wrinkled her forehead. "I don't know who's on duty on Sundays. I *could* ride over to the ranger station with him." Orren didn't say anything. "It's just over to Oasis, Uncle Orren," said Cindy, examining a pulled thread in the hem of her dress.

"But Joe wants to see where the ranger was murdered."

She sighed in exasperation. "Fine, I could show him how to get there. Then he could lock me in the car."

"Kinda pert, aren't you, babe?"

She pursed her lips but said nothing. Orren, too, sighed, cupping his forehead in his hands. "You know I just don't want you getting in the middle of anything."

"You know about the bugs, don't you?" the girl challenged Joe wickedly.

"What about them?"

"You're just going to the ranger station!" Orren erupted. "So you're out of the car five minutes!"

"But you said he wanted to see where—"

Orren stood up and stomped through the glass doors into the kitchen. Joe could see him yanking the refrigerator open. Cindy was watching him coolly.

"Sounds like you'd better not go," Joe said.

"Oh, he's okay." She flipped a hand dismissively, but she got up, following her uncle. For a moment he could see both of them framed in the doorway, the light from the refrigerator shining up on them, she with her thin body in her white dress, beside Orren's great height, like a pale swamp bird pecking at the heels of an angry bull. Then the kitchen lights went off and Orren came back out, heavily, alone. He started gathering the beer bottles. "You'd think a Latin man who raised two sons and helps run a whole south Florida crime bureau would be a pretty macho guy, wouldn't you? Now you know the truth."

"Is there something I should know about?"

Orren was on the verge of telling him, but Joe saw him consciously decide not to. "Nah, nah. I don't care if she goes. She'll be with you, won't she? Anyway, she loves that country." Joe picked up what was left of the chips. "She's special, that girl. Smart as a whip and don't take nothing off nobody. Ahead of herself in school, and straight A's in science. Jaime never had no sons; maybe that's the problem." He didn't stop to analyze his contradiction, but led Joe to the glass doors. "So what time you planning to go over there in the morning? nine?"

"Actually, I thought first I'd run down and say hi to Janet."

Orren stopped in midstride. "What for?"

"Courtesy?"

Orren shrugged, mystified. "Well, she'll be damned surprised."

11

HE DIDN'T DROP OFF TO SLEEP. THE house was shut up. Sealed. It was so cold he pulled up the blanket, while the sticky, insect-laden night beat itself against the icy plates of the windows, and condensation grew up the glass in a wintry map. Again he had the sense of not knowing what he had come for. In the night, alone, he could not dismiss his sudden fear that he had committed himself to a losing proposition. There was almost certainly no relation between the murder of the Wells girl and the other killings. He would come upon the guy and the Miller girl tomorrow—somehow in his mind they had started looking like an L. L. Bean–clad Jane and Tarzan, cavorting in a movie-set treehouse—and he would explain, embarrassed, that it had been conscience and duty that had driven him to barge in. They would all have a laugh over his folly, and he would flee, defeated, leaving Shorter to field the shame of his own damn lies.

But even as he came to terms with his image of the Miller girl, even as he dismissed her oblivious recklessness as nothing he should interfere with, his vision of Amy Wells intruded. So what if his crusade to catch up to Cherry and her boyfriend was a self-delusion? In his blundering, he might find out something that would help nail Amy's killer. He couldn't get over the idea that she deserved his help. He wished he had known her when she was alive.

Restlessly, he got up to go to the bathroom. He should have brought flannels, not these shorts and thin shirt. When he came out, he stole shivering to the window overlooking the pool, to breathe on the glass and trace a finger through the fog. He started; the pool lights had been turned off, and there was the unmistakable chiaroscuro shape of a spreadeagled body floating immobile in the water, just like one he had once been too late to pull to safety when he answered a worried neighbor's call in Jax. But then the body stirred, and he put both hands on the glass: it was the girl. She wore strips of black at her hips and chest, and the water washed over her, so that sometimes he could see every pale plane of her belly and other times she seemed to have no body at all. The mass of her black hair bloomed around her like ink running out of her, turning her to a jet-armed medusa. She kicked gently and fluttered her arms languidly and arched herself backward, so that the shadowy water that carried her rippled and played over her like a sea of lapping tongues.

Then, without warning, she righted herself and stood, chest-deep, her head thrown back, her attention directed up at him.

He felt himself flinch instinctively from the window, as if he had been doing something wrong. She made a pushing gesture with her palms. After a second he released the window catches and shoved the cold glass up.

"Come down!" Her voice was a theatrical whisper. "The water's wonderful! Come down!"

"I'm not dressed."

She floated forward, pulling herself with her slim brown arms. "Then get dressed! I'm coming up."

He started to protest that she shouldn't. He wasn't in the mood for chatting, and tomorrow he had a long day.

But by then she had snatched a white robe from one of the chairs and disappeared below him. He hurried into a shirt and trousers and opened the door onto the dark hallway. He would not let her stay more than a few minutes. He found himself arranging the two chairs in the room, positioning a little table with a ceramic rabbit planter between them, the way he might prepare to interview a witness. From what he had seen of her during his talk with Orren, he had best move fast to assert control.

When she appeared, winding her wet hair in a plastic clip, she had bound the short terrycloth robe securely around her. The opaque white cloth set off her tawny skin, her long, smooth dark shins, still sparkling with damp. She sat down in one of the chairs uninvited, doubling an ankle under her, totally unselfconscious. "It's freezing in here," she said. She extended her free leg. "Look. Goosebumps."

He took the other chair. Impatiently she shoved the ceramic planter out of her way, leaning across to him. Downstairs her eyes had been in shadow, but now he got his first clear look at them: They were miraculous, black and huge, and the harsh boniness of her pale features and her peace-rose coloring made a setting for them, so that her face was like a gold fretwork on a velvet backing, inlaid with chunks of a rare, aberrant midnight gem.

Well, he had known she was beautiful, hadn't he? Yet he was disconcerted. He had stopped thinking about Amy. A physical awareness of this girl's presence passed through him stealthily, a shudder of tantalizing discomfort. He thought, for God's sake.

But she didn't seem aware of any change in his expression. Her frown was innocent. "I came to explain."

"Why your uncle's so worried?"

"It's Amy Wells," she said with asperity. "All of a sudden everybody thinks any woman who goes into the woods like she did is going to get killed."

"But you won't?"

"Well, I don't know." The light hit her face, with its

mosaic of clean planes, oddly, so that one minute she looked mischievous, the next pensive. "I'm a lot like her. I take chances, too. So some people think I might."

Slowly the disquieting shudder ebbed. She became Orren's niece again, safely distant. Of course, his reaction was easy to explain. It had been a long time since he had known anyone quite like her, or like Amy: They were the kinds of girls you dreamed of when you were young, but grew up to relinquish hope of finding: fresh, idealistic, complexly intelligent—and brave. The only other person who had possessed those qualities in the degree to which he once desired them had been his long-dead dream of himself. What he had felt had been an infusion of possibility, another chance to enter a world he had failed to conquer, and from which he had long been shut out.

Well, he would stay shut out. At least for now. "So how well did you know Amy?" he asked coolly, platitudinous and grave.

She smiled, the black eyes gauging his defenses with a cheerful irreverence that went well with her tone of habitual challenge. "Ah-hah. The cop emerges."

"It's congenital."

"Tell me!" She rolled her eyes comically. "I know *he* dusts for my dates' fingerprints after we leave!"

She was probing to see if he would let her near him. And to see if he would hide behind stale answers: *Your uncle's worried about you. He wants you to be safe.* He recognized instantly, with a chill, that what kept him from choosing that option, so safe and proper, was an unwillingness, at least partly sexual, to let her see him as ordinary, to let himself down. It was her own damn fault, he told himself. It was naive and dangerous to dare people to be honest. "If you want help picking on your uncle just because he loves you, find someone else."

She sat up, stung. "I wasn't trying to make you pick on Uncle Orren."

"Yes, you were. Because you know he doesn't deserve it."

She shook her head sharply so that the clip gave way and the black tangles went tumbling. "Sometimes I just wish *nobody* loved me," she said.

He couldn't help smiling. "Oh, I have a feeling lots of people will love you," he answered more kindly.

But she didn't give him the reaction he expected, either. "Doesn't anybody love you?" she asked instead.

"Well, at the moment, not exactly an army."

"But you still know how it can feel."

"Yes," he conceded pointedly. "It can be messy."

She tilted her head to refasten the clip. He was sure she did it so he couldn't see her face. "You're not like the ordinary cops I've met at all, are you?"

Another question it would have been tempting to answer unwisely. He managed to play it safe. "I don't know what you mean."

But she seemed to be having trouble getting the clip to do what she wanted. He got up, drifting over to look down at the pool again. He had left the window open; the water was still now, with a chemically induced purity that made it impossibly clear. "So tell me about you and Amy," he said.

"Why can't we talk about you?" She looked up bluntly. "What are you so afraid of?"

"What I'm afraid of is that more people will get murdered."

"You seem to think I'm going to bite you."

"No, you won't bite me."

"I don't know." She slumped back, the dark eyes sparkling. "I have bitten people."

"You sound like you respected Amy," he persisted. "Were you friends?"

Abruptly she grew businesslike. "Not friends, exactly. We were on opposite sides in the darting controversy."

"Darting? As in the game?"

"The game of human omnipotence." Her gaze asked what hole he had been living in. "Darting panthers, of course. Amy was Park Service all the way: They think shooting panthers out of trees with tranquilizers and hanging radio collars on them is the best way to learn about them. The foundation I do volunteer work for believes the darting project is disruptive and stressful."

"A scientific foundation of some sort?"

"Oh, yes. A friend of mine who runs it is a Ph.D."

"And you're in college to be a biologist? Or so Orren tells me?"

She winked, teasing. "Next you say, you don't look old enough."

"You don't."

She, too, got up suddenly, restlessly, crossing to a big white-framed mirror over a bureau against the far wall. She bent over the hair brushes he had set out there, leaning close to the glass, the robe falling sharply away from the contours of her slender hips. He just could not tell if she was aware of her body. "As a matter of fact, I'm a sophomore," she said, talking to him through the mirror. "That's why I get so frustrated with Uncle Orren. I'm way past needing a chaperone who always wants me home before the *Ozzie and Harriet* reruns are over. I'm not used to that."

She turned, arching her back against the bureau. Now it was her breasts that the chaste robe defined.

"As far as I'm concerned, I'm already a professional. With a mission. Time is short here. Whole species, a whole part of the world, is disappearing. Amy took chances to save it, and I want to take them, except that I have to have notes to stay out late at night."

But he hardly heard what she was saying. The physical impulse, banished, had curled up outside his consciousness like a beggar, and he was growing more and more angry that he couldn't make it go away. How asinine to charge down here in a fury as if he had suddenly found it in his power to create a new self out of old failings; how idiotic to invest her with the raw youth and spirit he needed so desperately, replete with that one last catalyst, danger: the sense that letting down his guard, taking her on, would be tantamount to risking an intoxicating dare. He slammed the window down sharply.

"You haven't listened to a thing I've said," she complained.

"Of course I was listening." He went back to his chair, pulling it a couple of feet from the table before he let himself down in it. "So what kinds of chances did Amy take?"

"It *is* congenital. Like being deformed."

"Did she chase men?" he demanded. "Sleep with strangers?"

She narrowed her eyes, concentrating their darkness, and walked back to her own chair. "Do you seriously think he killed her?"

"Who?"

"Your Sinkhole Killer. The one you've been after."

"I don't know yet. Your uncle thinks it's unlikely."

"These people we're going to look for tomorrow—do they know anything about it?"

"I don't know that, either."

"That's right," she said, her voice almost imperceptibly prompting. "Cops don't know things, do they? They find out."

Maybe, he thought, just maybe, it was not there, after all, the innuendo, the challenge. Maybe he was just hearing what he wanted. But abruptly, alarming him still more, she twisted face front, put both feet on the floor, crossed, and dropped to her knees on the carpet before him. "I want to find out, too." Her voice had grown rushed and earnest, as if to tell him, somehow, that this person, this part of her, was the one he must listen to, must understand. "To be stopped because of *danger*— and I want the danger, too. I want to find out what I would do. Once I know that, I can do *anything.*"

He had been wrong to unleash this. "Get up," he said.

"You *are* just like the others, aren't you?"

"Come on. You need to go to your room. Go to bed."

Contact with her fingers when she reached up did not move him. He pulled her to her feet. "We're still going tomorrow, aren't we?"

"I haven't decided."

"You'll drive in circles without me."

"It'll probably be a big disappointment."

"Because we won't find out anything?"

"The odds are one in a hundred."

"Well," she said. "That's enough."

He got her to the door, but she stopped, turning. "It was my uncle who told me you were special. He says you're very good. At being a cop."

"I can be."

She caught the doorframe, resisting him. "Don't you sometimes think, when you catch a criminal, that you've caught up to someone who's taken the final . . . the really dangerous chance?"

"The victims don't always look at it so romantically."

"No, but what I mean is . . . if you really want to be able to catch them, you have to think like them, you have to have a little of that in you, too?"

"Maybe I'm not quite that good."

She hitched the lapels of the robe tightly together. They were standing very close. She put her hand out and touched his wrist, and then, in an ungainly hurry, as if not at all sure what she was doing, closed her fingers around it. It had been an uncalculated move, not bold because it was so awkward and childish. She looked down at her hand as if not sure it belonged to her. She took it away quickly. "Please," he said. "Go to bed."

She jumped back as if he had raised a fist to hit her. He realized she was shivering. He had conjured an image for what made her heedless sparring seem such a mortal risk. It wasn't just her age: He had dated girls who were twenty-one, twenty. Slept with some of them. But talking to her was like seeing a beautiful woman walk by on the street with some kind of monstrous and exotic animal—one of those panthers, say—on a leash. He couldn't help but react the way any man would: She was beautiful, and intriguing, and she was fishing. It was hard not to toy with the hook.

But what if he followed his exotic vision home and found the beast old and toothless, his goddess a fake who had simply found an easy way to make people stare? With Cindy, it would not be the anguish of uncovering a deliberate deception. It would be the disappointment of finding that she was just a child after all, her dares empty promises, her courage cheap. And his shame would be doubled because he was old enough to see through theatrics. Had seen through them. Had tried to make truth out of false promises, fully forewarned.

"Go get warm," he said.

"In this house that's impossible."

"Well, go try."

Leaving him, she made no sound. Then he, too, even in his shirt and trousers, was shivering. She had taken the big, hot-lunged beast out the door with her, and, heeding what common sense told him about what could be and what couldn't, he had let her go.

He went to the window again, as if hoping despite himself to get one more glimpse of her. Again he mustered defenses: She *was* too young, of course. And then there was Orren, his protective ferocity, his trust. And his own sense that lust was not the answer. Or would not be for long.

Tomorrow he would be more careful. *If* he let her go with him. He felt virtuous, but as he crossed back to the bed he could not deny that he also felt bereft, cheated. The room felt like an empty cave.

12

HOMESTEAD HAD ONCE BEEN A SEPA-
rate community, but Miami, like many big cities, had
forced itself onto everything near it, kicking tail like the
biggest and meanest of a sandlot full of dogs. Janet lived
on a narrow street two or three turns past prosperity,
where gates sagged and rusty mailboxes teetered, where
bristly dandelions overran the broken curbs. But against
all expectations, her house and one or two others near it
rose out of despair like junkyard violets: honeysuckle
swamped an arbor by her driveway, pink hibiscus flared
out of a green tangle, and well-trimmed azaleas marched
spirals around a flaming crepe myrtle growing from a
thick brown bed of mulch. Janet and Stacey, he thought
as he pulled up to the curb, shared this power to coax
things out in green leaves and flowers; whose fault was it
that for each of them, at that turn of her life where he
had come into it, the gift of nurture had finally proved a
crime?

Her car was the polished Honda with the sticker that
said, Nurses do it with care. Off to the side of the driveway sat an old Pinto with University of Miami parking
permits, very badly wrecked, so badly, in fact, that he

stood for too long entirely imagining the impact that would have rucked up the front end and twisted the frame cockeyed like that. No one in his right mind would have dreamed of repairing it. Hunter had lied.

She opened the old-fashioned screen door almost instantly, and his first thought was that she should have taken time to manner the tense lines out of her face. "Joe," she said with a bluntness that even for her was unexpected, "why didn't you call?"

"Believe me, I can go away."

But she opened the screen and marched two steps backward, as if they were awkward dancing partners. "You surprised me, that's all."

He followed her into an unpretentious living room off a tight foyer. Stacey had loved furniture, antiques especially, but Janet had always shopped at Sears; she was very good at it, and people generally thought she had spent more money than she had. Her glass doors opened not onto a pool but onto a screened patio, and in the tiny yard he could see a rock garden and bird baths. She turned to confront him. "So what's up?" she asked.

"Nothing. I was just in town."

"You've been in town before."

"So I've been thinking about you." He spread his hands. "I'm sorry. Okay?"

She gave in and laughed. She was like Stacey, yes; he had forgotten quite how much. She was prettier, more finished, with her chic red enamel earrings that matched her nail polish, her trim slacks and neat knit top, her brown hair sculpted off her face in chiseled waves. You would gladly buy real estate from Janet, he thought, or computers, or a dose of well-being; you would trust her. You would feel safe with her, just as you would with Stacey, because of the frank forbearance with which she faced you, her strength over you and much worse than you. "I've just been distracted. There's a lot going on."

He looked around, chose the couch, and crossed deliberately and sat down. She grimaced. "I guess this means you expect coffee."

"You could call the police."

"You are the police."

"Not officially."

"But you do have a gun."

He raised his arms over his head, showing his empty palms. But she walked over and hooked a finger in his belt and with one bright nail touched the butt of the .38 in its flat suede holster. He turned the raised hands into a shrug. She sighed exaggeratedly and disappeared into the kitchen; she returned carrying two steaming mugs, two coasters, and two perfectly folded cloth napkins. "Microwave instant," she said.

"Where's Hunter?"

"Oh, he stays at school."

The microwave instant was better than the coffee they brewed at the office. He was afraid to unfold the napkin. There was something forbidding about the perfectly matched corners. "How's he doing?"

"Fine. Growing up. You know he's eighteen."

He decided she did not know Hunter had been to see him. "That's not his car outside, is it?"

She raised her shoulders in deprecation. "I didn't say he wasn't a typical eighteen-year-old."

"How did it happen?"

"Driving too fast in a rainstorm. He was alone on the road. He walked away. Nobody was hurt."

"But he's doing okay, though? Grades?"

"Joe," she said with finality. "He's doing fine."

"Sometimes I think about him."

"You would do better not to." Her words took on a chipped finality that reminded him of bullets snapping into a clip. "*I* would do better if you didn't. Especially not now, after all these years."

He set the cup down, centering it meticulously on the coaster, and stared at her. She acknowledged her guilt with a tired flip of her free hand. "I know. I know. You did offer."

"Did you ever see that guy again?"

It seemed to take her a minute to decide he deserved an answer. "No."

"Hunter doesn't blame me for something, does he, Janet?"

"For what?"

Out of the corner of his eye he could see a circular bird feeder spinning gently under the patio eaves. A cardinal had dropped down in a crimson flurry, insouciantly riding the metal perch. He looked back at her. She was staring into the near distance, not seeing anything, tugging unhappily at her fingers. He was sorry he had come and knew she wished he hadn't. Maybe Hunter was right. You couldn't unsay some things, even if you wanted to, and for too many years neither of them had wanted to. Her tension reminded him of some of the things that had come between them: not only his obsessive tunnel vision, but also a secret, dizzying need in her he had not been able to define, let alone fill. He realized that it was her ring finger she was tugging at, and on it was a diamond in a gold setting. She looked down at it, then back at him. "I'm getting married, Joe."

He hesitated just a second longer than he had intended. He should have been more pleased to find that Zack had been wrong. "That's great."

"Kevin's a nice man. He's director of the clinic where I work. We love each other very much."

"I'm not arguing."

She sprang up suddenly, grabbing his half-empty cup and again disappearing into the kitchen. When she didn't come back for several minutes, he stood and edged through the swinging door after her. For some reason she had decided to wash his cup; she was rinsing it, her sleeves rolled up on her forearms. When she sensed him behind her, she turned off the water with a brusque twist of her wrist, brushing her sleeves down again and reaching for the jar of coffee. "Really," he said. "I'm coffeed out."

She put down the cup as if he had robbed her of a major purpose on which all her concentration had been focused. He came closer, and lightly touched her shoulder. "I think it's terrific," he said. "When's the wedding?"

"Next month."

"I'd like you to look happier about it."

"I am happy. I just suddenly started thinking about all the doors I'm closing."

" 'Opening.' "

"Of course," she said, to oblige him. "Opening. How'd you get so smart, Joe?"

He found himself thinking about last night, and Cindy. "Everybody's smart when it comes to somebody else's life."

She led him back into the living room. He didn't sit again. He was thinking that somewhere there had been a key, an answer, and sometime during those three years of their marriage he had kicked it through a crack. Now there was no finding it. "I'm afraid I haven't been a very good hostess," she said.

"It's okay. I should have called first."

She let him lead her to the door. When he turned to say good-bye she was smiling sadly. "I *was* glad to see you, Joe. I think about you, too."

"I'll try to get in touch more often."

Something gleamed in her dark eyes, something elusive and ephemeral as a reflection on water that can be destroyed with a breath. She touched his arm. "Wait right here." She turned toward the back of the house, leaving him alone.

There was a table along the foyer wall, with a flat mirror above it, and on each side of the mirror framed photographs of strangely muddy sunsets. Maybe Kevin had taken them. His gaze fell idly to a stack of letters. The top one had been opened and unfolded. He didn't mean to read it; it was the sight of her maiden name that caught his eye, unexpected even though he knew she used it. The letter was from the University of Miami, Office of the Registrar. He read it, bent closer, and read it again:

> Dear Ms. Jameson: On the basis of your son Hunter's high-school performance, we granted him early admission to our undergraduate program here at the University of Miami. We regret to inform you, however, that in his first term, Hunter's cumulative grade-point average fell well below the 1.5 required for satisfactory college performance. If, in his summer term, he does not succeed in raising his average to 2.0 or better, we will be forced to request his withdrawal from his course of study here at the university.

It jumped at him then, out of the corner where he had thought willpower could keep it, the whole picture: the affair Janet had had to punish him; the child she had waited too long to abort, thinking she could convince him it was his, even though she knew it wasn't, she who could never lie anyway; the child she had told him once, in those first angry years, that she hated, but who she had told him since was after all no one else's; the child she had come to love.

And coupled with that memory was what he thought he had glimpsed in the kitchen: a dark mark on her bare forearm, just the right size for a man's encircling grip.

Had it been his imagination? If not, was it his business? He shoved the letter out of sight under the others as she came back, handing him a sealed envelope with his name and address and even a stamp on it, the kind of embossed paper that told you unmistakably you were going to have to get a suit cleaned. "I was going to send it. One day."

"Thanks."

"Are you going to be back? I really would like you to meet Kevin. You could come and have din—"

"Janet, Hunter came to Tampa to see me."

Her mouth dropped open; she managed an answer in bits and pieces. "Why . . . but . . . whatever for?"

"Supposedly to bring me some information on a case down here that might tie into one we've been working on. He saw a piece in the paper."

"So that's why you're down here, then."

"On a very long shot. More for personal satisfaction."

"But why would Hunter do something like that? We hardly ever discuss you."

"I wondered myself. You're absolutely sure there's not something bothering him?"

She was shaking her head and frowning. Suddenly she stepped past him and pushed out onto the porch and reached for a single hibiscus blossom that had started wilting, with a quick jerk snapping it off. She stood with her back to him, looking around her, at this center of order and obedient grace she had created out of turmoil, and when she turned back the order was in her face once more, icy, ardently maintained. "I can't imagine," she said. "I'll ask."

"He's totally comfortable about your wedding?"

"Of course." Her tone was dismissive, as if no nerve had been touched. "He adores Kevin."

He found himself outside, the screen somehow closed, as if she had willed it. It seemed harder to press matters, any matters, with a door between them. "You know, if there's anything at all I can do for you—"

She crushed the faded blossom in her fingers. "Joe, thank you for caring, but you really don't need to worry. Kevin takes care of things now."

13

IN DAYLIGHT IT WAS A DISHEARTENING journey, westward down 41 with Cindy beside him. He felt hemmed in, blinded: on the south by unkempt willow and sumac and myrtle, on the north by a messy wall of Australian pines, beyond which stretched a barren canal bordered with chalky car tracks and an unassailable dike. Beyond the dike, the sky just seemed to keep on going. There was a lot of room out there, a brooding place for something feral you would not want to stumble over, something that surely must be fed sometimes, like a volcano starved for virgins, to make it sleep.

A car passed them without allowing enough room, and Joe had to bounce off on the shoulder. Cindy's lips tightened and she frowned behind her sunglasses. "The real Florida," she said.

She sat against the far door, congenial but distant. He had not been at all sure about bringing her, but she had apologized to him first thing, catching him alone after breakfast. "I'm sorry I upset you last night."

"It's all right."

"No, it's not. I was an idiot."

"I think we understand each other," he had said.

Her explanation, though, seemed to have had little to do with whatever he had imagined between them. She shook her head, retreating into her own issues. "I just get frustrated," she had confessed. "People treat me as if I'm a child playing games when I'm not. You know, I could help find out about Amy. But everybody keeps shutting me out."

"They just want to protect you."

She had made a face. "Thank you, Uncle Orren," she said.

So everything seemed okay; he had relented. Their new understanding was comfortable, if cool. For one thing, in khaki painter pants with steel-snapped pockets and heavy zippers, a yellow Banana Republic shirt, and pink high-topped sneakers, she looked decidedly younger. Neither did her fanciful yellow visor and the yellow ribbon twining in and out of her tangled hair recall the willful manipulation he had sensed last night. He was glad she had hidden her black eyes behind the big square sunglasses. The more barriers between them, the better. The glasses seemed to be her way of saying she too would just as soon forget.

They passed two bronze-skinned boys hitchhiking in front of a thatch-roofed Indian tourist village, their jeans hanging loose-butted, their shirts open, the sun striking sunrise-colored highlights from their flat Eskimo faces. Joe read aloud from a sign behind the hitchhikers: " 'Miccosukee.' Is that the same as Seminole?"

"No, historically they're two different tribes. They speak different languages. The Seminoles were originally Creek from up north, and the Miccosukee are descended from the native Calusa."

He had never thought much about Indians in Florida. He had never had any official contact with the ones in Tampa who ran a profitable bingo operation on a square of land near the interstate, and subconsciously he had relegated them to the status of a colony of Italians, vaguely different but pragmatically invisible. But the two boys had been vastly different, disjunctive, foreign, though of course they were not foreign. They were the natives, and he the one whose birthright was a lie.

"The Miccosukees have kind of been bastardized," Cindy went on, turning back to the window. "They're losing their old culture, but they haven't been assimilated into ours. Almost none of them move off the reservation to get jobs or go to school."

"But how do they live, then?"

She nodded grimly at the airboat concession they were passing. Monstrous signs promised horrors. "You see it right there."

Slowly, though, they put the depressing tourist clutter behind them. Joe found himself thinking of Janet. The contrast with Cindy was inescapable: Cindy in search of danger, Janet worn out with it, and marrying for safety. Or so it had looked to him.

But once—not so long ago, really—Janet had been as alive and impenetrable as Cindy, worse even: vehement and unyielding, a taut, dark-eyed scourge hurting both of them. "Don't you ever send him so much as a birthday card!" she had railed.

Maybe, looking back, he should be pleased he had been decent enough to get angry. "So what are you going to tell him, that the goddamn stork brought him?"

"I'll tell him his father's a bottle in a sperm bank. What difference does it make?"

"It makes a difference to me! Tell him *I'm* his father!"

That was when she had cried, reproaching him. "Oh, you'd like that, wouldn't you? So you could claim you had some responsibility for this marriage? When the truth is, you haven't even been here, you've never been here in your heart!"

He didn't know all the stages of her slow healing. He had seen her seldom, as her son grew up, and she moved, and Joe changed jobs. But their infrequent meetings slowly became less trying, less pregnant with her sense of betrayed passion; at those wide intervals he had watched her douse that slow fire until she no longer seemed sick on the fumes of it, and of Hunter he had glowing reports, belabored, perhaps, to drive home to him that this wonderful young creature was a miracle beyond any he could ever hope for, and in which he had had no hand.

For a second he wished he could meet this Kevin, assess him. There were questions that would bear asking. But Janet had made it plain she wanted him to stay out.

Cindy pulled him back to the present by leaning forward expectantly. "We're almost in Collier County now."

Collier County, seen in daylight, *was* different. Abruptly the Australian pines stopped, and the cypress scrub began once more to grovel up to the road: the trees sparsely leaved, stunted, and deformed like beggars, irregularly burdened with the dark round clumps of air plants, as if splotches of something that had been spat at them had stuck. Along both horizons lay sprawling strips of denser cypress, like the ribbed backs of dozing serpents, sometimes coiling their green tails around and smacking them across the road.

They re-entered the preserve, dodging the huge dead-black crows which strutted out boldly to snatch up smashed insects. When they reached the ranger station, with its dispirited flag flapping over it, Cindy led him along a chain-link fence toward a gate from which a path set off toward a shadowy wall of cypress. Beside them was a still slate-gray pond. At the gate, she lifted the lid from a weathered plywood box nailed to a pole. "This is the sign-in point for this part of the Florida Trail."

But there were no familiar names on the loose sheets of paper inside. "Can you get to a place called Fat Hog Camp from here?"

"I don't know where that is."

"Supposedly along a road called Eight forty-three."

"No, that's west of here."

She stepped through the gate. A little hesitantly, he followed. The heat seemed to steam up in layers, sticky around his ankles, blistering, scalding his lungs, higher up. Cindy drew away from him almost obliviously, although she kept decorously to the well-worn path.

They didn't have time, he thought, for random wandering. He started to call to her. But when she reached a place where the path climbed up onto a sort of sandy dike, she stopped and he drew even. From the dike, they could look out across a ragged gray-green expanse toward the dark cypress breastworks, a sudden out cropping of thick myrtle shielding them from the road.

"Can you walk out there?" he asked.

She took off the sunglasses, although he was just wishing he had not left his in the car. She didn't look at him, but across the grass prairie. "You could, but it's slow going. The limestone's pitted and close to the surface, and the saw grass cuts."

"It's not wet?"

"Not as wet as it ought to be."

"So where is the water?"

"Oh, drained off for sugarcane fields and people's swimming pools."

"But it's just June. It'll start raining."

She shook her head tragically. "Tourists used to come here for the birds, you know. Millions and millions of birds: wood storks and ibis and herons and anhingas and spoonbills and egrets. But in the last thirty years, ninety percent of them have failed to nest. Gone off somewhere. Died. Disappeared."

Her dramatic grief made him recoil even more from this strange land that trapped him on the fingernail scratch of civilization: to wander off the path would be to enter a scene of mass execution, where the somber domes were mausoleums and the long dim stretches of trees sinks where putrefaction piled up on putrefaction. "It's funny, I always thought of the Everglades as a big dark swamp."

She turned eagerly, her face brightening. "It is, in the big strands."

"Strands?"

"The deep troughs. Hardwood swamps. Like that long line of trees you can see over there. There's always water. The Indians used to canoe them like highways. You'll see, we're going to go into one."

"Will we see panthers?"

"We-e-ell. . . . Maybe some snakes and gators."

"Terrific."

"I love snakes," she said provocatively.

"Good. Then you charm them and I won't have to shoot them."

"No shooting!"

"Not even if something comes at me?"

"Oh," she said with genuine sadness, "things worth seeing never come at you. They almost always run."

That was what she was doing, he decided suddenly. Running. The realization made him react to her differently. What she had seemed to offer last night had not been so carefree, so easily surrendered, as she had wanted them both to think. He was indeed a chance she had taken, might still take, but not lightly. Just so, she had tried to make him see her as a chance for him. And facing him today, apologizing, would have been hard for a much more seasoned woman.

He realized she had not broken the silence. She was looking over her shoulder at him. She put the sunglasses on hurriedly, awkwardly, catching a stem in her hair.

"Don't do that," he said impulsively.

"What?"

"Put those on. I can't see what you're thinking."

She tilted her chin at him. "You don't want to."

He reached out and took the glasses off her. She didn't resist. There was nothing flirtatious in her eyes. Only tears.

"It's all going to be destroyed," she said miserably. "People have no imaginations. All they can see is concrete, condos, cocktails. The sense of mystery, the beauty . . . that has to be in you." She spread her fingers on her chest, a gesture so much a part of this side of her that it seemed natural. "Or else the most beautiful place in the world is nothing but a worthless swamp!"

He stood there with his heart unexpectedly aching, for her, for this doomed land she loved, felt himself giving in to unbidden emotion as weakly as if he were drunk. Now he almost touched *her* before he remembered he couldn't. She seemed to realize what his gesture, and his withdrawal, meant. She wiped her eyes messily, hurrying back behind the dense glass panes.

"Feel better?"

"You don't know what I mean, do you?"

"I'm not sure."

"You think I'm acting. You thought I was acting last night. But I wasn't. I never do."

It was true: Last night he hadn't taken her seriously, not the way she wanted, at least. It had been the sexual lure he had picked up and then hurled away from him, the hint of physical titillation, sharp but short-lived. This was an entirely different kind of passion, her sorrow and faith and the way he felt himself swept up in it, as if lust, too, could be preserved, made real, even transmuted into something golden, by an act of mind. As if you could infuse it with mystery from your own stock of dreams, make it rich and real and worth fighting for, like a crusade.

But mystery went out of everything sooner or later. At least it always had. Last night he had seen the risk clearly: that it was all an illusion. That despite your best intentions, your dream would die as the land was dying, and leave you stranded in the boneyard, both of you. What would he have sacrificed? Self-respect, friendship, her happiness. . . .

"We'd better go back," she said.

It had to be undone, of course, gotten back on a staid conversational footing so they could be comfortable together. They had a long afternoon ahead. He caught up when the path leveled out. "Maybe I do understand. A little."

"That's better than nothing." Her tone was blunt but civil.

"A friend of mine tried to tell me all sorts of terrible things about this place, but he was wrong. He said I'd hate it. I don't."

She stopped and looked up at him. He couldn't tell if she had decided to smile or not. "How encouraging."

"But he *did* say that all you did down here was drive and drive with the idea you were going to get somewhere special, but in the end every place you get to is more of the same."

"And where exactly were you thinking of getting?"

"I don't know. Someplace air-conditioned, I guess."

She did smile, shaking her head in resignation. "Most people don't recognize a special place when they come to it. Because they've given up looking, even if they don't know they have." When she walked on, she made room for him on the path beside her. So things were all right, then. "I'm going to take you someplace special. I bet you won't think so, though."

"The place with the panthers?"

"The place with the *possible* panthers. It's *always* possible." She stopped sharply, pointing skyward. "Swallow-tailed kite! Did you see?"

The black-and-white bird, evanescent, fork-tailed, had come swooping out of the sky like a stab of lightning, tracing a falling parabola so perfect it was almost fanciful, tilting upward and disappearing over the treetops just as he thought he could tell whether it was attacking or displaying, whether it flew on soft wings or bent scimitars, whether it was ordinary or something that couldn't possibly have been real. It had had a gently rounded, dovelike face and a black chip of an eye. "Is that like a pigeon or something?"

His ignorance flushed out dimples. "No, it's a raptor."

"Rapture?"

"The same root. Latin for 'carry away.' It's a bird of prey." Again she hurried forward. But as he caught up she turned impishly, her teasing suddenly probing. "They especially eat cute little baby rabbits."

"Fascinating."

"Pigeon!" she chortled. "Christ!"

Inside the big cool room, behind the high counter, the uniformed Park Service ranger looked up from his paperwork. "Howdy. Hot enough?"

Cindy took off her sunglasses. "I'm a friend of Dave Kang's," she said.

"Oh, yeah, you helped take out that cat that got his leg broke. Mr. Cruse over to Miami's niece, aren't you?" The ranger's assessment was discreet but appreciative. "Ain't seen much of old Dave."

"He's been up helping with the surveys on Alligator Alley." She gestured with the folded glasses. "This is a friend of my uncle's, from the Department of Law Enforcement. He has some pictures he wants to ask you about."

The ranger only glanced at the pictures Joe offered. "Will Gow's gonna love having you boys around."

"Will Gow the sheriff?"

"Yep. Seeing as it's Sunday, you better hope he went fishing today, like he usually does."

"You must have talked to Special Agent Portman."

"That his name? Well, I told *him* I hadn't seen hide nor hair of these people, and he told *me* I must've. Real trusting kind of dude."

Joe gave it a moment, thumbing open a brochure about trash disposal from a stack on the counter. "Then hikers don't usually check in here?"

"Now and again," the ranger conceded. "No law they

have to. The trail association maintains those trails, not the Park Service. Nobody has to maintain the ORV paths —or ruts, I should say."

"I'm not official," said Joe. "I'm not connected with Portman. We just work in the same office."

After a second, the ranger picked up the pictures once more, shuffling them and frowning. "Don't get me wrong. I don't mind helping out. At least when I'm asked nicely."

"Then you'll show them around for me?"

"I reckon so." He scratched his chin. "To drive back in the swamp, he'd have to have an ORV permit. Somebody might have seen him."

"You'd be doing me a big favor."

"I mean, I thought the world of Amy," said the ranger. "Nobody held it against her if she was a little crazy."

"Crazy?"

"You know, stormed off in them woods by herself and all. Least I didn't." He stashed the pictures in his pocket. "Yep, that Amy was one brave little gal."

14

OUTSIDE, A BIG FORD VAN WITH A MICH-
igan license had pulled in farther down the lot. Two
adults were reading the Florida Trail notice, while a couple of boys, thirteen or fourteen, had scrambled down
the bank to the pond, where they stood on the bank
heaving slices of sandwich meat into the water. Joe
started back to the car, but Cindy marched across to
glower down at the two boys like an aroused young
harpy. "What are you doing?" she asked.

The older boy squinted up at her. "Trying to get that
alligator to come over here."

There was indeed something gray-green that might
have been an alligator at the edge of the water far down
the pond.

Cindy's lips twisted. "Guess what will happen if he
does."

"Come on," said the boy warily to his brother, tossing
out the last of his meat. "Let's get out of here."

But they had to climb up the bank past Cindy. "Long
after you're gone," she told them, her tan face glowing,
"he'll remember that people mean food. One day some
sweet little child will wander down here, and that gator

will remember the food *you* gave him, and grab her, and eat her up." She raised her voice so that even the parents coming back down the path could hear her. "Then, of course, they'll shoot the gator, but who cares about that? Animals don't matter! Only people count!"

The parents hustled the boys into the van. Cindy turned on her heel and, crossing the lot, met Joe's gaze over the car roof. "Upset you again, huh?"

"At this rate I'll get used to it."

"It's very much against park rules to feed any animal."

"Then I'm glad you told them. They should know it." Mollified, she pulled open the door. "So who's this Dave Kang?" he asked.

"Someone else we're going to talk to. He works for the Foundation."

"Someone your uncle didn't mention for a reason?"

She paused, studying him for a moment. A calculated smile came and went furtively, and she seemed briefly to have put on her mask from last night, self-possessed and knowing. "Oh, but you'll keep me out of trouble."

"What kind of trouble?"

"Whatever we come across."

He wasn't convinced it was funny. "I have about as much control over you as I'd have over a hurricane."

"I *do* scare you, don't I?"

"Don't be so damn sure of yourself," he said.

Down a curving sand lane beside a boarded-up store sat a mildewed house trailer in a shady clearing. A young man was just climbing into a dusty pickup parked in the yard. He turned as they waded through the deep grass toward him, grinning past Joe at Cindy. Thin and angular as a twisted length of scrap iron, he had an unexpected sulky beauty, with his sunken black eyes, longish, thick black hair, and skin the color of rust. "How do, Miss Cruse."

Cindy lowered her sunglasses. Her lips had tightened again. "Do I know you?"

"I went out with you and Dave on a trip last winter. Remember? When we were looking for cat sign over in Fakahatchee?"

She frowned venomously. "Oh, yes, the *hunter.*"

It was a tilted, miscreant's grin the kid directed at Cindy. "You ate what I shot, didn't you?"

"Next time I'll take sandwiches."

The kid backed toward the open door of his truck. He wasn't retreating, just taking time out to scout his angles. "Nice seeing you folks," he grinned.

He pulled away in a blast of gas fumes. "He has pit bulls, too," Cindy sneered.

Joe wondered what it had taken to arouse her so deeply. "Who is he?"

She twitched her slim brown hand in a rigid dismissal. "His name's Jimmy Easter. He's a friend of Dave's. Maybe because they're sort of descended from the same tribal clan, which makes them sort of related. Anyway, Dave's much more tolerant than I am. About a lot of things."

"What does he hunt with that gun I saw tucked behind his seat? Elephants?"

She glared ferociously over her shoulder, but the truck was no longer visible. "He's not supposed to have guns in the preserve unless it's hunting season."

"That's the point. It wasn't a hunting rifle."

She snorted savagely. "Well, I'm not surprised."

A wooden porch ran the length of the trailer, its steps creaking under them as they climbed. Cindy jerked the door open and stuck her head in. "Dave?"

A welcoming voice hallooed at them. The little kitchen was a bachelor's mess, the sink stacked with dishes, half-filled coffee cups scattered around as if to collect drips from the roof during rainstorms, a heap of books and papers piled so high Joe wondered if the ones on the bottom might have started composting. The living room beyond was no less jumbled, but it looked bigger than it was because of the wide-open windows on either side. There was no domestic furniture at all, just bookshelves and filing cabinets and in a corner, an elaborate PC. A huge table filled what was left of the meager floor space; on it had been stapled a detailed, hand-drawn map bristling with colored pins.

"The only really complete map of the Big Cypress," Cindy told him as he lingered to study it. "Dave put it together himself from his own aerial photos and surveys. The pins correspond to all the current panther data. Decent, Dave? We're coming back!"

They passed a dim garret of a bedroom and a pit of a bathroom, and burst at last into another cramped but well-lit space. A rusty fan creaked unevenly in one of the open windows, its breath fitful and warm. The shelves and jumbled benches were crammed not with rotting books and papers but with jars and terrariums and aquariums, and Joe didn't have time to begin counting all the burrowing, half-seen creatures they contained. The little man behind the big easel grinned widely in welcome, and Cindy bounced over and kissed him soundly on the cheek.

Dave Kang had to be at least in his late fifties, and maybe older; his soft bronze Oriental features made it hard to be sure. His hair had gone so gray it looked white against his dark temples; his wrists poking out of the rolled-back cuffs of his khaki shirt were as thin and stained as sticks that had lain too long under water, and the backs of his wiry hands were as translucent and bold-veined as the wings of the huge flame-red-and-black butterfly trapped in the jar by his side.

It was the butterfly he was painting, and Joe caught his breath at the image: one so detailed and vibrant its web of color seemed to beat on the paper. "You're a very unloving young lady," said Kang, his voice gently musical. Like Orren, he had a twinge of an accent, but where Orren jumped off the ends of his words, Kang hung onto his, molding each of them into a circular tonal knell. He put down the egg carton full of paints and the soft-tipped watercolor brush with which he had been working and offered his hand. Joe took it. "Is this the reason I haven't seen you?" he asked Cindy. "A convert? or a new friend?"

"Joe's a friend of my uncle's. He works for the Department of Law Enforcement."

"No convert, then?" Cindy made a place to sit, a narrow three inches of bench beside a glass jar which housed an enormous black-and-gold spider. "Something official? I heard Will Gow was expecting somebody about the Wells case."

"That would be Special Agent Portman. I'm on my own time."

Kang looked at Cindy. She started to say something, but didn't. Kang's soft gray eyebrows rose.

"I promise, you won't be mixed up in anything," Joe said quickly. "Besides, it's almost certainly a dead end."

Kang picked up his brush again and dipped it in a jar of water, squeezing the bristles out carefully. Unasked, Cindy was arranging Kang's other brushes for him. "Well, you see, Mr.—"

"Hope."

"Mr. Hope, the fund I work for is also extraofficial. We're not connected with the DNR or Game and Fish or the Park Service or any other agency. This part of the world is a lot smaller than it looks. It's easy to step on other people's toes." He dried his hands on a torn towel. "It's not inconceivable Will Gow and this other man will come here and ask me some questions."

"We're just driving around," Cindy put in suddenly. "I'm just showing Joe the country."

Kang grimaced wryly. "Will Gow won't believe a word of it. What is it you think I can do?"

Joe produced the pictures. Kang studied them, nodding. Cindy jumped up and peered between them, interested in the photos for the first time. "Oh, yes, I saw these two," said Kang. "Three days ago. I'm afraid I wasn't very nice to them. I pretended I had the authority to order them out of the very sensitive area they were disturbing. But I'm afraid he knew I had no such authority. He said some fairly rude things of his own."

"Did he strike you as legitimate? Did he have equipment?"

"Maybe too much. Panthers don't sit still while you set up a tripod."

"Did they seem friendly? Comfortable together?"

Kang laughed softly. "*She* was ready to go back. She wasn't the type to sit for hours by a game trail, feeding the bull ants and the deer flies. I thought for a minute she was going to ask me to take her back with me, but she didn't."

"Can you give me some idea where they were?"

Kang moved the easel aside so he could edge past, and led them back to the room with the map. Without hesitation, he set a brown, reedlike finger down on a spot well away from the red line of the nearest road. "There."

Joe studied the map in silence. Not far from Kang's finger, he found a dot marked in prim, geometric handwriting, *Fat Hog Camp*. Without speaking, Kang moved his finger southwest toward the road, stopping on a tiny hollow circle, next to which had been pencilled, *Amy Wells*.

"So you can't get to Fat Hog Camp by car?" Joe asked.

"No, the bridge has been out for years."

"How long would it take to walk?"

"Well, it's low water," said Kang. "Better part of a day."

"Then they must have been camping back there. They might still be there."

"Maybe." Kang studied Cindy, who was hovering between them, bent over the map, unaware of him. "Mr. Hope . . . you like snakes?"

"Not especially."

"Cindy does."

"So she told me."

"Almost anything that comes out of holes, actually." Cindy straightened, pulling her hair back mischievously.

Kang's quick smile narrowed his eyes. "But she hasn't been here so that I could tell her that the scarlet king eggs she helped me collect have hatched."

"You're kidding!"

"Go see."

They followed her out onto the back porch. Impulsively she ran down the steps and across a grassy plot to a thatch-roofed Indian chickee, under which crates and various glass-and-wire cages were stored. Joe started after her, but Kang touched his arm. "I knew Amy very well," he said in a low voice. "I helped bring her out." Cindy was working her way in among the crates, well out of earshot. "You're planning to take Cindy there with you?"

"So far she seems to be doing most of the planning."

"Yes, she's very mature—and strong-willed—but this is a very bad business."

Joe propped his elbows on the porch railing. Cindy was kneeling in the shade under the chickee, lifting a glass pane off a wooden box.

"Already," said Kang, "there has been some unhappiness over some . . . grown-up . . . things that shouldn't have happened. I would not like to be responsible for getting her mixed up in any of this."

"Her uncle knows she's out here."

"He knows you've come to me?"

Kang's shining face was exactly the color of a big jar of sun tea when you held it up to the light and looked through it. Joe met his sad eyes in silence. "I didn't think so," Kang said heavily. "Well, as long as we understand each other . . . I'll tell you what I can. There's not much. They found no weapon. No cloth fragments caught on bushes, no skin under Amy's fingernails, nothing like that. There had been some rain that week, and the water had come up, and there were no foot-prints."

"The papers were vague. I have a friend who's a re-porter, and he couldn't get any details. She was sexually molested. If she'd been raped, there'd be semen."

"Rape," sighed Kang, "is not specifically what the ex-pression referred to. Whether she had been or not, the officers seemed to think it might be impossible to be cer-tain."

Again they met each other's eyes. Joe looked away first. "What about these kids who're supposedly sus-pects?"

Kang clasped his spidery hands together, the tips of his fingers tinged with the bright scarlets of his butterfly. "The Meacham boys are convenient suspects. They might have killed Amy in anger, if they were extremely drunk and she caught them a second time doing some-thing they should not have. But whoever did this was more than drunk."

"So who was it, then?"

"Oh, I wish I could tell you. Will Gow wishes someone could tell him." Again he considered. "You've heard Amy thought she was being followed, harassed, after dark? Of course, everyone thought in terms of the panther case, but although she never saw the car clearly, one thing she was very sure of was that it wasn't a four-wheel-drive pickup with mud tires, which is the only thing the Meacham boys would have been caught dead driving."

"Hmm . . . is there any possibility it could have been a sports car?"

"For example?"

"A red Karmann Ghia?"

"It does seem she would have noticed, had it been something *that* unusual, doesn't it? All I know is that it was a small car."

"Where do the Meachams live?"

Kang raised his eyebrows sharply. "You go there, you

will start trouble. Will Gow and Darryl Meacham have fished together for thirty years."

"That's all the more reason—"

"Not with Cindy. Please."

It was Cindy's movement, the bright pink-and-yellow flutter, that made them both glance simultaneously at her. She was leaning against a cage, staring at them, her mouth set. When she saw them looking at her, she straightened deliberately, fingering the sunglasses, and started toward them. She stopped a few feet away. "You must be talking about Amy Wells."

Kang didn't answer. He shuffled like a naughty child, looking down.

"See?" she said to Joe, her voice brittle. "Even Dave thinks I'm useless. Even Dave shuts me out."

Kang turned suddenly and went back into the trailer, leaving the door open. Cindy dashed up the steps, passed Joe, and disappeared after him. Joe did not know why it seemed important he should understand what was happening. He stepped into the trailer. But the map room was empty, the silence undisturbed.

Somewhere in the cluttered trailer, he thought, there was a magic cupboard, and Kang had whisked her through it, and while he stood here they were off somewhere living lives of wizardry he couldn't share. He took a step down the hallway, but then Cindy appeared at the end of it, pulling the door shut behind her. "That's okay, then. Let's go."

"He seems concerned about you."

"I know," she answered, shoving tendrils of damp hair under the visor. "Somebody else who *cares* about me." She made it sound like an execration. But because he was listening he heard her voice quiver, though she stopped it as sharply and firmly as she might have stopped a wedding peal by taking hold of the clapper of the bell.

THE TENSION HAD PILED UP BETWEEN
them again. He found himself driving pugnaciously,
while she stared out at the empty country beyond the
window as watchfully as a child who has been promised
her first sight of the ocean. The scrub gave way to untidy
walls of dense forest. She snapped directions, each word
an admonition. "Left. Slow down. Now right here." The
road they turned onto was 843: dusty white shell, true
as a gunshot, dying in the distance in a hot shimmer of
mirage.

"Who exactly is your friend Dave?" he asked her.

"I told you. Head of research for the Everglades Foundation."

"He's your Ph.D.? I thought you told me the Indians
didn't go to college."

At first he thought she was not going to tell him, but
his silence must have been persuasive. "Dave's mother
was Chinese. She worked in a bar in Miami, between the
big hurricanes."

"So he isn't Indian?"

"Oh, yes. His mother went off with a rich land specu-
lator. But he came back to Miami without her. He said

she took up with an Indian, but she told some missionaries she had been raped. She gave the baby to the Indians to raise, but then about ten years later she came back and took him away with her. She had married a rich man in California, and he sent Dave to school. So Dave is both Indian, and not Indian, and not white either—" Suddenly she sat forward, pressing her palms on the window. "Slow down. Here."

He stopped the car. The usual canal following the road was a shallow seep of rank black water. A red ORV permit sign screamed its warning from the bank; an uninviting timber bridge crossed to a one-lane puncture into the forest. She said, "You can drive in about a mile."

"Don't I need a permit?"

"Technically yes, but they'd just fine you."

"I won't get stuck?"

"Trust me, you won't."

But the bridge timbers rattled a warning. Cautiously he bounced the car up onto the sandy bank. "How far would *you* guess it is from here to Fat Hog Camp?"

"Judging from Dave's map? I'd say five miles." The overgrown pathway closed around them, and she frowned doubtfully. "You think this guy you're looking for hiked from Fat Hog Camp and caught Amy Wells back here and murdered her?"

"Possibly."

"But . . . I mean, given that he knew the country and was a good enough woodsman, you assume he just coincidentally stumbled out of the swamp in a murderous mood at the exact moment she happened to drive in?"

"I just assume there've already been a lot of coincidences: The kid in Chokoloskee who told me about Fat Hog Camp said the guy knew where it was because he'd already been back here, Amy Wells was killed here, your friend Dave found Sapia and Cherry Miller here—"

"And the Meacham boys have a hunting camp of their own not two hour's walk up the strand. That's where

Amy caught them with the cat. On the other hand, Eight forty-three cuts right into the heart of the Cypress. Lots of people use it. Tracks lead off all around."

"*If* Sapia's mixed up in the murder at all," he said, gritting his teeth as a limb smacked the windshield, "I think he's been hanging around down here for a while. I think he spotted Amy Wells and knew she worked alone and dogged her until he cornered her."

"Then why does he keep coming back here? Isn't that dangerous?"

"Like *you* told *me,* people who do things like this live to take chances. They don't always worry about whether something's dangerous or not."

The hardwoods thinned; once more they entered cypress, gothic and aerial, tall spare young trees growing straight to the sky out of a carpet of coarse knee-high grass. The sandy track turned dark and peaty, and he felt the car pitch downward, sinking. "We're coming into the strand. Water up ahead. You had better stop," Cindy said.

He braked in what looked like an often-used turning-around place. Lilies glowed like fireflies from the untidy grass, and heavy air plants weighted the frail cypress branches. "Isn't this where I lock you in the car?"

She turned toward him, anchoring the sunglasses in her hair above her visor, the twitch of her mouth suddenly insolent. "What for?"

"It's a murder scene. It may not be pretty."

"Do I really look that fragile?" She took his bemused headshake for an answer. "Besides, it's going to get rough. You need me."

"Oh, hell. Come on."

But he opened the door, took one dismayed breath, and shut it again. She laughed gleefully, bending to probe in the knapsack she had stashed between her feet, coming up with a plastic squirt bottle of insect spray.

"You first," he said.

She scrambled out; before her feet hit the ground she

was dousing herself, face, hair, back, legs, in an acrid fog. After a second he took his chance. She hurried around and drenched his back. The mosquitos screamed as they bombarded him, their million tiny howls merging to a supersonic whine. He slapped futilely. "We don't have to do this, you know," she said.

He looked around, rubbing his neck. In all that infinite forest nothing so much as trembled. "*We* don't. I do."

"You sound like somebody dared you."

"I guess I dared myself."

"Oh, well, that's different. Come on."

She spun and set off. He jogged and caught up to her. They had not gone far before he began to be glad she was with him. It had seemed so straightforward: getting out of the car, following the trim track onward. But it turned out to be very different from what he had planned.

For one thing, he had not fully planned on this devilish army, this plague of swarming creatures: motes of mosquitos with the bites of semiautomatic rifles, agile deer flies drilling his neck and shoulders, droning green-eyed horseflies big enough to land the whole bloodsucking invasion. The spray helped, the cloud of poison slowing the hordes, though it couldn't stop them. And quickly the forest changed. The trail wound down, out of sight of daylight, into a wet pitchy wasteland. The open woods darkened; sunlight crept in only penitently, and ruin rose on all sides. Ferns sprouted wantonly, rooted in rot, and water crept in to share in the carnage. The fall of the land was not perceptible, yet it was precipitous, a plunge of color and mind.

And still he kept thinking he would see things that moved. Sometimes he heard cries, far off, disembodied, and strange. But whatever was watching him was silent, hidden, or perhaps moving in another time frame, too slow for him to see it, or so vast he could not feel it, just as a diver in the ocean trenches can't feel the tides turn.

They came to a wide slough of inky water, an oily

tongue licking its way across the black, gummy guts of
the swamp bottom. Cindy turned, and her thin shoulders rose and fell, to his amazement, in an unmistakable
sigh of delight.

"Isn't it grand?" she said.

He jerked off his sunglasses and slapped a tickling
stream of sweat out of his eyes. "Yeah, a picture postcard."

"Did you see the big moccasin?"

He looked around hastily. In all the muck and tumbled roots nothing looked back at him. "Where?"

"Oh, way back. It was just crawling under a log. I
thought surely you would see it."

"All I can see is black spots. With wings on them."

"I didn't think you would like it."

"I didn't say that."

"You don't have to like it."

He took a step toward the water. Black mud
squelched up the sides of his shoe. "Well, it's not the
Alps."

"In the Alps they have to invent mysterious elusive
monsters for the tourists to watch out for. *We* don't have
to invent them." She pivoted on her toes happily. "Just
think of all the things that could be hiding out there!"

"Do we have to go through that water?"

"Oh, yes."

"Well, quit gloating. Let's go."

With a flick of her visor she plunged joyously forward,
pink shoes and all. He couldn't help hesitating. "Roll up
your pants legs," she told him. He bent awkwardly, balancing on one foot, then the other, feeling absurd but
obeying.

"You can take off your shoes, too," she called back.

He made a face at her and she burst out laughing. He
waded forward abruptly, catching up to her, almost losing his balance. When he felt himself firmly righted, he
realized she had caught his arm. He started to jerk away.
But then didn't. She put her palms on his forearms; this

time her grip was not awkward but fierce, unapologetic. Looking down, he saw the fine veins on the backs of her hands tighten and the sun-bleached hairs tremble. For a moment he felt dizzy, divorced from perspective. The punch of his heart changed rhythms. He drew his hands away.

But she caught his arms again. "No one will ever know if you kiss me," she said.

"I'll know about it."

She threw her head back, weighing him down. "You want to."

He said nothing.

"What is a kiss?" she demanded with a surprising undercurrent of urgency. "What will it hurt?"

He could, after all, be cold and uncompromising. "What I want is to do what I came for. I want to see where Amy Wells died and see if there's anything worth learning. Then I want to get out of here."

She backed away. "You think I'm too young. You think I have to be protected."

"I think you're looking for something I can't give you."

"How do you know what I want?" she demanded vehemently. "How do you *know* what you can give me?"

"Please," he said. "Please. Let's get this over."

"You don't know! You can't answer!"

He wheeled, heading back down the trail, up, out, away. For a second she did nothing. Then she called reproachfully, "All right. I get the message. I'll leave you alone."

He stopped, looking back and sighing.

"I won't hurt you." She turned a stiff shoulder. "Come on."

She marched off with Amazonian determination. After a long moment he shook down his trousers and followed. Her touch, her exhortation that was part accusation, had bruised like a kick in the gut. He was angry at himself because she was right, she had read his heartbeat: he had wanted to. He had wanted just a taste of her. For that unstable moment, she had been neither child nor woman but a *destination,* some place he might break through to that was not just more of the same.

But he was bitter, too, because he knew he must pass up all chance of being fulfilled *or* disappointed. Watching her slim, firm figure, utterly female, yet knife-keen and feline, glide ahead of him, he unaccountably grew angry at Orren. If she had been anyone else's niece or daughter. . . . But then he felt a slash of guilt that had nothing to do with Orren. She was playing at love without any idea of what she was getting into. If he had let himself kiss her he would have been hard put not to fuck her there in the mud, in the forest. At least that was what it had felt like. He felt like a predator himself, stalking after her. Crazy, blind little fool.

She led tirelessly. They slogged out of the mucky sink, through ankle-deep tar. Soon they came to another slough, a wider one. Greasy green scum roiled on the surface; drowned stumps poked out of the water like floating sentries camouflaged with feathery bonnets of fern. She didn't pause or glance back at him. "Watch where you put your hands," she said simply. This time the water came well over the rolled cuffs of his trousers, soaking his thighs.

At last the ground rose, and suddenly there was a reassuring profusion of heavy, geometric tread marks, her tracks marring them with light, patterned indentations. She trudged on, isolated and unspeaking. They entered a rout of tangled roots and stumps and fallen logs so enclosing and forbidding he felt that they were delving deeper, not emerging: burying themselves, not climbing free. The trail narrowed; the caterpillar tracks disappeared. Suddenly they found themselves in a water-laden glut of vegetation: green, bristly-flowered, thorned things that batted them reprovingly, bald runners of vines interweaving with tree roots, soggy overgrown timber warty with fungus. Cindy put a hand back coolly to slow him. "Through here."

They stepped out into a strange place, onto rising ground, a scab in the heart of the damp. It looked like a ruined pagan temple, a fit place for sacrifice. The floor was stained stone, pocked with deep black punctures; the walls were smooth-trunked trees which seemed to grow out of stumps they were choking, dripping their fluid roots earthward. The altar was the burnished copper root mass of a red-barked downed tree. Across the clearing, a desecration, stretched the yellow tape and flags the Collier County Sheriff's Department had laid out.

For the first time, Cindy hung back. He waited. She pulled the sunglasses down with a snap of her wrists. "This is the first time I've been here since . . . she died."

"Are you all right?"

She wrinkled her nose. "Of course."

The high-pitched mosquito jeer seemed to lessen, but not the grating plaints of the flies. He stepped over the tape carefully, leaving her at the edge of the forest. Dodging the pock holes, he made his way to the corner by the root-altar where all the tapes converged.

But whatever he was looking for, it was not here either, any more than it had been anywhere else. The stone fell off into a muddy hollow where every inch showed signs of having been raked and probed. Painted numbers marked discolorations; he couldn't be sure if any or all of them were blood. He peered down into one of the holes. It wasn't deep, and it was empty. It was all wasted, all empty. He straightened, suddenly aware of the heat, of the sweat inching down his body, of the indecipherable jeers of insects and frogs.

He heard a sound behind him. He turned. Cindy stood there, close enough to touch. She had pushed the glasses back again; her eyes were wide, as black as the holes in the lime rock, a distraught glimmer stirring in them. She jerked her head toward the stains in the rock. "Is that her blood?"

"It might be. I don't know."

"What are all those tapes and numbers?"

"That's where she was lying."

"Where she—"

He caught her elbow, supporting her. He turned her and led her away from the ominous profusion of markers. But she pulled herself up, pulse beating in her damp throat, her hand to her mouth. "Stop. I'm not afraid."

"Go sit down in the shade."

"I thought I could smell it."

"It's been too long. It's your imagination. It doesn't smell."

She turned, not away, but into him, ducking her chin so her tangled black hair brushed his throat. She didn't lean against him, but laid her hand suddenly, heavily, palm damp and trembling, against the hot flesh at the V of his shirt. She pulled her fingers down his chest slowly. He couldn't move to stop her, not until the tremulous, searching weight reached his belly. Then he caught both her wrists, and though she didn't fight, held her rigidly away.

"Cindy, how many men have you slept with?"

"If I tell you a lot, you'll hate me. If I tell you none, you'll think I'm a child."

"You haven't done it before, have you?"

She wouldn't look at him. "I have, I've—"

He shook her so that her head jerked back and she faced him. "Then what in God's name makes you think I'll be so damned different?"

"Isn't that kind of the point?" she whispered. "To find out?"

He wheeled, putting the breadth of the clearing between them. The rock, scoured clean and sterile, scraped under his feet. He leaned weakly against a tree, in its meager shade. She had not moved. But the crescent of sweat that had been inching down from the neck of her T-shirt had reached her breasts. Slowly, while he watched, she put her hands under them. She lifted them, in the translucent cotton, in the pale cups of her bra, squeezing, hurting herself with her dark fingers, the soft mass of her flesh heavy but buoyant, dense but molten, the nipples springing up as if driven by heat.

He closed his eyes. He heard footsteps. Not coming toward him. Going away.

He caught up to her and spun her. She didn't wince or run but looked up at him with a grieving insolence that made him want either to strike her or cry.

She opened her mouth and wound her hands behind his neck and kissed him. It was as good as over then, a suffocating moment when the livid heat overcame him; he took hold of the waist of her jeans and pulled her against his stiffening cock. She was wiry and taut, live with a tensile power, constricting yet fighting; she tasted sour, like the spray, not like a sweet fruit but a tart one, full of a fluid that quenched by intoxication, and with the alien taste of her came release and with that a purging indifference, to everything he had wanted to find and everything he had not. One of her hands clawed his shirt; with the other he realized he was fighting. She wanted to assault the bulge of his genitals through the cloth and he would not let her. Then she touched him, just the bite of a nail on his organs. His last doubts disappeared in a hot physical shudder: She was woman enough, goddamn her, and he clutched her hand to his groin, making her take him, her breasts hard knots against his body, between them but not dividing them the hard steel bulk of his gun.

He saw the movement, beyond the blur of her face and closed eyes, a lifetime before he heard the voice. "Bugs'll play hell with your bare ass if you do it, mister," the voice said.

It was not easy to come back from the choking sickness, get the ground to stop whirling, get his head clear. He let Cindy down slowly, feeling her breathing, like his, nearly stop. She tried once to pull away but he held onto her until she gave into him. The full-bellied man with the graying sideburns, in the fishing hat and stained green trousers and frayed shirt, put his hand to his jaw and scratched.

And behind him, slapping at his neck almost absently, his eyes bright and excited, stood Portman, his hair, usually so ferociously erect, drooping, his soaked trousers rolled up to midcalf, his lips open, his teeth clenched.

"Hello, Mr. Gow," Cindy said.

"Hello, honey," said the sheriff. "Your uncle know you're out here?"

"Yes."

"He know what you're doing?"

Her body against Joe's tensed resentfully. "I doubt it."

Will Gow stepped over the tape with slow dignity and turned to look back at Portman. Galvanized, Portman hopped over the tape, feinting close to Joe. "Well, I guess nothing happened," drawled Gow. "Yet."

Joe tightened his grip, jerking his rucked-up shirt down, and Cindy moved closer. "Nothing happened."

"Then maybe we won't have to tell nobody . . . this time."

"Tell who what?" demanded Cindy. "It's nobody's business."

"If I was your uncle—or your dad—it sure would be my business."

"Yeah," said Portman suddenly, cavorting up to them. "Sheriff Gow was telling me all about you . . . about how you sometimes forget to tell all the men you screw you're only seventeen."

Cindy shook free of Joe. Portman seemed to think she was going to spring at him; he stumbled back. Joe caught her arm. She was trembling. "You lie."

Will Gow stepped forward bullishly, separating the two of them from Portman. He glanced at Portman, then turned and spat; he looked long and hard at Joe. It was to Joe he spoke.

"You tell all those muckety-mucks at that candy-ass

agency of yours, when I want clowns like the two of you meddling in my jurisdiction, I'll goddamn ask."

Joe said nothing. Gently he pressured Cindy past Gow. Portman seemed on the verge of yapping after them, but Gow took hold of his arm. "You stick to business," the sheriff said.

16

HE THOUGHT SHE WAS GOING TO LEAVE him there in the woods. She walked rigidly, plowing through the mud and water, looking neither left nor right. Back at the car she climbed in her side and tossed the backpack onto the floor angrily. He got in and turned to look at her. She had folded her arms across her chest, curling up and hiding. "Please," she said, "take me home."

He slapped the car into gear and spun it around in the narrow space. Gow had parked his big four-wheel-drive mud truck behind the Izusu; there was just room to squeeze past. They bumped out along the rutted track, this time taking moss and limbs with them. He stopped the car where 843 joined the highway. In the rigorous daylight, everything—the road, the sky, her face —seemed two-dimensional, brittle as old paper, plastered to the same blank wall. She turned, openmouthed, the sunglasses helpless to shield her.

"Talk," he said.

In answer she kicked open the door, springing out into the gritty junction of shell road and highway. He bolted after her, vaulting the car hood. He caught up to her, grabbing her arm, just as a minivan shot past them; it braked, stopped.

"They'll think you're raping me," she said.

"Is that what you want them to think?" he demanded. "Do you want them to come back and save you?"

She wrestled her arm free, ignoring the van. It drove slowly on, its occupants clearly watching. "You believe them," she accused him. "You think I'm some kind of whore."

"Did you sleep with Dave Kang?"

The sunglasses were dead reflections. He didn't ask her this time, but reached out and took them off her, putting them in his pocket. "I wanted to love somebody," she said.

"You've got your whole life to love somebody."

"I thought I could love Dave. He loves me."

"What am I," he demanded, his voice cracking, "part two of the experiment? Or part ten?"

Bereft of her defense, she whirled from him. "Why am I explaining all this to you? You're going back to Tampa. It's all meaningless anyway."

"It won't be when I have to explain to my boss and your uncle."

"Oh, is that it? Your *honor?* Well, I'm fucking sorry."

"You should be."

She spun back. Tears had started down her cheeks, wearing away her beauty. "It isn't the least bit possible I could really love you? That I could mean it?"

"You don't know what you want. You're just running around in the dark. You're a child."

"A few minutes ago I wasn't. A few minutes ago I was worth loving."

He couldn't look at her. Cars were still whipping past, so fast their tailwinds almost sent him staggering. Dust clogged his throat, a choking powder. "Why didn't you stop me?" she demanded. "You're so perfect, why didn't you say, 'Cindy, don't'?"

He put both hands over his face. He wanted to turn

his back on her and start walking—off, anywhere. He wanted to walk out into the muck until it claimed him. She stiffened, an impulsive defense that somehow made her seem taller.

"I'll tell Uncle Orren anything he wants to hear to get you out of trouble."

"That's not necessary."

"I'll tell him I lied. I'll tell him when you asked I said I was—"

"Cindy."

She broke off, chewing her lips, her fists clenched. He said, "Don't."

She stared at him, face strained in the harsh sunlight, then brusquely marched past him. She was already in the car when he reached it. Though she huddled away from him, he caught her wrist, fighting her into acquiescence, then stretching for the seat belt and fastening it securely across her. The car leaped, spinning gravel, as he stepped on the gas.

He was right: it was Orren's department Chevrolet, the tall radio antenna jutting off the trunk hood, he saw parked in front of the little roadside store. He pulled up beside the Chevy and got out. Cindy, ignoring him, slumped down into the harness of the seat belt, bracing her knees on the dashboard. The breeze grumbled through a row of squat palms and ruffled the peeling, long-out-of-date inspection stickers on the rusty gas pumps. From beyond the dingy screen door, he could hear raised voices. As he started forward, the door swung open and Orren hurried out. "Joe! It's a damn good thing!" He took Joe's arm, pulling him back toward the Isuzu. "Why didn't you tell me about this jerk?"

"I don't have any control over Portman. He's Kaplan's—"

"I don't mean that jerk. I mean this other one. This

guy with the hots for the chick from Tampa you're looking for. Why didn't you tell me about him?"

A truck went by, pelting them with dust and gravel.
Joe took a long breath. "Shit."

"Shit is right. He came busting in here, collaring people, telling them they had to know where she was. When
nobody knew what the hell he was talking about, he
started bashing heads."

"It never occurred to me he would be such an asshole."

"Then you know him?"

"I knew him in Tampa. I left him in Tampa."

"And you're gonna take him back to Tampa."

"Where is he now?"

A rangy man in jeans and a white undershirt, his
dark hair growing down his weathered cheeks in long
sideburns, pushed the screen door open. He raised a
wiry fist, showing raw knuckles. "Down the road as far
as his ass could haul him, I guess."

"Then he didn't do any damage?"

The man grinned slowly. "No more'n he got."

"That's not the point," said Orren, glancing through
the car window at Cindy. He lowered his voice. "The
point is, the last thing anybody needs is some jackamo
with crotch itch running around starting brawls."

"I'll call Kaplan and tell him I—"

"I called him. At home. I told him you won't be setting
a foot out of Collier County until you can take this jerk
with you in cuffs."

The thin man was scratching the shaggy nape of his
neck languidly. "Which way did he go when he left here?"
Joe asked.

"Thataway," said the man, pointing east.

"Driving a red Ford pickup," said Orren. He took a
scrap of paper out his pocket. "License. Had a bunch of
stickers on the windshield, a Reese hitch, a dent in the
right quarter panel—"

"I know it. How long ago?"

The man shrugged. "A while ago. Two hours."

Joe sighed. "You'll find him," said Orren. "Won't you?"

"Yeah, I'll find him."

Orren glanced again at Cindy, who had moved her hand to the door handle. "Take her home first."

"Orren, there's something I have to—"

"About this mess?"

"No, it's personal, it's—"

"Do me a favor, save it. Jesus. I got to find Will Gow before he hears about this from some dipshit with an ax to grind. Jeez. Already he's gonna be on the phone to Tallahassee, and now this."

He was turning away. Joe folded the slip of paper and put it in his own pocket. "You do *me* a favor, then, Orren."

"Yeah, Joe, what is it?"

Joe opened the door of the Isuzu. Cindy was sitting up, chewing her lip, looking from one to the other. "Later on, you remember I tried to tell you."

Orren paused in midstride. He frowned. He met Cindy's eyes. When he turned back to Joe, his face had crumpled, as if someone had flung a big chunk of mud at it. He rubbed the narrow space between his eyebrows wearily. "Get her home."

At the house, Nita was out in the driveway, in gloves and a sunhat, trimming the hibiscus, piling the sheared branches in a basket at her feet. Cindy didn't speak to her, but hurried inside, slamming the door. Nita raised her thin gray brows at Joe. "We had a disagreement," he said.

"Well. No matter. Sometimes kids just turn up the heat to see the pot boil. Don't you remember doing that yourself?"

"Nita—"

She stepped back, squinting at the branches, selecting one more to sever. "Yeah, Joe?"

But he shook his head. "Anybody call for me?"

"Nobody. Why, you want a date?"

"Not the one I think I'm lined up for."

She chuckled. "Yeah, I heard from Orren it was turning into a party."

The house was quiet. Cindy had disappeared. He climbed to his room, fished out the Beretta and his shoulder holster, and selected a coat. But it was too hot to wear the coat unless he had to. He preferred not to imagine having to shoot Shorter, and if he did have to intimidate him, surely the .38 would do the trick.

He found he wanted desperately to tell someone about Cindy: Nita, anybody. Until he did, the afternoon's grief would go on fermenting inside him. On the way back downstairs, he almost made up his mind to risk it, but when he went outside Nita was not there. It was nearly five o'clock. There was no telling what Shorter was up to. And taking the time to find Nita and confess to her would not save him from facing Orren, nor would it pad his fall.

He was stashing the Beretta in the lock box in the Isuzu's console when he heard footsteps on the pavement, coming toward him. He looked up. A man he had never seen before was approaching him, a slender, well-dressed, comfortably handsome man with an un-memorable face.

"Excuse me." The stranger put out his hand. "Are you Mr. Hope?"

"Yes, but I'm in—"

"Please. My name is Kevin Landry. I'm planning to marry Janet, your ex-wife. I understood from her that as long as you were in town you would probably be staying here."

Any impulse he had had to meet this man the day's turmoil had driven out of him; he wanted none of it. "I don't mean to be rude, Mr. Landry—"

"Please." The stranger had stopped in front of the car,

almost pressing against it. "I'm not here on a call. It's important."

Janet had said he worked at the clinic. Urgency, Joe decided, might well be a commodity this man would call on freely. Yet Landry bothered him. His hands had found each other, and Joe had the distinct feeling they were trying to comfort each other, stop each other from shaking, though the man looked calm enough.

"It won't take long," Landry said. "Ten minutes. Fifteen."

If he found Shorter, Joe thought, he would have to hang onto him. He had the confrontation with Orren ahead. It would be hard to get back to this man. The man's fingers were grinding into each other now, the nails leaving visible scars.

He looked at his watch. Three and a half hours of daylight. "So what is it?"

"Not on the street." Landry looked up at the blank windows of Orren's house. "There's a Wendy's up on the corner. Let me buy you a cup of coffee."

Joe found himself looking up at the windows, too. But nothing stirred.

"One cup," he said.

"I'm grateful." Landry wasted no time. He crossed to a Lincoln parked by the opposite curve. Joe got in the Isuzu and followed. At Wendy's, Landry was waiting for him on the sidewalk, hands on his hips, palms turned outward, hollow-chested and meager despite the well-cut suit.

"I'm *very* grateful," said Landry as Joe stepped up onto the curb. "I like to sleep nights. I know this is an imposition, but it's the only thing I could think—"

He had stopped talking. It was the oddest thing Joe had ever seen. It happened so quickly, so silently, that for a minute it seemed as if the thing had been there all along and Joe just hadn't noticed. Landry did not fall. He simply went on staring ahead of him, his mouth still shaped to form the next word, with half his forehead blown away.

For one long lifetime there was utter silence. Then the bullet hit the glass behind them. The glass seemed to break far away. With that sound, as if he had been waiting for it, Landry toppled. He fell neatly and meekly—probably, Joe thought in a cold haze of horror, much as he had lived.

ALTHOUGH HE HAD WASHED HIS FACE
and hands in the Wendy's washroom, Joe kept finding
new spots of Landry's blood on his body. His nails were
rimmed with it; he had rubbed his neck under his collar
and dislodged a big caked smear. Outside it was late evening, not dark yet, though the dark was coming. The
shooting had occurred just inside the little west Miami
municipality of Windwood; downstairs in the compact
neo-Spanish city hall, was police headquarters. Upstairs, Orren, Portman, Will Gow, the taciturn local lieutenant who had handled the shooting, and another man
Joe didn't recognize sat around a much-doodled-on, li-
noleum-topped table that took up most of the floor space
in the bleak conference room.

He knew it was not the only inquisition he would face.
Any shooting involving a special agent automatically
triggered an executive investigation. Planes from Tallahassee and Tampa were even then en route, with Kaplan, and probably Win Haggertie, on them. Kaplan,
maneuvering for promotion, would be livid. An agent—
his agent—in the middle of a spectacular public killing.
With or without authorization, innocent or not, from

Kaplan's viewpoint, Joe had gotten himself into a mess.

Now, in the Windwood conference room, the only chair left was one at the head of the table. Gow kicked it back. The sheriff wore the same plaid shirt and bleached-out pants he had worn when he cornered Joe in the forest. He was portly, more solid than fat, with an authoritative immovability in his ruddy, full-fleshed features. "So you're one of Cruse's best men."

"Did he say so?" Joe asked politely.

Orren was worrying a paperclip, trying to straighten it. He frowned. Gow put his hands on the chair arms, bending forward intently. "So who tried to kill you, Hope?"

The lieutenant slumped with his eyes closed; he, too, had blood on his shirt, had helped bag the body. The strange man hitched his chair closer to the table and waited.

"I haven't decided," Joe said.

"You damn well stirred up somebody," snapped the stranger.

"Chief Akins, Windwood police," Gow told Joe, jerking his head across the table. "He suggested I might come in and help him. Seeing as how there might be a connection with Amy Wells."

Joe was looking at Orren, but Orren would not look back. "Here," the police chief said, flipping Joe a pad and pencil. "Make a list. Everybody you've talked to about the Wells case or anything mixed up with it, starting with Tampa."

Joe picked up the pencil slowly. "There's not the faintest chance the shooting had anything to do with Landry?"

Gow pushed out of his chair, lumbering to the small high window and snorting in disgust. "Why should it?" demanded Akins.

"You've read my deposition. I told you what he said, how he acted."

"Bull," said Gow. "The man was as plain as white bread. Everybody we've talked to says so. He probably wanted to know if your ex was playing with a full deck before he married her."

Orren looked up from the paperclip.

"That was fifteen years ago," Joe said. "She wasn't crazy. She was just upset."

Orren put a weary hand on Joe's arm. "Just do what he says, Joe."

Portman, sitting close to the door, was the only one among them perched upright, notepad at the ready. The day's events had made him forget that junior officers did best to keep their mouths shut. "Joe likes to run his own show," he said.

"Well, *here* I run it," the police chief retorted. He turned to Joe insistently. "And what about this lunatic from Tampa who's running around loose down here?"

"But why would Shorter shoot me?" Joe asked. "I'm his best bet to find this Miller girl he's looking for."

Gow had peeled a loose flap of weatherstripping from the window frame and was tearing it into strips and dropping them.

"There's got to be somebody!" Akins moaned.

"What about these Meachams?" Joe asked tiredly.

Gow's head snapped up. "What about them?"

"I heard you were friends with the father."

"Oh, balls and a bull's cock! Why should Darryl Meacham shoot at you? He don't know you from a pig's ass."

"But *did* you tell him about Hope, Will?" Akins demanded, thumping a fist on the table.

"I told him Hope wasn't official and he didn't have to talk to him if he came around sniffing. Those are plain facts, and he was entitled to them." He circled close to Joe, leaning on his hands, his weight, his insistence, oppressive. "Besides, *you* talked to Dave Kang."

"What does Kang have to do with it? Is he a suspect?"

"Anybody who's ever set foot in Collier County is a suspect."

"It sounds to me," said Joe, "like you've only got one set of suspects, and they give you gas."

There was a silence, during which Akins worked his fidgeting hands into his armpits. Portman clicked his pen point in and out. The chief finally blurted, "Oh, back off, Will. The one person who probably isn't a suspect is Hope himself. Maybe we'll get somewhere if we can talk him into cooperating. What about it, Hope?"

Yes, what about it? At first, lying in the hail of broken glass on top of the stranger's still-warm body, he had been not afraid, but angry. It really had not occurred to him that it might not have been Landry the shots were meant for. All he could remember thinking was that, after all, Landry had seemed harmless, and whoever had killed him had done something very unfair.

So he wanted to help. Certainly. Gow's face, near his, exuded indignation. They were south Florida cops, all of them; they weren't unused to death, to street fights and drug deals souring. But Landry had been a respectable citizen, a visitor to Akins's territory, and Akins was looking glum, as if his honor as a host had been impugned.

"There's only one problem," Joe said. "Since six this afternoon I've been answering questions, not asking them. So why should I be the one who knows what's going on?"

The silent lieutenant roused himself. He needed a shave badly; no doubt he had been dozing in front of a ball game when the call caught him. "Because if you don't, nobody does."

"We got a crime scene and witnesses, don't we?" interjected Gow briskly.

"Sure," said the lieutenant. "At least ten who saw the whole thing. Four saw the car. One said it was a black Cadillac, two said it was a white Datsun, and one said the shots came from a Greyhound bus."

"A Greyhound bus?" queried Orren incredulously.

"It didn't. There weren't any."

"The white Datsun, then."

"A hatchback or a plain coupe, take your pick. They couldn't come within a mile of each other on the year or the license, and one said it took off east, the other west."

"Bullets?" said Gow, drifting back to the window, eyes narrowed.

"We found three. Thirty-eights. Some people said they heard six or seven."

"Hope?"

"I heard two. I heard the second one from the ground."

Orren leaned forward. Portman, behind him, had to crane to see around him. "Since the way you tell it, we can't count on witnesses, how do we know the shots *were* fired from a car?"

"If the shot that hit Landry was the first one," supplied Akins, "then the way they lined up was consistent with a car going east."

"Seems like another driver would have seen the gunman," Gow objected. "It was daylight."

"I dunno," the lieutenant countered. "Traffic's like my kid's video games in that intersection. When I drive through there it's all I can do to dodge all the hotdogs."

Akins leaned toward Joe, stopping just short of prodding him. "These people you were looking for. They know you?"

"Not to my knowledge."

"Maybe someone told them about you. Someone from Chokoloskee. Or Kang."

"You got pictures of these folks?" Gow asked.

Joe fished out copies. The sheriff inspected the shots, then stashed them in his shirt pocket. Akins looked at his wristwatch. "You won't find them today, I don't reckon."

"I don't know." Gow hiked his trousers as best he could under the overhang of his belly. "I just might turn them up—now that we're all through running around in the woods like rutting hogs."

Another silence fell. If he listened carefully, Joe thought that off in the distance he could hear incoherent shouts of warning, but no one else in the room seemed to notice. Portman was watching Joe hopefully. "Give him a break, he coulda been shot," Orren said.

"Well, if he gets shot out in that swamp," said Gow, suddenly cheerful, "he won't get no funeral."

"He gets the damn message," barked Orren.

"I reckon he better," said Gow, heading out the door with a grin.

Portman had settled back cozily. Orren glared at him, moving his chair an inch closer to Akins. "Get on the car," Akins said to the lieutenant. "The car's important."

The lieutenant yawned. "Probably won't tell us jackshit."

"So far," growled Akins, with a sideways glance at Joe, "nobody's told us jackshit. But we gotta find it. And we need a witness." He turned to Orren. "So do I get that list from Hope or not?"

"You'll get it," conceded Orren.

The police chief nodded, placated. "You know, this ain't a big town, Cruse, and I'm not as proud as Will is. How many men can you give me?"

Portman tried to look doubly alert, but Orren hiked his chair around even more brusquely, turning his broad back on him. His gaze met Joe's. "You got blood in your hair still."

Numbly, Joe put his hand to his forehead.

"Go wash some more," said Orren. "I'll see you downstairs."

Unsteadily Joe pushed away from the table. Portman rocked back in his chair as Joe approached him, so that the door would not open quite all the way. Orren turned on him, bristling. "Will you sit up and pay attention?" Joe slid past, carefully not letting the door slam.

. . .

In a Dade County police station, there was no such thing as Sunday, and Landry's death had set the big room downstairs to churning like sand under a breaking wave. Typists were pounding statements into hungry computers, while every few seconds an anonymous phone pulsed a nerve-drilling electronic summons. Printers clacked prophetically, and reporters scurried from phone to printer to typist, as if waiting for something succulent to pop out of a hole.

They engulfed him the instant they saw him. It didn't take any effort not to tell them anything. It would have taken more effort to put two words together. Through a gap in the scramble, he saw a dull green gnomish shape like a mutant mold from a horror movie: Zack, sitting on a desk, watching delightedly and swinging his shabby heels.

Joe pushed blindly through the crowd. "It's your fault," he said.

"I hadn't looked into first causes," Zack answered immovably. "Except that somebody's obviously scared of you, but from the looks of you, God knows why."

Joe blinked, and blinked again, and shook his head.

"Hey," said Zack suddenly, sliding off the desk. But Zack wasn't big enough to give him that day back. Joe elbowed his way through the reporters, heading dumbly down a side hallway in search of a bathroom. But through a glass pane in a door he saw something that drew him irresistibly. The door was locked; he took hold of the door handle and shook it hard.

She crossed quickly, letting him in but slamming the reporters out. She gripped his bloodstained shirt and twisted obliviously up against him, so limp and warm he could have folded her in half. "I'm sorry. I'm sorry," he repeated senselessly, as if it were a chant in one of those wishful religions. He didn't notice Hunter until her sobs began to slow to spaced, hard gasps. Hunter rose from his chair at the small bare table and, as Janet slowly felt her way free of Joe, she turned to him and let him take her. Suddenly it seemed to Joe the kid had grown; suddenly he seemed the most solid of them all.

The boy looked levelly at Joe. "It's pretty bad."

"What did Kevin come to see me about?" Joe asked gently.

Janet shook her head, her whole body swaying. "They've asked me. I just . . . just don't know."

"She's been answering questions for hours," said Hunter.

"I wouldn't mind answering," she said. "I just don't know what *to* answer. I just don't know."

In dark, baggy trousers, a soft white shirt, and a black string tie, Hunter looked nearer forty than eighteen. He had not shaved, and his beard was scratchy and threatening. His eyes looked as if they would need a major jolt of drugs to clear them. He ushered his mother toward a pair of chairs in the corner, where he sat them down together, united and self-absorbed.

But Joe pulled a chair up close by. "They think it was me the guy was after," he said.

"Wasn't it?" Janet stammered confusedly.

"It's just that there doesn't seem to be much motive. What did you and Kevin talk about when he came to see you? about me?"

"I told him you had been over."

"Was there anything you had been arguing about?"

She laughed unsteadily. "Whether I should wear white at the wedding."

"They've asked her all this," Hunter said.

She freed a hand from her son's grip and caught Joe's and squeezed it. To Joe's surprise, one of the tears lodged in Hunter's eyes broke free and streaked down his cheek. Joe got up heavily, turned his back, and crossed the room, feeling there was something he ought to be doing, if only he could figure out what. After a moment, someone breathed beside him; he turned and found it was Hunter. "You get used to your mom being in control," the kid said. "It's weird."

"You seem to be taking good care of her."

"Yeah, but I feel funny. I'm not sure what to do."

His lips were parted, his face softened by his unspoken plea. Joe wished crazily he could take on both of them. Suddenly it seemed that whatever it was they needed, he had and could give in abundance. "You seem to be doing okay."

"I haven't been a very good son. She deserves better."

"Maybe now she'll get something better."

"I haven't been doing very good in school. But that's going to change. A lot's going to change." He was watching his mother intently. She had reached for her purse and was sorting through it restlessly. "Does all this have something to do with that Wells girl's case?"

"Everybody seems to think so."

"You're gonna find the guy who shot Kevin, aren't you?"

"Someone will."

"Listen," said Hunter, his words coming more harshly, "if you find him, when you find him—you'll let me know, won't you?"

"When they get a lead, they'll tell your mother."

"I mean me, especially. You'll tell me," Hunter said.

The heat in the boy's dark blue eyes came from somewhere beyond the bounds of what he or the kid or anyone else had any power over. "It's an official police case, Hunter. I probably won't be in a position to make that kind of decision."

Hunter glanced at his mother again, catching something between his clenched teeth. He turned back to Joe, shrugging his strong, young shoulders. "I just feel like I ought to do something."

"So do I," Joe said.

Hunter caught Joe's wrist abruptly and held onto it, just for a second, a brief, secret gesture, man-to-man. Joe nodded. Silently Hunter crossed back to Janet and sat down beside her. There was a rap at the door. Joe saw Orren's face in the window. He opened the door, and Orren jerked his chin at him; he stepped out, pulling the door to.

Miraculously, the reporters had disappeared. They entered another of the little interrogation rooms. Orren shut the door.

18

YES, KAPLAN. LOOKING DISHEVELED, despite the flattering fit of his suit. And Win Haggertie, a well-built man with a trim cap of near-white hair. It had been Haggertie who, eight years before, had hired Joe from the Jacksonville force. Joe had hoped Portman would not be there, but he sat in a corner nursing a clipboard, ready to take his eternal notes.

"Well, Joe," said Haggertie, starting things off with one of his diplomatic smiles, "you could have planned better. Cubs were playing."

There was a table here, too, but other than Portman, no one had sat down. Kaplan was walking back and forth jerkily like a mechanical bear on a track at Disney World. Orren had tucked his hands into his armpits, tired and withdrawn. Joe would have given a lot to sit, but until the others did, he could not.

"Anyway, late as it is, we'll keep this short for now, barring complications." Haggertie opened a folder on the table. "Orren's filled me in, Joe. I've read your statement. Thought you'd like to know they've turned up a new witness." He selected a sheet, holding it at arm's length to skim it. "I've just glanced over this, but I gather this man claims he saw the shots fired. He was right behind the car. Says it was a white Datsun, an '81 coupe. Reported stolen just this afternoon by a family who had left it in the parking lot down at Matheson Hammock."

"He saw the gun?"

Haggertie let Orren pick up the narrative. "Says at first he didn't know quite what he was seeing. The stupid people had had the windows tinted." Like many cops, Orren deplored the practice. "Says he saw a flare, then he heard the shots and made the connection."

"So who was driving?"

"Naturally he can't tell us *that*. Another car cut in front of him and by the time he got back on the Datsun's tail, it had a half a block on him. All he'd say was that he was pretty sure it was a man."

"White, black?" interrupted Kaplan. "Dark hair, light?"

"White man with dark hair, he thinks, but he wasn't positive." Orren humped his shoulders. "He thinks whoever it was expected to be followed, which wouldn't be surprising. Says he had tailed it up across Forty-one, he was in the left-hand lane and the Datsun was in the center, and he was speeding up to close in, when the Datsun cut across the right-hand lane and took off up the ramp onto the Palmetto. The witness couldn't get out of the box he was in in time to make the exit. Had to go back. Of course, by that time the Datsun had burned rubber."

"The car'll be useless," asserted Kaplan. "It'll turn up soon enough and it'll be spic-and-span clean."

"What does *she* say?" Orren asked Joe, shifting his glance toward the door to indicate Janet.

"She couldn't tell me anything she didn't already tell Akins's people."

"It's too bad. Poor girl."

Kaplan, Joe knew, was in a box. He had to disclaim responsibility for Joe's meddling in a case in Miami when he was officially off duty, but he could not appear vindictive before Haggertie. "What *is* too bad," he said, succeeding in sounding impersonal, "is that no one seems to know what Joe did to provoke this attack." He managed to prowl close enough to Joe to give him a private glare. "Just maybe there's something you forgot in your deposition you've remembered in time to tell us?"

Joe was careful to answer him directly, without looking at Haggertie or Orren. "If you mean something that might help us in our case but doesn't pertain to theirs, no, I haven't. But I'd like to get on record."

"Naturally," said Kaplan. It was a careful response, pointed but just short of offensive. "Go ahead."

"The only thing I managed to convey to anyone all day —not as much by anything I said as just by being here— was that there might be some connection between this Amy Wells and the sinkhole murders. Nobody fired those shots deliberately expecting to kill me or Landry. You can't shoot a thirty-eight from a moving car at that distance and expect to hit a target as small as a single man. Those shots were meant as a warning. That Landry got hit was an accident. Somebody doesn't want us investigating this case."

Kaplan flapped his fingers behind his back. "There are other possibilities," he objected. "What if the person firing those shots didn't realize he could never expect to hit you or Landry? Landry getting killed could still have been an accident, a lucky one, even if Landry was the target. And if you ask me, it would be nice if he was."

"Or," said Joe, "I stirred somebody up, somebody connected with either case, or both—"

"Or neither," insisted Kaplan.

"Or neither . . . who's just plain crazy."

"And the shooting was a psychotic episode," concluded Orren.

"One day they're going to prove you can catch psychoses from drinking water." Haggertie pivoted, surveying all the agents, including Portman, who looked up alertly.

He singled out Orren. "I guess Sheriff Gow and Chief Akins have suspects? Any you especially like?"

"A couple. Without more data, no front-runners."

"And Akins wants us to work with him?" Orren nodded. "I'll talk to him in the morning," said Haggertie. "Lean a little to make sure your favorites don't get neglected. Norman, anything else you see as urgent tonight?"

Kaplan looked at his watch. "Remembering to call for my phone messages." He bent over Portman, then tapped the notepad with a stubby forefinger. "Get this typed up by the morning."

"Yes, sir," said Portman. "You're staying?"

"Overnight, anyway," Haggertie responded. "Vern might be right: this mess may be none of our business. It's much more likely to be their killer than ours." He touched Orren's shoulder for a second. "I have a one o'clock conference in Tallahassee. We can talk early tomorrow?"

"Yes, sir," said Orren.

Haggertie swung to face Joe. The smile he had started with came back again. "The sooner *you* get yourself to neutral territory, the better off we'll be all around."

He swung the door open so Kaplan would have to go out it. Orren signaled with his chin to Portman, who took his time leaving but finally made it. Then, sooner than Joe would have wanted, he and Orren were alone.

A silence Joe did not like fell quickly. "That was relatively painless."

"It may be just starting," said Orren.

"Especially if Haggertie's reamed Kaplan out for letting me come down here."

"My understanding is, he didn't 'let' you. He washed his hands of you in front of witnesses. It's your ass that's in a sling."

The silence began again. Slowly it began to ache, like the air in your lungs when you know you have been underwater as long as you can manage. Gow had surely told Orren what he had witnessed in the clearing. But Orren just stood there, waiting. The hell with it. "I tried to tell you," Joe said.

"Yeah, sure. You tried."

"I'll get a motel."

"Yeah, you better."

It would have been best to shut up. But he didn't. "She's not a child, Orren. You can't just order her not to do things."

Orren spun on him, incendiary and Latin. "I don't want to hear it! I don't want to know how it happened! I don't want to know anything, you hear?"

"Orren, have you sat down and had a talk with her?"

"Just who the hell are you defending?"

He didn't know. Even without closing his eyes, he could go back there, to that infinite wilderness where it seemed something should have been living, and yes, something was.

Orren was waiting, every vibrant hair on his stirred-up body bristling. "What happened between her and Dave Kang?" Joe asked.

Orren wilted. "It was a helluva mess."

"Whose fault was it?"

"He's a weird dude."

"He looks harmless."

Orren wiped his face with a limp hand. "Yeah, you'd think so."

"She gave me the impression she started it."

Orren flared up again, almost automatically. When Joe didn't flinch, he kicked at a chair. "Nobody even knew about it, me and her aunt knew nothing about it, until she tried to break it off. Then suddenly Kang was all over the place, hounding her. I had to have a talk with him."

"Where was her father? Why didn't he have this talk?"

"He was in Honduras. I've been like her father."

"I guess Kang listened?"

"You'd think an Indian woulda been tough. The guy's crying, Joe."

It would have been hard on Orren. A grown man's open passion, inconsolable. "I just don't think it's as simple as you think it is."

"Look, Joe." Orren took on a judicial patience. "She's young. She still dreams a lot of shit. She doesn't understand that everything she dreams won't happen."

"Maybe I don't completely understand that either."

"No." The word was heavy, airless: a weight that made its way straight to the bottom. "Well, anyway. We all want you back in Tampa as soon as possible, Joe. Haggertie and Kaplan'll see you up there."

"Yeah, sure, Orren. Whatever."

"Gow'd like to hang onto you for a few days, but I told him he can get hold of you up there when he needs you."

"What about Shorter?"

"They can pick him up. Or we will. Now we've got plenty of reason to look for him."

"He didn't have anything to do—"

"It's not your case," Orren said.

After a minute, Joe shrugged submissively. "I want to go to this guy Landry's funeral on Tuesday."

"That's not smart."

"I can take a personal day. Janet won't understand if I don't."

"And Kaplan will understand if you do?"

"I'll ask him."

"Sure, Joe, you ask him." Despite the bite in his voice, Orren seemed to have used up his objections. "Your stuff's at my house, but get it tomorrow. If the bosses are going to bed, so can I."

"Yeah, me, too."

"And Joe—"

He looked back at his old friend from the doorway.

"I want that list Akins asked for."

"You know everybody on it."

"Write them down anyway."

Not tonight he wouldn't. But he said, "Okay."

So he moved into the Vista Motel. He wasn't sure what vista he was supposed to have paid for. Outside his window, all he could see was a Hess gas station with Miller Lite and Bud signs in the window. He had with him a cheap toothbrush, a package of plastic razors, travel samples of shaving cream, deodorant, and toothpaste, the clothes he had nearly died in, and his two guns.

The guns had proven singularly useless. No villain had presented himself to be fired at. But there was a villain somewhere: that he knew. He inspected the motel room carefully, looking behind the shower curtain, even kicking under the bed to make sure it was too low to the floor to conceal an intruder; he fastened all the locks and pulled the skimpy curtains shut.

Whom had he aroused? Who was frightened or offended? He believed what he had told Kaplan and Haggertie: His questions, of the kid in Chokoloskee, of the ranger, of Dave Kang, had been innocuous, meandering. And yet someone had panicked. For someone, a whisper of discovery was enough.

He hung up his clothes conscientiously, despite the wrinkles and bloodstains. Tomorrow he would put them on just long enough to find his way out of them again. It seemed that the faces he had seen that day, one of which might be *the* face, were hovering just out of swatting range like a new swarm of voracious insects, each one starved for his will and courage as well as his blood. In the early hours, lying awake in the frigid blast of the air-conditioning, he found that the more he batted them away, the more tenaciously they pressed in on him: Gow, Kang, Orren, Landry himself—all, all wanting something out of him, sustenance from some vital vein.

And in an even colder hour, in a chill measured not by the clock or the tremulous a.c. shudder, but by the

slow dead sifting of his sinking thoughts, he thought of
her. He thought of the ease with which he could have
made love to her, and the ease with which he had been
stopped. She had been right: for him, it would have been
meaningless, except that he never would have forgotten
it and would have surely done penance for it on many
more cold lonely mornings. For her—despite her resolution, her courage, her determination to seize life hard by
the balls and hold on, all the things that had drawn him
to her—ah, for her, it would have been a crevasse on the
unfinished map of her young life, one she would have
spent far too much time and tears climbing out of, if in
fact she had not been killed outright by the fall.

He wondered if he were giving himself too much importance. She might have slept with dozens of men. He
didn't want to believe it. He wanted to believe what she
had cried out to him with so much heat, that she had
wanted to love, had thought she could love as soulessly
as she could drop coins in the March of Dimes can, that
it would have been that easy, and the payback that uncomplicated; that she was just a little girl who did not
know that when you gave love, something else far less
expendable was often rooted out as well.

Orren, of course, would have left for work by the time he
reached the house Monday morning. Nita would be
home. Somehow seeing Nita did not seem as frightening
as meeting Orren. But her black Chrysler was not in the
circular driveway. The front door was soundly locked.

He considered his blood-smeared clothes and, as he
had no choice, decided they were not so awful he
couldn't wait another half hour to change. He turned
away. But then, unmistakably, the locks began clicking
open. He waited with his hand on the door handle of the
Isuzu. She came out on the porch, holding the screen
back. She looked calm, though there seemed to be a
shade or two missing from her floral coloring. "It's all

right," she said coolly. "Aunt Nita thought I shouldn't be alone with you if you came by. But I told her that was nonsense. I see no reason why I shouldn't be allowed to give you your things."

He crossed to the porch. "No one's here but you?"

Her mouth set suddenly, like a crack in sandstone. "Yeah. And don't forget, I bite."

She wore gym shorts and a loose pullover. It was the first time he had seen the full length and leanness of her dark, smooth legs. Inside it was dim and freezing, and the plants on ceiling hooks, in the kitchen where she led him, seemed to strain for the weak daylight from the screened pool deck. His bag waited on the table, with his extra shirt, still on a hanger, laid respectfully over it. She stood nearby, her hands on her hips, while he unzipped the bag to check his belongings. Nestled between his shaving things and clean underwear was a plastic Baggie, fastened with a wire twist-tie, and in it were a half-dozen chocolate chip cookies, still faintly warm.

Suddenly he felt wearier and sadder than he had getting up from Landry's body yesterday. "From Nita?"

She nodded. She turned suddenly to the refrigerator and took out another bag, full of peaches and plums and a couple of big green Granny Smith apples, and, of all things, a Snickers bar. She offered it solemnly. "From me."

The fruit was icy, and even though the air in the room had been dehumidified, some damp warmth, perhaps from their breath, settled on the plastic, jeweling it. Surely a few chunks of fruit meant nothing. He took the bag without touching her and stowed it in a zippered outside pouch. Abruptly she pulled out a chair, folded a long leg under her, and sat. "You don't have to talk."

"I don't think everything was said yesterday that should have been said."

She raised a straight, strong brow. "Something I neglected?"

"No, something I did. I shouldn't have been so angry with you."

"I did mislead you."

"Let's don't play martyrs. I'll take the blame."

"I'm not apologizing." She changed legs, grasping a hard brown knee. She seemed all sharp bones and angles, elaborately arranged to ensure distance. "I wanted to make love to you. I still don't see why it's such a sin."

"Goddamn it, Cindy, what happened to all the boys your own age?"

She snorted, an unladylike sound she must have inherited from her father or from Orren.

"There have to be some boys with brains," he persisted. "What about in your science class?"

She made another noise, this one her own, as if something distasteful had been squeezed out of her. "At the University of Miami?"

"So apply to Harvard."

"What's wrong with you?" she snapped.

He zipped the bag shut with finality. "Twenty-five years."

"You make it sound like a disease."

"We have nothing in common."

"We do. We care."

The appalling irony of that judgment seemed beyond explaining. She had never looked younger. He wanted to leave, but instead he sat down across from her. He could feel his face not doing what he had intended, going infantile on him instead of turning knowing and cold. She clasped her hands seriously in front of her, within reach of his if he wanted them. "Cindy, I'm not in love with you."

She stopped herself from laughing. "You do feel something."

"It's called lust."

"I know about lust."

Somehow he didn't doubt her. For a moment, eyes meeting, they did have something in common, the same thing they had come so close to sharing yesterday, the same strangled need.

"We both thought it would answer for something we wanted," he said. "But it would only start something that would be no good."

There must have been a distance that was just right, safe, yet close enough to reach her, but somehow he had misjudged it. He was much too close. He could see the tears lying in glittering rows, melting into each other, on the rich black curve of her lashes.

"You deserve to be loved," he told her. "You deserve someone who can love you."

"Oh, stop being so damned sensible!" she said.

It was so seductive, hanging just off to the side where he had only to turn his head to choose it. Last night he had dozed, wandering in and out of places with strange colored skies, dreaming of making love to her, and when he had awakened, the dreams had clung to him like a scent. She sat looking at him, and for just a brief moment, the flowers seemed on the verge of opening again, inviting that one swift drunken plunge.

He stood and gathered his possessions, and she watched him, hands tense. She didn't follow right away, but when he began wrestling with the locks she appeared beside him, and when he moved aside, she helped him, working down from the top while he worked up from the bottom. But when he had the door open and was reaching for the screen, she was there, between him and daylight. The tears had soaked into her skin, so that they hadn't disappeared, but had given her features a silken texture.

"You'll thank me," he told her.

But she opened the screen for him. "Come back in thirty years," she said bitterly. "Maybe I'll be old enough then."

19

NEVER HAD THE ROAD TO ANYWHERE
seemed so straight and compelling. Onward it rushed,
back through the cypress, cutting in half the flat blank
plain and the sky. He had decided not to go to the funeral. He had left Cindy shut in behind him, had had a
long, slow, thoughtful breakfast, and had decided to go
home.

He felt wise at last, though not at peace, and his pain
was what convinced him. The right thing, the thing he
ought to do, was whatever felt the worst. The sky had
turned dour; up ahead he thought it might be raining.
Though the windows were rolled up, he could feel a low-
pitched shudder in the air, as if the invisible beast curled
around the rim of the world did not sleep well.

He was zooming along, not watching, when suddenly
he passed a shell road shunting off into the wetlands; a
sign told him it was 833. He had a sudden unbidden
flash of Dave Kang's map: 833 and 843. Two parallels
scored on that green patchwork with the pins stuck in it.
One on one side of Fat Hog Camp, one on the other.
Other wandering fingernail marks leading through

Kang's widespread, hand-drawn, topological circles, some of them from 833, working their way in.

He slipped off onto the shoulder and spun the car around. He reached the shell road and turned onto it. It was one-thirty. Orren still thought he was staying for the funeral on Tuesday, and had surely said so to Kaplan. So no one was looking for him. The road ran off northward, toward a sky that was still blue, a thin used-up color like the memory of an ungranted wish.

But he had not quite talked himself into starting forward when he saw a truck rattling down the road toward him: the faded pickup the young Indian, Jimmy Easter, had driven out of Dave Kang's driveway yesterday morning. In the bed, atop a crude tool box tacked in under the cab window, an enormous dog paced. It was a squat pit bull, not quite white, not quite brindle, its massive head on its fighter's shoulders as square and solid as a block chopped off a primitive neckless statue, desecrated with mismatched eyes.

The truck slowed for the turn, the dog wheeling back and forth on the box, perfectly caged by its balance. The truck had to pass very close to where Joe was parked; Easter recognized him instantly when their eyes met.

The young Miccosukee pulled to the side of the road. Reluctantly Joe opened his window. Easter hooked an elbow over the truck door and bent down to him. "Hey. I saw you on TV last night. You were with that guy that got shot."

"That's right."

"Miss Cruse wasn't still with you, I don't guess."

"No, she was home."

Easter's tan, drawn hide, against the richness of his thick black hair and the ebony pits of his eyes, made Joe think of oil seeping into clay. The dog stopped pacing and leaned out over the side of the truck, dripping spit in the heat that settled between them. Easter beat a rapid lick on the truck metal. "So how come you're running loose around here? Aren't you scared somebody might take some more pops?"

There was something jabbing, personal and pointed, in his insolence. Joe shrugged. "So far nobody seems to want to."

"Found your lost campers?"

"Why, have you seen them?"

"No. Dave told me about them."

"I quit looking for them. I'm heading back to Tampa."

"And you done took Miss Cruse home."

Yes, personal. The truck's exhaust made him nauseated. The dog drooled foamy streaks down the metal. "By the way," mused Joe casually, "what do you shoot with that M16 you've got stashed behind the seat?"

Easter's dark gaze never shifted. "Whatever I have to."

"Ever shot it at anybody?"

"Once."

"What happened?"

Easter pumped the gas. His teeth when he smiled were white as bits of filed shell. "They quit doing what they was doing. Say, you're not heading back out in them woods, are you?"

"I'll take care of myself."

"Well, if you don't," said the kid, "them woods will."

The pickup's dust left him still sitting there. His mind was playing tricks on him, trying to write Easter into the murders. Why? Because he knew his way around Collier County? Because he had been within a hundred miles the day the Wells girl died? No, it was just because he disliked him. Not the kind of tired impatience he felt with Portman, but a crawling uncertainty, a feeling that when he was near Easter, he was clinging to an unsettled bit of the world that might willfully tip him off.

Finally, ignoring Easter's warning as well as his own judgment, he shifted gears and set off. His dust smoked up behind him, a dry, untalented genie. He had to keep putting away from him the carping voice that kept warning him back.

He drove much longer than he should have—a good hour. He had no idea where to find the mysterious camp. On his left, the direction he wanted to go, there was no canal, only an easy bump over a ridge of sod into the forest. He passed dozens of overgrown trails and car tracks, at long last coming upon one that had been gnawed raw by a double slash of recent tire marks. He could still see the imprint of tread.

So he turned, too, down a dim tunnel where the ground rose and fell under him with a malicious inconstancy, and every turn of the path brought him face-to-face with the place he had just been. Soon, as on his trek with Cindy, he came to a place where the path did not so much sink as the wet came up. The tire tracks, though, pressed on, cutting deep black gouges in the mud.

Here, although the forest had grown dimmer, it was not really so grim; color held its ground against the encroaching wet and dark. The woods on both sides were full of surprises, sunny licks on ferns and tree bark, bare roots twining like poured copper, purple flowers shooting out of green distances like slim jets of very cold flame. In the midst of the silence, he heard a living bird calling, its chill, clear note like a hollow artifact falling on stone.

But it all seemed so empty, as if what lurked there was too horrible to bear in full daylight, the kind of thing that would grab what it craved from behind.

He began to press forward once more, keeping his small car to the highest ridges of the pathway. One more curve, he was thinking, when he saw the flash of color. No bird was that particular machine-dyed Prussian blue. He knew instantly it was a man moving quickly through the trees. In his mind, he began instinctively checking the disposition of his guns.

But the man didn't appear again right away. Ahead, the path rounded a bend. Joe tried to calculate. Had the man been on the path? He didn't think so. But on both sides was morass.

He stopped the car. He thought he could see the mosquitoes, ubiquitous and caught up in their vibrating Brownian flurry. He had no spray, nothing. He sat still, waiting. He could not see anything. Reluctantly, he got out of the car.

Instantly the pricks started, on all sides, through his clothes, aiming for the most inviolate zones of his flesh. He slapped and waved his arms and began moving. The grass on the trail was high, dry enough that his footsteps rustled. He rounded the bend, and then he saw the blue again, off the trail, low to the ground, in a puddle of fallen night that had gotten trapped in the forest—a man's torso half-submerged in a stagnant pond.

He couldn't see a face. Between him and the pond and the blue thing was a wide swath of militant-looking green spear points, just lush enough and verdant enough that he knew they were rooted in water, too. Wading through those sloughs yesterday had been distasteful. But there, in open channels, you could at least tell what might be slithering toward you. He stood in the road and shouted. The blue torso didn't move.

So, even though he didn't want to, he went. On the first step the ground grabbed him, and he never really felt bottom, just a boggy engorgement that stopped him from being devoured. The reeds themselves were alive, trembling with crawling things. He blundered through them, trying to look where he stepped, but he couldn't see a solid surface, only the convergent stems of plants and, out of the corner of his eye, the things that hurried out of sight at his fumbling and splashing. Where the jealous grass freed him at last, with the body just a few feet away but still partially hidden, the water began, platelike and depthless. Blindly, he floundered into it. Instantly he sank up to his crotch in a cold and unforgiving pool.

He forced a leg forward; he felt something solid: a log,

a rock. He trusted his weight to it but the slippery, unseen surface dumped him backward, so that he plopped into the water like a flung scoop of mud. He grappled with his hands and touched slime and jerked them away again; he fought for a hold with his feet and heard a sound like the yelps of a whipped animal and couldn't believe he was making it and shut up. Finally he found a trembling balance, straightening with his shirt dripping and the gun at his belt cold and waterlogged.

Now, at last, he could see beyond the line of reeds; he could see Ray Shorter's chafed hands clutching at the mud bank, could look down into Shorter's pleading, swollen, red-mapped eyes.

For a moment they just stared at each other. Then, soaked and filthy, Shorter pushed slowly out of the water, and opened his mouth and began moving it. At first Joe thought he was cursing, but then Shorter raised both hands and held them out, and Joe saw that he was pleading. There was still a long, uncertain distance between them. Joe did not want to cover it. But Shorter wasn't coming forward. Joe took a lurching step toward him. The logs and mud gave; he floundered. Shorter said, "God. Oh, God."

Joe heaved himself across the distance. Shorter put his arms around him and fell against him, laying his head feverishly on Joe's wet chest.

Joe hooked an arm around his stout neck. The water buoyed Shorter, and Shorter's weight steadied Joe. "Did something bite you?" Joe asked.

Shorter gaped at him vacuously.

"A snake? Did a snake bite you?" Joe said.

"Snake?" Shorter began thrashing and babbling. "Snake, snake."

"There's no snake, goddamn it." Shorter's struggles had carried them backward. "I asked did one bite you? Are you okay?"

"Snake," said Shorter again, sobbing, as if whatever

wanted him would finally get him, no matter how hard he fought or where he ran.

"Shit," said Joe. He paddled awkwardly, dragging Shorter with him. Shorter's face looked inflamed, with scratched-open sores. They reached the reeds, Shorter as limp and inert as if he had swallowed half the pond. "Help me, damn it," Joe told him. Shorter just coughed. Joe sat down in the reeds; inch by inch he hauled him, flattening a swath through the grasses, until finally, exhaustedly, they lay together on the roadside, oblivious to everything but the feel of solid ground.

"Dead," said Shorter suddenly. The word exploded like an engine backfiring.

"Who's dead?"

"Dead."

"Who's dead? The girl is dead? Cherry?"

But Shorter only groaned and rolled over and buried his face in the grass.

THERE WERE DOZENS OF LITTLE MOTELS
on both sides of the highway, no doubt dating back to
the days when 41 was the only way down and across the
state. He chose one called the North Glades that looked
clean and inviting. Shorter had drooped down in the
seat, apparently dozing, but when Joe opened the passenger door, the trainer hoisted himself out with a grunt
and made it inside on his own.

On the way into town, Joe had tried stopping at a
phone booth to look up a walk-in clinic, but Shorter had
roused himself groggily, staggering out onto the pavement after him. "What are you doing?"

"Trying to find you a doctor."

"I don't need a doctor. Don't take me to the police.
They'll send me back."

"What does your wife think? Shouldn't you call her?"

"Don't tell anybody," Shorter begged.

Had he been sure Shorter was okay, he would have
driven him to Miami. But what if something happened to
the trainer on the open highway? He tried getting some
drive-through food into him, but nibbling the ham-

burger, Shorter had a fit of dry retching. "Haven't eaten. Since I left Tampa."

"When was that?"

"Don't . . . Saturday. What day is this?"

"Monday. Shorter, who's dead?"

"Don't know. There was just . . . blood."

"Human?"

But Shorter had just shaken his head fitfully. "Don't let them send me back."

The motel was older than it had looked: the air conditioner rattled, there were cigarette burns in the carpet, and the bath fixtures practically twisted off in his hands before the hot water started coming. But there was a phone; he could sit down in peace and call Orren. First he filled the ice bucket with warm water and stripped Shorter down to his wet boxer shorts and bathed him. Shorter's flesh was soft, warm, and pink, more unnerving somehow than the cold hides of corpses. There were no swellings on him, nor anything that looked like bite marks. Joe put him in the single bed and covered him with the thin blankets, then jerked the curtains shut on the daylight, pulling up the single chair. "Shorter. Tell me. What did you see?"

But Shorter started up from the bed feverishly. "They'll arrest me. They'll send me back."

"Forget about that. All I'm asking you is what happened."

Shorter struggled wildly, kicking at the covers. "Don't tell my wife. Don't tell Lyssa."

Joe stood up. Shorter grabbed his wrist. "Where are you going? You're going to call them to come get me, aren't you?"

"Lie down."

"Maybe it's nothing. Maybe I dreamed it. Sleep. An hour. Then I'll take you."

Joe sighed, freeing his wrist gently. "Go on, go to sleep," he said.

The red-rimmed eyes closed slowly, reluctantly. Shorter tumbled and twisted, fighting the onslaught of peace.

And Joe sat gnawing his knuckles, shivering in his still damp clothes. Orren's number buzzed in his brain like a mosquito that had sneaked in out of the dusk.

But if he called Orren from the room he'd scare Shorter. He decided to wait until he was sure Shorter was asleep, then call from the outside pay phone. A long time passed; he dozed off a little. When he woke, a particularly suffocating darkness had finally fallen. He stumbled outside. There was no moon, just a strange auroral flickering along the horizon. By his watch it was ten. He punched Orren's number and then his credit card number into the pay phone; Orren answered drowsily on the third ring. "I've got that guy Shorter," Joe said.

"Jeez," said Orren. "I'd finally found five minutes to crash. Where are you?"

"In Naples. I found him wandering around in the woods. I thought I needed to get him cleaned up and in bed fast."

He could hear Orren yawning. "Well, is he hurt then?"

"I don't think so. He's just delirious. He's spinning some kind of tale about stumbling over something dead out there."

"Dead?" said Orren impatiently. "Like a human body?"

"He's mostly babbling. He did say he didn't see a body."

"Jeez, Joe, it could be a deer, a pig, anything. What time is it?"

"Tenish."

"That funeral's tomorrow. At eleven. You think that guy's off his nut, or you think there's something to it?"

"He's pretty delirious."

"Well, can you get him over here by ten? Not that I'll be able to get any sense out of him."

"Sure, Orren."

"I'll call Gow, then. I want you to stay out of it. Deliver him and get packing."

"Sure, Orren."

"And whatever you do, don't let that prick get away."

He hung up, still nodding. Yes, Orren. He took a deep breath. The humid air was full of gas and rot.

He went back inside and into the bathroom. Shorter's clothes, as wet as his and dirtier, lay in a sour pile on the floor. With a sudden gush of anger, Joe picked them all up and flung them into the bathtub. He ran warm rusty water over them and swabbed with his hands until the black pond muck floated out of them. Then he drained the filthy water and wrung out the shirt and trousers as best he could, draping them over the curtain rod. They wouldn't be dry anytime soon. He would have to find an all-night laundromat. What a bitch.

He went back into the bedroom and stole one of the blankets off the mound of Shorter's body and pulled it around his own shoulders, drawing his long legs up and settling uncomfortably against the wooden arms of the chair. Just for a precious minute, he closed his eyes.

It was three when he woke. The blinds were drawn, and the lamp was still on, and it might have been a day in a nuclear winter, when dawn did not plan to come. His chilled muscles were so knotted up he could barely rise, but he managed. "Shorter!" The trainer's gummy eyelids fluttered open. "Shorter, get up! Come on!"

Shorter's puffy lips began to move as consciousness came back to him. "Gotta find her. Gotta find her, Hope."

"I know. We don't have long. Come on."

In the bathroom, as Joe had expected, Shorter's clothes still dripped. He gathered them in a motel towel and went back into the bedroom. Shorter had slipped his legs out of bed and he sat looking up at him, shirtless and mournful, like a big sea mammal, all flayed blubber with eloquent human eyes.

"Get that blanket around you," Joe ordered. "Let's get out of here and find a place to get these dried."

It took Joe longer than he had hoped to find a laundromat that was open. He left Shorter huddled in the car while he took the clothes in and parked them in a dryer. From a vending machine in an alcove he bought them both weak coffee, and he microwaved them greasy fried pies. As he climbed back behind the wheel, Shorter reached out voraciously and took the food from him. "I have to deliver you to my boss at ten," Joe said.

Shorter almost dropped the coffee. Joe caught it and set it on the dashboard. Shorter was fumbling to escape, but he couldn't figure out how to open the door. Joe gripped his arm, digging his fingers into the muscle under the blanket. "Listen. You want to know and I want to know. We've got five hours. Now what the hell happened out there?"

Slowly the quivering under his palm died down. Shorter reached tentatively for his coffee, almost spilling it; he sipped it cautiously. "Parts of it I don't remember," he said.

"Where were you? Where's your truck?"

But with his free hand Shorter just rubbed his eyes. "I changed my mind. I can't go back out there, Hope."

"Shorter. You've got five minutes to start talking sense. Then I put cuffs on you, and you're out."

Shorter hiccuped. Joe waited. Shorter risked a bigger, sloppy sip. "Someone told me there was a hunting camp out there where people always went to see panthers. I thought they might be there."

"Did you find it?"

"I found something. A camp of some kind. Looked like rats lived in it."

"You walked in?"

"No, I drove all the way there. Sometimes it was hard going but the truck made it."

"And?"

But the memory of it seemed to stop him. Visibly he

projected whatever he was seeing into the distance, as if only by reducing images until they were unrecognizable could he bear them. "It smelled awful. Like the mares' afterbirths when you don't bury them right away."

"Blood?"

"Everywhere. The ground looked like it was moving. It was all the flies."

"Could it have been an animal? deer blood?"

"There was a shirt."

"A girl's shirt? Hers?"

Shorter's hand tensed around the edge of the blanket. "I couldn't tell what color it was."

"Did you look for a body?"

"I was sick."

"I know. Did you look for a body?"

"I don't remember. I think I passed out. When I woke up, it was dark . . . things were all over me. I must've run around in circles."

Joe sighed. He hadn't meant to. Shorter wrenched around to face him, baring his teeth. "You think you'd be so tough, in the middle of the night, with all those bugs biting you, and snakes all around, and . . . knowing any minute you were going to stumble across a dead. . . ." He started weeping.

"So you got lost?" Joe pressed.

"I didn't have the faintest . . . I don't know how I got so turned around."

"You didn't see anybody else out there?"

"I thought I saw a fire."

"Like a campfire?"

"Big fire. Through the trees."

"Did you get close to it?"

"Things were . . . I was scared to move. Things were everywhere."

"In the morning?"

"In the morning I couldn't see it."

"You didn't try to look for it?"

"I didn't know which way to go."

Day seemed to ooze up out of the concrete, chill and gray. The fluorescence from the laundromat was colorless. Instead of warming him, the coffee made Joe shiver, as if the rising dawn had swept him farther than ever from the last kind pass of the sun.

Shorter smacked at the back of his neck. The sores where he had clawed the bites had scabbed over. "Will I get some kind of disease or something?"

"No. Why should you?"

"You can. You can get all sorts of things."

The dryer had stopped tumbling. Joe got out and retrieved the shirt and trousers. Shorter accepted the garments with the stultified obedience of a prisoner being handed his uniform. "What about after? Are you going to turn me in?"

"I don't know yet."

"They'll tell me I'm crazy. They'll screw it all up. They don't care. They'll never find Cherry."

Joe just put the car into reverse. He was impatient. The mission he had sold himself on in the small hours looked more and more like an arrogant miscalculation. Gow and Orren could solve it; Gow and Orren had the men and machines to solve it. He was as crazy as Shorter; the whole thing was crazy. "Maybe you *did* imagine it," he told Shorter. "Or maybe we'll find deer guts."

Shorter stared at him hopelessly. "How will we know?"

Joe frowned.

"I wouldn't know deer guts from—from. . . ." Shorter swallowed, his face blanching again, and Joe thought he was going to faint. "I won't know the difference. Will you?"

They did not have to wake up Dave Kang. The little man was outside in front of his trailer as they pulled up in his overgrown yard. He was watering tomato plants, adjusting the wire frames around them. In a box at his feet were freshly picked bananas and mangos. He snatched up the box when he saw them, then set it down again self-consciously. There was no tangible sign under the oaks, in the sweet wet grass, that anything had been damaged, yet there was a feeling of hurt, of things said and done that had not yet quit throbbing in the stillness. He blinked at Shorter, whom he did not know, then turned to Joe. "So the unpleasant things did happen?"

"Who told you?"

"Will Gow, of course. I'm more or less his burden." He picked up the still-running hose and flung it far from him, then hoisted the box of fruit to his slender shoulders. "Or I should say, something he would like to settle with, but can't."

"Did he tell you about Landry?"

On the lone picnic bench by the trailer, Kang set down his booty. "The man who got killed? Yes."

At Joe's shoulder, Shorter's body was humming invisibly with reawakening impatience and anger. But he didn't speak. Instead he nudged Joe urgently. "This is Ray Shorter, from Tampa," Joe told Kang. "He's a friend of that girl I've been looking for. He thinks he's found some sign of her, and she may be hurt."

"She may well be," said Kang. "It's easy to get hurt around here."

Shorter moved inside his clothes, a clenching of muscles that put a blip in the low, ugly signal his nerves were sending. "We need someone who knows his way around out there, who can tell what he's looking at if we find anything," Joe persisted. "Will you come?"

Kang blinked again, this time at both of them; Joe could not have said why such a small motion, from such a slight and civil creature, should have seemed so foreboding. "Agent Hope, my concern is not people. My concern is snakes, birds, and panthers, and once in a while an alligator. You're a law enforcement officer. Why didn't you take Mr. Shorter to the sheriff? You want Will Gow mad at both of us, is that it?"

"There's nothing illegal about driving out to this Fat Hog Camp with us."

"You can't drive to Fat Hog Camp."

"Shorter drove to some kind of camp."

Kang frowned, slapping a mosquito off his shoulder blade. "Where?"

"West of one of those shell roads, Eight thirty-three."

"Ah. The Meacham camp. That's even worse."

"You're afraid of the Meachams?"

"Terrified of them," Kang said soberly. "Or else they're terrified of me. Either way, it's the same."

Shorter had started moving, though apparently he was not going anywhere. Apparently he was just trudging the confining ring of the clearing, swaying from side to side as he walked, the way zoo elephants do, a monotonous, deliberately numbing performance of despair.

"Go back," begged Kang suddenly, in a low voice that could not have reached Shorter. "Do what is expected of you. Don't take this chance."

Shorter had come up against a small lean-to. Amidst the clutter, the picks and rakes, the unused lawn mower, the lengths of hose and rolls of wire, sat a mud-spattered canvas-topped Jeep, a relic. Shorter had paused by the open rear of the Jeep, peering in. Suddenly Dave Kang plunged toward him. Joe was tired, and slow. Before he could even begin to follow, Shorter had pivoted toward them, a rusty, black-barrelled shotgun pointed at them. His aim was straight, the shake of his hands lethal. Joe stood stupidly, and Kang hesitated. Abruptly Shorter let the gun thump to the ground like something that had died in his grip. Kang hurried to him and picked it up, breaking open the action and dumping the shells. He put them in the pocket of his khaki trousers. "Everyone will be at the funeral," Joe said.

"Not the Meachams."

"Good. I'd like to meet them."

"Is it likely people will be shooting at us?" Kang laid the rifle inside the Jeep. "The way someone shot at you Sunday?"

He had almost forgotten that he was a figure in the puzzle, not the one outside it, solving it. "Nobody's after me."

"Will seems to think so."

"Nobody's paying any attention to me."

Kang took Shorter by the arm. But he was too small to move him. "Help me," he sighed to Joe. "We should get this over fast."

21

KANG STOPPED THE JEEP. AHEAD OF them, out of place and derelict, Shorter's faded red truck blocked the forest trail. Instantly, over the muted sputter of the idling engine, came a constant whine from the forest. Shorter slapped his neck convulsively. Kang twisted to look back at them. "Does he have the keys?"

Joe had fished them from Shorter's pockets when he rinsed the trousers. But when he offered them, Kang only frowned. "Maybe we better walk in. It's only a hundred yards."

He edged the Jeep into the soggy ditch from which the elevated trail had been dredged, keeping just one wheel on the high ground. Joe wished that Shorter would not come, but of course, he was the first one out of the Jeep, though he still held onto it, letting go only long enough to slap at mosquitoes. Joe felt the first stinging welts rise on his own neck. "Where is your spray?" Kang asked.

"I forgot it."

"You should be more careful." He leaned back into the Jeep and sorted through a cluttered dashboard compartment, offering a tiny glass bottle filled with oily liquid the color of urine. "Don't use much. A little goes a long way."

The scent did not drive off the insects, any more than Cindy's sprays had, but it granted a thin bubble of peace. Kang, a few steps ahead, ignored the barrage. Joe followed, and finally Shorter let go of the Jeep and hurried after them. They edged past the mute hulk of the truck. A litter of dead cypress fronds, delicately multilobed as the snapped-off arms of burnt snowflakes, had collected on the dusty hood.

"What was it he told you he found?" Kang asked Joe quietly. "Just signs of blood?"

"I think he found some clothing."

"The Meachams wouldn't do that. Murder on their own doorstep."

"If there is blood, it's important not to touch anything."

"I wouldn't think of it." Kang eyed Shorter behind them. "Is he all right?"

"I can't cuff him to the Jeep."

"Well . . . he's her friend? Then he has a right to come."

The ground crested slowly, shaking off the black, puddled cloak of the low-lying swamp. In among the twisted shrub and burl-cankered hardwoods were yellowed palms, sere and drooping. Overhead something rustled fearlessly, then landed on a swaying branch in the pathway, a masked black-handed creature like an infant monkey, piqued at their intrusion. "Fox squirrel," Kang volunteered. Ahead, the woods gave way to a clearing, a raised patch of earth and shell pounded smooth by use. Off to one side someone had erected a ragged Indian chickee. "A midden," Kang told him.

"A what?"

"An ancient Indian refuse heap. Built up out of discarded clam shells from Florida Bay." He wrinkled his nose. "Something is dead, all right," he said.

Joe stopped him from entering the clearing with an outstretched hand. The chickee's uneven plank platform supported random heaps of Visqueen-covered camping equipment: a dented Coleman stove, lanterns, propane tanks, a rusty metal gas can, a folded canvas tarp. In the center of the clearing was a blackened fire pit stacked with half-burned logs damp with dew and trussed with spider webs. Beside the pit was a board table, heavily scarred with knife gouges. Half-rotted ropes were strung from one side of the clearing to the other on tree limbs. The sun was low and mote-filled, and the air was still.

Shorter had exaggerated about the blood. There was no carpet of it, no knee-deep carnage. But on the gouged table, clearly, something had been messily butchered. Blood had soaked into the wood and dripped down the unplaned trestles, caking in coagulating rivulets like streams of red wax down the sides of a candle. In the cool dirt of the table's shade a few wet patches still glistened. There was a sweet smell, like crushed flowers. About the flies, Shorter had been right: they swarmed greedily, too engorged to rise.

The musty perfume was not the smell, though, that they had caught coming in. That smell came from somewhere outside the clearing, less tangible but undeniable: a fetid belch from that silent sleeping creature somewhere out in the trees.

Kang turned to Joe. "We've lost your friend."

Joe had only to go a few steps back down the path to find Shorter. The trainer sat in the dirt, out of sight of the blood, his head buried in his arms. "You okay?" Joe asked.

"I don't want to find Cherry."

"Maybe it's not Cherry. You don't have to come into the clearing. But get up and help us."

Shorter flung off his grip, rocking his head.

"Where did you see the fire?"

"I wasn't in the camp then."

"Which way did you go?"

"I don't know."

He could see that Kang had edged forward and was standing over something that looked like the flayed pelt of a dead animal. He hurried back to Kang's side. There in the shell lay the T-shirt Shorter had described, brown with bloodstains, so dry and stiff it looked petrified.

"It could be a man's shirt," Kang ventured throatily.

"Possibly. But it's on the small side."

Kang's face had lost its sunny rose-tea translucence. "We have no business here," he said.

"Shorter said he went stumbling off into the woods. Maybe if we skirt a little way along the edge of the clearing, we'll find his footprints."

But Kang faced him stubbornly. "I said, this is not my business. This is the sheriff's business."

"I agree. Go get him. We'll stay here."

Kang's worried gaze ranged past him, down the gap where the pathway opened. "He's not well."

"So take him with you."

But Kang stared at the ring of still trees surrounding the clearing, licking his lips.

"What are you afraid I'll find?" Joe asked.

The little Indian's head jerked around, but his gaze kept shifting. "Trouble," he said to the trees. "More and more trouble."

"But not *your* trouble, right?"

Abruptly, the little man took the glass bottle from his pocket. He offered it. After a second, Joe took it. "Do what you must," said Kang. "But you are a dangerous man."

He turned, leaving Joe in the clearing. Joe saw him stop and bend over Shorter, who blundered to his feet. Leaning on each other, the two disappeared down the trail.

So now he knew: he had routed Kang out that morning not to guide him, but so he would have someone on whom he could wish Shorter. But soon enough, they would return with Gow, and Shorter would become his burden again.

Kang was right, of course. Looking for evidence, even Shorter's footprints, was not his job. Blood and hair and sifted dirt would speak volumes to a crime scene unit, but not to him. What he should do was park himself on a mossy log that lay near the entrance to the clearing and wait, for the sheriff, or perhaps for Orren. Make sure no one came along and disturbed anything. Make sure *he* didn't accidentally disturb anything.

But the temptation to see what he could learn was enormous. Whatever he didn't discover for himself now, no one would ever tell him. He looked at his watch. He had at least an hour. And the woods, so far so unyielding, seemed to mutter an unexpected promise: Out there just out of sight was something important, something only he could discover. An accomplishment that would earn him the indisputable right to stay down here and finish what he had started. That the promise was probably a lie didn't make it less enticing. He ached to set out into the woods.

He indulged himself with a very careful circuit of the edge of the midden. In the almost impassable ring of stunted hardwoods surrounding the hummock, there were only a few breaches through which Shorter could have fled into the forest. He knelt by one gap, peering down a short crumbling slope and across the swamp floor.

Here, as in the open woods, the ground was grassy, but Joe could see smooth surfaces of impinging water like a tarnished silver sheet. The woods did not help him. As always, he could see a long distance, but what he could see was meaningless, tree upon tree, overlapping, images superimposed and embedded, until the proliferation became as impenetrable as a solid wall.

He eased around the clearing to another trail. This one was more rewarding. The water came up closer, seeping in between the grass roots, and at the damp edge of the mound he spotted the unmistakable print of a big man's shoe.

If Shorter had wandered off this way, then somewhere out there in the variegated monotony, he had seen—or thought he had seen—something on fire. Joe drew in a deep breath. The rotten smell seemed stronger, but he could not tell that it was mixed with any scent of smoke.

He peered out into the forest. Part of him argued that it was just as well he did not have to go out there, give himself up again to unseen nastiness in waist-deep water, risk his hands and feet to carnivorous horrors. Another part scoffed: For a long distance, the grass grew out of that shallow inlay. If he really wanted to know what the forest could tell him, he could find his way without risking more than dirty palms and wet feet.

But as he stood there trying to decide to be sensible, he started; something stirred at the green edge of perception, rustling the tangle of tree limbs, briars, and vines. There was a crash of brush, then another. Then silence. He craned to see, almost losing his balance. He saw nothing but the unending puzzle, the striations of tree trunks, the hodgepodge of overlapping leaves.

But then the crash came again, reckless, more distant. Something—someone?—in a panic, fleeing. That he could not see a man's form meant nothing. Someone was out there.

He stepped down the slope, straddling the footprint, watching for others. But the muck quickly grew so amorphous an elephant wouldn't have left a mark in it. He tried to make his way carefully, looking for logs to step on, or firm clumps of grass, at the same time keeping an eye on the forest ahead of him. His own wallowing and groping made noise, so it was hard to listen, but once when he paused, grabbing for balance at flimsy brambles, he heard the crashing again, closer, more frantic. But still he saw nothing, not even shaking limbs.

The rotten smell was growing stronger. He looked at

his watch; Kang had been gone less than thirty minutes. Just as he started forward, there came a rattle of leaves so close he was sure his prey had doubled back to attack him. Ahead was a big slanted windfall of a toppled tree. He plunged toward it, surrendering caution, sinking heedlessly in the pernicious footing. With the tree as a shield, he crouched, listening over his heartbeat. The crashing stopped. He levered himself slowly above the prone trunk . . . and laughed.

The ground beyond rose slightly, so that the humus among the tree roots was drier and the fallen leaves had not rotted to mush but had spread in a brittle brown carpet. There, rooting busily, was a nickel-shelled armadillo, plowing into thickets with the determination of a drunken gate-crasher, then retreating blearily, scattering leaves with its thick scaly tail. If it heard Joe laugh, the sound didn't register in any sentient layer of its brain. It was making a terrible racket, unwatchful, unalarmed.

Sinking against the tree, Joe decided he had not really been such a fool. How could he have told Gow or Orren he had seen movement and heard rustling but had not tried to find out what was making it? What he had done was logical. On the way back, he would be observant, watch for footprints or evidence. Maybe he would find that luck had made him a gift of the chance he wanted. He pivoted in the soggy weeds and prepared for his hike back across the marshland—and realized with something like a knife jab to his belly that he did not know where the clearing was at all.

Impossible, he thought. The wall of hardwoods ringing the clearing would be unmistakable against the gray-trunked cypress. But somehow there were more hardwoods than he remembered, closer together, big knots of them merging into indefinable tangles in the distance. He looked up. He could see bits of sky, weak white like stained linen, but no sun.

This was stupid, he thought. And solvable. The clearing had to be right there, right in front of him. All he needed to do was keep the big fallen tree at his back and walk straight forward, still, of course, watching for any sign that anyone had been there before him. He could see a cypress stump at the edge of discernible detail, one that had been logged perhaps half a century ago, and that now had sent up new shoots that had grown together about twenty feet overhead, making a spindly H. He hadn't noticed the stump on his way out, but then he'd been watching out for whatever he was pursuing, and besides, things could look different from different sides.

He would use the odd tree as a marker, he decided. From there he would surely be able to pinpoint the high ground of the camp.

But somehow, as he started forward, it seemed the ground had changed. Perhaps before he had been too caught up in the chase to notice, but now it seemed that solid footfalls were impossible to find. And now that he was watching, every narrow black gap between grass blades held something that roiled and shivered and plopped. A whiplike shadow exploded out of a treetop when he was not looking; spinning, overbalancing in a shifting mudhole, he tried to glance up, and thought—*thought*—he saw the brigand face of the big belligerent squirrel. But then it was gone, with a starchy leaf-frond rustle and a pointed little patter of loose twigs and bark.

He was finding it hard to worry much about spotting evidence. Resolutely, he refocused on the cypress stump, dodging nothing, mincing and stumbling straight ahead. The ground, the woods themselves, seemed to resent his progress. He lost his temper with a waist-high patch of tendrils that wouldn't part for him. A mistake. They were armed with mean spines and caught at his shirt and his flesh under it. He had to stop and disengage himself carefully, and when he looked up at the stump again, it seemed farther away, not nearer. Too, there was a narrow, dark moat ahead of him, deep, with a visible current stippling its surface. He was sure he hadn't crossed any-thing like it on his way out.

He pivoted thoughtfully, holding onto logic. Now he could make out a dense clump of myrtlelike bushes; the sun had begun to shift overhead, and beyond that green myrtle wall the light was noticeably brighter. Surely that thickening and brightening marked the mound of the clearing. In fact, he thought he could see the shell slope blaze white. He fixed his sights on that cool lure in the green and amber infinity. He must go straight for it, quickly, before the light changed.

That elbow of deep water still blocked him. By veering off course ten yards to the left, he thought he could avoid it, but he ordered himself not to. A few steps, he argued, and he would emerge in grass again, into what looked like a solid, uncomplicated stretch that would take him right to the flash of white. The heat would dry him. The hell with hanging back.

He put a foot out into the open channel and instantly sank to his knees. He could feel the current tugging him. Three steps, he told himself. He took another step. The mud had no bottom. It gripped his feet, sucking at him. The water rose halfway up his thighs.

"You can fucking swim, can't you?" he said aloud. He started forward again, the water licking up to his crotch, absurdly cold.

He had a sense, within seconds after it happened, that he had known it was about to happen, as if a quick film, subliminal brain litter from another existence, had been reeled and rewound before him, then played once more in its entirety so he could get a good, close look.

He saw, then and ever afterward, the white foam of disturbance, as chaotic as panic. He saw, or dreamed he saw, a big bladed wedge, steel-colored and glinting but nubile as if warped by supersonic forces, spin through the air in a strangely fluid, weightless arc. But it hit the water with tons behind it, an animal strength that shattered his self-control just as it cratered and fragmented the putty-blank surface of the water, so that calm and peace and courage seemed like illusions, tricks of physics, alive in the heat of a hand but brittle as cold glass when dropped. He could not clearly say he saw the teeth, but he thought he saw them, the eyes, too, close-set, chert-yellow, with black disks of Jurassic hate set in them, from a time before heart and heat came about.

He might have screamed, but he couldn't remember. He leapt backward, finding handholds in air and flowing water; he landed in the shallows with a force that knocked the breath out of him; the brush opened for him as he kicked and churned and crawled backward on his hands and butt. Through the swath he had slashed in the grass and reeds he could see the narrow slough plainly: the plate-black water, trembling softly with its own sluggish pulse, its wound healed over, its ebony surface untroubled and still.

He gulped until he could breathe. A dragonfly, all blue like a dangling chip of Wedgewood, hovered at eye level. He laughed suddenly and crazily at its benign, pop-eyed inspection. When it landed on his knee, he didn't even brush at it. It tested its long clear wings lazily, lapping with its strange mouth parts at the soaked cloth.

How big had the thing been? He got flabbily to his feet, angry at the way his knees wobbled, peering at the smooth swell of water, wanting another look.

But the water had taken it back completely. In all the forest, things had tucked themselves away from him. Once more nothing stirred.

Only then did he remember that he was lost. And being lost was suddenly the simplest of problems, the kind you could only encounter in a world with destinations, where there were road signs and maps and logic, in a sane world, on solid ground.

He pivoted slowly. There was the cypress stump, still beyond the deadly water. Where was his myrtle patch, his white flag of shelly bank? The sun had changed, cutting through the canopy at random angles. He blinked, and then jumped, in a rush of new terror: It was a long time before he could convince himself the two men were really standing there, and were really alive and breathing, and not visitations from somewhere much farther away than the mucky bottom of a pond.

THEY WERE BOTH YOUNG, STOOP-shouldered, the threadbare seats of their jeans hanging almost to their knees. Their grease-splotched T-shirts sported faded beer logos, and their billed caps advertised chewing tobacco and auto parts. Both had boils of sticky blond curls, but one of the men had a skimpy beard that dangled from his chin like a clump of undercooked noodles. The other, somewhat younger, had the same blue eyes, their outer corners downturned a little, the same sunburned dollop of a nose stuck between his high cheekbones, but where the bearded brother's face was lean as a peach pit, his was round as a melon, his reddened skin tight and shiny. The thin one unhooked a grimy thumb from his jeans pocket and began digging thoughtfully at a big raw pimple in the limp fringe of his beard. "You out here all alone, friend?"

"Your name wouldn't be Meacham, would it?"

The younger one swaggered forward aggressively. "Who wants to know?"

To Joe it suddenly seemed crucial to get certain facts out in the open. "I'm a law enforcement officer," he said.

"Well, you're one wet law enforcement officer." The

thin brother gave up on the pimple with a disappointed glance at his fingers. "What was you trying to do, arrest old Tom Gator there?"

Joe looked over his shoulder, but there was no sign of the gator. "Yeah, I saw him." He brushed a frond of slimy weed off his forearm. "He ever killed anybody?"

"Not today!" the chubby brother guffawed.

"Let's don't stand out here all day in the chiggers jawing," ordered the skinny brother. "Will Gow'll be here directly."

"You talked to Gow, then?"

"Heard him on the CB. Sounded like we better get out here."

"So what have you been doing, running around in that clearing screwing up evidence?"

"The hell you say." The younger brother folded his tattooed arms belligerently across the beer ad on his stomach. "Sheriff Gow knows me and Lee ain't mixed up in no killings. Somebody's always trying to stir up shit that ain't got nothing to do with us."

"Oh, hush up, Wesley." His brother slapped at his neck, then glanced at his palm, wiping it on the hanging seat of his jeans. "Like I said, no sense in getting et up out here."

He turned, jerking his hand elliptically. Wesley, the plump one, closed in behind him, smelling of day-old sweat. They marched in charged silence down a path that mockingly opened up for them, and after an easy, dry walk of less than two hundred yards, climbed back into the clearing through the exact gap from which Joe had climbed down.

The only change Joe could see in the clearing was the presence, in the opening to the little road, of a huge yellow vehicle, almost completely covered with dried mud, crouching over a set of immense, splayed tractor-treaded tires, with headlights the size of small moons.

"How did you drive that thing in here without me hearing you?" Joe asked incredulously.

"The noise you make splashing around in the bushes?" said Wesley.

"How do you know how much noise I make?"

"We set up here fifteen minutes watching," said the older brother, flashing a mouthful of gold fillings. "Lots more fun than messing up evidence."

"How did you get it past the red pickup?"

"Moved it," the older brother said.

Wesley had picked up a stick and was poking at the blood-stiffened shirt. "Don't touch that," Joe snapped.

The kid blinked at him blandly. He didn't drop the stick.

"Do what he says," his brother ordered.

"When was the last time you two were out here?" Joe asked him.

"I reckon that's one of the things Will Gow'll be asking."

"Probably."

"Then I reckon we'll wait."

The older brother climbed up into the swamp buggy and slouched in the seat behind the steering wheel, propping a cracked cowboy boot on the dashboard and dragging his billed cap down over his eyes. Wesley began whacking at leaves along the edge of the path with his stick. Joe sank down stiffly on the fallen log by the gap to the pathway, resorting to Dave Kang's magic bottle. The heavy kid curled his nostrils scornfully, reaching behind him and digging at the crack of his buttocks. "That don't look like deer blood, does it?" he asked.

"Can you tell the difference?"

But the kid just shrugged distantly. "Did you know I was named for a preacher? And my great-granddaddy was a preacher."

High up on the swamp buggy, his brother sat forward, the cap pushed back, frowning. "Don't bother the man, Wesley."

"Just talking."

"Well, I'm trying to sleep. Shut up."

Wesley frowned down at Joe. "Your brother's kind of mean to you, isn't he?" Joe asked him.

"You think you're gonna find out things from me by being nice to me?"

"Like what?"

"Well, you're not. Lee's sleeping, so shut up." He began working his way down the path past the buggy, swinging the stick from the shoulder, *whack, whack, whack.*

He was trapped in muck, up to his heart in it, and Orren and Gow and Kang were standing around watching him, all having decided there was nothing they could do. He knew he could open his eyes and stop it, but he didn't. He kept going, watching himself drown.

What woke him was a smell, a man's cologne, of all things, and suddenly there was Orren's hairy face glowering down at him. Orren's nose wrinkled in disgust. "Jesus, how can you sleep?"

It was noon. The sun, cooking down from a sky as white as concrete, had steamed the blood and mixed the two smells, the sweet one and the fetid one, and Joe, still caught in his dream, felt his stomach turn. His head hurt bitterly and his clothes had dried to a rigid crust that crackled when he moved.

"You really followed directions, didn't you?" snapped Orren. He was wearing a dress shirt and trousers, but he had tucked his pants into heavy work boots. *"And* you left the crime scene. You left the place so those two nimrods could drive in here and fuck up anything they wanted! How can we claim chain of possession when—if! —we get to court?"

"I saw something moving out there," explained Joe tiredly, trying to wipe the ache out of his eyes. "It turned out to be an armadillo." In the face of Orren's indignation, his defense did not have the force he had imagined.

"Besides, if the Meachams killed someone here, they've already had all the time in the world to fuck things up."

But Orren just shook his shaggy head. "What the hell is the matter with you, Joe?"

Beyond the swamp buggy Will Gow and the two Meacham brothers conferred in murmurs, with Gow doing most of the talking. The skinny older brother listened with his arms wrapped around his sunken chest and his big, flat-boned hands shoved into his armpits. Wesley was trying to peel a scrap of torn rubber off the buggy tire, sullen as a kid dragged along on a shopping trip. Joe unkinked himself and stood. "Where's Kang?"

"He and Shorter are getting the pickup out of the swamp where Mutt and Jeff pushed it."

"What's the matter with the fat one? Is he retarded?"

"Not by no judge's definition. He tell you about his cat that got run over?"

"No."

"Well, keep your distance, he will."

Gow drifted across the bow of the buggy toward them, leaving the Meachams pantomiming what looked like an ill-tempered disagreement. At the sight of Joe, the sheriff puckered his downturned mouth. "You still trying to be a hero, huh? Stomping around in the woods on your own?"

"I was curious."

Gow spat expressively. "You were looking for the fire."

"I don't know that there was a fire."

Gow jerked his head toward the path, presumably indicating Shorter. "He says there was."

"He could have been hallucinating."

The sheriff put his fingertips on the crown of his hat and pushed it down on his head, hard, as if he had felt a bad wind coming. He screwed up his nostrils at the stench from the forest. "Man, you think they been throwing coon guts to the gators?"

"I sure hope so," grunted Orren.

From Gow's grimace, the smell was not something he expected to acquire a taste for. "Come over here a minute, Cruse."

The two of them moved off along the rim of the midden. Joe couldn't hear what they were saying. Every now and then Gow glanced back at him, and once, so did Orren. Suddenly Gow wheeled. "Lee! Wes!" He met the brothers near the swamp buggy. Heads bent, the three of them reached some sort of cryptic understanding; Lee looked up, inspecting Joe with a hangman's eye. Then the young men grabbed on to the scaffolding of the buggy and scrambled up onto it. Gow turned back to Orren. "Don't stand around scratching your butt."

Then he, too, climbed up, and the machine shuddered to life, backing out of the clearing, its passengers bouncing with the lurches. "What the hell was that all about?" Joe asked as Orren rejoined him.

"Gow's cooperating on the Landry killing; I'm cooperating on this."

"Where's he taking Lee and Wesley?"

"Supposedly out to show the lab boys where the turn is. So Kang will think we've cut him some slack."

"Kang?" said Joe incredulously. "Why not the Meachams?"

"Because the sheriff doesn't think those boys are quite dumb enough to make themselves look like murderers by accident, and I don't either. At least Lee isn't."

"But is he smart enough to do it on purpose so we'll *think* he's not that dumb?"

Orren shrugged. "Gow knows him. I don't."

Through the trees, Joe saw the buggy crowd Kang and Shorter into the ditch as they trudged along on foot, a giant and an elf. The roar receded. "They hunt off those bulldozers?" Joe asked.

"No, mostly just tear around and run over things."

"You really think it's Kang?"

Orren was frowning distantly. He didn't glance at Joe. "One of my men saw him driving out of Windwood about six on Sunday."

"I still don't believe it."

"Oh?" said Orren, not nicely. "You read his mind?"

"Of course not."

"Then shut up."

Kang led Shorter up to them, charily as a kid who has brought home a stray mastiff. From far off on the fringes of awareness came a low-keyed, hungry rumble. "Thunder," Kang said.

Orren shrugged. "Not close."

"I'm afraid not." Kang clicked his tongue. "We need the rain."

But Orren looked over his shoulder at the black rims stiffening around the shrinking dollops of blood. "Not till we get this checked out we don't."

"Do you think the sheriff is dragging his feet on these killings? Is that why you got rid of him?"

"I didn't get rid of him. He'll be back in a few minutes."

But Kang ruffled his peppery hair skeptically. "The Meachams would not have left so willingly if there had been anything here you might stumble over."

Orren still had on his tie; he took it off and stashed it in a pocket. "You don't think it's human blood?"

Kang seemed to have conquered the distress he had felt that morning. "I think it must be. No one would butcher a game animal so cavalierly."

"Well, we'll figure out who did it later. Now I want you to help us."

"How?"

Shorter was standing close at hand with his head bowed, frowning, and Orren ducked his chin to look into his face, as if calculating how hard a poke it would take to wake him. "Gow says there's another trail that comes in not far north of here."

"Yes. I know it. It turns off the shell road quite a ways up toward the Alley, then dead ends in the slough just a little northwest of here."

"Gow thinks we ought to get there double-quick and see if there's any sign anybody's been there recently. He thinks we can get there faster on foot than he can in a cruiser if you lead."

Kang was sanguine. "Possibly."

"I want you and me and Mr. Shorter here to work our way up there. On the way we'll fan out and keep our eyes open. You stay on the right, Shorter can keep you in sight, and I can watch him."

Kang blinked, impassive as a diminutive Oriental merchant waiting for them to talk themselves into some gingeroot or rhino horn. "What are we looking for?"

"I don't know. Signs of a fire, maybe."

"And Mr. Hope?"

"Agent Hope will guard the crime scene."

"Veering east is slightly farther, but it will take us across drier ground than trying to follow a beeline," said Kang blandly.

"Whatever you say," Orren agreed.

"There's a damn big gator out there," Joe interrupted. They all looked at him as if he were a pack animal that had suddenly spoken. "It jumped me."

"You probably scared it," Orren reproached.

Kang led the trio out of the clearing. Shorter followed him, staying close behind him with a fawning dependence. Orren turned back on his way out of the clearing. "Don't you move so much as a gnat's teeny eyelash out of here," he told Joe.

"If you're so sure Kang knows something, why let him pick the direction?"

"I'm not. As soon as we get out there, I'm gonna fade around to the left. You keep your eyes open. Try to keep him in sight."

"It's easy to get lost."

"Jeez, I'm not a birdbrain, Joe."

. . .

From the tree line he watched Orren blundering heavily from hummock to hummock, from lightfall to lightfall. He should have been glad, he told himself, not to be forced back out into it. His clothes, his body, reeked of humus, sour earth, and standing muck.

But the sense that there was something out there, something Orren wouldn't know to look for, still taunted him. And Orren was crazy to trust Shorter to keep up with Kang. Kang was moving fast, and behind him Shorter sank and scrambled up and sank again like a floundering bull moose. The Meachams had been right: someone plunging through the swamp did make a lot of noise. Kang, far ahead now, flickered in and out of the sunlight, while Orren, already trying to work his way left, turned long enough to wave Joe back again.

Disgusted, he circled the rim of the midden, looking west and south through a gap in the tangled brush, in the direction opposite the one Kang had chosen. Somewhere off to his left, high overhead, something shrieked in the treetops. How big, he wondered, were these damn panthers? The shriek rose again, maniacal, invaded. Something as brown as the undersides of dead leaves rose from a branch startlingly nearby: a hawk of some sort, voluble in its disruption. Raptor. Flesh eater. He wondered if Cindy had gone to the funeral. The mosquitoes were finding him; he took out Kang's bottle, dousing himself in the oily dope.

Suddenly, from the forest behind him, arose a harsh, frightened wailing that came from no bird in a treetop, no cornered armadillo: a bawling senseless and panicked, inchoate and inhuman, a yowl that started deep and tore deeper—Shorter, screaming for help.

He wheeled precariously, almost sliding down the midden bank. The shouting didn't let up. Where Shorter had been, now there was nothing but forest. How could he find him in time to help him? Even if he could figure out which direction he ought to go, how could he shove through the muck and brush fast enough? Then, through the still bars of the trees, Joe saw something pale flapping and thrashing. He plunged down the slope, crashing into water up to his knees, wrenching himself loose again. Abruptly he caught sight of Orren pushing in from the left ahead of him. The screaming stopped. Orren flickered in and out of view, then vanished. The silence was horrendous. "Shorter!" he screamed.

"Over here!" Orren stepped out from behind a big stump, dragging Shorter with him. They were both batting at the air around them. "Damn hornet nest!" Orren said.

"Do you need help? Do you want me to—?"

"No," said Orren. "Stay there."

They made their way up to him laboriously, skirting brush, climbing falls of timber like piled mammoth bones. Shorter was whimpering in the grip of his latest misfortune. Orren's broad face had reddened dangerously. "We've lost that goddamned Kang."

Joe peered around unsteadily. Orren was right: In the green and gold grid of the surrounding woods, nothing moved.

"So help me God," Orren said.

A couple of foul-tempered hornet scouts had come with them, their off-key hum twanging in Joe's ear. Shorter was having a hard time standing still. "For God's sakes, quit slapping!" Orren commanded brusquely. He sucked in his breath and let it out in a shout. *"Kang!"*

No one answered.

Shorter quavered, "I'm not gonna die, am I?"

"No, you're not gonna die." Again Orren put his hands to his mouth, threw his head back, and bawled, "Kang!"

But still, as far as either he or Joe could tell, there was no answer.

"Fuck it all to Christ," Orren said.

With Neanderthal grace, Shorter was trying to flounder his way over a nearby log, though he couldn't have had any idea where he was going. "This guy's a walking disaster," muttered Orren to Joe. "How do you tell if somebody's allergic?"

"They stop breathing."

"What if one of us is allergic?"

"Did they sting you?"

"A couple of them."

Shorter had dropped to his knees in the mud. "A snake'll get him next," Joe said.

Orren lurched forward, grabbing Shorter's collar. Moaning, Shorter drooped against the log. With a rough hand, Orren tilted his jaw to the light. The flesh around his throat was beginning to puff up and tighten. "That hurts," he said.

Orren's eyes met Joe's. "Do you know your way back?" Joe asked him.

They both looked around. The forest was featureless.

"That way," Orren said, not quite under his breath. "That cabbage palm. I'm pretty sure."

In fact, Joe did not think they should head for the cabbage palm, but he let Orren pick the path. Shorter wasn't helpful. He swayed, lost his footing, hung back, whimpering. The skin beneath his eyes was beginning to glisten, and stings on his lips made his mouth a lumpy nest of lesions. Once, glancing back over his shoulder, Joe caught his breath. Orren heard him, and looked, too. But by then there was nothing. "Kang," Joe said.

"What was he doing over there? He should be east of us."

"This place spins you around until you don't know which way you're going."

"I know which way I'm fucking going," grunted Orren. "Out."

Joe kept a watch behind him, but he did not see Kang again. The whole thing was incomprehensible. If Kang had done this strange killing, why hadn't he covered his crime? Why—when he had been so distressed this morning—had he now taken off so confidently? To do what? Scout on his own? Destroy evidence? And why risk arousing their suspicions? Did he suspect someone he wanted to protect? Someone from the Park Service, who had worked on the panthers? Someone who had known Amy Wells?

They were close to the palm now; the going had gotten wetter, once more obstructed by rotten tree falls; the three of them were clambering feebly through the mess, taking great care where they stepped and what they grabbed onto, when Joe, slightly ahead, looked up into the narrow Chinese eyes of Dave Kang.

"Jesus Christ," said Orren, stopping short beside Joe.

"Did I scare you?" smiled Kang. "I'm sorry. What happened? I heard shouting."

"And you're gonna hear more of it! Where the hell did you get to?"

Joe saw Kang take in Shorter and deduce what had happened. "I thought I saw something through the trees," he explained amiably. "I thought Mr. Shorter would stay with me. I had to watch where I was going. There were quite a number of snakes."

"I didn't see any snakes," said Orren.

"Perhaps not." Kang did not quite smile.

"What was it you thought you saw?" Joe persisted.

"I wasn't sure. Possibly signs of gator poaching."

"You found whatever it was, didn't you?" snapped Orren.

"No. I came to a slough, and was just deciding to cross it, when I heard your shouts."

"Why didn't you answer?"

"Because I was listening."

"For what?"

"For someone out there."

Orren sputtered indignantly. "There was no one out there."

Kang shrugged lightly. "If so, when you shouted, they took cover."

"I saw you," said Joe. "You were directly behind us, not off to the east of us."

"I found I had wandered back toward you. There was a lot of wet ground in my way. I had to circle back."

"You know," said Orren, using his size as Joe had seldom seen him do, "you should be keeping me on your side. Not pissing me off. Right now I'm pissed as a cat in a cesspool."

Kang nibbled his pale lower lip resignedly. "Mr. Shorter looks uncomfortable."

"We're all uncomfortable!"

Kang gave a meager indifferent shiver. "Then let's go."

He turned coolly. Orren jerked a foot out of the mire and feinted at his retreating backside. "Cocksucker," he breathed.

They had not been so far off. Kang led them a hundred yards to their left and the clearing materialized before them, perfectly distinguishable, like a mirage that grows plainer the closer you get to it rather than disappearing. It was afternoon now, and the flies were congregating with a nasty mob vitality. The sun shone straight down, and again came that guttural sob along an unseen horizon. "Jeez," said Orren. "I hope they get this site worked before it rains."

Kang was inspecting Shorter's welts, waving his fine-boned hands over them without quite touching them. Magically, he seemed to calm Shorter, who stood with his swollen eyelids closed. "At the emergency room they'll pull these stingers out."

"Is he in any danger?" Joe asked.

"I don't think so. His breathing would have shut off by now."

Orren took Joe's elbow, drawing him away. "These damn mosquitoes. Didn't I see you with some bug stuff?"

"Kang's."

"Let me have it." He pounded the mouth of the little bottle against his palm until it was empty, then smeared the juice on his neck and cheeks.

"There's something out there, and Kang knows it," said Joe. "If it's the girl, will you believe it's our case?"

Orren crunched his heavy brows down grimly. "Personally, I hope it's deer blood. Then it's nobody's case."

"But if it isn't—"

"Didn't you fucking hear me, Joe? You've got to quit thinking you're the only one smart enough and tough enough to solve this."

"That's not what I was thinking."

"Balls. Sure you were. Only this time you've dicked your way into a corner. You just better hope Will Gow don't blab."

Kang, who was sitting on the log by the pathway, perked up, sighting back down the road. Shorter heard it too, and began gathering himself like a traveler arranging baggage. So the swamp buggy came in from the east, ahead of the cruisers and staff cars, and the thunder muscled toward them from the west, off the gulf. And when the buggy churned into sight, and Lee Meacham, still in the driver's seat, cut the motor, there was an abrupt silence like that of a pair of bulls pawing. The thunder threatened from deep in its unsettled gut, but Lee Meacham just grinned.

23

THE HOSPITAL WAS THE NOISIEST PLACE
he had ever been. He decided it was loud because of the
way the rooms branching off the central nurses' bay all
cast scraps of disquiet into an invisible convection. People came and went in a hurry, as if in the world outside a
war had just started. In one of the rooms was a squalling
baby. Sitting there in his chair against the wall, he tried
to feel sorry for the unseen mother, and succeeded to the
point that he wished he could go and take the baby from
her. When the baby abruptly stopped crying, he wanted
to go see what had happened to it. He watched the room
from which the sound had been coming, but no one went
in or out.

He started to his feet at a movement near him. A
young deputy stood there, not one of the ones he had
seen at the camp but a stranger with fair-skinned Irish
good looks and a restless way of rocking just on the edge
of motion. "I'm here to take over," he said, in the sliding
rhythms of his southern country dialect. "Sheriff Gow
said you was to go on home."

Home could mean many things. Probably it meant
back to Tampa. The deputy didn't take the chair Joe had

vacated, but stood with his back against the wall, his strong arms crossed.

As he headed for the corridor, Joe saw the doctor to whom he had entrusted Shorter, a dark-skinned Cuban named Piniero, whose long white coat, so immaculate, looked like the uniform of a religious order. But he was brusque when Joe stopped him. "No, no. I told the police already, he's all right."

"You think he's in his right mind? You think he knows what he's doing?"

"He's exhausted," said the doctor. "Dehydrated and hungry. After a day's rest he will have to be taken elsewhere. You'll come back for him?"

But Joe gestured to the young cop. "It's up to them now."

It had not rained. Stars had come out, an immense random fleet of them. At the motel they gave him another room, with a quieter air-conditioning unit. There was a tree frog in the bathroom, virginal green like a leaf that had just begun unfurling, with big, startled black eyes and a visible heartbeat. He tried to catch it but missed with two grabs, and let it stay; for the few seconds he lay in bed conscious he heard it splatting from tile surface to tile surface, probably feeding on minute insects that had weaseled in through gaps in the window frames.

When he woke up, it was with the sense that he had known something was going to come and get him, driving him out of bed with staccato raps as brusque as landed blows. He was at the door and turning the knob before he realized that it was a sound he was hearing. "Come on," said Gow. "We got a squad car. Get dressed."

Outside, two of the sheriff's deputies in their severe uniforms blocked the sidewalk. Joe clutched the warmth of his bare ribs under his palms, realizing only slowly that he had no clothes on. "What's going on? What do you want?"

"We found something."

"It's two—somebody or some*thing?*"

"Something. Not your gal. Hurry up and let's git."

So Joe gathered his wrinkled, dirt-smeared, air-dried clothes from the floor where he had thrown them and went in the bathroom. The frog had disappeared.

There was no moon tonight either; the stars looked like the shards of something phosphorescent that had dropped on the dome of the sky and shattered. The place Gow took him was not the hunting camp they had been in that afternoon, its scent sugary with animal effluvia. Instead it was a huge vault chiseled out of the dark swamp by a profusion of floodlights, in which trees towered like fluted rock. Shadowy figures danced between the gray columns. The air vibrated with the leaden hum of a generator, and the smell the car's air conditioner sucked in was acrid, civilized, and polluting: a fire smell, poisonous. Joe and Gow got out. The hot night air, clogging as ether, replaced the fake a.c. chill.

Gow measured him in the glow from the floodlights. "You always start things you can't wind up?"

"I'd wind it up if you would let me."

"Your bosses don't think so."

"Then why didn't you let me get some sleep?"

Gow yawned pointedly. "Because this damn case won't let *me* sleep. You brought something down here, friend."

"I turned over a rock you've been dancing around, that's all."

"Yeah," said Gow, "and ever since, all I've had time to do is squash bugs."

He started forward into the forest. "What did the lab report say about the blood in the camp?" Joe called. "Was it human?"

Gow wheeled, meeting his gaze stolidly, his narrowed eyes chipped reflections. "You think I'd be up at three in the morning if somebody'd barbequed a pig?"

A man accosted the sheriff. "We got them planks laid," he said to Gow.

"You got the number off it and all?"

"Got a crew out there now taking pictures."

"Well," said Gow resignedly, "let's get our boots wet."

There were not as many mosquitoes as Joe had expected, but around the strung lights armies of fat, winged creatures twirled in blind spirals, loop-the-looping, colliding, and getting nowhere. Ahead, on the far side of this new well-lit clearing, was a Japanese lantern walk, a double row of planks laid from hummock to hummock down a soggy lane through the trees. Following Gow, Joe tried the planks and found them slick but sturdy. Up ahead, flashbulbs fired relentlessly from all directions like guns blazing. In a pool among the trees, under the barrage, lay a motionless black hulk. Gow edged out to the end of the planks and stepped off on a tree root, inspecting it skeptically. "Recognize it?" he shot at Joe.

"Why should I? It's burned to a cinder. There's not a scrap of paint left on it."

"Yes, there is. It's white."

"But why drag me out here? I never claimed I saw it."

"Thought I might jog your memory a little."

"There's no memory of it to jog."

Gow swatted a bug that had landed on his jaw. "You say today when you were all out tromping around, and Dave Kang got separated, you saw him coming back in from behind you? Instead of northeast, like he started out?"

Ignoring the water soaking into his trousers for the thousandth time that day, Joe blundered off the planks. Gow watched like a scientist measuring a reflex. Joe splashed between the bulb bursts and laid his hands on the car hood. It was cold and cindery, already oxidizing, definitely a Datsun. "How did he—they—get it out here?" he called to Gow.

"Dragged it down the track from Eight thirty-three with a buggy, then pushed it into this hole."

"Tracks?"

"Not yet. Too wet."

"One man?"

"Could have been. It ain't much car."

He eased around to peer inside. It was dark, but he could see that the water had flooded in, covering the floor. The steering wheel was a naked shaft, the seats piles of seared stuffing. The windshield glass had cracked. He couldn't pull the door open; something had fused. There was no point in asking if Gow had seen the way the shoulder belt had been pulled under the front seat back and jammed into its catch to stop it from buzzing. But he did ask, "Was the guy who owns it the one who left this belt this way?"

"Not the way he tells it," Gow said.

He edged sideways, sinking to his knees in a hole. "Is this the road Kang was supposed to lead us to today?"

"Except he led you northeast, the long way, then from the sound of it, he shied around west northwest. *I* think he could have made it all the way here between the time you missed him and the time he caught up."

Joe shrugged. "But why would he risk making us suspicious?"

"He didn't figure to. He heard Shorter shouting and figured you wouldn't be paying any attention." Gow swatted both sides of his neck at once. "What gets me is why *you* didn't see it. By Lee Meacham's reckoning, you got within a few hundred yards."

"I saw mud," said Joe coldly. "I saw trees. I saw water. I saw the biggest alligator I've ever seen in my life."

"Yeah," said Gow, with a chuckle. "Lee told me."

"And I think it's strange when people think that's funny."

Gow shrugged. He didn't stop smiling. "Well, let's go

get dry. Ain't no use in squatting down and praying over the thing."

Back at the cruiser, the sheriff conducted an unintelligible interchange of terse barks and crackles on the radio while Joe tried to squeeze the water out of his trousers. Then Gow hung up the mike and propped his elbows on the car roof, full jowls on his fist, hat brim shading his eyes from the floodlight glare as he studied Joe.

"This Shorter could have killed her as easy as anybody," he ventured.

"Then you know the blood in the camp came from a woman?"

"Female Caucasian."

"But no ID?"

"Cruse is getting us a hurry-up job from the state lab. If we're lucky, the gal in Tampa'll be a secretor, and she'll have left her toothbrush at home."

"But why would Shorter kill Cherry Miller? And why would he shoot at me, for that matter?"

"Because he's loony."

"How would he get hold of a swamp buggy? How would he find his way around?"

Gow tapped a quick one-two on the car roof. "That's right, you've got your own suspect."

"Well, where is he? Have you looked for him?"

"The guy that was with her? You sure there was one?"

"I'm not the only one who saw him. And Sapia knew this country. He's been down here lots of times. His credit card record proves it."

"Well," said Gow curtly, "maybe he's dead, too."

Joe was thinking. "Finding the car out here ties whoever killed Landry in with this murder."

"But it don't tie either of them in with Amy Wells."

"Let's say the girl who was killed in the Meachams' camp *is* the girl from Tampa—"

"Then," said Gow, yawning, "it looks like we're right back where we were the other day at the meeting. You stirred someone up, let them know you were interested in these people. They took a potshot at you, but they missed. So then—or maybe before, it don't matter—they kill her, to make it look like you're on the right track, make it look like *he* killed her. That's why I say he's got to disappear, too. He's got to be dead."

"But if whoever fired those shots and killed this woman in the camp is that desperate to throw me off the track—"

"Yeah," assented Gow. "Then there's a connection with the Wells case he—or they—don't want you to find."

"Sapia could still be alive. He could have done all of it."

"But that would be putting you on the track, not leading you off it."

"Maybe that's what he wants."

"Maybe so." Gow shrugged.

Joe didn't see the signal with which he summoned one of the deputies. The deputy hurried to the driver's door, opened it, and then waited. Gow circled the car slowly. He set his hand on the passenger door handle. "Get a piece of paper, Hope. Get some authorization."

"And if I did?"

"This is a big county. Full of tourists and drug runners. I don't have the time or the manpower to chase around out here in the pond apple and the palmetto."

"What about the official department liaison?"

"I sent that turkey back. I told Cruse I wanted you to stick around."

"Orren didn't warn you I'm a troublemaker?"

"Who needs warning? But you're either stubborn as hell, or slicker than Cruse gives you credit for. Either way, like I said, I'm interested to see what else you stumble into."

"Unfortunately, I can't ask Orren for favors. There're complications."

"Yeah," Gow sighed grimly. "And I could kick your butt for that."

Gow did not ride back to Naples with them. Alone in the car with Joe, the deputy began talking eagerly about fishing, first of the days of his not-so-distant childhood, of snook and redfish by the carload, of tarpon so big you couldn't get them in the boat with you. But it seemed that it was much harder to catch anything than it used to be. The fish were dying. The bay was dying. The deputy personally thought a new plague was coming. The fags in Key West were part of it. Nobody read the Bible anymore, that was why things were so fucked up, the deputy said.

24

HE WAS NOT PREPARED TO WAKE UP again what seemed like scant seconds after he lay down, and certainly he wasn't prepared for what woke him. Gow's knock had been placid compared to the frantic banging that drove him out of the bed he had barely gotten warm. He lost his balance struggling back into his trousers, stumbled over his shoes, and cursed when he knocked his hip on the chair. He was still cursing when he jerked the door open. Cindy stood there wet-eyed in the daybreak, in a U. of Miami sweat suit, her black hair thrust up in unruly curls. "Oh, Joe! They've put Dave in jail!"

And behind her stood Hunter, looking much as he had when he had hitchhiked to Tampa, ruffled, sloppy, a little drunk with indefatigable purpose. It was light, but just barely. No one else seemed to have woken up; no one was glowering at them from the other windows. "Get in here," Joe said. "Jesus." When he had them both inside, he slammed and chain-locked the door.

He caught up his shirt and hurried his shoulders into it. "What did you tell them?" Cindy demanded. "Why did you get him involved?"

On the veneer desk by the TV there was a plug-in coffeepot and courtesy servings of instant coffee. He took the pot into the bathroom to fill it. Cindy followed him. "Why, Joe? Why?"

Her cheeks were streaked with tears. He had to shove his way out of the bathroom past her. He took the pot back to the desk and plugged it in, then broke open a packet of coffee and spilled it into the plastic cup. The water showed no signs of boiling. "Cindy, I asked Dave to go out there with me because I needed his help. From that point, he was on his own. He got himself in trouble."

"But what are they . . . what happened?"

"To tell you the truth, I really don't know."

Cindy turned her back unhappily. The coffeepot began to mutter and cough; he thumped it impatiently, then suddenly spun on Hunter. "What are you doing here?"

"I—we met yesterday. At the police station in Windwood, when my mom and I stopped by to sign for Kevin's—"

"So what have you done, left your mom alone?"

"Her friend's with her."

"And she thinks you're in the dorm? As usual?"

"What is it with you anyway?" Hunter demanded. "I haven't done anything wrong."

No, no law said an eighteen-year-old and a seventeen-year-old couldn't be out driving around together at six A.M. No law said they couldn't wake up an undisciplined and unhappy cop who was the one, in fact, who had gotten everyone in trouble. The water finally started the insistent gurgling he had been waiting for. He unplugged the pot more decorously than he had plugged it in and filled the plastic cup. Cindy had gathered her courage again. "Don't you think you could get him out?"

He backed toward the rumpled bed. Hunter watched him with cold curiosity, as if he knew there was a trap door under the carpet and wanted to see Joe crash through. "How did you find this out?" Joe asked Cindy, sitting down.

"Dave called me."

"And he told you I had gotten him into this?"

"He said he thought you were suspicious of him about something."

"He went off and left Orren and Shorter out in the middle of the swamp for no reason. Did he explain that?"

She and Hunter glanced at each other. There was more to the look than Joe had really wanted to see. How long had they known each other? Twenty-four hours?

Cindy made the decision. "Yes, he did. He thought some Indians had been using the camp. He thought maybe they had been poaching gators, and he thought he knew where they might have gotten rid of the . . . of what was left, if they were."

"Did Kang tell Gow all this?"

"He doesn't want to. He thinks Mr. Gow might make him tell who he thought had done it."

"Gow's not interested in gators."

"But he doesn't like Dave."

The coffee was growing cold fast. "He'll have to tell if there's any chance of Gow bringing a charge against him."

"But. . . ." She looked truly alarmed. "A charge of what?"

"Obstructing justice, for one thing."

"Oh," she said, suddenly confident. "Dave wouldn't care about *that.*"

Hunter moved. All he did was cross his arms, but to Joe it seemed he had shifted closer to Cindy, closer to a zone of contact he had no business entering. Hunter said, "He still hasn't told you whether he's going to help or not."

Cindy frowned at him, then turned back to Joe. "Joe, Dave shouldn't have to be in jail. He doesn't know anything about any killing. Can't you get him out?"

He didn't look at Hunter, at his strong, youthful,

flung-back shoulders, at the clean, righteous line of his jaw. "I'll talk to Gow."

For a moment she didn't seem to realize he had answered. Then she reached for his forearms and bent toward his unshaven, unwashed cheek. But he tensed against her. Their eyes met, and he realized that what he had stopped would have been innocent, but what his resistance had called up between them was not.

"Don't you think we'd better hurry if we want to catch your uncle?" Hunter asked her.

She straightened reluctantly. Joe got up and went back into the bathroom, turning on the cold water and dousing his face. Cindy appeared once more in the doorway. He glared sideways at her, water trickling down his cheekbones. "Joe," she apologized, "I have nowhere else to turn."

"If there's anything I can do, I'll do it."

She pressed forward suddenly, this time more determined, landing a kiss that started sweet and cool on his cheekbone but ended wet and startled on his sour mouth. He was exhausted and disoriented and for a moment it was no different than it had been in the forest: He didn't know who was holding whom, or whether he was clutching her or repelling her. Hunter came to the doorway, frowning, perplexed. Joe twisted her around and forced her on him. "Take her. Hurry. Take her away." Awkwardly, Hunter stabbed an arm around her, and the momentum of Joe's shove sent her with him. He heard them go out, and swung around against the cool tiled wall, sweating and hating himself, hating it that he had gotten caught up in this mess he couldn't shake free of, hating this thing he wanted so much that all truth said must not be done.

Next door to the Collier County Criminal Justice Center, he spotted a K Mart. Suddenly the urge to be clean again, really clean, was overwhelming. He bought a cheap pair of slacks and a plain blue long-sleeved shirt and changed in the restroom of the Hardee's facing the highway, cramming his old clothes into the shopping bags and tossing them into the back of the Isuzu. He could smell them when he climbed back in, although he had rolled the bags up tight.

The Collier County Criminal Justice Center turned out to be a concrete conglomerate on which the dust of construction had not fully settled. A short L surrounded by a high chain-link fence with coiled wire on top was clearly a holding facility. He headed for the dark-tinted doors with the gold stars on them, choosing the one marked Sheriff's Administration, only to find himself beaten to the entrance by a pair of Indians. The young one was flat-chested, wearing opaque gold-stemmed sunglasses and a faded red U2 T-shirt; the other was grizzled, squat, and square-bodied, with eyes as black as beadwork, and marks like shovel chops scoring his grim earthen jaws. He wore a plaid western shirt with a string tie knotted with turquoise. Both wore jeans.

"Excuse me," Joe said.

The kid turned, catching the old man's arm. The old man, alerted, seemed to grow stiller, more poised and cautious. His black eyes flashed like glass in rock.

"Were you going to see Dave Kang?" Joe asked.

"What about him?" the kid demanded.

Joe focused on the old man, whose defiance, at least, was mute and calculating, not foolhardy. "I'm a law enforcement officer from Tampa. I want to talk to Kang."

"My grandfather don't speak English," the kid said.

It had never occurred to him that a south Florida Indian would not know English. "Are you from Kang's clan?"

The old man responded sharply but unintelligibly, in short, bitten-off sounds.

"If you're the law," the kid argued, "why're you outside, not inside?"

Joe took out his ID. The old man ignored it; the kid shrugged.

"What's he charged with?" Joe persisted.

"Nothing. He's going to talk to the state attorney. Because he's a *citizen.*" The kid made it sound like a sickness. "Because he wants to."

"I'm a friend of a friend of his, someone who cares about him. If he's innocent, anything I find out will help."

"Fine." The kid fingered the expensive-looking stems of the sunglasses with loving precision, settling them above the umber swell of his cheekbones. "You help the part that takes up with white girls and alligators. Not the part that's kin to us."

They moved. Joe moved, too, blocking them. The old man made a sound like a branch snapping. "Excuse me," said the kid. "My grandfather wants to sit down."

Joe moved again, but this time they were ready, and when the door swung shut again, they were gone.

Maybe the smell of him had signaled the truth to the Indians, that he didn't care about Dave Kang at all. He reached for the tinted door again. This time it was someone coming out who stopped him: Janet, blinking at him curiously. "Joe!"

"Hello! How did you get here?"

"Drove. How else?"

He had envisioned Hunter using her car that morning, but Cindy and Hunter must have been in one of Orren's. Irrationally, he didn't want to tell her about the two of them arriving together to see him. "Did you come about Kang?"

But she was perplexed and innocent. "Is that someone who has something to do with Kevin?"

"Nobody's sure. They've picked him up for questioning."

"Well, do you know where I'm going now?" she said. "To find a fortune teller. It's the only way I'd know if the sky was falling." He had not realized how close she was to crying. "No one will tell me anything."

"Maybe there's nothing to tell yet."

"*You* know things, don't you?"

"Not much. In fact, I've come to try to find out a few things from the sheriff."

"He's not here. Or at least they say he isn't."

He surely was, thought Joe. In with Kang, probably. And probably out of bounds for both of them for now. Janet's simple dark clothes, her air of mourning, made her look like a pilgrim. "Listen, there's a Hardee's over there," he urged. "By the time I buy you a cup of coffee, maybe the sheriff will be back."

She made herself smile. "You want to comfort me with fast-food coffee? Didn't I read it causes cancer?"

"Worry causes cancer," he said. "Come on."

But Janet hesitated again at the door of the restaurant. "Oh, Joe, these places always remind me of . . . I always expect any minute to have to throw myself to the floor."

"Lightning won't strike twice," he encouraged her.

She grimaced. "Lightning will strike where it damn well wants."

She let him usher her inside, though the set of her shoulders stayed wary. He bought a Styrofoam plate of pale eggs served over a Brillo-like sausage. She refused half-and-half and sugar, and beside his cork-colored coffee, hers looked pungent and hot.

Her thin dark brows drew together. "I read in the paper that Sheriff Gow had been called in because there might be some connection between . . . Kevin, and that girl, that ranger, who got murdered."

"Unfortunately, I'm afraid I'm the connection."

"But . . . that means it *was* you the killer was aiming at."

"Gow thinks it was."

She fingered the perfect little square she had made of her paper napkin. "They treat me like a suspect. They won't even let me read the depositions."

"Your lawyer could probably make them."

"My lawyer charges by the second. But if they keep on telling me the sheriff's not in. . . ."

"Probably he isn't." Unfortunately where his reassuring lie led was not so pleasant. "They found another killing, and he was up all night."

"A woman?"

"Apparently so."

But she had drifted off, in heart and mind, out of the reach of his comfort. "We were all so happy, Joe."

He pushed the Styrofoam plate away. "I know."

She didn't catch the dry bite in his voice. "And Hunter and Kevin were such good friends. They both loved computers and video games. Every time we went out to eat! All those wasted quarters!"

"For a while I thought it might have something to do with Kevin," Joe said. "Hunter's coming to see me in Tampa that time."

She looked up at him with the same unequivocal gaze her son had inherited. "Well. . . . Maybe, seeing me starting off in a new direction, maybe he felt a need to confirm some things about himself."

"To make sure I wasn't his father."

"To make sure he didn't have a father somewhere, I guess."

In this, he thought, she had not changed: this willingness to be fair, to delve deeply, to know and tell the total truth. To take blame where someone had to. He had been right to come here with her; she was doing him good. Innocence and integrity were qualities you could catch from being around her, and no one would feel the need to cure you of them. He tested the sides of her coffee cup. It was growing cold. "Drink."

She obeyed, unconsciously making a face. "This sounds terrible, but I think this awful thing has helped Hunter. It's given him a chance to see himself as strong."

"He is strong. He just hasn't known what to do with his strength yet."

She smiled seriously. "I'm glad you like him."

He put his hand on top of hers suddenly. "I see you in him."

He could almost feel the question they were both thinking take shape between them.

"Would it be different?" he asked.

In answer she moved her hand slightly, not taking it away, but changing it, so there was not so much heat from the places their skin touched.

"Orren was talking to me about you," she said.

He gripped her hand even harder. "Janet, if anyone ever finds out who did kill Kevin—"

She freed her hand gently, waiting to be sure he was not going to finish the sentence. "For a second I thought you were going to say, you'd be the one."

"I thought better of it."

"You *would* have said it eighteen years ago."

He looked at his watch. It had been just twenty-five minutes since he had talked with the Indians.

"But you're as restless as ever, aren't you?" she asked.

"I just thought of something—probably nothing—I want to check before Gow does get cracking."

"Uh-oh."

"Nothing dangerous."

"Just illegal?"

"Why do you want to know, then?"

She stood up emphatically. "I don't."

"Unless you'll let me drive you back to Homestead?"

He thought he saw her eyes sparkle. "If I let you take me home, would it stop you?"

"No, just slow me down a little."

She gathered their litter decisively. "We'd better get in trouble separately, then."

But on the way out she took hold of his arm, slipping the tips of the fingers of her right hand into his hip pocket, a proprietory gesture with which, in the first good months of their marriage, she used to make him feel warmly in charge. As they neared his car, she tugged him suddenly to a stop and bent to the sidewalk. When she straightened, she held up a penny, a little dark, but with shiny edges.

"You can't even buy bubble gum with that," he teased.

"I don't try. Whenever I find them, I put them in jars. When the jars fill up, I take them to the bank and put them in a secret account for Hunter. I have almost a thousand dollars." She took a plastic aspirin bottle from her purse, pried off the top, and dropped the penny in. "Kevin laughed at me, like you did. But for a while there, he was doing it, too."

For a minute he could see it, the pennies pinging one by one, piling up infinitesimally, through the wide mouth of the two-thirds empty jar. He took a penny out of his own pocket and dropped it. But it rolled up under a car. "Doesn't count anyway," she said.

"By whose rules?"

"It's like the difference," she said, "between finding a perfect seashell, and buying one."

"Someone else will find it."

"And feel very lucky."

He thought again of the jar, and how slowly it was filling. The emptiness seemed to echo, and each ring of a coin to sound like something breaking.

"Don't worry." She was laughing gently. "It won't go to waste."

Back at the sheriff's administration building, he made no attempt to accompany her inside. He had started out feeling bad about deserting her, but now he didn't. Janet was the one person out of all of them he was being foolish to worry about. The jar might be filling slowly, but it was filling. It was his own sadness that echoed. She had plenty of provisions, and the compass of her grown-up common sense. He was the one who was sucked up, swept away, and moorless.

And what he was going to do next could only make it worse.

25

IT WOULD NOT HAVE SURPRISED HIM TO find that Gow had thought of it first, but there was no one in the clearing. The lock on Kang's trailer was the simplest discount hardware dead bolt. He fished in his pockets, digging out a little set of wire hooks folded like a plug gapper. He seldom had to use it, but he had not quite forgotten the trick of it, and within seconds he was inside.

It was not the first time he had broken into someone's home illegally, but it was the first time he had done it without being sure he wanted to. He would not have been surprised to find elves at work, or at the least, mice and spiders and roaches, stitching up the tailor's devastated life for him when his back was turned. So he paused, trying to see out of the corners of both eyes at once. And there were little, barely perceptible movements, little shudders, secret doors closing, and then a cold silence, a nay-saying and shutting out.

The cluttered kitchen, where stacks of opened but undisposed-of mail and half-read newspapers covered every available surface, did not look like the place to start. In the sunny main room, the map seemed bigger than he remembered it. He marvelled at it. Was this how you found your way, then? Make charts; piece your way through an inch at a time? Maybe, he thought again, Dave did not learn the forest. Maybe he drew a line on this tabletop, and out at the end of consciousness a trail came into being, or a cypress dome, or a pond. Joe could not tell from the map exactly where they had been yesterday. Maybe the Meachams' camp was not something Dave had invented. Maybe the Meachams had their own map, and in their own dark hours alone were drawing just as fast as Dave was, and it was a silent race to see whose world would cut whose off first.

He edged past the computer and file cabinets, down the narrow hallway to stand in the doorway of the cubby-hole bedroom. Nothing mystical came chattering out at him. It just seemed the most probable place, that was all.

The room was cleaner than he had expected. There was no dust on the linoleum, no stain on the braided carpet, and the red-and-gold coverlet on the single bed had been carefully smoothed over the pillow. An issue of *Audubon* lay on the bedside table, on the cover white geese with sunset on their backs flying over water. In the drawer, alongside a rusted case knife and a rolling cat's-eye marble, was a little inlaid wooden box that looked as if it ought to contain secrets, and in fact, it held a Ziploc bag of marijuana and an ornate ceramic stone. Joe closed the box carefully without disturbing anything and put it all back.

Without his knowing it, his mind had loaded up with possibilities, and intuitively he followed it. At the same time, he was listening, and again without even knowing it, he had made plans: if Gow drove up in front, or an Indian, he would go out the back. No one need know he had been inside. His body kept on moving. In a niche in the wall was a built-in chest of drawers, and on its top ordinary clutter: clean socks knotted together, loose change in a plastic dish, a few tinny keys. There was, however, a very big hunting knife in a worn leather case, whose blade gleamed like a diamond right down to its perfect edge. He took out his pocketknife and scratched at the juncture between the hilt and blade, but the thing was antiseptically clean. Next to the chest of drawers, a second niche served as a closet. Kang's clothes, it seemed, were all khaki. The space beneath the shirts and doubled-up trousers housed an elaborate radio-stereo system, including both a CB and a police-band radio, as well as a cheap TV set. There was no VCR.

The top drawer in the chest held odds and ends: cancelled checks rubber-banded together, a sewing kit that looked as if it had never been opened, an unused birthday card still in the Walgreen's bag. Most of the checks were to the electric company. Deposits and withdrawals were meticulously recorded in dogeared checkbook registers; large sums at regular intervals, it seemed, arrived from something Kang designated the HFTE Fund. The cancelled checks bore the address of a Naples bank.

In among their clothes, especially their underwear, was where people with only minor secrets to nurture seemed to think their treasures would be safe. Kang's underwear was neatly stacked, his T-shirts folded. Joe found nothing. The next drawer held only shirts and jeans.

It was the bottom drawer that dismayed him. It contained box after box of color slides. He held one set up to the light from the window, amazing kinetic images of a snowy fork-tailed bird like the one he had seen with Cindy, against a sky so blue it was depthless. A second, chosen at random, held breathless mosaics of sunsets seen through palm trees. Dutifully he poked behind the rest of the boxes. Again he found nothing. Okay, if not in the bedroom, then where?

Temporarily he passed up the bathroom, as he had the kitchen. He made his way along the narrow corridor to the back room, where all the unnamed things in the glass jars and cages and aquariums dreamed in silence.

The easel stood where he had last seen it, but now from the creamy sheet of thick watercolor paper leered a coiled snake, whose body and the leaf bed beneath it blended together like the pieces of a liquid chocolate, umber, and sand-yellow puzzle. There was something remotely satisfying about the image and the blended colors, and he knew Kang had painted it because he had thought it was beautiful. He circled the room slowly. Most of the containers seemed to be empty. One jar seemed like a jumble of leaf litter, but when he peered intently he made out the shiny, half-buried carapace of a very big beetle. In another, when he took the time to focus, he discovered a tiny brownish snake with a perfect gold ring around its neck, its hide smooth and shiny as Naugahyde, its pinhead eyes benign. There was a glossy salamanderlike lizard with an electric blue tail, and a huge, velvety, zebra-marked moth on a square of bark. None of the creatures looked dangerous. Most of them looked like toys.

Under the south-facing window stood a wooden table with three crookneck lamps arranged strategically around a platform in the center. Leaning up against the wall were a tripod and a white screen. Here, perhaps, Kang staged close-ups of his specimens. Under the table was a large cardboard box, and in it were mounted paintings. Joe crouched and began flipping through them. The first one was a pose of the blue-tailed salamander. Joe knew only a little about painting, but Stacey had had a sophisticated eye and had taught him to recognize talent. Kang's style was free and expressive, yet at the same time, vividly detailed and precise. The lizard was *that* lizard, and yet more than that lizard. It was movement and history and future, a universe of lizards, and other beautiful, elusive things, all caught up in a few quick strokes that looked as if they had been discovered rather than made. The second painting was of a deer, perhaps done from a photograph. The third was of cypress trees, stately and stoic. He forbad himself to linger and flipped the prints more rapidly. At the very back was a big watercolor tablet. Joe eased it out and rolled back the cover. The tablet was full of nude pictures of a girl.

It was not Cindy. It was a girl with flowing hair—presumably, from the way the lucent washes were handled, a blonde. In all the sketches, her face was just a hint: a shy dash of color. The sketches were not lascivious, but chaste and worshipful, studies of form and not detail, yet, in Kang's style, definitive enough, concentrated enough, that it was impossible to believe they were not done from life.

He inspected every single picture. None of them could have been of Cindy. Most likely, as best he could tell, it had been blond Amy who had posed. He put the tablet back, relieved, but also disappointed—because somehow he felt that had Dave painted Cindy, Joe would have known something about her he could not have found out any other way.

Turning, thinking, he backed up a step too far and bumped against something heavy behind him. It was a glass case, and he had dislodged the wire lid. He reached to ease the lid back over the opening—and stopped. It was the snake of the painting. It was less colorful than Kang had painted it, as if it had cloaked itself in dullness, like a peacock or some other creature that would only display itself when prayed to with enough reverence. It stared at him unblinking, the black-slit eye dirty yellow like a rotten lemon. It was powerful in its muddy inertness, a coiled black muscle, clenched for the silent punch.

He eased his hand around to the side of the case. The snake, awakened, began to feed its coils over each other, the somber markings riding the scaled flesh the way foam labyrinths ride the top of a water ripple. He tapped the lid forward. The snake drew its head back, hunkering down in the dark knot of its body. He tapped the lid again. The snake doubled its neck back on itself, jaws spread like a fist flying open. Its throat flashed, tissue-white hide stitched to the roof of its mouth with two wicked, back-curved needles. Heart pumping, shivering, he lowered the wire lid into its groove.

He could see down the silken throat. That blow would be final. He backed away, suddenly not sure he wanted to know any more about what might be here, what was hidden. Leave Kang to his rites.

He even made it halfway down the hallway. But then he stopped, the bedroom on his right, the map room ahead of him. The place had what Terry Bessel, back in Tampa, liked to call the stink of innocence about it. It was the kind of place that simply refused to justify what he was sensing. The clinically polished knife, the virginal reverence of the paintings, promised a morose counter-point, like extremes of piety. He knew from experience such an awareness usually meant one of two things: either the assumptions that had brought him here were garbage, or the person whose premises had yielded so little had something really serious to hide.

He had been in the trailer half an hour. A half hour more was all he dared risk. Assuming Kang did have guilty secrets, how good was he? An amateur, or a professional dissembler? If Kang was a professional, good at secrets, Joe would not find what he needed in the time left to him; it would take a trained team days to rip the trailer apart. So Joe's only practical choice was to consider Kang a driven victim of his passions. Then there would be a standard set of places his own training told him to look first.

In the little kitchen, he opened the cabinet beneath the sink. The drain pipes were corroded, stuck fast, with no signs of recent tampering. Nothing had been taped inside the walls of the cabinets or under the table or inside the other cabinets where the dishes were stored overhead. He wrapped his long arms around the refrigerator and felt along the dusty edges. Inside the freezer were plastic packs of frozen body parts that looked like chopped-up squirrel or rabbit, and a couple of cold bricks of hamburger. If Kang had stuffed something inside the hamburger before freezing it, Joe would just have to not find out what. The refrigerator itself was largely empty. He poked down into containers of cottage cheese and moldy stewed tomatoes with a dinner knife he took from the drain board. The fresh vegetables in the crisper had not been hollowed out. There were far too many empty beer bottles, stacked in bags along the wall, color-separated for recycling, to go through. His body was moving automatically again, his brain casting around him. They would be letting Kang go soon, if they hadn't already. Ten more minutes. He looked behind a corkboard on the wall. Nothing. His hunch seemed a washout. Five minutes more, that was all.

Kang, of course, had more places than most people to hide things. He had places where one would not only not *think* to look, but would not *want* to look, either—

He slipped the roll of paper towels whose core he had been inspecting back on its rack and walked rapidly down the trailer. The snake had retreated once more into its deceptive coma, its eyes open but lifeless. When Joe had knocked the case, he had moved it out from the wall just enough that by crouching under it he could see that it was floored with thin wooden slats. It appeared to be lined with plastic. Crouching lower, and with tense fingertips easing it another half inch off its shelf, he could see through the narrow gaps between the slats.

And there was something there, something white, contrasting with the dark humus weighing down the plastic. He could see only a sliver, but he hoped profoundly it was what he thought it was—an envelope itself wrapped in plastic. Was finding out what was in it worth what he would have to do?

The snake stirred again as he straightened. Once more its hinged jaw flew mindlessly open, as fixed as a piece of machinery which had slipped its gears and jammed. Joe backed slowly out of what he was sure was striking distance. Slowly the snake collapsed into a dark tangle in a corner, pretending a dead branch could hide it. Joe took the painting off the easel without looking at it. The legs of the easel slid together easily. It was heavier than it looked. From its full length of six feet away, he fitted the end of the easel between the snake's cage and the wall and pried. The glass case scraped to the edge of the shelf. Almost resignedly, the snake began to coil again, working its head free. Joe pushed hard. The case balanced a second, then plunged.

It struck the bench below with a sharp crack. The lid flew off, dumping dirt, paper, plastic, and snake. The snake seemed to come off the ground striking. It was slow and clumsy, like a limp rope cast by a weak hand, but its white mouth homed blindly. Joe flinched backward, dodging cages and shelves and clutter. The snake leapt, thudded against the floor, then leapt again. Joe caught himself up in his own feet and crashed to his knees in the narrow hallway. When he got up, he ran. Only in the kitchen did he stop, gasping. He was shivering. But when he turned, as far as he could see from where he stood, the trailer looked utterly peaceful. He could hear only the indolent, summer-weary whine of a single fly buzzing against a window screen.

He retraced his steps cautiously, poking his head around the corner into the back room. At first, among all the benches and shelves, he couldn't see the reptile. He exposed himself an inch. And there it lay, now beneath a bench to his right, head still laid back, foamy mouth still stuck open in a pantomime of outrage, body brown as dung, guarding a narrow gap between two low tables through which he would have to pass.

He could see what he had dared all this for. It was what he had thought it was: a legal envelope, plenty big enough to contain photographs, lying about ten feet from him, in a heap of broken glass and humus. Ten impassable feet.

He took out his .38 and leveled the barrel. His target

was just a white scrap of flesh, but at this distance, he wouldn't miss.

But he didn't shoot. The snake's head swayed a little, testing the air for him. But he was still too far away; it couldn't lock in. Joe moved into the room, edging along the wall, measuring distances. When he reached a table which blocked him, he set the gun down, carefully, very carefully, and worked the table sideways until he had cleared a gap he could squeeze through. He picked up the gun again, and crept along the far wall. He knew now that if the snake struck, it would come through the air sluggishly, and he was sure one of the five rounds he could pump out would stop it. But though it turned its head slowly, tracking his scent and heat, it did not strike.

At his left, against the wall, sat a bar stool, on it a flimsy wire cage which seemed empty. He tapped the cage with the nose of his gun. The leaves stirred and slid off the glossy back of another huge beetle. He lifted the cage with the tips of his fingers and set it on the bigger table. He put the gun in his left hand and with his right picked up the stool. With one of the legs he slowly raked the packet toward him, out of what he judged to be the snake's best range.

He knelt and reached forward. Something—heat, motion, sound—set the snake off so that it came up at him like firecrackers thrown on a fire. The two reflex shots he got off shaved wood from the legs of the bench beneath which the snake had been coiled. The snake fell short of his wrist by a foot, rearing back again, drawing its long, thick, hauserlike length to it, its tail snapping against the floor. On his butt and heels Joe scrambled sideways under the table, rolling. When he got his feet under him and straightened, he looked down and realized he was clutching the plastic-wrapped envelope in his shaking right hand.

The snake was winding itself back up slowly, nesting its lethal jaws with those unspent fangs once more against the tense spoor of its body. Joe edged sideways toward the hallway. Once there, he stopped, leaning against the wall, the gun dangling from his left hand and the booty from his right. It was hard to get enough strength back to push the safety into place on the pistol, harder to find the coordination to get it back into its holster. But finally, with both hands free and his heart quieting, he grappled his way into the plastic and worked the pictures out.

THE SHERIFF'S DEPARTMENT IN NAPLES had let Dave Kang go. No charges had been filed against him. Gow, insisted the woman at the desk, was truly not there. It seemed a plane full of drugs had crashed in the middle of Golden Gate, and there had been a general exodus of able bodies to the scene, the sheriff and his lieutenants among them. Joe did not know where Golden Gate was. He showed his ID, thinking it might make a difference, but it didn't. She would tell the sheriff Joe had stopped by when he called in.

He went back out into the heat, sweating as if he had a fever. He had not passed Kang's Jeep on its way home; he was sure of it. So Kang must have gone into Naples, and it might be a while before he realized what had happened. Joe had rewrapped the trisected black-and-white contact sheet he had found in the envelope, and two of the three five-by-seven enlargements; scouting quickly, he had rehidden them under the sink, working them into the hole the sink fittings came through, between the wall and the cabinet. The third picture, the one that best showed Amy Wells's face, he had stuck in his pocket.

Would Kang guess who had stolen it? Maybe the snake would tell.

He barely saw the traffic. He was not sick now, although leaning against the wall in the stuffy trailer, he had thought he was going to vomit on Kang's hall carpet; he had had to sink to the floor, and sit sweating, until the nausea at the sight of those images had cleared. Tough cop, he had berated himself, wiping the bile from his lips.

But now he had gotten over it, over the feeling that even though he had never seen that brave face except in pictures, he had known her. The anguish of recognition had given way at last to a low-key, heart-jerking excitement. Now his mind was intoxicated, racing. He did not think Kang had snapped the pictures. They were amateurish, the white flesh overexposed, the staring eyes, charged with awed terror, crazed glaring dots. Nor did he think Kang had developed them; they were shadowy, overdeveloped, grainy—probably made from color negatives by a careless hand.

But Kang knew who *had* taken them. The excitement boiled to a slow, delicious anger. Damn politics. Damn people's feelings, their sensitive egos. There was only following the trail, finding out.

Then he did see Kang's Jeep, approaching on the left side of the road in the rushing traffic. But Kang zoomed past without catching sight of him. Joe managed to get over, but he would have had to do a U, and the traffic headed south was impassable. Suddenly it struck him that Kang might well have been coming from his motel, just ahead. Maybe he had left some message, a request for an assignation. Joe cut back into the right-hand lane, and when he reached the motel, turned into the parking lot.

His room door was locked, just as he had left it. Not that the ancient lock would keep an intruder with any determination out, any more than Kang's door had. He saw no sign of a message. He opened the door impatiently. What he really wanted was to see what Kang would do when he found the pictures gone.

But as soon as he stepped into the closed, dim room, he smelled it, at first subtle as the whiff of ocean that penetrated from the gulf through the gas fumes, then hitting him, dilating his veins, speeding his pulse, lacing the roots of his hair with adrenalin. He went back and bent over the lock. Sure enough, faint bright scratches ringed the keyhole. The room itself looked untouched. He crossed to the bathroom first, but it was clean, cloying with disinfectant, the tub dry and empty. He looked in the closet, pulled down his overnight bag, and looked in it. He moved with quick dread, impatient. He looked in all the drawers. Nothing. It was under the bed, then. But it wasn't. He could smell it more strongly than ever, a presence now, conjured out of a sewer. The bed had been carefully made up, the two pillows pressed together. But between them was a sag, and in the sag, an unevenness.

He decided he really had not liked the girl in Shorter's fantasy. He hardened his natural empathy. She was what her sister had said she was, and like all her kind, she had asked for it. He waited, and the low-keyed rage and the eagerness came back, overwhelming horror. He jerked the spread clear.

At his first stupefying glimpse of the dark hair spreading gummily over the pillows, he thought it was Cindy. But Cindy could not have been dead long enough to start stinking. The stump of this creature's neck had long ago quit bleeding; the hair, tangled nastily like rotting seaweed, stuck to the decomposing tissue. He could see the big severed veins, purple at their hearts, still faintly glistening. The eyes were open. He had not realized they would be blue, like cornflowers. The skin was white and taut, the face staring, amazed, bereft, and still.

He covered it back up again, though he didn't tuck the spread under it. He sat down in the chair, by the window, and for the second time in as many hours had to wait for a room to stop spinning. In the end, it was Orren's number he dialed.

Orren's greeting was harsh. "It's a good thing you called. *Now* what's going on with Cindy? Is that kid related to you? He's not, is he?"

"Orren, something's happened."

"You mean something *else* has happened. It's been like a damn earthquake since you showed up."

"Get somebody over to my motel room," Joe told him. "I've got some new evidence."

"Joe, don't you listen to anything I tell you? Quit messing in things that are none of your business. It's not your case."

Joe looked at his watch, envisioning Kang speeding back down the open highway. "Orren, listen to me. I have found something in my motel room. Gow is supposedly off somewhere investigating a plane crash. Someone's got to process this thing."

The change in his tone must have worked. More cautiously Orren said, "What is it?"

"Not on this phone."

Orren made a noise like a big cat in a zoo cage fed up with being poked at. "Jesus, Joe. All right, all right. What motel is it?"

"The North Glades. On the west side of Forty-one about three quarters of a mile down from the police station."

"You stay there. It'll take at least two hours."

He took a breath. Now for more trouble. "Orren, I know who left it. Kang."

"I thought Gow had Kang."

"They let him go. I passed him coming back from here. Orren, somebody ought to be after him."

"You stay the fuck where you are," said Orren belligerently. "You stay with that . . . evidence."

Joe sighed. He looked at his watch again.

"And incidentally, what *about* this kid with Cindy—?"

"Orren, why don't you just lock her in a closet and be done with it?"

Now he *had* pushed too far. Orren slammed down the phone.

He started to sit down on the bed, but remembered in time and switched to the chair. He had been in the motel room twenty minutes. Kang was probably on his way back to the trailer. The Indian would realize instantly that someone had been there. He might do anything. Fish out more evidence and destroy it. Head for a hide-out, possibly where he had disposed of his victims' bodies. And if Joe waited for Orren? The chance that lay before him now would be lost for good.

How much trouble was he in already? He had broken and entered. He had confiscated evidence without a valid search warrant. Orren and Gow might cover for him be-cause of the lead he had found for them, but how far would that dubious charity stretch? No point in lying: not far.

But if he could close the case? in an hour? now?

He stood up and took the picture out of his pocket. Aligning it carefully over the edge of the bureau, he tore it right down the middle of her face. He weighted it with an ashtray and left it there. Then he peeled a page from his pocket notepad and scribbled on it, "Gone after him. Will call in. Sorry. Joe." He folded it over twice, wrote Orren's name on the outside, locked the door behind him, and jogged down to the motel office. A woman in an electric blue blouse, unnaturally black hair piled elabo-rately on her head, was talking on the phone in Spanish. He had to wave his ID at her to make her cover the re-ceiver. "I'm Joe Hope, in twenty-seven. Did an Indian in a Jeep come here looking for me?"

"I just got here," she said flatly, as if the phrase would explain anything.

"Well, in about an hour there'll either be a sheriff's

deputy or a plainclothes policeman here, big guy with a mustache driving a Chevrolet. This note is for whoever gets here first."

She lowered the phone, her opaque charcoaled brows lifting. "Something the matter?"

"Not if you deliver the note."

He left her fingering it. She was going to read it, but it would tell her nothing. She could call the cops, but the cops were already coming. He jumped in the Isuzu and bounced out of the driveway, recklessly breaching the wall of hurrying cars.

But there was no Jeep at Kang's trailer, no sign of life. He hung a hard U and roared back out onto the highway, passing a Camaro with inches to spare. Vultures flapped belatedly off a dead armadillo, one wheeling right at his windshield, its lizard eye fearless in its filthy wattles. The barren road dismayed him. What was he doing? Getting into deep shit for nothing. *Go back,* said his nerves. *Do it the smart way: Let Kang go.*

But then a black Chrysler passed him, not going very fast, and the driver was Cindy, her clean young face pinched in concentration. She saw him. She spun around behind the wheel, mouthing something. The car was Anita's. Watching unhappily in the mirror, he realized what she had been slowing for: to spin the car around on the narrow highway between the guard rails. Once back out on the roadway, she crowded the Chrysler in behind him, keeping pace with him. He could see her dark frown, the determined hunch of her shoulders. And up ahead of him, suddenly, he saw a brown dot, bouncing and sailing: Kang.

Damn her. She had passed Kang, and had deduced that Joe was following him. He couldn't outrun her without putting her in serious danger and in the bargain, giving himself away to the Indian. Up ahead, on the right, he saw an oak-shaded picnic table. He put on his signal so she wouldn't slam into him and skidded off into the shell.

He jumped out of his car and was leaning over the Chrysler before she came to a full stop. She looked up, tense sweat on her bare throat and upper lip. She had changed into jeans and a loose blouse with flamingoes stenciled on it. He demanded, "What are you doing here?"

"Looking for Dave. They told me they had released him. Why are you following him?"

"Where's Hunter?"

"He had classes. He took me home. What's wrong, Joe?"

"Nothing you can help with. Go back home."

But she shook her dark head, her glower the image of her uncle's. "I refuse to let this happen to Dave."

"It *has* happened. Go home."

But she set her jaw, eyes narrowed. "Joe, why are you doing this? Are you jealous? Is that it?"

It was time she learned to hate him. Kang's Jeep had faded from sight among the heat bars on the highway. There was a gap in traffic, no one to see them. The door was unlocked. He jerked it open, reached in, and hauled on the hood release. She scrambled out of the car after him as he circled to the hood and flung it open. She grabbed his elbow, but he caught her wrist in his right hand and held her off him. "What are you doing?" she cried. He pulled the plug wires off all six of her cylinders. The car coughed, backfired, and died. She threw her hands into the air, speechless, exactly, he thought, like a bird coming home to find all its eggs smashed.

"Turn off the ignition before you put them back on." He headed for the Isuzu.

"Joe, *why?*"

"And if anybody stops to help you, get in the car and keep the door locked."

She caught his sleeve. "Please listen. Dave wouldn't—"

He didn't expect her to fall down in the shell when he shoved her off him, but she did. He almost started back to her, but stopped himself. As he got in his car, she was rolling over, scrambling to her feet and cursing. He had noticed before she did not curse like a child. She ran at the car as he pressed the accelerator, only stopping when he outdistanced her, her fingers ravaging her hair. Though he told himself it was an act of conscience to disillusion her, to hurt her, he found himself hoping that whatever happened next would be pretty awful, that people would turn out to have died by the millions, and he would discover more than enough bodies to absolve him of this crime.

KANG HAD DISAPPEARED UTTERLY. JOE
could not spare the energy to curse. He shot past another of those narrow shell roads slicing toward the pale
horizon and saw far down its length settling dust smearing the tree line. He braked precipitously, wheeling
around in front of oncoming traffic. This road had not
been maintained; holes like small amphitheaters swallowed his car and then spat him out again. The little road
led north a half mile, veered right, then left, and north
again. A faint chalky haze still drifted in the sweltering
air.

He took his 9mm in its shoulder holster out of the
center compartment and set it on the passenger seat as
he turned the second corner. Ahead there was more
dust, thicker, a quivering plume of it. He eased his car
around the left-hand turn, out of the shelter of the ragged cypress forest. A quarter mile away, the Jeep was
weaving brashly around the holes.

Joe stopped short, letting the Jeep draw away behind
its dust cloud. In the hard sunlight the road was like a
spill of white paint through the trees. Up ahead, the
woods gave way to open prairies littered only with a few

pines and dwarf cypress. The dust obscured the Jeep. He let the Isuzu slide forward again.

They drove a long time. The current of his excitement stalled. What if there was a shoot-out and he killed Kang? Who would back him? He wished for a dose of sure and carrying elation, but it didn't come. Still, he did not turn around.

Abruptly, he realized that there was nothing behind the thinning cloud of dust between him and the horizon; somewhere, Kang had turned.

Or was waiting. The Isuzu bottomed out noisily on a big rock at the edge of a pothole as wide as the road was. Yes, waiting, with the old shotgun cocked and pointing. He bumped along soberly and watchfully. He came upon only one turn into the woods, posted with one of the big red-and-white ORV permit warnings. Grimly, he pointed the little car into the dappled shade, turning off the a.c. as he bounced along and winding down the window to listen. The hot air flooded in, but he heard only his own breathing and the growl of the car.

Sure enough, the trees soon began to thicken, but they weren't warped cypress, they were tall pines, spear-leaved palmettos, and palms rustling their collars of dead fronds in a wind-stirred dance. The trail was too narrow to dodge the gaping craters. It was hard to watch all around and at the same time watch where he was going. He transferred the gun to his lap.

The trail forked, the left branch pushing deeper into the palmetto. On his right, a gate stood open, and to a fire-scarred pine had been nailed a hand-lettered sign, Private road. Joe pulled the car into the V between forks and got out. In a bit of mud at the bottom of the first big hole in the right-hand fork, the Jeep had left tracks. The car couldn't make it through the deep pits ahead. He put on the shoulder holster, pocketed his keys, and left the locked car nosed into the palmetto. Batting absently at deerflies, he started softly down the sandy lane.

With the chest-high palmettos protecting him, he saw

the structure before he stumbled over it. Unlike the Meachams' deep swamp camp, this one was clean and well built, a screened cabin sitting in a tended glade. Laden fruit trees shaded the grass: citrus and banana and avocado. A garage housed an airboat on a trailer. Bird feeders swayed gently from the eaves.

He could see no sign of Kang or of the Jeep. The sharp-smelling palmetto shielding him, he crept forward until he had a good view of the side of the cabin. Something moved: as Joe watched, Kang came out on the screened porch.

The little man appeared to be peering around him at the porch itself, on which Joe could see vague humps of clutter. Kang wheeled suddenly and bent, opening the lid of some sort of large chest or storage locker. He began taking out what looked like folded blankets and stacking them on a table beside him. Apparently unsatisfied, he put them all back. In a haggard motion, he dragged a hand over his face, peering around once more. There seemed to be another chest; this one, too, Kang emptied and refilled.

Overhead in the shadows under the roof were dim rows of shelves. Kang began to take things down and shove them back. Twice he stopped abruptly, looking off to his right and freezing as if listening. He did not look toward Joe. So Joe had an uninterrupted if shadowy view as Kang suddenly strained on tiptoes, reaching far back into the overhead dimness, then sank down holding an envelope somewhat smaller than the one that had held the photographs, innocent and white.

He turned toward Joe. Joe dodged behind a sumac, but Kang did not see him. Kang was taking small, densely orange strips from the envelope and holding them to the sunlight. Color negatives. Kang went through them hastily. He folded the flap of the envelope and jammed it into his shirt pocket. Then, galvanized, he trotted to the porch door.

Joe huddled under the sumac and myrtle. A wind had

started up, a steady gossip in the palms and palmettos. Kang emerged from the driveway that led to the cabin, veering right, away from Joe, his back turned. Joe followed. He was almost close enough to grab Kang when the Indian cast a startled glance over his shoulder. Joe dived, but Kang scrambled forward. He was quick and nimble, and even with his longer legs, Joe took four strides before gaining on him again. He didn't shout; there was no need to, nothing to reassure him about, nothing to warn him of.

The little man suddenly dodged sideways, straight into the chest-high palmetto. Joe overbalanced, recovered, and plunged after him. The knife-edged fronds stabbed into him, blocking him; the thick, ridged, above-ground roots caught his shins. Kang gained five feet. Up ahead, the sea of spears ended under scrub oaks. Well camouflaged in a clump of dense myrtle and Brazilian pepper was the rusty fender of Kang's Jeep.

Kang scuttled under the curtain of leaves and vines. Joe straightened to his full height, jerking out the Beretta. The Jeep coughed, the engine turning over. Joe aimed just below the bit of fender he could see, hoping to hit rubber, but the bullet zinged off metal. He fired again. This time, under the pop of his gun, he heard a second explosion: the tire blowing out.

He floundered forward just as the myrtle began to quiver. Kang was going to drive out, flat tire and all. Joe ducked around in front of the thicket. He could not see Kang himself, just the square of the grill and the front tires plowing toward him. He fired between and above them, into the engine block. There was a heady bang, and then silence. Then scrambling and crashing. He ducked under the cloak of myrtle in time to see Kang darting off through the dense scrub and seedling pines.

So Kang was not armed; if he had been, he would have stood his ground. Joe plunged after him. But Kang had other weapons: his size, his forest coloring, his agile grace. For fifty yards, Joe kept a bead on his flickering form as it dodged in and out of the trees. Then Kang worked his old magic. The woods grew denser. Ferns sprang up among the brambles. Joe suddenly realized he was sloshing through muck, in deep grass, with no way of judging what lay under it. He stopped, catching his breath convulsively, starting at the threat of a sinuous streak underfoot that turned out to be a tumbled branch. When he looked up again, he found himself facing an impenetrable wall of vegetation, through which he could just make out the flat, plastic green of a slime-coated pond.

The Indian could not have gone straight forward. The grass would have been trampled, the surface of the water stirred and broken. Joe backed up tensely, studying the mud. He found a print, a slurring near a tree root, pointing off to the right, that might have been Kang's. But the ground rose sharply, and he found himself back among palms and pines. He couldn't read tracks in the firmer footing. He found, though, a sort of trail, a beaten-down place. The palmettos began again, the trail threading into them. The gun butt damp in his grip, he veered down it, scanning the woods across the top of the stiff green fans.

And instantly heard a rattling rush behind him, and felt something blunt strike his thigh. He twisted, too startled to cry out, reflexes jerking. It wasn't a snake, it was a vision of dirty white, a lunatic writhing and growling, a brown eye and a blue one, both glazed with rage. He lowered his gun hand, aiming blindly. Something dark and quick caught his wrist, and a hard weight slammed him into the palmetto. The gun went off, the bullet slicing the fronds. A man dropped on top of him, wrestling for the Beretta. On top of both of them, tearing at his face over the man's shoulder, piled the snarling dog. He put out his left arm to fend it off, and in that instant the man pried the gun loose, leaping backward. The dog caught Joe's arm, worrying it, spit dripping from its licorice-colored gums. The man, a dark blur of motion, cracked the dog in the skull with the side of the gun. The dog's wet grip broke. The man lifted it by the choke chain around its throat until its fevered wail died.

"Get up," Jimmy Easter said.

Joe got his legs under him, watching the dog. With a short laugh Easter freed it, kicking it in the ribs. Muttering in its throat, the dog slunk away.

Joe jerked his shirt sleeve back. Blood welled up, threading across his palm, but it wasn't spurting. There was one puncture that was deep and not bleeding. Easter pulled his T-shirt out of his jeans and tore a strip off the bottom, tossing it to him. "No veins." Gingerly Joe bound the strip of T-shirt around his forearm. "Get back to the cabin. That way." Easter gestured with the gun.

The path they followed wound left and finally broke clear of the palmetto right behind the cabin. Joe led, dashing the sweat out of his eyes with his good arm; then Easter, Joe's gun at his lean hip; and then, ten feet back, where Joe could only catch glimpses, the venomous wraith of the dog.

"Go around front," Easter snapped.

He followed Joe up the steps and onto the porch, kicking out a folding chair beside a rickety plywood table and waving him into it. The dog came in, too, pushing the door open with his head and dropping on his belly in the shadows. "You wait," said Easter. He disappeared into a dark niche that looked like a kitchen. Joe leaned back, mopping his forehead. Above in the shadows were, indeed, rows of books and boxes. He could see the marks of Kang's probing in the disturbed dust.

Easter reappeared with a bottle of peroxide and a packet of gauze, setting them down on the table. He did not seem to have the gun with him. His dark, still eyes made Joe think of the hard-shelled beetles in Kang's jars.

"So this is your place?" Joe asked.

"You didn't know that?"

"No."

"Then you just poke around in people's shit for the hell of it?" Easter sat down catercorner from Joe, taking his time uncapping the bottle. "What were you looking for?"

"Whatever you're hiding, I guess."

There was something stagnant about the black eyes. "Somebody else was here, wasn't there? Friend of yours?"

Joe sat back. From somewhere in the forest came a drumming as staccato as machine-gun fire, except that it was richer, as if coming to them from underwater. Joe started. Easter laughed.

"Ever seen one of them woodpeckers?"

"Yes."

"Used to be two kinds of them. The Crackers called the one that's gone extinct the Lord-to-God bird. My granddaddy once told me that every tap you hear when one of those birds is drumming stands for something you coulda done but didn't. Like right now, I guess I shoulda waited here at the cabin for you to come back and shot you dead."

Joe's arm was throbbing. He unwound the strip of shirt and peeled his sleeve back. Suddenly Easter grabbed his fingertips, flattening them. To free himself, Joe would have had to punch him. Easter poured peroxide liberally into the gashes.

"That dog's the one that's going to get shot one day," Joe said.

Languidly Easter recapped the bottle. "Dog's no damn good sitting in the truck."

He went back into the kitchen. Joe pressed the clean gauze against the cuts, then redid the crude T-shirt bandage. When he finished, he looked up to find Easter leaning against the doorway, twirling the Beretta by the trigger guard.

"You know, there's no law up here," Easter said. "Sheriff's got his hands full fishing cars out of the canals and rock pits. Park Service's broke half the time. Florida

Game and Fish don't like making people sweat, so they stay in the air-conditioning. People pretty much do what they want."

"You're wrong. There's law up here right now," Joe said. "Me."

"You're a trespasser and a law*breaker*. And I got your weapon."

The .38 at Joe's stomach would stand up to the Beretta, but he did not want to use it. "I didn't come in your place."

"And you're not gonna tell me who did."

"I thought maybe you might already know."

Easter crossed suddenly and yanked his chair close to Joe's. He pulled the gun from his pocket and tossed it onto the table. The clip had been taken out of it. Without warning, he grabbed Joe's hurt arm with the hard claws of his fingers. His skin was the color of a particularly violent sunset. Joe didn't move.

"I bought this place with my own dough," said Easter. His voice was dead and dull as the sound of a stick beating hide. "Money I made driving a bulldozer in hundred-degree weather, building cesspools for white people in Naples. In-holders could sell to the Park or to who they wanted to. This one sold to me."

"Fine," said Joe through clenched teeth.

"The Park wants all the in-holders out."

"I don't know anything about it."

Easter dropped Joe's arm in disgust. "Framing me for killing Amy would be a good way to get my land away from me."

"That seems like a lot of trouble for a couple of acres."

"Not if there was bad blood to settle."

"Whose bad blood? Because you're an Indian?"

"Never you mind," Easter said.

Claws raking across the plank floor, the dog twisted around to gnaw at its tail bone. "How well did you know Amy Wells?" Joe asked.

"Not good enough to kill her."

"Did you ever take any pictures of her?"

"Pictures?"

"Snapshots. Photographs."

Easter's lips, pale in his dark face, twisted. "Dave Kang's the picture taker. Ask him."

"How well do you know Dave?"

The woodpecker drummed again, farther away. But the sound still had that resonance, like something blind mining underground.

"I'm the one asking questions," snapped Easter.

"Except you know some answers. I don't."

Easter growled the same way the pit bull had, as if hate was what he was bred for. He pounced for Joe's arm again. Joe was suddenly sick of it. He jerked away, kicking the chair back. The dog leaped up, spine bristling. Distracted, Joe spun toward him, snatching the .38 out of its holster. He got a shot off; he knew he had because he heard it. And kept hearing it. It kept reverberating in the sudden darkness, sharper and sharper until it became a staccato pounding, not on the outside but on the inside, resonant and resounding, as if it were his own head being chipped out from its hard center by something with a taste for stone.

NEVER LOOK DIRECTLY AT THE SUN, HE had always been told. But the problem was, the sun was hanging there, looking right down at him. He put his hands up to shield his face and smelled the scent of someone else on him. When he opened his eyes again, he saw the strip of Easter's T-shirt still bound around his wounds.

He sat up, grunting. For a moment his vision blurred. The ground under him was hard and dry and prickly. He blinked the motes of dizziness away and found himself in the middle of a hot grass prairie, sitting on limestone with a cracked, scabby soil spread over it, withered stalks of some brown grass offering a spare cushion, and the cloud-choked sky overhead. Cypress domes marred the horizon. They seemed to waver, bearing down on him, then browsing away again.

Slowly he began to remember that something had happened with Easter. He had shot at something; something had struck him. The hard lump under his armpit, to his sluggish surprise, was his Beretta. To his surprise, Easter had reinserted the clip. And the .38 had been slipped back into Joe's waist holster. Tremulously, his left hand stiff and tender, he eased it out; it had also been reloaded. What was Easter trying to tell him? That he was going to need loaded guns?

The light dimmed. He looked up. The cloud that had crept up overhead had a thick gray bottom. Stiffly, unsteadily, he pushed to his knees and got up. Waves of pain washed up against the front of his skull like liquid sloshing in a glass.

Horizon to horizon, grass and cypress ringed him. He had no idea which way to go. He realized that he was thirsty. Could you drink the snake-roiled water in those thickets? He would risk it. Maybe as his head cleared, something intelligent would come to him. For a change.

He decided to go east because that was where the nearest shade was. He found out right away that even had he not been half stunned, it would have been hard going: the wispy grass in which he had been lying thickened to waist-high saw grass, its serrated teeth snagging his shirt and cutting the backs of his hands. Underneath, invisible, was pitted, knife-edged rock. With its barricades of myrtles and brambles, the cypress dome ahead of him did not look cool and welcoming; it loomed like a fortress. He whacked his knee on a wicked, upright slab of the riddled limestone hidden in the grass.

He decided he hoped very much it was Easter, not Kang, who had done the killings. He hoped he would be the one to pin them on him. The sun scuttled under a cloud again, and the grass turned dishwater gray, the horizon gun-metal. Suddenly he realized his foot was sinking. He drew back and looked up. The cypress dome had inched up on him. A breeze passed, and the tops of the tall straight trees grumbled to each other overhead.

Fifty yards ahead of him suddenly there came an explosion of motion, an eruption of inhuman squeals, grunts, and barbaric belches: not demons but an assortment of pigs, one of every size and color, whinnying babies and bellowing grown-ups, black, mottled, tan-and-white, plain gray. They were running straight toward him, away from the thicket, the coarse hairs on their ridged backs rising like quills. They fanned away from him as they saw him, giving him a good look at their dirty ivory before disappearing into the parched cover with a rattle of brutish sobs. Then all fell silent, and the grass righted itself behind them. He let his breath out, shaking, his heartbeat wild.

It came to him in a hot rush that he was going to see a panther. Surprised to find himself so eager, he struggled, hunched down, into the first scattered ring of dwarf cypress, blundering into mud again, working toward a low gap in the myrtle. The mud silenced his footsteps and the breeze came back; the branches crackled like torches. He edged forward into the deepening, oily water. The heart of the dome was colonnaded and hollow. Across it, really not ten yards from him, staring straight at him, stood the thin, upright, dirt-colored splinter that was Kang.

For a long moment, like an animal assessing what and who Joe was, Kang froze. Then he turned. One second he was a shadow between trees; then the grass beyond stirred and closed, and as was his maddening talent, he simply wasn't there.

Joe gave up caution. He plunged straight through the open dome. Submerged cypress knees tripped him and downed logs snaked past him, but he floundered on. The rush of blood and determination drowned out the relentless ache in his arm and the plaintive boom in his head. He burst between trees at the spot on the edge of the dome where Kang had vanished and found himself following a swath of beaten-down grass.

This time Kang's progress was direct, devoid of cunning, and Joe shoved his way brutally after him. Kang was making, it seemed, for the open prairie where the grass was shorter, the line of sight clearer. A foolish move: in an open chase, Joe would have him. He vaulted a sudden upwelling of jagged boulders and saw Kang burst out into the broad savanna, running without look-ing back to see how closely he was pursued.

Here, Joe realized, the grass was shorter because wide furrows had been beaten into it, a gouged, rutted track where something ponderous had worn its way along. He didn't bother shouting; the only thing he feared was running out of breath before Kang did. The sun had come out again, hurting his eyes.

Up ahead, the ruts and tracks all seemed to converge in a shadowy copse from whose heart the crowns of oaks towered. Joe made himself breathe regularly, asking not more speed but persistence. He gained on Kang, and ran faster. The cool of the trees poured over him, chilling his sweat.

The trail wound into a cloister of big-boled hardwoods where air plants proliferated like cancers. Through the hoary trees he could see Kang sprinting steadily, follow-ing the track as it doubled back, so that they were actu-ally close to each other, with only the impassable tangle between them. And he realized unexpectedly where Kang was heading: toward the back of a lopsided lean-to propped between tree trunks. Joe quickened his pace, but Kang darted out of sight behind the dark blind.

Joe stopped, panting. Clearly it was another camp of some sort, and clearly Kang had known about it and had fled straight for it. Which could mean he thought he could ditch the negatives, but could also mean he had a weapon of some sort cached in the shelter. Reluctantly Joe took his Beretta from its holster. If Kang wanted shooting, fine; let him start.

But as he rounded the curve, treading carefully, he heard a man's voice, not Kang's. "Come on, fella," it was saying. "You Park Service, or what?"

A second voice, still not Kang's, answered. "He's got to be Park Service. What else is there?"

"Could be Game and Fish," the first argued.

A third said, "He looks like one of them damn Mig-gasuggees. Or a Seminole."

The voice that had spoken second put in, with just a hint of disquiet, "Well, we got to do something with him."

The first voice retorted, "Like what?"

Joe saw them before they saw him. There were four of them, one older and gray-haired, wearing glasses; one in his mid-forties; the others possibly twenty-four or -five. Though they all wore brimmed caps and camos and snake boots, they were all clean-shaven with square-cut Caucasian features, more like Palm Beach lawyers than woodsmen. They had been sitting in the clearing, shielded by a wall of the lean-to, in lawn chairs, ice chests between them, emptying and piling up beer cans. The shed housed several varieties of three-wheeled all-terrain cycles with balloon tires and, in a corner, a stack of automatic rifles. One of the younger men had a big M16 slung over his shoulder. Hanging from the shabby roof were four softly jewelled rattlesnake skins.

They had Kang arraigned between them, the older man clutching his arm. Kang was sweating, his brown skin blanched beyond weariness. "Come on," said the man, more roughly. "Who's after you? Somebody chasing you? What do you want?"

Suddenly the man with the big army rifle tapped the older man's shoulder and pointed, leveling the heavy gun at Joe.

Immediately, reflexively, Joe holstered the Beretta, lowering his arms, palms outward, to show his empty hands.

"Two of the fuckers," whispered the younger man who was not holding the rifle.

"Shut up," snapped the older man. Turning to Joe, he slowly rearranged his features into a crisp, gratified grin. "Come on, friend. Join the party. You boys Park Service, or what?"

"No," said Joe, carefully casual, "just a little personal problem."

"Well, don't hog the fun. Come on over," the man said. "Maybe we can help."

Common sense argued that the men would not dare to harm either him or Kang, yet every instinct told him not to walk to them. Kang's face was impassive. If he was frightened, only the clench of his small dark fists showed it. Joe fixed a grin on his own face and took a step forward. As he did so, a brown thin-fingered hand settled on his shoulder from behind, gently warning. He smelled Jimmy Easter before he heard him. "Hello, hombres. You guys want the prize or what?"

"Oh, it's you," said the gray-haired man, almost deflated. The younger man lowered the rifle with a grunt. "What prize?"

"Prize for catching the little fucker. Caught him pilfering parts off my buggy. In plain daylight." Easter let his hand trail off Joe's shoulder and sauntered forward, dangling his own M16 by its strap. "Can you beat that?"

The gray-haired man studied the three of them judiciously. "We thought he might be Park Service," volunteered the middle-aged man.

"I bet you did. You'd'a been up shit creek, huh?"

"You seem a little too damn sure he's not."

Easter just walked straight up to Kang and took his other arm. "Me and my buddy here been chasing this prick for a half hour. I got some words to say to him when I get him alone."

For a moment, he and the gray-haired man contended mutely. Kang didn't struggle, but stood only half-breathing, an animal with all his systems shut down and death still in sight.

"What if he starts talking?" the gray-haired man demanded.

"He won't," said Easter. "Not to nobody about nothing."

"I thought you might be planning on turning him over to the sheriff."

Easter just snickered again, low in his throat. "Now

you know what the sheriff told me about sneak thieves out in the backwoods." He scratched his rib cage idly with his free hand, giving Kang's arm another yank. "Sheriff's a busy man."

Abruptly the man let Kang go, crossing his arms on his green-clad chest in an empty swagger. Easter pushed Kang cruelly into Joe's arms.

"Indian?" the gray-haired man asked.

"If he is, he's a damn sorry one."

"Maybe he's one of them East Coast Seminoles," said the young man with the rifle.

But the middle-aged man had started rubbing his tidy upper lip thoughtfully. "You know, Jimmy, your tall friend here looks a little nervous. Bet if we patted him down, we'd find a badge."

"That so?" Easter grinned, this time a smile that might have been boyish, except that it was still too hard and white. He drifted to Joe's side, the black eyes expressionless. Before Joe could move, Easter dipped his quick brown hand into Joe's breast pocket, pulled out the ID in its case, flipped it open, waved it around casually, and stuck it back in Joe's pocket. "You're gettin' to be a bunch of old ladies. He's damn DEA. He's not sweatin' no illegal vehicles or game violations. He could give a shit about a pack of sand fleas like you."

"Damn!" said the gray-haired man. "I hate that drug stuff."

"Ruining the country," said the middle-aged man. "Japs are gonna take us over."

"Drug dealers should all be shot," said the kid who had not spoken. "Lined up against the wall and shot."

"Say," said Easter, "how come you ain't offered us a couple of cold ones?"

"Give the chief some beers, Ricky," the middle-aged man ordered. Ricky, the kid with the rifle, dug in a cooler and tossed Easter two Buds. Easter passed one to Joe. "Must be the same snake I had in my yard the other day." He pointed with his gun. "Can't be two diamond-backs on Lightnin' Prairie that size."

"We'll make you a wallet out of him," said the gray-haired man, not quite smiling.

"Yeah, so the next time I take you out for deer out of season, I'll have somewhere to stash the money." He shoved Kang up the trail ahead of him. "Well, thanks for doing my job for me."

"Take better care of your belongings," said the middle-aged man. "Next time we might not give them back so easy."

"Don't talk shit, bro," grinned Easter. "You know the rules around here. Whoever gets there first and holds on longest gets the best pickings."

"That's you—this time," the gray-haired man said.

Easter winked at him and took a long swig of the beer. He jerked his head at Joe, giving Kang a shove. "Move it, asshole."

"Don't forget what you said about not turning him over to the sheriff."

"Hey, like I said, don't sweat it."

But the last Joe saw of the gray-haired man, he was adjusting his glasses, as if he were not sure he had seen straight at all.

THEY HAD NOT GONE FAR, WALKING IN silence, before Easter touched a finger to his lips and waved them off the trail. They slid into a pit full of Styrofoam flakes, plastic soda bottles, and rusty metal, where they ditched the beer cans. Easter ahead and Kang in the middle, they emerged on a trail through a luxuriant fern garden, where mosquitoes hummed at ear level among the brilliant fronds. In a pool of sticky sunshine they came upon a swamp buggy as big and grotesque as the Meachams'. Easter half lifted, half shoved Kang into the front passenger seat. "You get in back," he ordered Joe.

Joe obeyed. Kang sat silently. Easter swung up behind the wheel. Unmuffled, the engine backfired and coughed. "Hang on," Easter said.

The big machine ground down into the wet holes and oozing ruts, dropping one lurching wheel, then another, tilting and slinging its helpless cargo backward and sideways and forward, awkward and evil and bizarre. They came to a big palm trunk toppled across the trail. Easter stood and wrestled with the stiff gears, forcing one front wheel, then the other, over the log; the buggy hitched its rear wheels after it, grinding to itself in a low, Neolithic mutter. "We'll go through the strand," said Easter over the engine sputter. "Make double sure they don't come after us."

"Weren't they your buddies?"

Easter made a noise with his tongue, part suck, part spit. "Weekend warriors. They finish their nine-to-five jobs on Fridays and then come out here and play desperado."

"That shack belong to them?"

"No, it's an old trespass camp. Park Service'll tear it down soon."

"So what were you doing?" Joe demanded. "Sitting here in the trees watching?"

Easter glanced back, the corners of his sullen eyes crinkling, but the white teeth hidden. "I thought you might flush something I wanted."

"Did I?"

Kang, who had been morosely picking burrs off his shirt sleeves, met Easter's gaze. It was Kang who looked away. "Not exactly what I woulda asked for," Easter said.

The track led down into a wet black heartland, where their approach disturbed a dozing gator, a soot-green bullet-shape nose down on the mud bank. It launched itself soundlessly into the water, sinking as if sucked under, leaving not a ripple.

"Arm hurt much?" Easter shouted.

"No."

Kang said nothing. He did not look around.

"We'll get a breeze on us directly," said Easter. "Bugs'll leave us alone then."

Sure enough, they soon lurched into open cypress, where the shallow water, mirroring the sky, stretched silken and glittering in all directions under the tangled, random stitchery of the pale grass. A big ash-blue heron got up out of reeds in front of them, croaking its disgust. Easter stopped the engine, hiking up his T-shirt and scratching his flat stomach. Kang leaned back, clutching the low roll bar. "Get down, Dave," Easter said.

Kang just blinked at him.

"Hurry up," said Easter. "I'm going to search you. I want to know what you took from my house."

Kang moved, so fast he slipped and tumbled off the buggy ass first into the saw-edged grass. He got up, struggling backward, but Easter vaulted after him, landing on top of him. Easter had height and weight on Kang and soon wrenched his arms behind him, but Kang kept writhing and clawing and biting so that Easter could not get a hand free. Joe climbed slowly down into the mud. Easter slung Kang around to face him. Kang's narrow eyes had gone blank, the gleaming bronze skin beneath them swelling to mask them, like a third eyelid. Joe slipped the envelope of negatives out of Kang's breast pocket. Easter tossed Kang aside coldly, advancing, one hand clenched, the other outstretched.

"Don't do it," Joe said.

"Gonna shoot me?"

"It's a temptation."

"What are they?"

"You don't know?"

Easter just jabbed out his hand.

But Joe eased the first strip of negatives from the envelope. Against the white backing he could distinguish the images clearly. Instead of giving Easter the envelope, he slipped the torn photograph from his own pocket and offered it. Kang hunkered down in the muck, his gray head bowed.

Joe had hoped that Easter's face would change, but he had underestimated him. The young Indian examined the photograph stolidly. Then he turned with it delicately arched between his grimy fingertips, bent over Kang, and took his arm. "Get out of the dirt, Dave." He backed the older man up against the buggy. "Your friend thinks one of us did it," Easter said.

"Ask him about the head," Joe prompted.

"What head?"

"The dark-haired girl's head."

"Tell the man about the head, Dave."

Kang did not look up. Suddenly Easter grabbed Kang's collar, slinging him back and forth. Kang clawed at his throat to stop Easter from choking him. "Tell him!" Easter spat.

"I don't know what you're talking about."

"What were you doing at my motel?" Joe demanded.

Easter stopped shaking Kang. "Looking for you," the little man gasped, meeting Joe's gaze finally. "I prayed you would help."

"For somebody that wants help, you've sure done a lot of running." Joe shouldered closer. "And why were you hanging around out there on the prairie? What would you have done if I hadn't spotted you? Waited till my back was turned and finished me off?"

The little Indian flushed, abruptly angry. "I was waiting to see if you were hurt. I would have come back for you."

"Shut up, both of you," interrupted Easter. Suddenly he tore the photograph into shreds, dropping them into the grass and green roots and dark water.

"Dave did not do this," he said flatly. "But some of us" —he looked at Kang, pointedly—"are not so sure about *me.*"

He jerked Kang away from the buggy. Kang staggered in the mud, recovering shakily. "Get clear," Easter said to Joe.

"You're leaving us here?"

"Get back. You want mud on you?"

"So how do we get to my car?"

"Follow the leader," said Easter. The engine roared to triumphant life, farting fumes. "Get clear or get buried. And go get a tetanus shot for that arm."

. . .

He should not have been surprised that Kang knew the way. But it was not a congenial walk. Kang did not speak; he just started slogging. Joe made no effort to question him; that could wait for Gow or Orren now. They didn't follow the trail, which had been churned to mush by Easter's buggy tires, but set off across the wet prairie, through stunted open-country cypress and tall dome cypress, and always, the villainous surfeit of grass.

At last the ground quit sucking at their ankles and filling their shoes; they emerged onto the higher plain again, then entered a long line of trees which fell across their track like a tongue of green spoil. Soon Joe saw the glint of his car's roof through the spaced pines, around a curve in the trail.

But as Kang led around the turn, Joe saw the glint came not off the roof of his abandoned Isuzu, but off the roof of a black car parked across the trail behind it, blocking it. Kang stopped. Cindy slid off the hood of the Isuzu, where she had been sitting. The black car was the Chrysler, spattered with mud and dust.

Cindy crossed straight to Kang. She started to touch his arm, but the simple distress on the Indian's face must have stopped her. He walked past her, to Joe's car, pulling on the door handle. But the door was locked. He turned mutely, sagging against the car.

Dirt and what looked like grease smeared Cindy's white T-shirt. "How did you find us?" Joe demanded.

Anger cracked her voice. "I know my way around. I didn't need an escort."

"Does your uncle know you're here?"

"Of course not."

Joe turned from her, unlocking the Isuzu. Kang circled to the passenger side, holding to the car. Joe opened the door for him. They could not squeeze past the Chrysler without scratching it. "Is there another way out?" Joe asked. Kang nodded. Joe jammed the key in the ignition.

"Don't do that," said Cindy.

Joe ignored her. He started to turn the key.

"I took your oil filter off," Cindy said.

After a long silent moment Joe put the keys back in his pocket, released the hood, and climbed out. Below the bare filter gasket, a thick smear of oil soaked into the sand.

He lowered the hood, turning to lean against it. He was tired, sweat- and mud-soaked; his arm throbbed.

"I learn fast," she said.

"Where is it?"

But she squared herself, inviting the worst.

"Fine," Joe told her. "Let's all stand around wasting time, so more people can get murdered."

She widened her eyes sarcastically. "But Joe—we have the killer right here with us. How could anyone else get hurt?"

Overhead, building up out of the silence, came a slow rising rumble, like a series of explosions set off in the distance.

"It's going to rain," said Cindy with chilly satisfaction. "And when it does, all the holes in this road will fill up with water and the ruts will turn to mud and we'll spend the night here. All three of us."

The air was still, growing thicker. The woods darkened.

"It's perfectly simple," she said. "You tell me what Dave is supposed to have done, and I'll take you to get a filter and some oil in Aunt Nita's car."

Thunder popped again.

"Tell her!" whispered Kang suddenly from somewhere behind him. "Tell her, so all this will stop!"

"Dave." She turned on Kang. "I know about her, I've always known. I thought you realized. It's all right."

But Kang shook his head. Joe did not want to look at them. The vacant distances between the pines seemed safer. "Dave," she pleaded, "did you kill her? Is that what this is all about?"

For a moment all three of them hung there in the stale silence under the still treetops and the massing clouds. Joe thought that if Kang was ever going to say yes, he would say it now. But he just shook his head.

The wind started, chasing a sense of harm through the trees. The first wave of air was hot, but behind it came a chill.

"Get in the Chrysler," Joe said abruptly.

"Then you'll tell me?"

"Yes, damn it, I'll tell you." A whip of sound came cracking down out of the sky at them. Joe felt the tense muscles in the back of his neck flinch. "Let's get out of this weather."

"We can go down to Fanny's place on Twenty-nine. It's not far by the—"

"Fine. Anything. Anywhere," Joe said.

But after all it was only a feeble shower. It cleansed nothing. The derelict restaurant, a sagging heap of boards and blocks, looked as if it would soon subside to mold if it wasn't torched first. Cindy braked under a straggling oak by the roadside, and Kang, in the backseat, reached for her futilely. "Cindy—"

She turned at the desperation in his voice. "Are you backing out, Dave?"

"This is not a snake that might bite you if you step on it," Kang said urgently. "This is something that will pursue you until it devours you."

"He's right," Joe told her.

But she dropped the keys into her pocket. "You said you would tell me."

"Go home," Joe said adamantly. "Stop interfering."

She got out, slamming the door hard. "We had a deal." Neither of them answered her. Her eyes were as black as Easter's, as Kang's, but there was no caution in them. "We had a deal," she said again. "When you're ready to honor it, come inside."

Her long dark hair swung between her thrown-back shoulder blades as she marched away. Heat descended instantly, and the hot engine pinged. Abruptly Kang pushed out through the back door. "I'm going to tell her about the pictures. Someone has to."

Joe jumped out after him. He caught him by the collar, jerking him back against the car, his fingers coiling around the butt of the gun in its holster. "You move and I'll shoot you."

Kang went limp, raking his thick-veined hands over his polished idol's face. "You wouldn't, but it doesn't matter. I don't have the guts."

"Then quit talking about it."

"But I should do it. She is just a child who doesn't understand her own hunger. I should do something to convince us both she cannot possibly love me anymore."

Joe let go of him warily. Kang had recovered some of his cunning, retreating behind the inanimate copper face, the infinite resignation. Only the eyes, watching Joe the way a cat watches someone it wants to run from, betrayed his cautious human fear.

"Why don't you try telling the truth?" Joe challenged.

"I have told the truth."

"Then answer my questions."

"I don't want to make trouble for other people."

"What other people?"

"For Jimmy," said Kang tiredly. "But now it's not just Jimmy. Now it's Cindy I have to save."

Joe backed up a step. Kang made no attempt to move. Delicately Joe inspected his sore arm under the wrapping. It was tender around the puncture, but when he didn't think about it, it didn't hurt him. A car rushed up the long, straight road toward them, starting off as a sliver of light in the distance, then materializing into a whistling torpedo: a silver Nissan pickup, zooming past them at eighty. "So that was why you tricked her into bringing us out here," said Kang. "You had no intention of telling her anything. You hoped a deputy would see us, and settle this for us."

Joe didn't bother to defend himself. Still slouched against the car, Kang sighed, just a touch too heavily. Joe said grimly, "You can tell me who the hell Jimmy Easter is, for a start."

Kang's answer was meek. "I think he is my cousin."

"You think? You don't know?"

"It was never proven who my father was."

"Then who was the old man who came to see you at the sheriff's station this morning?"

"My stepfather. The one who accepted me into the clan. Jimmy is his nephew."

Joe retied the strip of Easter's T-shirt. "Miccosukee?"

Kang nodded. "By blood. None of us are tribe members."

"How can you not be members?"

"The tribe is an organization. You have to choose to join."

"So Jimmy's independent?"

Kang shifted. Joe touched his gun, but the little man just felt his way around to the back of the car and let himself down on the bumper. He didn't look comfortable there, either. "Jimmy is even independent from his family. In some ways he's less Indian than I am."

"Because he works construction instead of selling garbage to tourists?"

Kang looked up at him. Sweat had beaded on his bronze forehead. "Some among us believe the independent Miccosukee are better off. The tribe is highly socialized, but those who have had to make their own living have not learned to take handouts." He pushed up to look toward the restaurant. "If anything happens to Cindy, I will hold myself responsible."

"What about Amy Wells?" Joe asked him. "Were you responsible for her?"

Kang only sighed. "What happened to Amy is over. We should give our thoughts to the living."

"Did Easter sleep with her, too?"

But Kang lifted an indifferent shoulder. "You must ask him that."

Another car passed, from the opposite direction, a Cadillac de Ville with a CB antenna. The windows of the Chrysler rattled in its scalding slipstream. "So Easter lives in that cabin?"

"No, he lives with his mother in Ochopee. He goes to the cabin whenever he can. Sometimes I go with him. Today I thought he would be in Naples."

"And you found the pictures there?"

The little man closed his eyes and swallowed. "Yes. Under a mattress, when I spilled a beer and had to take off the sheet."

"And when you got back home this morning and found out somebody else had gotten hold of them, you thought you'd better hunt down the negatives before the sheriff did?"

Kang moved his shoulders helplessly.

"Or," Joe went on, "you hid them there yourself, thinking that if you got caught, you could use them to turn the heat onto Easter."

"I see." Kang nodded. "You think I led you there on purpose, to point a finger at Jimmy. But why would I remove them? Why wouldn't I just tip the sheriff off to go and find them?"

"But why take these risks to protect him?"

"I watched him grow up. I'm fond of him. As I told you the other day, it seemed to me a lot of people have been ready to grab at the most convenient answers. I didn't want Jimmy to provide a new one."

"So that day at the Meachams' camp—"

"Jimmy often hunts around there. If I had found any sign of him, I would have destroyed it."

"What do the Meachams think of Jimmy?"

"He is everything they wish they were."

"Like above the law?"

Again Kang brushed off facts beyond argument. "In

some ways Indians are above the law. We can hunt, and cut cypress—"

"And murder?"

Kang shifted his slit, cold eyes. "Of course not."

"When you went to my motel room," Joe asked him, "did you go inside?"

"No, you didn't answer."

"Were there other cars there?"

"One. A blue Ford at the end with a Michigan license." The fathomless eyes darkened. "That's right, something else has happened."

"Yes."

"But you don't trust me enough to tell me what."

Joe's arm twinged. No doubt Easter was right, it was full of infection, already working its way up inside him. He shook his head. "No."

Kang planted his spidery hands on the bumper, hoisting himself to his feet. "I'm tired of this. No police are coming. No one will relieve *me* of my duty."

Joe moved, but Kang dodged. "And what will you tell her?" Joe demanded. "That you killed Amy?"

"I'll tell her whatever it takes." Kang looked at Joe's gun, against his ribs in its holster. "If you decide it will help to shoot me, go ahead."

Of course he didn't shoot, neither did he run after Kang; he just watched him stagger into the restaurant, a depleted, pallid figure. Had the little Indian murdered? With what resources? That hidden alien cunning? The sun had dropped toward the tree line, doomed by its own weight, but it had not mellowed. He took off the shoulder holster, dropping it through the car window onto the seat, and put the Beretta in his pocket. It made an uncomfortable, and probably obvious, lump, but he did not want to leave it in a car to which he did not have the key.

The restaurant was unexpectedly big inside, dark, lined with wooden booths as deep and shadowy as coffins. An old man on a stool behind a counter nodded to him as he entered, then went back to threading a dish towel through palsied hands. Cindy sat in one of the booths, an unopened can of Coca-Cola and a tumbler full of ice before her. Kang, standing over her, looked around at Joe desolately. Otherwise the room was empty. "Why don't you call the sheriff?" Cindy demanded intractably. "Or my uncle? Tell them where to come."

Kang tensed. "Show her the pictures, Agent Hope."

"Yes, I think it's time you showed me," Cindy said.

After a second's hesitation, Joe took the envelope from his pocket and dropped it on the table in front of her. He expected her to pounce on it, but instead she just put her left hand over it, pulling it toward her. "Maybe Jimmy Easter killed those women," she said perversely. "He likes to kill things."

Kang's dark eyes moved, but he didn't challenge her.

"And what happened to all the other suspects?" Cindy went on, guarding the envelope with her spread fingers. "Why couldn't it be the Meachams? They could have planted these pictures to implicate Jimmy Easter and Dave."

Joe just nodded toward the envelope. "Quit stalling and look."

But though she thumbed up the flap, she didn't open it. "Or what about this man you came down here looking for, that photographer—did the ground swallow him up?"

Kang bent over her suddenly, planting his palms with assertive finality. "Cindy, Cindy, listen. Listen to both of us. You must stop this foolishness. You must *not* get involved."

She shoved the untouched Coke away abruptly, levering herself up, the negatives palmed as if she intended to slip them out of sight and bring them back as doves.

"I can't see in here," she said. "It's too dark."

Joe followed her to the door. She stopped with the screen at her back. "Don't take those negatives out of here," Joe ordered.

"So now I have to beg to go to the bathroom?"

"Give me the envelope and go."

But she only glared at him, backing outside and down the steps. Joe followed. At the gas pump in front of the restaurant sat a rusted-out Dodge with a low front tire and a roof held together with duct tape. The wormy little man wrestling with the gas hose was watching them. "This wasn't part of the deal," Joe said.

But she kept backing. Out of the corner of his eye Joe could see the bathrooms in a separate shed to the left. Behind him, he heard the door creak as Kang came out of the restaurant.

Suddenly Cindy turned, heading for the bathrooms, clutching the envelope in front of her. Joe caught her arm and turned her; he snared a corner of the envelope, trying to twist it away from her. She jabbed at his eyes; he dodged, feeling the blood well on his cheekbone. Her body was sweaty. He felt the envelope slipping free, crumpled but whole.

He hadn't heard the chatter all around him, the demented urging. He didn't know what it was that climbed on him suddenly; it felt light enough to be Kang but it stank like a dead fish dragged through cow shit; it went for his throat with hard brown bony forearms, encircling his waist with monkey's shins. Cindy fell to the pavement, tearing the envelope. Joe thought only of holding onto the rest of it as he beat at the arms that hugged him, spinning round and round, feeling the mad grip give.

Other voices were exhorting. Cindy scrambled to her feet, darting in to pry at his fingers. She kicked at him, cruelly, and this time didn't quite miss. The creature on his back whooped, and then something snatched his ankles, and in a welter of pain and rage, his hurt arm throbbing, he toppled to the gritty concrete, the crushed gem of the envelope rolling away from him; he saw her scoop down for it, saw her feet running, and then he felt himself swamped, buried, the fuzzy little gut, excrement-sour, pressing against his jaw. Thighs like posthole diggers straddled him, locking his neck in a clamp in which he simply could not breathe.

"Hey, there, Eugene," a voice interceded over the inhuman caterwauling. "Don't go hog-wild, boy. Let the man up."

"Beatin' up on a goddamn lady!" squeaked the monkey's voice above him.

"Yeah, I seen him. She's out of reach. He won't get her."

"There's a damn gun poking out of his pocket," said the squeaky voice. "Let me get a hold of it."

"No, you just hang on. Now, mister," it called, more loudly, "I'm'a taking this gun away. You just play possum."

He felt prying at his hip. He grunted and grabbed but the hands worked the gun free. The grip choking him loosened.

"Fancy-dancy," said the squeaky voice.

"Now let him up, son. Come on."

The weight tipped, descended once on his rib cage, jolting him, then lifted. He pushed weakly at the pavement and rolled over. Standing over him were two shapes, one knobby, unkempt, and trembling, the other big and blue. The big one was a rotund stranger with close-cropped blond hair and pink shirtless flesh under stiff overalls who balanced the Beretta comfortably in a shiny palm; the other was the weedy little man from the gas pumps, his sweat-stained T-shirt hanging off him and his greasy trousers torn. Beyond them, on the steps of the restaurant, stood the mournful dishwasher, still kneading his towel, and Kang.

Unsteadily, Joe stood up. Kang met his eyes for a long second, then abruptly turned and walked to the Chrysler. "Stop him," Joe heard himself croak, but not surprisingly, no one obeyed him. Kang got in and the Chrysler shot off down the road.

The beat-up Dodge still waited by the gas pumps, and

an antique truck sat pulled just off the highway, its driver's door hanging open. Live chickens wriggled their necks through the slats of crates piled in the bed. Joe turned to find that the big man had followed him. He had slipped the clip expertly out of the Beretta and was emptying it. He dropped the shells into his overalls pocket, snapped the clip back into place, and handed the gun to Joe.

Joe jammed the useless weapon back in his pocket. Then he took the .38 from his belt. "This your truck?"

"Yep." The man smiled benignly. He had but one front tooth, a gray chip in his gum line.

"I have to catch them. Let's go."

"Can't," said the man mildly.

"Why not?"

"Well, it won't start. It don't never start when you stop it after it's heated up a little. It won't start for an hour or more."

Joe stared at him, uncomprehending.

"Go on," said the man. "Key's in it. Give it a try."

Joe turned to the Dodge. The left front tire sagged almost to the rim. The right front was worn to the cord. Something was pooling beneath the car, dripping from the chassis. The gun grew heavy in his hand.

"Look, mister," said the denim-clad farmer gently, "believe me, I got some idea what you're feeling. But don't you think maybe this time you better let her go?"

THE SUN WAS BECOMING A PERSONAL enemy. It tracked him as it sank toward the treeline, growing nearer and bigger, threatening a slow, dry death. Along the highway the intermittent rain had made the pavement steam. It was not getting cooler. Before setting off on foot, he had doused his head with the water hose beside the gas island, drinking as much of the hot, rubbery-tasting fluid as he could stomach, but it had not helped.

He had not been hurt, just scraped up a little. It was the arm that bothered him, not because it was especially painful, but because his imagination kept turning it into a bloated, pus-filled club. It surprised him every time to peel back the fragment of T-shirt and find only a tiny halo of inflammation spreading from the single wound.

Very few cars passed him. None stopped. He had given up rehearsing what he would say to Orren. No manner of phrasing could make it sound like sense. He began, inexplicably, to find the brawl at the restaurant funny. He kept seeing himself hopping around in circles gurgling, that filthy ape on his back.

That he was right, that he had learned something Kang might never have told them, would make no difference on paper. Without doubt they would fire him. But then the risks would be very different ones. All he would have to worry about would be getting killed. He began to walk faster. He wanted to get there, to where what mattered would be reduced to something he could manage: not letting someone shoot him before he could shoot back.

There was a shaving of sunlight on the road ahead. Another car coming. He threw his arms up mechanically, then lowered them. It was the Chrysler. Cindy was driving, alone.

She pulled up beside him. The window hummed down three inches. They looked at each other for a moment. "Are you hurt?" she asked.

"No. Where did you take Kang?"

"Home." Her voice had tightened. "That was what he wanted."

"Where are the pictures?"

"I destroyed them."

"There is such a thing as obstructing justice."

"Then I guess I've done it," she said.

After a second, she punched the button that would unlock the door. He got in beside her. It was ice cold in the air-conditioning. "I'll take you to your car."

"There's not enough oil in the pan now."

"I bought some. Five quarts."

"Where is my filter?"

She had stopped looking at him. "In the trunk."

"I thought it probably was."

"You should have beat me up for it."

"Is that a joke?"

"I don't know. Is it?"

"Don't hold your breath, I'm not going to," he said.

She let the car roll, her face sandstone, alive to corrosion. From beneath the seat she extracted a can of Coke with the chill still on it. He drank it without pausing.

They passed the restaurant. The old truck still sat there, lame and untended, but the Dodge was gone.

"Do you think this is going to stop your uncle from finding out what happened?" he asked her.

"I'll tell him myself."

It was perhaps five miles back to the shell lane that was the first of the many deserted and twisting paths that would return them to Easter's. For the most part the highway ran straight, but there was one long, sweeping curve they had to negotiate, and it was midway along that curve that the deputy's cruiser appeared, racing toward them. Cindy took her foot off the accelerator as it passed them, then pressed it down again. But Joe said, "Stop."

She glanced at him, then at her mirror, her brown jawline setting.

"He's braking," Joe said.

"So?"

"The best way to make a cop mad is to make him chase you."

"If he catches you."

"Of course he'll catch you. Don't be a fool."

She pushed the Chrysler faster. They had rounded the curve, so that for a brief stretch they could not see the cruiser, but if it had turned to follow them, it would soon gain. The speedometer climbed to ninety. He thought of grabbing the wheel. But she looked at him as if she knew what he was thinking. "You want him to catch us, don't you?"

"Sooner or later he's bound to."

Her grip on the wheel tightened. "Well, I pick later," she said.

She hit the brakes. The car slewed sideways, tires yelping. He thought for a moment she had lost control. He dived for the wheel. But she was still fighting for it, turning it, her foot down hard again. Ahead of them was one of those rickety, impossible wooden bridges, its gray planks sprung, its edges crumbling. They had not a hope of making it across. The scummy water below was shallow, but the sandy bank was steep. He let her have the wheel, bracing against the dashboard. But with a loud brief rattle like an artillery burst, they were over, skidding up into the trees out of sight of the highway. "I knew what I was doing. I've been across that bridge before."

Then they could hear the siren, crescendoing toward them. "What makes you think he won't be right behind you?" Joe asked.

"Because he'll be like you, he won't think we could have made it. He'll think we turned on the shell road."

The siren peaked, and then came the long whining shift as it faded. She drove on into the woods, taking a left fork, then a right. Her black eyes smoked with perverse delight. "He'll get back-up and come after you with a search party," Joe said.

"They won't catch me. I know where this trail comes out."

Ahead of them loomed a scar in the forest: a trashy clearing, frame walls slowly toppling, a stooped chimney collapsing a brick at a time. Knowingly she threaded the car between an abandoned freezer and a pit full of glass and scrap metal. Behind the ruin was a tilting latticework that might once have been part of a garage. She nosed the car behind it, out of sight of the main trail. After a second, catching her breath, she cut off the engine.

"Is this another one of those places the Park Service hasn't gotten around to burning?" he asked sardonically.

"It's not in the preserve. It belongs to the Foundation."

He got out of the car. Vines wound through the battered lattice, tugging at it. The remains of a concrete walk led to tilting stone steps. Beyond was a porch, rot-eaten and treacherous, but through another door he found a room with most of a roof over it, its linoleum floor still intact. He knelt, crushing a scrap of paper and a bit of ash between his fingertips: a roach end from a joint. In a corner, the gummy jellyfish shapes of discarded condoms littered a pile of trash.

Cindy had followed him; she stood just inside the doorway, her frown intense and innocent. For the first time, he got a good long look.

"So you just dropped Kang off at home, huh?" he asked.

"Of course. What about it?"

He walked up to her and grabbed her wrist before she knew what he was doing, and when she struggled, pinned her other hand, pushing her against the wall. She was strong and lithe and angry, and it was not easy to trap both her hands with one of his and jerk her shirt open, but he managed. Her breasts, full but still youthfully blooming, hung free. He forced his fingers deep in her right jeans pocket and wormed out her lacy, hastily crumpled bra.

She lunged at him so furiously he almost lost her. To keep her from clawing and kicking he bore her backwards, forcing her up against the rotting wall with his own weight. "Couldn't he think of any other way to say thanks?"

"I just let him kiss me," she spat. "I told him not to."

"You weren't exactly in a hurry to stop him."

"He fucking *loves* me!" she said. "Or haven't you noticed?"

"Too many goddamn people love you."

"So you get to tell me who to love?" she asked.

He let go of her, pushing her away from him. Who had she been across that bridge with, Kang and who else?

"I won't get pregnant, if that's what you're afraid of," she said behind him, her tone suddenly brutal with that ultimate, unanswerable dare.

"That's not what I'm afraid of."

"No," she said bitterly. "You're afraid for you."

He had thought from her voice that he would turn and find her crying, but she wasn't. She was glaring straight at him. "No man is going to give you that," he told her ferociously. "It will never be like that."

"You always sound so *certain.*"

"You'll get the same thing you got from Dave, and you'll hate it."

"You know an awful lot for a coward," she said.

A single blow would have done it, knocked the thought of him out of her. But he didn't do it. Again he turned away. But she seized him from behind, tearing his shirt out of his trousers. Her nails tore into the meat of his rib cage. And then as he wheeled, she hit him, a hard hurtful claws-extended blow. "Go," she said. "Go play it safe. Go."

Suddenly the only way he could hurt her back was to kiss her, and before he had stopped digging his teeth and tongue into her she was kissing him. Her shirt was still open, his arm inside it, taking the wet pendulous weight of her breasts. The buds of her nipples hardened against his muscle. She sucked in breath, fumbling at his belt buckle. "Don't," he told her, drawing back futilely. She touched the .38. He took it away from her, tossing it across the room, skidding it into the pile of litter. Then he was helping her instead of fighting her, his curses twisting in his throat as she assaulted him, striking deep between his legs and offering her body. "Don't," he said again, and then uselessly, "Don't."

So yes: He did want to make love to her, had always wanted to. Had wanted from the first time he saw her to feel the clench of those feline muscles entrap him, and with that stabbing pleasure, surrender the last sense he had of himself as decent and lawful, as responsible, rational, and sane. And surrender to *her,* not to a child, but to something finally stronger than he was, a demon let loose at him, irresistible, unconstrained by any rules he knew. But love was the wrong word, that wasn't what she wanted, that wasn't what they were doing; she seemed to want instead that ongoing battle, a brutal breaching of each other's defenses, a searching deeper and deeper into each other after something beyond kindness, and whenever he tried to bring charity into it, she hurt him, deliberately and provocatively, as if only when they both fought all out would victory be final, only then would they break through to that unreachable thing kindness and caution could not keep alive.

At least that was what it was like for him, a new breed of love he could not stand up to, a new self he could not have soberly set free. The man who rammed into the wet flesh between her legs was a man who could fight into her, invade and be dispossessed by her, while she drew blood and arched and twisted to feel him pound all the way to the base of her heart.

And even when she had settled against him, licking the dirt and sweat off him and brushing his chest with the still tense shafts of her nipples, she would not spare him; she wanted even more of him, no kiss or caress but violations there was no point in shirking now.

Then outside it was getting dark, and mosquitoes, drawn to their sweat, descended out of the dusk in a loud miserable torrent. He grabbed up their clothes in wads and carried her naked to the car.

"What are you going to tell them?" she asked.

"I haven't decided."

"You don't have to tell them anything."

He used the tails of his shirt to wipe the dirt off her face. No, he would not have to tell them anything. They would know.

"Promise me one thing," she said.

"What?"

"That even if they fire you, you won't give up trying to find out who did it. You're the only one who can clear Dave."

"Why do you care so much about Dave?" he asked her, although he had asked her before and still hadn't believed what she told him.

"He's my friend."

"That's not good enough."

"The only thing he's done wrong is love me."

But he wouldn't let her turn away from him. "But what about sex with him? He couldn't satisfy you?"

She pressed herself against his bare chest, her own flat belly trembling. "Oh, Joe, why do you have to know?"

The last light had gone, and he couldn't see her. He turned on the dome light. A mistake. In the dark they had been presences, penetrable and unbounded. In the light they were shells of bodies, opaque and apart. He found himself thinking again, how many others? With a cramp in his chest he envisioned Hunter's bare back and driving buttocks, nailing her to that grimy floor.

But her eyes were deep and earnest. "I don't love Dave," she said. "But if anything happened to him, I would feel like I had done it. He's my friend. I can't abandon him now."

He wound his fingers in her hair, clutching her to him. "Cindy, I have to know what you're looking for."

"I hurt Dave," she said at last. "I wanted things he couldn't do."

"Like what?"

She didn't answer. She shook her head free and stretched her arms until she lay flat across him, breasts molten, her flesh golden with a liquid sheen. He pushed his hand between her thighs and she spread her legs to take him, arching her back and shuddering. "More than just sex," she whispered. "I can't explain."

"Then how will I know how to do them?" It seemed vital to make her tell him. "How will I know what you want from me?"

Suddenly a tear broke free of her lashes, streaking her temple. She curled up into him, her hand finding his cock, importunate, demanding. He could barely hear her muffled whisper. "For now let's just fuck again," she said with a sigh.

31

HIS CAR STILL SAT NOSED UP IN THE palmetto where he had left it. By the Chrysler's head-lights he reinstalled the filter. "Will I see you tomor-row?" she asked before she left him. He knew that it would depend on what her uncle did to them, but he said yes anyway. When they kissed good-bye, they had to deny the urge to go on kissing. It was getting very late.

He was no longer in a hurry to go back. He had passed the point where turning himself in could save him. He did not want to sit in a lighted room, exposed, and tell what had happened, but neither did he want to be hunted down by his oldest friends. He told himself that if he went back now, willingly, and faced it, he might still help bring down a murderer, and save lives. That show of righteous courage was comforting, though whether it would sustain him he did not know.

With the help of a phone book in a roadside booth, he located a twenty-four-hour walk-in clinic in Naples. He told the doctor who gave him the tetanus shot and dressed his arm that he had jabbed himself on a nail. He was sure she didn't believe him, but it must have been

near the end of her shift because she wrote him a prescription for antibiotics anyway. He had the prescription
filled at a Walgreen's, then made his way back to the
motel. The parking lot was full of cars with county tags,
not to mention two department cars—one, ominously,
from Tampa—but by then his dread had aged to a kind of
devious resignation: he climbed from the Isuzu calmly
sorting facts into those he would offer, and those he
would not.

There was a police tape along the sidewalk; his room
door wasn't sealed, but a uniformed deputy was guarding it. No light shone through the curtains. As he hesitated, figures detached themselves from the lighted rec-
tangles of doorways farther along the motel L. He sighed:
reporters. Just in time, the door of room 26, next to his,
opened and Portman emerged, quivering with vindictive
energy. Behind him, sweet square face the color of dirty
eggshells, came Hube.

Orren, third in line, dwarfed both of them. The deputy
was hovering, uncertain. But then Hube, seeing the reporters coming, ducked under the tape and took his
arm. Joe didn't fight. A woman juggling a videocam
jumped up on the sidewalk. Portman swung sideways,
slamming the door as Joe passed.

There were two double beds in this room. Gow sat in
the one cushioned chair watching the late news and eating potato chips from a plastic bag. On the little table
beside him were the soiled wrappings of deli sandwiches.
He glanced at Hube, who was peeping through a crack in
the curtains. "They still out there?"

Hube nodded.

"Maggots," said Orren crossly.

"When it comes to a good tale we're all maggots," said
the sheriff sedately. He turned back to the TV, granting
Joe a sliver of his attention. "I was beginning to think the
next time I saw you, you'd be floating in a rock pit." He
pawed deep into the bag. "I can't ever stop wondering if

that's how come the catfish get so damn big in those ponds."

He was wearing a dress shirt and a tie that he had pulled down from his collar. He still wore the silver-buckled belt. Portman had pulled his tie down, too, but Orren and Hube had taken theirs off. Orren had rolled his sleeves up on his dark hairy arms.

"You're under arrest," squeaked Portman, his back to the door. "Leaving the crime scene. Two counts."

Hube stood hunched like a turtle sucking itself into its carapace. "Just shut up, Portman."

"Look, Habin, I'm sick of your attitude." Portman jutted his chin forward, his narrow face pinched with enmity. "I was given a commission and I intend to perform it."

"We were *both* given a commission. And like it or not, I'm the senior officer. We'll perform it when I'm good and ready."

Portman looked at his watch. "Fine. But I'm leaving out of here at eight o'clock in the morning. Whatever you plan to do, it better be done by then."

But as he lowered his arm, Orren edged in among them. He held, between just the tips of his blunt fingers, a folded sheet of paper with its edges taped together. At the sight of it, Portman froze, his sneer wilting. Hube swallowed, taking a step backward. Inside the paper Joe could see the dark shadow of the halved photograph. Even Orren's gaze couldn't hold steady. "Where's the rest of it?" Orren asked.

"There isn't any rest of it."

Gow stopped watching the TV. Orren gripped the folded sheet more tightly. "So what happened? Where did it go?"

"It's a long story."

Gow got up and turned off the set. He eyed the sheet. So, thought Joe: Even the sheriff, despite his well-honed and cynical self-possession, was not proof against horror. But then, Gow had known Amy. In the silence, the four men stood looking at Joe.

"I know where there are more of them," Joe said.

"All like that?" Gow's query was authoritative, but his voice was shaky.

"Yes. Some worse."

"Pretty calm about it, aren't you?" barked Portman.

Joe just looked at him. Orren had started sweating. Gow turned away. When he turned back, his full, stalwart face was set, professional, as Joe had expected it would be.

"They're in Kang's trailer," Joe said. "A whole contact sheet and two more enlargements. Figure out a way to get a warrant and I'll tell you where to look."

"Was Kang by any chance standing there while you found them?" the sheriff challenged.

"No. You had him, questioning him."

"Typical! When he does find something, it's fucking inadmissible!" Portman rolled his eyes.

"Contact prints," Gow speculated, ignoring Portman. "Meaning somebody had access to a lab. Were they all as badly processed this?"

"Pretty much. They were all overexposed."

"The sixty-four thousand dollar question—who else was in them?"

"As far as I could see, nobody but her."

It took a moment for the men in the room to struggle free of the dark tangle of images his words summoned. The one who finally found his way back to the surface was Orren. "How well did you search the trailer?" he asked.

"Not well. I quit when I found those."

"Then maybe the negatives are there, too. Maybe they have more detail in them."

"No, the negatives aren't there." The nearest bed looked solid; he backed and sat down on it. Orren was snapping the sheet of paper back and forth in his fingers. "I caught up to Kang after he realized someone had been in his trailer, and followed him."

"Yeah," said Orren, "after I expressly told you not to."

But Gow wasn't interested in Orren's indignation. "And Kang led you to the negatives?"

"He went straight to a cabin in the preserve that belongs to an Indian named Jimmy Easter. That's where he claims he found the prints, and that's where the negatives were. He had to search to find them and I don't think he was faking it. He claims it's Easter he's been trying to protect."

"So where are these negatives now?" demanded Gow, jamming his thumbs in his belt.

"They got destroyed."

Of course the next question came hard on the heels of his evasion. "By who?"

"As far as I know," Joe said plainly, "by Orren's niece, Cindy Cruse."

Her name in the sticky little room rang like an imprecation. "Goddamn it!" bellowed Orren, suddenly twisting the sheet of paper so convulsively Gow made a little move as if he wanted to take it away from him. "She was with *you* all day!"

"Orren, I did the dead level best I could to keep her out of it."

Orren waved the folded sheet of paper. "And she's seen these? You let her see them?" He advanced, more appalled than angry. "How could you, Joe?"

"Let's get this straight," Gow imposed forcefully. He managed to get his hand on the paper and photograph, and after a brief perplexed resistance Orren conceded it. The sheriff used his own bulk to ease Orren back a step, planting himself face-to-face with Joe. "You went this morning while we were questioning Kang and searched his trailer and found a set of photographs of Amy Wells, apparently taken as she was being murdered."

"Yes. Then I came back here. But as I drove up Forty-one, I passed Kang heading the other way. I went in my room and found the girl's—"

"We know what you found," interjected Portman. "And then you disobeyed orders."

Joe spoke to Gow and obliquely to Orren and to Hube, who had worked his way deep into a dim corner and stood there, letting the wall support him. "At that point I was sure Kang must be the killer, and I wanted to know where he'd go or what he'd do when he knew I'd found the prints."

"So how the hell did Cindy get mixed up in it?" Without the paper to twist, Orren looked disoriented.

"She passed me on the road. She was looking for Kang, and she realized I was following him. I tried temporarily disabling her car to stop her, but she had figured out where we were heading. I saw Kang take the negatives from a hiding place in Easter's cabin. I chased him, but he got away from me. Then Easter came along and sicced his dog on me."

"Yeah," grunted Gow. "That's one hell of a catch dog, ain't it?"

"So you talked to this Easter," prompted Orren.

"He claimed he knew nothing about what Kang was looking for. He helped me run Kang down. I got the negatives away from Kang and let Easter look at the other half of the picture. He tore it up."

Gow stroked his full upper lip. It was soft and hairless, as if he'd just come from an expensive shave.

"But if you had the negatives," said Orren, "how did Cindy get them?"

"It was Kang's plan to show them to her, to scare her into staying out of trouble. I'd tried talking, and so had he, so I decided maybe he was right. But she took off with them. And with Kang. When she came back for me later she told me she'd destroyed them. To protect Kang."

"You know," said Gow glumly, "if everybody con-

nected with this case would stop protecting everybody else connected with it, maybe I could get somewhere."

"What is it with Cindy?" Orren asked, as if one of
them could answer. "What does she see in that little
chink?"

"Apparently," said Gow, "the same thing Amy Wells
did."

"But what the hell is that? Can't somebody tell me?"

But Joe said to Gow, "Easter denied having had anything to do with the Wells girl." Gow just raised his
brows, waiting. "He seemed to think the pictures had
been planted as some kind of harassment, by somebody
trying to get the cabin away from him."

"But he didn't say who?"

"He said the Park Service or some of the local hunters."

"Well," said Portman, "anybody crazy enough to do
this—" he jabbed a thumb toward the torn photograph,
"would be capable of anything."

"I don't think Kang developed those photos," said Joe.
"He does a lot of photography. He'd have done a better
job of it."

"You're right," conceded Orren. "They're pretty
grainy."

"That's because the negatives were color. Color film
always does that when you print it in black and white."

"Kang doesn't use color print film, anyway," said
Gow. "He uses slide film. And he sends it out to be developed. He almost never does black and white."

"How do you know that?" asked Hube. It was his first
contribution.

"Because since this case started I've been nursing a
file on Kang so thick it even tells what size underwear he
wears."

"Still," suggested Orren, "if Kang did somehow get his
hands on these pictures—however it happened—he
could get to a black and white lab, couldn't he? Just

because he doesn't usually do black and white developing doesn't rule him out."

"Hope's right, though," said Gow. "These are overexposed *and* underdeveloped. Kang would have done a better job."

Portman had been listening with arms crossed, butt propped on the bureau. Suddenly he interrupted. "Hope's been gone a hell of a long time. Am I the only one who thinks he hasn't accounted for all of it?"

"I don't know," said Gow. "Searching the trailer, driving back here, chasing Kang, talking with Easter, chasing Kang again, then the deal with Miss Cindy—sounds like a day's work to me."

"What about it, Joe?" asked Orren. "Anything else you want to tell us?"

Shaking his head proved easy. Gow crossed the room and reached for his coat. "There is one thing you could account for—if it's not too much trouble." Joe couldn't guess what was coming. He said nothing. "Where's your buddy Shorter?" Gow asked.

Joe had almost forgotten who Shorter was. "The last time I saw him you had him. In the hospital."

Gow worked his way into the coat. "Yeah, I know you delivered him. But this morning he just up and walked out."

"Right past your deputy?"

"I ain't saying we did a great job of guarding him. We'll do a better job of finding him. I just thought maybe he'd hitched back up with you."

"I don't claim any responsibility for Shorter."

Portman straightened. "You don't even claim much of that for yourself."

Gow eyed Portman like a man appraising a useless object that had unaccountably fallen out of the sky into his driveway. He sighed visibly and confronted Orren. "Look, Cruse, I know you got business to conduct with your boy here, but you mind if I run him next door and show him that stain?"

Joe was surprised by the request, but Orren seemed prepared for it. "Take him. Take him."

"Well, come on, too," said Gow, "if you'd rather not lose sight of him."

But Orren brushed him off moodily. "Why? Don't I trust you?"

"I sure hope so."

"Then what do I care? Take him. Go."

The night had thickened. Sweat condensed on them like a web they had walked into. Now there were two deputies patrolling the sidewalk, both smaller than Joe but stouter, one of them carrying himself like a wrestler. The reporters must have retreated; there was no sign of them. Gow unlocked the room next door, flicking on a light. The floor with its cheap dingy carpet had been covered with plastic. Gow shut the door behind them. He gestured brusquely. "Come looka here."

The bed, too, had been shrouded in a protective covering. Joe hoped Gow was not going to make him look under it. Against the wall, by the head of the bed, was an exposed strip of carpet covered by a separate square of clear vinyl sheeting. Poised over it was a chrome floodlight on a tripod. Gow switched it on and peeled back the plastic. "Can you explain that?"

He pointed to an amorphous rusty stain about a foot square. For the most part the discoloring was just a trace, but in a couple of spots the drying red smear, whatever it was, had caked on the rug fibers. "If it weren't for the light, I wouldn't even be able to see it," Joe told Gow. "I didn't see it this afternoon. I didn't make it. I assume it's blood?"

"Yep," Gow assented. "Hers. And you're right—the carpet's so dirty we didn't see it either until we brought the lights in. How do you think it got there?"

"He set down some sort of container he was carrying the head in."

"Like what?"

Joe shrugged. "A paper bag."

"Too much blood. Seems like it would have split the bottom."

"Then one of those canvas totes."

Gow rubbed his chin, using his talent for rendering his well-fed features impassive; his smooth rosy skin shone softly, as if time, running over it like water, had worn its contours away. "Too bad he didn't dip his fingers in it, huh?" he mused.

Joe had edged back to the door. Gow was rearranging the plastic and turning off the floodlight. "I suppose you hope I'll tell you things I wouldn't say in front of Orren," Joe said.

"Oh, he knows you lied to him," rejoined Gow placidly. "Believe me, he's just as happy."

"He asked me if there was anything else I wanted to tell him," Joe snapped. "I didn't lie. I said no."

The sheriff crossed and opened the door, a hand on Joe's arm steering him outside. "Listen, Hope." His tone was a mix of argument and lecture. "I'm not calling you a liar. Anyway, Cruse knows anything you say to me about his case will get back to him. But he wants to wash his hands of *my* case if he can."

Joe faced him. "Your case? I seem to be in the middle of it."

Gow put a finger to his lips. He drew him down the sidewalk away from the deputies, pressing on with what was, for him, uncharacteristic vigor. "Listen, all day you been out there. Seeing, listening, thinking. You made it sound like for a while you were sweet on Kang, then maybe a little on Jimmy Easter. But I know what you been chewing on." He rolled his head back, so that his words took on the force of an accusation. "You came down here to tie in this photographer, this Sapia. You can't let go of him because you know you could get off the hook if you could prove that the fella who did your sinkhole killings, and killed these two girls down here, Amy and this Cherry Miller, is one and the same."

But Gow's assessment was not quite accurate. The day's events had not given him time to think. They had been like a freefall, tumbling him indiscriminately from one blind supposition to the next. He supposed in the back of his mind he had remembered that tying either Kang or Easter to the sinkhole killings would earn him the vindication he so desperately needed. But today it had not been his own survival that obsessed him; it had been Amy Wells, her tortured face, her stripped, mutilated body; Cherry Miller, the blank but much too human stare of her glazed blue eyes from his pillow; and finally Cindy, alive, compelling, the scald of her sweat still on his hands. . . .

"So you been holding out for this Sapia, haven't you?" Gow persisted. "Well, what if you thought back over everything you saw and heard, and everything that happened, only this time with the idea that Sapia couldn't possibly be your man?"

Joe pivoted. "So they've found him."

"He's dead. They found both bodies."

The revelation struck Joe harder than he had expected. He heard himself breathe, "Shit."

Gow let his guiding hands fall, but stood with them poised, as if Joe were a spinning top he had finally and tentatively balanced but which might whirl out of control any minute. "The point is, now your department don't give a damn. But I still got a mess to unravel. Before Cruse boots you out of here, think about it. If it wasn't this Sapia, then who?"

It was as close as he had come to pitying Gow. But pity did not guarantee trust, for either of them. Gow was handling him carefully, like a newly tamed leopard that might still bite.

"If what you're saying is true," Joe argued, "you think I'll have to admit that the sinkhole murders and these two killings down here are separate cases?"

"This Sapia was your connection. If he's out—"

"I'm a connection myself. Hube and Orren really think it's accidental that since I showed up to tie the cases together, at least three more people have died?"

"But like we've said before, that could just as easily be somebody down here—Amy's killer—trying to make you think there is a connection when there isn't. *Her* killer's probably got an ironclad alibi for the sinkhole case."

Joe took a turn away, looking for a breath of fresh air in the night contagion. "One person doesn't: Shorter," he said.

Across the parking lot, two male figures, presumably reporters, slipped out into the uneven glow of the signs and streetlights, staring at Gow and Joe with unconcealed curiosity. One of them lit a cigarette. Gow frowned.

"Shorter," he repeated. "Yeah, pinning both cases on him would save your butt, all right. But it'll take some doing. How do you figure to make it work?"

"I just wonder if I asked his wife the right questions. There're racetracks in Miami. What if Shorter's been coming down here fairly often? What if he knew his way around down here a lot better than he's been letting on?"

"Well, God knows he's not wound up too tight." Gow rubbed his chin thoughtfully. "But he doesn't look like your suspect in that composite."

"There's no real evidence that suspect is the right man."

"But then if Shorter is your killer, calling your department's attention to himself by accusing this Sapia would have been pretty risky. Is he that dumb?"

"You told me yourself it wouldn't be dumb—especially if once he turns me onto Sapia, the Miller girl gets murdered and Sapia himself conveniently disappears."

The sheriff took a moment, processing possibilities. "Under this scenario, Sapia's resemblance to your composite is just a coincidence. Well, if we assume Shorter is the killer, isn't it just a little too much of a coincidence that he and Sapia suddenly stumbled into each other's paths?"

"Maybe. But if you do allow it, then it might have been bumping into him, into somebody who looked like the composite, that gave Shorter the idea of using him to put us off the trail."

"I still say he would have been smarter to keep a low profile."

"Not if something—anything—had happened to make him feel threatened. Murderers get paranoid, you know. Or maybe he just likes seeing us chase our tails."

But Gow folded his arms uncommunicatively. "All right: We know Shorter was in the clearing where the Miller girl was killed. We don't know where he was when Landry was shot, but then we haven't asked him. And if you're right and he knew the country, he wouldn't have had any trouble getting from the Meacham clearing to where we found the stolen car. I guess he'd have had to do some maneuvering to get the car out there—access to a buggy or tractor, for sure—but so far the one thing he's been is smarter than he looks." He tilted his head, and though for the moment Joe couldn't see his eyes, he felt the sheriff's concentration. "But you have to admit you're biased—you like him because you can connect him up with both cases. Can't you do that with anyone else?"

"I haven't tried. But if I could—whether it was Shorter or Kang or the mayor of Miami—you'd almost certainly have your killer."

"Or," said Gow, "if I could find my killer, you'd have a name, a face, to zero in on when you get back to looking for yours."

In fact, Joe didn't need the incentive of self-preservation to help Gow; had he known how to help, he would have gladly. But he didn't see how the day's scramble was going to benefit either of them. He had opened up

Gow's case, yes, but now it was more, not less, complex, and the galling sense of unfinished business, of a plunge arrested before the telling impact, was beginning to nettle him. Watching him, Gow prompted, "Sunday you thought I was neglecting the Meachams. Since then you've met them. What do you think now?"

"The same thing I've thought all along, that for these cases here, nothing really lets them out." He spoke briskly, ticking off the points. "For Amy they have an unassailable motive. They have an alibi, but it sounds like it's pretty much in the family, so it would probably break. They might have shot at me to scare me, and they knew about me because you told them. They could have killed the Miller girl to throw suspicion on Sapia, and they killed him to keep him from turning up. It was pretty daring, doing the killings right in their own camp, but look how confused it's made us: So far we've mostly used it as a point in their favor. Maybe it wasn't so much daring as smart."

"You're right, Lee can be smart. How smart he's been this time, I'm not too certain."

"I suppose Wesley would do what Lee told him?"

"Wesley'll do what anyone who's got him by the ear tells him." He stared off into the distance; the watchful loiterers were still there. Possibly they could overhear snatches of the conference. "What about our friend Kang?"

Kang. Joe pictured again the little man's closed, cunning features. "Kang is weird."

Gow nodded. "Snakes. Bugs. Lizards. He's weird."

"He doesn't really have much of a motive, for killing Amy or any of the others."

"Does this killer really need one?" The sheriff answered himself with a headshake.

"And Kang is a photographer," Joe went on. "So he'd be as likely as anyone to take those photos, and he could have developed them. And I've already wondered if he led me out to Easter's cabin on purpose, not to protect

Easter but to make sure the negatives got found." He cupped his jaws in his hands, trying to sort out connections. "He's denied it, of course. He said the reason he cut off by himself that day at the Meacham camp was to destroy any signs of Easter's presence, but that could have been meant to throw suspicion on Easter, as well."

"It could have been signs of himself he was after."

"And at Easter's this afternoon, Kang could have gotten away, but he didn't. He hung around. He said he wanted to make sure I was okay. But it was almost as if he had to know what was going on."

"And he was the first person Sunday to find out about you, and as a matter of fact, he was the only one who had seen you."

"And with Amy, at least, there's the sex."

Gow drew himself up sharply. "Oh? Taking up with girls like Amy and Cindy proves a man's abnormal?"

"I didn't say that. I just said there was a pretty intense attraction, one that obviously got disappointed. You and I both know where that kind of situation can lead."

"I wouldn't have held the girls against Kang," said Gow, more mildly, "if it hadn't been for everything else. Sure, he likes them. Why not? They're young, smart, pretty. But as far as what happened with Amy—and with Cindy—the girls themselves are partly to blame."

"They're the only ones? No others?"

"The only ones *I* know of. Believe me, it's a question we'll be asking."

"So what did he do, hypnotize them?"

"No," said Gow soberly, "they hypnotized themselves. The truth is, Hope, Kang's done a lot to try and save this country, the park, and the girls got caught up in it. Taking up with Kang stood for something. But you're right— he can't hang on to these girls once he gets them." He fingered his lip, his attention once more drifting. "Yep," he said slowly. "I like Kang."

In the pensive lull that fell between them, Joe noticed

that the reporters had crept closer, cueing the deputies to fade out and intercept them. "What about Easter?" Joe said. "You've left him out."

"I don't think it is Easter."

"I get the impression he doesn't restrict himself to bulldozer driving."

"No, he guides hunting parties. He's good at it."

"Just say he guides a few poaching parties, too."

"What does that have to do with—"

"Suppose Amy Wells found out about it. Suppose she threatened to turn him in." He found his mind stringing conjectures nimbly. "Then Sapia and the Miller girl come along and stumble over something he's mixed up in. And I'm likely to stumble over the same thing they did if I poke around long enough."

"He wouldn't have tried to gun you down on a city street."

"Says who?"

"Says me. And besides, if he had all those logical reasons, why the Sam Hill did he take those pictures? A crazy man did that."

Joe envisioned again the oily, airless depths of Easter's black eyes. "Okay, suppose he is crazy. Suppose he killed Amy and Cherry for the same reason we've suggested Kang did—for kicks. Suppose he had his eye on Cindy, for whatever reason, and all of a sudden here I am going around with her. A man who's already killed for the hell of it wouldn't stop at murder to get me out of the way."

"I think *you're* getting a little crazy."

"You asked what I think."

Gow tugged his coat into place. It was a tight fit on his robust torso. "One thing we're both still assuming: that it was you that sniper was aiming at when Landry got killed."

"If we don't, though," argued Joe, "we have to assume that somebody, for some totally unrelated reason, decided to try to kill Landry, and picked the exact moment when so many people had a motive and opportunity to try to kill me."

"Or that a random killer with no connection to you *or* Landry picked the exact moment when so many people had a reason to go after you to start blasting away. You're still sure Landry didn't give you a hint what he wanted?"

"No, he didn't. The best I've been able to come up with is the possibility that he wanted to make sure Hunter really wasn't my son."

"He's not, is he? Orren says he isn't."

Joe lifted his shoulders. "Janet told me repeatedly he wasn't. He doesn't look like me. There've never been any particular ties between us. If Landry wanted more proof, I couldn't have helped."

Gow sighed now, hugely, thumping the heel of his hand against his temple. "I could get some of this worked out if I could sleep on it. Except I can't sleep."

"What keeps worrying me," said Joe suddenly, "is that there's somebody else. Somebody totally different, coming at me from an entirely different angle. Somebody I've completely overlooked."

"Except that people who get mixed up in things like this almost always leave footprints. From the sound of it, you didn't come across any new ones."

"You still like Kang."

"Kang just keeps getting himself hung up in the brambles."

"Personally, I'd like a line on what's happening with Shorter."

"Yeah, if it was my butt, I wouldn't blame you."

"Besides," said Joe in a tone that sounded oddly like confession, "I've already had to deal with the probability that my coming down here was what dragged Landry into it, got him in the wrong place at the wrong time. But if the Meachams or Kang or Easter killed Amy, then I have to accept the possibility I gave the kiss of death to the Miller girl, too. But if it's Shorter, she was probably already marked."

"We all do it, don't we?" ruminated Gow. "Solve cases the way we'd like them to turn out."

"That's all you think I'm doing?"

"Like I said, it's normal."

"Well, I am normal."

Again Gow adjusted the set of his coat. "All too normal." The gesture might have been some kind of signal; the deputies redeployed themselves again, one backing down beside the sheriff's unmarked county car, the other easing down the sidewalk. Now there were three reporters, not two, and they exchanged fragmented comments with the deputy, whose blunt negatives plunked like bass notes in the still air. "You say you think Kang's home?" Gow asked.

"That's where Cindy said she took him."

The sheriff lowered his voice nearly to a whisper. "Think about this, Hope. You didn't go in Kang's trailer this afternoon. Instead, you'd been out to breakfast; you saw Kang leaving your motel, you found the head, you took off and followed him to Easter's. You saw the negatives then, when you and Easter caught him. That's enough to get a warrant."

"Except that I had to knock over a cage to get at those pictures. Kang will testify I was in there."

"Yeah, but maybe you lied to us, huh? We didn't know it."

Joe shrugged. "It can't hurt me. It might even help. If you can sell Orren. And shut the others up."

The sheriff took his arm again, delaying their parting. "And listen, Hope. There's gonna come a time when you want to get hold of me. For whatever reason."

Joe was not sure what Gow was asking—or offering. "Tomorrow I'll probably be back in Tampa."

"That don't mean your brain'll stop working."

"Maybe I'd be better off if it did."

The sheriff persisted. "If you need me, my office'll get me. Don't take no for an answer."

"Good," said Joe dryly. "I'll call you when I need to make bail."

The deputy opened the door for them. Orren, sitting in the chair Gow had vacated, had turned the TV back on, but clicked it off and stood. Portman and Hube were lying on the beds, Portman reading the paper. He, too, got up. Gow said, "Cruse—come out a minute and sit with me in my car."

Orren obeyed a little hesitantly. Gow was right, thought Joe; Orren wasn't sure he wanted to hear what Gow might say. Joe shut the door behind them. Hube, whose eyes had been closed, opened them and rolled to a sitting position, looking wasted. He got up and hurried toward the bathroom unsteadily, as if afraid he might vomit. Joe settled onto the bed where Portman had been lying. He thumbed through the paper listlessly, picking up the comics. Several silent seconds passed. Joe was trying to make sense of the words on the page when he sensed motion, and looked up to find Portman standing over him. Hube came out of the bathroom, kneading his temples with stiff fingers. "You fucked her brains out, didn't you?" Portman asked.

Hube started. Joe felt his muscles clench, but he didn't rise.

"You fucked her," said Portman, bending over, his face temptingly near. "And after I deliver you to Kaplan, I'm going straight to Tallahassee and tell Haggertie you fucked her, and if she admits it, you're going to jail."

"I thought that was where I was already going," said Joe quietly.

"Oh, for God's sakes!" cried Hube, charging forward. "Who fucked who is not department business! Now will you keep your personal grudge out of it?"

Portman drew himself up. "Statutory rape is a felony. If he admits it and you don't turn him in, you're an accessory."

"I know all I need to know about the law."

There was a sound from the doorway. Orren had come back into the room. How much he had overheard, possibly only Portman knew. He crossed between them, with slow effort, as if the force of gravity in the room had suddenly been doubled, and picked up the phone. He had to go through the operator to call long distance, and no one said anything while he waited for the connection. Then he said, "Hello, Nita? Listen, babe, is Cindy home? . . . Yeah, I just wanted to make sure. Listen, did she say where she'd been?" He stroked dust off the phone cradle with a forefinger while he listened, not looking around. "No, don't hassle her any more tonight. I'll talk to her later. Yeah, babe, in a few minutes. Same to you. 'Bye."

As he turned, his dark, sad gaze passed over Joe remotely, the old flame of disgust smothered. He focused on Hube. "Did you tell him?"

"Not yet."

"I got a long drive ahead of me. I want to get out of here." He turned to Joe, running a hand across his brow as if he were still sweating. He said exactly what Gow had promised: "They found the bodies. What was left of them. The photographer you've been looking for and the girl."

"Positive ID?" asked Joe, though he knew the answer. "Especially him?"

"They had his teeth. Brunswick faxed his dental records to Gow this afternoon. As for her, we've got almost all of her. Enough to be sure there's a match between the head and the rest. But that's one reason Gow wants Shorter—to get a positive make."

"But where . . . ?"

"They'd been thrown down that big gator's cave. There was some sign they'd been weighed down, but they must've broken loose when the gator started working on them."

"What's the matter?" taunted Portman from Orren's elbow. "You don't look so tough all of a sudden. Ground sinking out from under you?"

"But nothing says the Sinkhole Killer didn't murder Amy Wells and Cherry Miller . . . and Sapia," Joe said to Orren. "It just means it wasn't Sapia." An option he had not thought to pass by Gow occurred to him. "Or for that matter, he could still be the Sinkhole Killer. It just means these killings down here were done by somebody else."

"Hope oughta be tired," went on Portman irrelevantly. "He's had what you might call a fucking big day."

Orren slapped him, open-palmed, the smack oddly muted, like a loud kiss. He backhanded him on the return stroke. Portman was so startled he toppled backward, tripping over the little table and crashing against the wall. Orren crossed in two strides and picked him up by the front of his shirt, spun him, and pushed him to the door, holding him with one hand while he opened it. "You got a room, don't you?" He didn't give Portman time to answer. He planted a shoe the size of a game board on Portman's backside and shoved, propelling Portman out into the darkness. "Then go to it. Now." He shouted after him: "And don't talk to those reporters!" He wheeled back, not looking at Joe, and said to Hube, "Lock this door so he can't come back in." Hube moved quickly, taking the door from him. "And be by the phone in the morning." Hube nodded, almost desperately. But then Orren seemed to lose momentum. He sagged, brushing at his rolled-up shirtsleeves, as if contact with Portman had left some sort of grime on them. "You tell him the rest, Hube."

"Yes, sir."

Orren turned almost drunkenly. "Good night."

"Good night, Orren," said Hube, shutting the door.

Joe did not watch as Hube fastened the dead bolt and

chain carefully. Then the sounds of motion stopped, and Joe turned. Hube was leaning against the door, his face haggard and wistful. Joe said, "Do you have a question you want to ask me, Hube?"

"No," said Hube immediately. "I'm not interested."

"So what is it you have to tell me?"

Hube drifted forward, hands digging into his pockets. He stopped when he got opposite Joe with the bathroom behind him. "Let me have your gun."

Without protest Joe took the Beretta out of his pocket. He handed Hube both empty clips. Hube said, "Where's your ammunition?"

"I lost it."

Hube's mouth wrenched, but he said nothing. He stashed the Beretta in his own pocket and dropped the clips on the bureau. "You've got another gun, don't you?"

"That one's mine."

Hube put his hand out in silence. Joe did nothing.

"Do you want me to go get Portman?" asked Hube. "So he can search you while I sit on you?"

He gave Hube the .38. Hube unloaded it. He put both gun and shells in his other pocket. "And your badge and car keys."

After a moment Joe tossed both items onto the bed. Hube had to come forward to get them. He did so cautiously, stretching an arm gingerly, then backed away.

"You got dirt all over you," said Hube. "Why don't you take a shower."

"Is this it? Is there more?"

"Get cleaned up first," Hube said.

WHEN HE CAME OUT OF THE SHOWER,
Hube was taking his own clean shirt out of his overnight
bag to hang it in the alcove. There was a glint of metal
and a faint, familiar clang. Hube met his eyes, and
crammed the handcuffs into the bottom of the bag before
zipping it firmly.

"You have to come on back," Hube said.

"I thought I was fired."

"You're not fired yet. You're on temporary leave."

"What if I want to be fired?"

"That's what Haggertie sent me along for, to keep you
from wanting to be."

"You think putting cuffs on me would make me want
to get fired less?"

"They were just for an emergency."

"And what would constitute an emergency?"

Hube massaged one hand with the other. "Listen,
Joe, the cuffs were Kaplan's idea, not mine."

Joe sat down on the bed nearest the window, claiming
it. Hube didn't argue. Joe's own overnight bag, salvaged
from the room next door, had been waiting for him in the
small bathroom. In it, along with his wrinkled clothes,

had been a last fresh change of underwear, so at least in that way he was clean.

"So now that Sapia's dead," Joe asked, "you're just closing down the operation?"

"Closing down *this* operation," said Hube. "Yours. Sapia is not our guy."

"So what's happened?"

"A lot. First, Kaplan sent Natalie up to Lake City to show a picture of Sapia to that girl Portman got the description from. She said he definitely was not the man who abducted her."

"Is that the only picture Natalie showed her? She didn't show her any others?"

"What others? Who is there?"

Joe didn't answer. His mind was working.

"You should have done that yourself, before you came down here, and you know it," Hube reproved.

"But there's *something* going on down here."

"Hell, yes," said Hube. "And I'm goddamn glad I'm not on it. Orren took me and Portman down to the city morgue and showed us what they dragged out of that swamp."

"How did Portman handle it?"

"I don't know. He had to go to the bathroom. I had to sit down and drink a glass of water. You know, Joe, this friend of yours, Shorter—"

"He's not my friend."

"Thank God for small favors," Hube sighed.

Joe lay back on the bed. He was no longer thinking about Hube. He was thinking instead that Gow was right: For a dumb fuck, Shorter had found it absurdly easy to outwit all of them. Where was he now? Who was he stalking? Where had he holed up?

"There's more," Hube said.

Joe moved his eyes without rolling his head over. Hube settled onto the other bed, a benign egglike figure on which someone had strapped the farcical gun. "Juan finally got the go-ahead to work on that project we were discussing at Sydney's. We started running TV spots, asking people who'd been approached by suspicious characters in interstate rest areas to come forward. So far we've gotten about thirty calls."

Joe listened politely.

"Most of them," Hube went on, "Juan decided were just people turned paranoid and overreacting. One of the so-called potential abductors was a woman, which seems unlikely. He came up with about six possibles. Two people gave descriptions that sound like the same guy."

"The guy in Portman's sketch?"

"No. Younger. Apparently light-complexioned, good-looking. We're working on a new composite." He loosened his shirt collar. "We got some car descriptions, but the only ones who got tag numbers were a few of the rejects. In any case, there's nobody down here who fits the new description. And no sign of a connection with this Wells case." He left a small silence Joe didn't fill. "You see that now?"

Joe turned off the light over his bed. His heart was tapping out a muffled, heretic litany: *unfinished business.* "When they pulled those bodies out, what did they do about the gator?"

"Oh, they shot him," said Hube. "I saw him."

"How big was he?"

"Twelve feet. Supposedly way off the record."

"What do you suppose they'll do with him?"

"Gow seemed to like the idea they might sell him. The hide, and the meat to restaurants."

They were both silent for a few seconds.

"That's bullshit," said Joe. "Gow's sense of humor."

"I never order that stuff anyway. Give me steak and potatoes," Hube said.

But Joe had moved on now from thoughts of death. He had begun again to think about Cindy, about making love to her in the warm wet sea of the prairie, in the hot fecundity of the forest, in the deep oblivion of a fern-bordered slough. Being places of his imagination, they were culled of all discomforts, of all distraction, of all except the quick hot exultation and the exotic glow. Yes: unfinished business. As he mused, lightning began to knife through the slits in the curtains, as if the beast out there, the one he had so often sensed, had come prowling, sweeping its searchlight gaze ahead of it, searching for prey.

Toward daybreak it rained. Joe sat up in bed and opened the curtains to watch it. The lightning flashes against the darkness were so bright the only color in them was an obliterating whiteness. Between blasts, the rain blew horizontally in the chintzy glow of the streetlights, in solid repeated waves like surf. The thunder was sharp and immediate like limbs snapping. Joe heard Hube roll over in bed, but he didn't turn to face him. Hube had lain down with his clothes on, Joe's guns still in his pockets, his own under his arm. The bag with the handcuffs in it sat on the floor beside him. Once Joe heard him push up, perhaps to consult the watch he had taken off and set on the bed table, then sink down again. Then Hube didn't move anymore, but Joe knew he lay with his eyes open, on guard.

The rain stopped about five. Lightning still raked the sky, but now with thin, shrunken claws of color, cloud to cloud. Even with the streetlights still burning, it was possible to make out textures overhead: the shadowy thundercloud remnants, the open dawn-filled air pushing in behind. If he waited too long, worried too long, Portman would come and it would be too late.

Hube did not wake when he stood. Quietly he inched around the bed and knelt by the overnight bag. The zipper unzipping sounded like a train passing. He lifted the cuffs with both hands, so they wouldn't clang against each other. Holding them in front of him, he straightened over the bed.

Of course Hube jumped at his touch, for just a second too long letting disbelief overcome him. By the time he did believe, Joe had his right wrist in a twisting grip and the handcuff around it. Hube reached with his left hand and closed his fingers awkwardly but solidly on the loaded 9mm in his left armpit. He had the gun juggled around and leveled as Joe snapped the other cuff through a decorative slit in the headboard. Joe put his hand on the barrel of the automatic, wondering with half his mind what lunacy kept making him think guns could not kill. Hube thumbed down the safety. Joe did not try to dodge his aim, but just sank to the edge of the bed and waited. Hube let go at last. The butt of the gun as Joe took it dripped with the sweat of Hube's hand.

They were both shaking. "She must give damn good head," Hube said.

Joe didn't answer. He moved fast now, to the beat of something pounding inside him, behind and inside all his organs, something alive that had gotten trapped inside him and was rattling his ribs to get out. He reached into Hube's right pocket and took out the .38 and his car keys. He had to dig for the shells. Hube neither fought him nor helped him. Joe put Hube's Beretta and his own down on the bureau. The K Mart clothes he had worn yesterday hung on the back of a chair. He stepped into his trousers, dived into his shirt, and slipped the .38 into its holster. "I'm leaving the department gun and the badge."

"What the hell difference does it make?"

"Call it a point of honor."

"Bullshit."

The phone on the night table was almost within Hube's reach. Joe moved it to the other bed.

"Kaplan won't have to cut your balls off," said Hube. "Orren will."

Hube's hurt and anger were beyond the reach of explanations or promises. Joe said nothing.

"And you think they won't pick you up?" Hube demanded. "You think you'll get more than a couple of hours out of this?"

"That's all I want, a couple of hours."

"Maybe I would have found a way to give you a couple of hours."

"Well, it's too late now."

"Got that right," Hube said.

It was close to seven when he reached Miami. The clouds had retreated inland beyond the rim of buildings; the clear sky was smoky, not quite blue. Trying to breathe the air was like trying to breathe seawater. Would Nita be up? Would Orren have already left home? There was no way to time things, or plan. Not with this need driving him. He knew which window fronting the street was hers. He found that he was making a kind of test out of it: If she managed to get down and see him, it would mean she did love him. He told himself that he wasn't being fair to her, but all the same it was something he needed, to see her risk for him at least some fragment of what she had risked for Kang. He would not ask her to go away, not now, would not ask her to become a fugitive. He would see first what he was to be charged with. It depended on Hube.

He stopped far up the street, startled. She had managed to get out, all right: for somebody before him. Jimmy Easter's pickup was parked at the curb. Easter himself stood there, facing Joe, leaning on an outstretched arm braced on the truck cab. And Cindy, slumped against the door, her back to Joe, fit perfectly in the angle of Easter's arm and body. Too perfectly. Joe, coasting slowly toward them, realized suddenly that for all the enmity they had spent on each other, they were unaccountably alike, blood and soul related, their jagged contours pieced together in the early morning sunlight like two halves of the same scrap of brittle iron.

Easter saw him, and the look on his face made Cindy turn. Joe braked and cut off the engine. Cindy was wearing her sweat suit. Easter wore black: black T-shirt, tight, dark unfaded jeans. His black hair framed his lean face like harsh strokes laid down by an unmannered child's crayon. The expression on Cindy's face when she saw Joe climb from the Isuzu was one of someone just waking in an unfamiliar room.

She took a hesitant step toward Joe, but glanced back at Easter, as if he had thrown out an invisible noose. She was almost to Joe before she seemed to break free.

And Joe realized that, despite what he had told Gow, up until that moment he had not fully believed that Easter could have done the murders. There was something so honestly violent about him that it had seemed that no homicide he would commit would be in secret. He would blast his victims to smithereens in a revolution, but never cut a heart out in stealth. But now the young Indian straightened with enough obscene self-celebration to plant a thousand severed heads in motel rooms in broad daylight. Joe thought he would have made a perfect target for the .38.

He wasn't sure she was going to kiss him. Neither was she, but then she did, standing on tiptoes. He had desperately needed the taste and feel of her. It was the only thing that could have made his night visions seem real. Her mouth was sweet and civilized, tasting like toothpaste. Easter, still watching, crossed his arms on his chest.

Joe's heart would not stop its destructive pounding. "What is he doing here?"

She looked back doubtfully at the Indian, as if there might be another "he" to whom Joe could be referring. "He was asking questions about you."

He felt himself move a little. Easter's stance, too, changed slightly. "Cindy, he's dangerous."

"I thought it was Dave who was dangerous."

"Until the case is solved, they're all dangerous."

"Why is everyone so afraid of him?" she asked, suddenly exasperated. "If it turns out he did do it, at least that would clear Dave."

He didn't understand how it had happened, but he could feel the sudden tug of war for her attention. He caught her hand, turning her toward him. But there was a rough edge to her impatience. "I know," she said. "You want me to be *careful*. You all always want me to be *careful*."

"Cindy, there are two sets of cops and the whole South Florida Department of Law Enforcement working on this case. If Kang is innocent, they'll clear him."

"So far they've been doing great, haven't they?"

"I love you," he said vehemently. "I'm trying to keep you from getting hurt."

Easter had slumped back against his truck, head cocked to watch them, his slack pose derisive. But then the young Indian's gaze shifted suddenly, and following it, Joe realized that the door of the house had opened. Anita emerged, in slippers and bathrobe, her hair in curlers under a gauzy bonnet. She came silently to the end of the driveway. Easter touched a brown hand to his forehead, irreverently. Anita turned away from him coldly to look up the street at Joe and Cindy.

"You see?" said Cindy, her voice unexpectedly tremulous. "*She* loves me. *They* love me. I know, I know, you all do."

"Cindy, what's so awful?"

"They locked me in my room."

Reason told him none of them had done anything the danger she might be in didn't warrant. But he couldn't help feeling she had laid out a test, and he was failing it. All the definitions of love he had ever known would have failed it.

"I took the doorknob apart," she said. "With a fingernail file. Nobody's locking me up."

"All we want . . . all I want—"

"You want me to be a good puppy," she spat, suddenly savage. "Daddy's sweetheart. A good little girl."

He had been going to say that all they wanted was for her to do what was sensible, but between the thought and the words rose the vision of Hube cuffed to the headboard.

"Cindy!" called Anita plaintively. "Cindy, before your uncle wakes up . . . please come back inside!"

He caught her hand again, and held on when she stiffened. "For God's sakes, listen. You want to make up your own rules. Fine, we all do. But it's dangerous. That's what you don't see."

"You're afraid of them, aren't you?" she demanded. "Of *their* rules."

"If I was, you think I'd be here?"

She was scornful. "Then kiss me. In front of Aunt Nita. Kiss me the way you did last night."

For one second he looked past her, down the street to Anita, into Anita's accusing eyes.

"Goddamn you," said Cindy. She couldn't quite get her hand away from him. He pulled her to him, covering her mouth with his. He felt her founder, for an unsteady instant bereft of anything to defy. But then she pushed away from him so indignantly he could only think that her anger was what mattered to her, not him.

"Cindy," he said, to hold her, to stop her. "You asked me to promise I would try to help Dave."

"I guess I shouldn't have bothered."

"I'll do the best I can."

"So far that hasn't been very much."

What had happened to the clean passion he had spent last night reliving? He had jumped from a high place, thinking that when he fell so hard he must surely hit bottom, but the ground had gone on giving. He had come looking for something he could be sure of, and all he had unearthed, from that first day, going underground in the sunlight, was the oldest and purest sort of doubt.

"Swear to me," he said, "you'll stay away from Easter."

"I'm not afraid of Easter. *Some*body has to find out about him."

"Cindy, if he's the killer—"

"You don't think he's the killer. You're just jealous."

"That's crazy."

She didn't deign to answer him. Nor did she go to Anita. She walked back down the street toward Easter.

"Cindy!"

She ignored him. Whatever she said to Easter, it just made him grin.

"Cindy," Anita echoed. "Honey, please be good."

But she spun and marched past her without speaking, letting herself brusquely into the house.

Anita stood there what seemed like a long time, staring fixedly at Joe. But Joe couldn't move until Easter did. Finally, with that enraging, languid confidence, Easter climbed back into his big truck. He drove by Joe fast, so that the wind rattled him. When Joe turned back to the house, Anita had gone inside.

THE SKY OVER MIAMI WAS CLEAR, BUT HE
could hear the thunder, not too distant. He couldn't tell
where the sounds were coming from, so there was no
chance of driving in the other direction. He was in a
hurry, with nowhere to go, and all around him these
grunting coughs of doom.

The first thing he had felt as he left Orren's was rage.
Easter hadn't been there to ask questions. Easter had
been there to drive home a challenge. You accuse me,
Easter's smile had said. Look what I can do to you.

Why, *why*, hadn't he gone after Cindy and jerked her
away from Easter? Betrayal—his of Orren and
Hube, hers of him—dragged on him, his guilt a burden
he had picked up all too eagerly but now couldn't cast
off.

She wasn't to blame. He was. He had aided, abetted,
shored up, an insanity, all the while knowing exactly
what he was doing. Last night, for which he had spat on
his conscience, seemed nothing more now than a horrible illusion. A lost and hungry girl had given him a
chance to feed her desperation, and he had seized it, savagely. Now because of him, she might be in mortal dan-

ger. Only one way to save her, to fight free to forgiveness: find the killer and find him fast.

Above all, he must not let Hube or Orren or Portman catch him. This was his mission, his duty, his atonement. He decided he would give himself twenty-four hours. If by then he had only made things worse, he would turn himself in.

He realized as he drove that he wanted it to be Easter. But if it *was* Easter? What had Cindy said to him—*promised* him—that had made him meet her eyes and smile?

No, he didn't want it to be Easter. But slowly a fatal terror settled over him. Of course it was Easter. He deserved for it to be Easter. So of course it was.

He found a twenty-four hour Albertson's that sold plain cheap shirts in plastic packages. He bought a couple, as well as oversize bandaids and some ointment. His arm didn't hurt much anymore, and normal color had come back around the edges. In the store's rest room he put on one of the clean shirts, rolling the sleeve down over the fresh plastic square.

He sought out a gas station that still did repairs. There were so few of them left. He needed one with lots of parking space and a generous bustle of business. He was in a hurry and decided to consult a phone book, but the first phone he saw sat right on the apron of a Mobil station that suited his purposes perfectly. After a wait that seemed endless, he rousted a blue-uniformed mechanic, infuriatingly lethargic, from under one of the half-dozen cars lined up in the two cluttered bays.

Tomorrow night, Joe said, flashing his credit cards, he had to drive to North Carolina. The car needed an oil change, and the timing belt was nearing its recommended limit. If he left the car till tomorrow noon . . . ? Well, said the mechanic, masticating every word, they were pretty busy. A timing belt was a big job. But grudgingly he let Joe fill out a work order. Joe gave a false name, making up an address near Orren's. He ditched the Isuzu in an angled slot far back in the ranks of waiting cars.

The cab he called came within minutes and took him by devious ways to the airport. The girl at the Hertz counter accepted his VISA without question. Hube knew the ruse, but he also knew others, and just maybe it would take him a few hours to settle on this one. Another option was to go to a bank and use his card to get some cash to buy a used car, but he was going back out into that trackless nowhere, and he needed safe transportation. They gave him a dark blue Nissan Sentra with ten thousand miles on it. It was peppy and agile and if he had to, he could double up and sleep in the back seat.

He began to feel good, driven, in control. Not far from Orren's was a strip mall he remembered. At Winn Dixie he bought a big can of insect repellent. The bookstore carried a wide choice of tourist maps, including extensive fold-out maps of all the counties. He bought four: Collier, Monroe, Lee, and Dade.

The next move was trickier. Walking back to the car, he thought it out. The ruse with the pictures would work; he would make it work. So far he was the only law enforcement officer who had seen the photos, the only one who knew exactly what horrors they contained. And somewhere out there was somebody who must be growing more and more paranoid. Worrying. Wishing he had never taken those pictures. Peering at his copies, if he had some, night after night, not looking now at the sheet-white figure in the foreground, but searching for dimmer, more awful ghosts in the backdrop of dark.

Unlocking the car door, he felt his hand hesitate, but willed it to keep moving. He climbed inside without a break in his motion. No, he hadn't imagined it. That same car, a nondescript tan Pontiac, had been parked near him at Albertson's; now it sat off by itself, several rows away, recognizable by the half-peeled-off radio station sticker in the window. Shorter needed to learn that when you followed someone around, the first thing you did was disguise such obvious identifying marks.

The racehorse trainer was wearing a brimmed hat and sunglasses. As the tan car followed Joe out of the parking lot, he put on his own sunglasses. So that was what Shorter had spent part of those stolen hours doing: staking out the North Glades Motel.

Joe had picked the tracks leading out to Easter's as the scene to which he would lure the trainer. He almost missed them: once he passed the place he'd turned around yesterday when he was tailing Kang, he dodged north on the first shell road he came to, and he wasn't really certain until he was already well down it that he'd made the right choice. He had to take his foot off the gas and coast until he saw the beige nose of Shorter's car ease off the highway.

It was time to decide whether or not Shorter was a crazed killer—who might well be armed. The cops had impounded his truck, so if he'd brought a weapon from Tampa, they had it. But in Florida it was as easy as getting your feet wet to find a pawn shop that would sell you a handgun over the counter, no waiting period, no questions asked.

The site he'd picked was even better than he'd remembered. He drove on by, as he'd planned, until he rounded the next curve. He edged the Sentra into a particularly opaque stand of viny brush, cut the engine, and listened. His heart boomed; otherwise he heard nothing. He doused his arms and throat and ankles with insect repellent and got out.

The repellent, he decided, had been meant for evenings by the barbecue grill, not for jungle warfare. He batted his way quickly down the trail to the little built-up hump of the culvert, where a crumbling concrete pipe cut under the ruts. The bank was steeper than he remembered, and brush-clogged. Water seeped through the pipe, but this once he didn't intend to wind up in it. He dug with his toe among the weeds, hoping to roust out any snakes, but he scared up nothing worse than a big harlequin grasshopper which sluggishly thumped out of his way. He crouched below the road level and took out the .38.

In less than a minute° he heard Shorter's car. It bobbed into sight, complaining in every joint and spring. Shorter was being careful, as careful as Joe had been yesterday. Joe let the car pass. It rocked and plunged and wove toward the curve. Then Shorter saw the Sentra. He stopped.

Joe stepped out into the path twenty feet behind the Pontiac. He wanted the bullet to pierce both the rear and front windows, well clear of Shorter's head. He placed it perfectly, sliding back down into the culvert as the neat hole pocked the glass. Stretching so that he could see above the bank, he watched the shadow of Shorter's head, in its floppy tourist hat, freeze. For a moment nothing happened. Then, with a jerk, the shadow above the seat back disappeared.

Now the question was how much of a waiting game Shorter would make him play. But after only a few seconds Shorter bawled with a quaver, "That you, Hope?"

He didn't answer. The hat, trembling a little, reappeared in the slit of the windows. "For God's sakes, don't shoot me, Hope! I was trying to catch up to you! I want to talk!"

Shorter had had plenty of chance to catch up to him. "Sit up where I can see you!" He balanced the gun where he could use it in a hurry. "Face the front."

Shorter's big round head, without the hat, inched into sight. He was trying to sneak a look over his shoulder. "I said, face front!" Shorter's head jerked back into line rigidly. "Get your hands above the seat where I can see them." The hands rose eagerly, growing up into the light in speeded-up motion. "Use your left hand to open the door," Joe told him. "But then get it back up again.

Keep both of them up, keep your back turned, and get out."

Shorter maneuvered himself as ordered, grunting and grimacing, his thick frame cowed. He wore the same filthy clothes in which Joe had delivered him to the hospital Tuesday evening. Joe waited until he stood with his empty hands elevated. "Now turn around."

There was no sign of a gun in the tight waistband under Shorter's belly. "Walk around to the trunk and spread your legs and put both hands on it."

"Don't you believe me?" pleaded Shorter, not budging. "I was trying to catch you to talk to you."

"Why didn't you flag me down?"

"I just wanted to see where you were headed. I mean, nobody ever tells me anything. I have to find everything out for myself."

Joe jerked the gun. "I'm doing the finding out now. Move."

Abjectly Shorter stomped around to the back of the car. He was just positioning himself with feet and hands spread when the car began to rock and bounce with the violent struggles of something inside it, something that banged and thumped and let out nasal wails. Shorter stared down at the car as if he had involuntarily conjured this uproar without any idea how he had done it. Then, abruptly as it had begun, the display stopped.

"What the frigging hell have you done now?" Joe asked.

Shorter started to pivot toward him, but at a twitch of the gun he lurched back into position, lowering his hands gingerly to the trunk. The banging and bumping didn't start up again, but from the trunk came an asthmatic keening. Joe inched forward with every trick of caution he ever learned. At first he thought it was the trainer himself who stank, but as he drew close he realized it was the car that gave off the sour miasma, seven-eighths whiskey and one-eighth vomit. Shorter's waist, pockets, legs, and chest were clean. He had nothing on him but a wallet, a pocketknife, and some loose change. Joe backed away.

"It's the Meacham kid," volunteered Shorter, boast- fully defiant. "The stupid one."

"How the hell did that happen?"

"Can't I turn around?"

"No."

"You think I killed them, is that it?"

"Killed who?"

"That guy and Cherry. Don't waste your breath ask- ing me how I knew. It's all over the news."

"You seem to be taking it calmly."

"I knew she was dead from the start," said Shorter bitterly. "When I first saw all that blood I knew it. You fucks wouldn't listen to me. You just called me crazy."

"Yeah, kidnapping's a lot saner."

"So's pointing guns at people," Shorter snapped. "I want the guy who did it. I'll do whatever fucking works."

The wheezing was getting weaker. "Is he all right?"

"He's breathing, isn't he? I didn't hurt him."

"He climbed in there by himself, that it?"

Shorter sighed. The thick beard springing up on his jowls was gray, tipped with silver. "Yesterday—before I knew they'd found the bodies—I wanted to go back to that place. You know, that camp." He rolled his head stiffly on his thick neck without turning. "I wanted to poke around and see if I could find anything the cops hadn't. But it was full of them—uniforms, cruisers. I had to back out in a hurry."

"I can imagine."

"This kid almost crashed into me driving in." He sucked air up his nose, wrinkling it distastefully. "I'm not sure how he knew about it—I mean, it hadn't been in the news yet, had it?"

"He probably got it off a police scanner."

"Anyway, he got a fucking kick out of telling me all about it." Shorter's voice thickened with disgust. "I told him I'd give him a hundred dollars if he'd come back out and tell me anything else he could find out from the cops."

"He fell for that?"

"I had it. I showed it to him. I figured it couldn't hurt to try him. Anyway, I waited up the road at that store. He came right to me. I had bought a bottle of whiskey. I figured I might need it to make me sleep later. But he saw it on the seat and I could see he wanted some. So I offered it to him. I figured it might make him talk better."

"So you got him drunk."

"How was I to know he can't handle liquor? The next thing I knew he was passed out. But he had told me . . ."

"Don't stop now."

"Goddamn it, you think I'm made of wood? This smell is killing me."

"How long has he been in there?"

"All night. But I cracked the trunk sometimes. I didn't want him suffocating."

Neither did Joe. "So what had he told you? Talk fast."

"He was getting pretty boozy. But he told me he and his brother knew who had done the killings, and his brother could prove it. He started telling me all this shit about the other killing, the Wells girl."

"So who did he say did it?"

"All he would say was that it was an Indian. He started telling me Indians are . . . they're big as horses, and when they . . . do it to white girls they. . . ." He choked, faltering. "He made it sound like he goddamn saw it."

"So you decided to hold him hostage?"

"You think I was going to let him waltz off? I tried to get him to call his brother. But after all that, he wouldn't do it." Shorter's voice rose indignantly. "After all that, he told me his brother wouldn't tell me. He said his brother was waiting until he could really nail this Indian. I couldn't believe he would do that, tell me all that shit and then back out on me."

Joe wiped sweat off his upper lip. The mosquitoes were beating about his ears, batting against his eyelashes. "So you're meeting Lee somewhere?"

"I haven't called him. I hadn't decided the best way to do it. I started thinking about you."

"Where are the keys?"

"In the car still."

Joe backed up the trail, keeping the .38 leveled. "Turn around."

Shorter faced him, watchful but acquiescent.

"Walk toward me," Joe told him. He kept backing, letting Shorter get about fifty feet from the car. "That's far enough. Now lie down on your stomach with your hands behind your neck."

"For Pete's sakes, Hope—"

But grumpily, Shorter knelt, then flattened himself, squirming to find a bearable position in the dirt. Joe skirted him as widely as the road would allow, holding the gun on him. "Don't twist around," Joe ordered tersely. "Lie flat."

The car began to bang and rock again as Joe approached. The keys were in the ignition. Joe crouched and peered under the seat, then circled and rifled among the maps and packs of tissue in the glove compartment. He found no weapon. "Where did you get the car?"

"Lady left it running outside of a post office in Windwood. Changed tags with another car in a mall parking lot."

"Is he tied up?"

"He was."

Joe stood well clear when the trunk flew open. Yes, Wesley was still tied. His feet and arms had been anchored to the struts of the trunk, and he had been gagged with a strip of his own shirt. He had been crying, and the eyes he rolled at Joe were bloodshot and caked with dried mucus. The boozy vomit had spread under him, sticking in his already greasy, tangled, cornbread-yellow hair. And he had pissed on himself. The piss, too, stank of whiskey. He was breathing heavily, nostrils pumping in his pink hot face.

Joe used a cautious thumb and forefinger to work the gag out of Wesley's soft red mouth. The taut cloth had dug raw gouges into the corners of his lips and along his jaws. The first sound out of his mouth was a full-throated bellow. "Shut up," Joe told him. Wesley wailed louder. Joe slapped him, hard enough that the bellow died to a gurgle. Joe wiped his hand on his pants and held his breath and bent close. "Who killed Amy Wells?"

The pink-rimmed eyes searched Joe's face. The mouth worked, but only drool slid out of it, plopping in the congealed vomit. Joe waited. Wesley began to wail again, not loud, but deliriously. "Who?" Joe said again.

"He wouldn't talk to me anymore, either," said Shorter. "All I could get out of him was gibberish."

Joe straightened. Wesley began flopping, but Shorter had laced him into the trunk so intricately the strong nylon cord only tightened with his struggles. Joe reached up to close the trunk lid. Wesley managed his first intelligible word: "No!"

Joe frowned. "No what?"

Wesley just slammed his head from side to side, as far as the cords would let him.

"I'm not turning you loose until you talk."

"No!" Wesley drooled more, food bits and blood trailing down his cheeks. He thrashed against the cord that bound him. "Don't shut . . . can't stand . . . dark. . . ."

Joe bent over him again. "I won't shut it if you tell me who killed Amy Wells."

Wesley rolled back and forth in the vomit. He drew his lips back and formed a word. Joe had half-expected it, but still it startled him like the sharp impact of a thrown rock. "Eas . . . ter."

"And your brother can prove it?"

Wesley nodded savagely, then closed his eyes and coughed.

"How?"

"No—no—no—"

"Who did he say?" Shorter twisted out of the dirt.

"Nobody you know."

"Damn it, Hope!"

Wesley's broken protests decayed slowly into mindless ululations.

"Get up and come over here," Joe told Shorter.

Reproachfully dusting the dirt and burrs off his clothes, Shorter obeyed. Joe kept the gun on him, giving him plenty of clearance. "Gag him again."

"Christ, Hope. I don't like to touch him."

"Neither do I. You started this. Now finish it."

Wesley twisted and kicked, but Shorter was stronger. Reluctantly he resecured the mucus-smeared strip of shirt.

"We'll leave this car here," said Joe. "We'll put him in the backseat floor of my car."

"He's heavy."

"You got him in here."

"I was smashed. I didn't know what the fuck I was doing."

Joe shoved the .38 into its holster. "Between us we'll have to manage. You'll drive and I'll keep an eye on you both."

"Where are we going?"

"Where I tell you. We don't have much time, so come on."

34

THERE WAS A PHONE BOOTH OUTSIDE the ramshackle restaurant. Sweetwater information gave him the number of Meachams' Body Shop on the first try.

A gruff male voice answered. "Lee ain't here. Who's this?"

"Is this his father?"

The voice grew harsher. "What's it to you? Who are you?"

"My name is Hope. Lee knows who I am."

"Are you the cocksucker that's got Wesley?" The voice didn't wait for an answer. "You harm one hair of that boy's head, mister, and I'll troll for sharks with your balls."

He was in too big a hurry to argue. "You got ninety seconds to shut up and listen."

There was a dense silence. He could almost feel the man at the other end wrestling with his fury.

"What kind of truck does Lee drive?" Joe demanded.

Still the man didn't answer.

"Sixty seconds," Joe told him.

"A yellow GMC with mud tires."

"Tell him to come west out Forty-one and drive north on Twenty-nine," Joe said, "about fifty miles an hour. If he hits Alligator Alley, he should turn around and drive back. He should reach Twenty-nine by eleven. If he's not alone, he'll never see me. If he is, he'll bring Wesley back with him."

"What did you say your name was?" the man asked. But Joe hung up.

When he stepped back out into the sunlight he was shaking. If Lee answered the summons, he would do so for a reason. He would come because he was worried about something, something he didn't want to share with the cops. If he didn't, Joe's part in the game was over. Whatever happened to Cindy would be up to the official army, not to him.

Over Shorter's protests, he left both of them in the tumble-down building across the rickety bridge. It was shady there, if not exactly cool, and he doused them both generously with his bug spray. Wesley's gaze was clear now, but when Joe ungagged him, he only pursed his cracked lips and tried to spit. Bruises Joe hadn't noticed before were popping out around his eyes. "What if he tries to get away?" Shorter asked peevishly.

"He won't get out of those knots."

"You should leave me some kind of weapon."

"We're in enough trouble without that. Sit down and get some rest. It may be a long day."

He drove back down to 41, glad to be free of them. At a big roadside airboat concession, he parked among the tourists and the charter buses, the Sentra pointed toward the busy highway. Most of the people piling out of their vans and campers and Cadillacs were elderly, the men knobby-kneed in their plaid walking shorts, the women sunhatted, blue-veined bare legs richly dimpled. The men superintending the big airboats moored in the stagnant canal used megaphones to bark off the minutes between departures, and each boat that burst into throbbing life carried a full load.

Joe began to feel sleepy. He did not know how long he would have to wait. Lee might have been all the way down in south Miami. When after forty minutes there was no sign of him, Joe knew he was going to have to risk ducking into the gift shop to buy a cup of coffee. He could watch the road through the shop windows. But as he pushed the Sentra's door open, Lee did pass, driving fast.

Joe slammed the door again, ducking, though Lee couldn't have seen him. He didn't follow right away. A Lincoln passed, crammed with tourists in sun visors; next came a beat-up station wagon with two cadaverous dogs hanging over the tailgate, then a Mercedes pulling out dangerously, a Hertz truck, more tourists. If there were cops, they were well-disguised or well back. Joe eased out into a long gap in traffic. He couldn't see Lee ahead of him any longer, but it didn't matter. When he reached 29, he turned north.

He had not paid cash for Wesley's revelation. If Lee really had the evidence to convict Easter, why hang on to it? Why wait until his brother's safety and silence were threatened to trot it out? Joe had been prepared for a fight with Shorter and hadn't gotten it. With Lee Meacham, he might be walking into all the fight he wanted. Lee almost certainly went everywhere armed.

He caught sight of Lee's bulldozer-yellow truck shortly after they had passed the restaurant; as usual, there were few other cars on the narrow two-lane highway. No one seemed to be following. Joe began to close the gap.

As he drew closer, he saw the silver glitter of a CB antenna. He had known there'd be a glitch. Lee could radio Gow anytime he wanted, giving him a description of Joe's car and a fix. Gow could have driven out the Alley; he could be up ahead waiting. If so, there was nowhere to run to. Joe saw Lee glance in the mirror. There was just room to pull off on the shoulder. He gave Lee twenty yards and stayed in the Sentra, his gun on his lap.

Lee kicked the truck door open, then stuck both hands out so Joe could see them. "I'm coming out, Hope." His voice was twangier, more phlegmatic, than Joe remembered it. "I ain't got nothin' on me. Don't shoot."

He slid down from the high seat warily, hands held high. His beard and hair looked softer, almost downy, and his plain white T-shirt was spotless. But he wore the same baseball cap, and below the brim his pale eyes, so much like his brother's, had narrowed, fawning. "I ain't looking for no trouble," he said, lips stretching off tobacco-stained teeth. "Fact is, I've been wanting to talk to you."

Joe got out of the car, letting Lee see the gun, but keeping it angled down beside his thigh. "Step away from the truck."

Lee sauntered obediently to the center of the highway. "You don't want to fool around too long out here in the open. No telling who might come by."

Joe hoisted himself up into the truck cab. The CB was crackling on what sounded like the police channel. With his free hand, he punched it off. "Get in my car. You're driving."

"Now why should I trust you?" asked Lee. "Word is, you're crazy. Maybe you done killed my brother already."

"I thought you had something you wanted to tell me."

"I can help you solve this case," Lee drawled amiably.

"Then get in the car and take your chance."

Lee clicked his tongue and shrugged. He ambled to the car, treading on the droopy cuffs of his too-long jeans. Sliding in beside him, Joe laid the .38 on his lap. Lee, he decided, smelled cleaner than he did. "Never drove one of these Jap jobs," Lee said.

"You put the gear shift on *D,*" Joe said curtly. "It means drive."

On the shell road to which Joe directed him, there was no sign it had rained. The dust rose like a scalding fog behind them. They entered the preserve and Joe picked one of the wooded turns at random. It was all random now, anyway, throws of game pieces. As soon as the trees shielded them from the road, Joe ordered, "Stop."

Lee hit the brake and the car stopped hard, its nose dipping. He turned toward Joe, flexing his thin brown hands on the padded wheel cover. "Is this when I get my brother back?"

"You'll get your brother back if I like what you tell me."

"I ain't responsible for your likes and dislikes."

"Well, I don't like wasting time, you can bank on that."

But Lee sat stiff and still, and for the first time Joe realized he was nervous. "You think you're so goddamn smart."

"I'm smart enough to wonder what it is you're scared of."

"I'm just warning you. This ain't no city sidewalk."

Joe thumbed down the hammer on the revolver.

"Okay, okay," said Lee. He let his breath out. "I got to reach in my pocket."

"What for?"

"Not no gun. A little pill bottle."

"Get it out slowly. Let me see it come out."

The label on the vial of amber plastic had Wesley's name on it. It had held a depressant, used, Joe thought, to control mood swings. Now it contained a bullet, a .308 Winchester, bedded in clean cotton, scored but perfectly preserved. Lee dumped the slug, let him look, then closed his palm.

"You dig that out of Amy Wells's body?" Joe asked.

"Nope. Out of a man's body. His name was Walter Cantrell." He accented the last syllable. "Two l's. I know because he was a county commissioner from Broward, and it was on all the news shows when he didn't come back from a hunting trip."

"Who shot him?" Joe asked obligingly, although he was pretty sure he knew the answer.

"That ass-kissing, cunt-licking Miccosukee bastard. Shot him and four others in the back from a hundred yards with a semiautomatic sniper gun."

"Easter."

Lee snorted, as if the breath it took to say the name gave off a stench that scorched his nostrils.

"But why?" Joe asked.

"Same reason he does everything. For the hell of it. He thinks he can do any damn thing he wants."

"And you were there?"

"I was in a blind watching." He blinked, a mechanical click of his chapped eyelids. "He dumped them down a gator hole, just like he did those other bodies. But they didn't stay there either. I brought 'em up."

"Then why isn't Easter waiting for the chair?"

"Because I didn't report it."

"Because you can't prove it."

"Monkey-fuck," snapped Lee, opening his fingers and closing them convulsively. *"This* proves it. I buried them bodies with the rest of the bullets still in them. Anytime I want I can take the cops right there."

"But you haven't."

"I wanted to wait." His eyes themselves were like the butt ends of bullets, steel circles with round percussive centers. "Until he got really sure of himself. Really sassy. Until he really had something to lose."

"Why do you hate him? Because he's an Indian?"

Lee shook off the accusation with a shiver like a wet dog. "Indians can be okay. Him I hate because he's a goddamn hypocrite. It was him fed that Wells girl a bunch of lies about me and my brother, so she could stand up in court and claim she figured it all out."

"So he knew Amy?"

"Sure he did. I seen her lots of times at his cabin."

"With him?"

"Sometimes with him, sometimes without him. That's probably why he killed her, because she was two-timing him right there in his own place, with Kang and anything else with a pulse. And then her standing up in court and acting so pure and fine!"

The tan hooks of his fingers had clenched around the bullet, but the eyes were still metallic, closed, their explosive force capped. "Why bring this to me?" Joe asked. "Why not go to Gow?"

"Because you got my brother, stupid."

Joe ignored the epithet. "What made you so sure I have him?"

"One of my buddies saw him last night with that other crazy bastard from Tampa. He's your stooge, ain't he?"

"Just what is it you're afraid your brother might spill?"

The centers of Lee's eyes seemed to deepen slightly, as if they had been tapped by the action of some lightly falling hammer. "He don't know nothing *to* spill, so get off it."

"So you're giving up your hold on Easter out of brotherly love?"

"Look here, dumbass," Lee hissed. "My brother ain't like other people. He can't take things like other people. You got him locked up somewhere, he's probably beat hisself to death trying to get out. He's probably already dead."

How true was it? Wesley was delicate, claustrophobic; he was in danger; Lee wanted to rescue him; and this was all he had to bargain with, this long-held secret evidence against an enemy he could not get at any other way. "Do I get the bullet?"

"What are you going to do with it?"

Joe tilted the gun up, leaning back thoughtfully. "This slug, and what you saw, has nothing to do with

Amy Wells. Or with these other two murders. Or with the guy who shot at me."

"So you don't fucking believe me."

"Not completely. I think you're hiding something."

"Oh, I'm hiding something, all right. I'm hiding my goddamn temper."

"But I think you're right. I think if Easter's that kind of murderer, he's probably *the* murderer."

"Think what you motherfucking like."

"I'll trade you."

"The bullet for my brother."

It worried Joe to realize that Lee wouldn't be making the deal unless he thought he was getting the better part of the bargain. But he had no choice, he had to keep pushing. He had a lot less than twenty-four hours now.

"All right," he told Lee. "I'll take you back to your truck. Go back to that restaurant down the road and wait by the phone booth. As soon as I can I'll call and tell you where to find him."

"No go," said Meacham forcefully. "You take me right to him."

"You've got your CB. If I don't come through, call Gow. How far can I get?"

They sat looking at each other, each plucking, testing, tugging at, the network of facts and lies and half facts between them, each listening for a single true note.

"All right," said Lee.

Joe put out his hand. Lee dumped the bullet into it. It was heavy, precious. "Can you back out of here?"

"You take me for a jerk?" Lee said.

HE AND SHORTER DEPOSITED WESLEY AT the mouth of the lane where Joe had parked with Lee. Wesley was docile, but mute. Shorter did not want to leave him. "He knew more than he was telling. It was an act."

"Well, you had tried beating it out of him, hadn't you?"

Self-consciously Shorter licked the scrape on his knuckles. "Damn it, Hope, this is a murderer we're after. A crazy man."

"I know that."

"Then don't preach, for God's sakes." He cut his bloodshot eyes sideways as they sped north up 29. "What are you going to do with that bullet?"

"I haven't decided."

"I say let's go round up this Easter."

"I don't think the two of us will be 'rounding up' Easter."

"Are you scared of him?" demanded Shorter nastily.

Joe said nothing. The bullet weighed in his pocket: useless, because it had no apparent connection with the

Wells case. Useless, unless. . . . "When you get to Alligator Alley up here, head back toward Naples."

"What are we going to do, turn ourselves in?"

"I hope not. Watch for a phone."

Lee was waiting as instructed. His responses were terse and ungrateful. "Yeah . . . yeah," then *click.*

Joe had taken the car keys away from Shorter. The trainer sat in the Nissan watching Joe sort out change. "It's hot in here," he said.

"So get out and walk around."

"It's hot out there, too."

"So shut up."

"Damn it, Hope. If you weren't so fucking scared of this Indian—"

Joe dropped a quarter in the slot and started dialing.

"You've got a gun," said Shorter. "I could buy a gun. We could take this guy. He can't be that dangerous."

But Joe didn't answer him. He expected the worst when he heard the sheriff's department receptionist. But Gow was true to his promise: The woman said, "One minute," and in considerably less than a minute Gow's gruff voice came over the phone. "Well, Hope, what took you so long?"

"It takes time driving back and forth across this damn county. Think of a way I can see you."

Gow fell silent. Joe let him think. "You got a car, right? You've seen the post office in Ochopee?"

"The one-room place? Where the tourists take pictures?"

" 'The world's smallest.' I'll drive out there. I'll sit there from noon to twelve-thirty. You drive back and forth. If you're not satisfied, don't stop."

"That's no guarantee."

"Much as I like hearing from you, you're the one who

wants the meeting. I assume you have a good reason."

"I hope we both want it."

"What I want is a break." Gow didn't say good-bye and Joe didn't either. Of one mind, they hung up.

Joe left Shorter back at the tumbledown house across the wooden bridge. He didn't like the idea of leaving him; he wasn't ready to lose him. He wanted Gow to respond the way he had planned, and do it in a hurry. But as usual Gow seemed to be on his own schedule. He was sitting with his legs out of the door of his car, in a coat and tie but hatless, his thin hair ruffling in the slipstream of the passing traffic. He looked less formidable than he had last night in the darkness. He squinted up at Joe dolefully. "Today's my birthday."

"Congratulations."

A load of tourists had pulled up at the tiny shack that served as a post office and were crowding past the mosquito netting to pose with the postmistress. "So let's see what kind of present you brought me," Gow said.

"I brought you a bullet."

"Where did you get it?"

"From Lee Meacham." Gow raised his brows. He clearly had not had any more sleep than Joe and his eyes had gone basset-hound heavy. "He *claims*," Joe went on, "he dug it out of a corpse he had fished out of a gator hole."

"Ah, shit," Gow said.

"Apparently you would have preferred a bottle of Jack Daniel's."

"Let me guess," said Gow. "Walter Cantrell."

"Allegedly."

"And who allegedly killed him?"

No, thought Joe, there was no bottom. You sank and you dug and you tunneled and it all just kept on going.

"I think you know," he said.

"And you also think," said Gow, "that I could use this bullet and this story to get a warrant to search the cabin, and maybe find something else that would tie Easter to Amy or to one of these other killings?"

"Call it a wish."

Gow took a big, sad breath. "You don't by any chance have a tape recorder in your pocket, do you?"

"Why should I?"

"It has occurred to me—a little late, I guess—that just maybe you're not quite what you say you are. Not that I don't trust Cruse."

"This isn't a department sting," said Joe. "This is you and me. Do you want to search me?"

To his surprise, Gow levered himself out of the car, a little sheepishly. "Where's your gun?"

"Belt holster."

"Stick it in your shirt pocket."

After a second, Joe wedged the .38 barrel-first into his empty shirt pocket. Standing there in the bright sunlight, with all the tourists' cars passing, Gow patted him down. He even jerked the shirt open as if to look for wires. "You'd never tie that slug to Easter," he said when he had finished. "And if by some chance you did, he'd be dead within a week."

"Then he did kill Cantrell?"

"I don't know if he did or not."

"Who does know?"

"The *story* is, he came up on this Cantrell and a whole bunch of others out on Snake Woman Prairie one day. They liked to go out there and shoot out of season, drive their ORV's around, get drunk. They'd been cited but they were hot shots over in Broward and they just laughed at it. This day, though, they'd strung up a live doe by her back legs, and they were using her for target practice, shooting parts off her, one at a time."

"So Easter fired to scare them and accidentally hit one of them?"

It might have been the pinging gravel thrown up by a passing car that made Gow grimace. "The story is . . . Easter picked them off one by one."

"Where's the gun?"

"My best guess? In a lake."

"What lake?"

"I didn't pick it. I don't know."

Joe heard his own resigned sigh, the hiss of faith and resolve escaping. He scratched his forehead in exasperation. Gow walked a few feet away from him, scuffing the graded sand and pebble shoulder. "Who in God's name *is* Easter?" Joe asked.

Gow overturned a worn bit of shell with his toe. "You know, Hope, in 1947, when Congress set up Everglades National Park, there was a law passed. The U.S. government swore to preserve and protect this land—this part of the world, which at the time at least was absolutely unique—*in perpetuity*. I think that means forever." The ironic snort that would have cheapened the weight of his voice went unexpressed. "When you read something like that nowadays, all you can think about is how simple-minded people are. Here we've got bad water pouring down the state on us, when we can get water at all. We've got people pressing in from both sides like a cancer, people who don't understand why if they've got the bucks they can't live wherever they want, even if they have to drain a town's well field dry or plow under the last six-hundred-year-old-stand of virgin cypress to do it. We've got the goddamn melaleuca tree out of Australia. Fire don't kill it, chopping it down spreads it, and it wipes out everything it moves in on. On top of all that, we've got the sea level rising, salt water backing up under us right now while we're talking. Thinking about it just makes me tired."

"What does all this have to do with Easter?"

Gow bent with a grunt and picked up a bit of shell, then dropped it. "Thought for a minute that might be a shark's tooth." He reached inside his coat and scratched his rib cage. "When I found out—never mind how—that Jimmy might have shot those men, I felt the same way I felt when I smelled that little girl on you last night, and maybe a lot like you felt about yourself."

Joe did not have time to brood over the condemnation. "Easter works for you. Undercover."

"We've got a serious poaching problem in the park. He's cut it in half almost singlehanded. We've tripled our drug arrest record since he started feeding us information. He saves lives, too: He helps us keep up with all these weekend warriors who forget what their daddies taught them about loaded guns when they get out in these woods and get drunk."

"Lee thinks he's the one who tipped off Amy Wells."

"She stood up in court and said she was the one who figured it out, but he did all the legwork."

"And you think that's worth Cantrell's life?"

Gow grunted heavily. "Well, whoever killed him, Cantrell's not coming back."

"You can't tell me Lee doesn't know all this."

Gow grimaced. "The way Easter's played it, Lee thinks Easter don't like him because Easter just generally don't like white people. And Lee don't like Easter because, among other things, Easter once ran him and some friends off when they tried to crash the Green Corn Dance the Indians hold every year."

Joe wished there was somewhere they could go, into shelter, out of the glare. "None of this settles the question of whether or not he murdered Amy Wells."

"I don't think he killed her. Why would he? He liked and respected her."

"And slept with her?"

Gow shook his head unhelpfully.

"If Lee Meacham talks—"

"If Lee talks—forget whether or not he can prove anything—we'll have reporters divebombing us like goddamn deerflies. Somebody'll crack some records and put two and two together. Once Easter's in the spotlight his cover won't last a week."

"So it's never been the Meachams you've been protecting, it's Easter."

Gow got belligerent. "Until and unless there's some real proof against him, I haven't done anything wrong."

"But it would be convenient, wouldn't it, if it was Lee who killed Amy?" The sheriff sighed and nodded. "Except you need proof he's guilty before you provoke him. Otherwise you won't have anything to buy him off with. So you don't want to pick me up yet. You need time."

"The minute I pick you up," Gow agreed, "he'll expect me to go after Easter. When I don't, God knows what he'll figure out."

"On the other hand, what if it's not Lee?" Joe challenged. "What if it's Easter or Kang or somebody else? What will you have to hold over Lee then?"

Gow had wandered back to his car, which, like the sheriff himself, showed the nicks and scratches of wear. He rubbed pensively at a gouge on the fender. "If it is, I guess I'll have to live with it. Maybe I'm sort of hoping for a miracle."

"You keep acting like you think I'm it. If you do, you're hard up."

"Well. . . ." Gow's face broke up in a slow smile. "When these old boys go after a big gator, the gator usually don't want nothing to do with them. He just crawls up in his cave. But the hunters, they go around on the bank and ram big poles through the muck over the cave and pound the gator in the back until he comes out again. They don't have to worry about whether the gator might whirl around and take a chunk out of one of the poles."

"If somebody wants a chunk out of me, I won't make it hard for them."

"No," said Gow. "I'd say you were sticking more than your neck out." He touched a finger to his tongue and rubbed at another mark on the car. "Just do us all a favor, and leave Miss Cindy Cruse at home."

"I've tried to. I want to."

Gow didn't look at him. "She reminds me a lot of Amy. Same heart. Same crazy spirit. I hope she don't learn what Amy did."

"She thinks she can help Kang."

"Well, maybe that's another reason somebody better get that gator out of that cave."

He climbed into his car, handing Joe a stiff little card. "My home number, and my mobile number. You need me, you call."

Joe took the card reluctantly, turning it in his fingers. "If Easter killed once, he'll kill again. What if he did kill again—when he killed Amy—and you could have stopped it?"

Gow blinked, drawing his legs in. "If I thought you were right—but I don't. If you are, well, I expect I'll pay for my lapses. But I have a feeling all the ones in my life I don't know about will cost me a lot more than the ones I do."

Joe felt that he should go on arguing, that there was some boundary of accountability he should defend. But the sheriff's solemn gaze had steadied, and for a second he saw himself as Gow must see him, gaunt, derelict, fugitive, and branded. "You want me to be of any use to you," he told Gow, "keep Orren and Hube off me for twenty-four hours."

"If I were you, I'd get rid of that rental. That was the first thing your buddy from Tampa thought you'd do, dump your car." The sheriff had reached to turn up the crackling radio, but turned it down again. He took a scrap of paper from his pocket. "Oh, that reminds me, your ex from Homestead has been calling for you. This is the number; she's not at home."

"Janet?"

"She sounded upset, but she said it wasn't anything to do with the Landry case. She wants you to get in touch."

He didn't have time for Janet. Gow saw him frown. "Promised I'd tell you," he said.

"What are you going to do?"

"Go back and sit on Kang some more."

"He hasn't told you anything?"

"Not enough to buy a cow turd. Oh, by the way, I've got my warrant for his trailer. You never told me where to find those pictures."

"Under the sink. Behind the plywood. I didn't want him accidentally dropping them in the toilet."

Gow speculated. "You saw them. You think if we look at them close we'll learn anything from them?"

"I don't know. I've been wondering myself." He shuffled in the shell. "I still say you could get a warrant for Easter's cabin. You could keep a lid on it."

Gow slammed the door, poking an elbow out of the open window. "If twenty-four more hours go by like this, and we don't make any progress, I'll have to, won't I?" he said.

36

DRIVING BACK TO PICK UP SHORTER, JOE started thinking about Janet, and about Gow's warning about the car. Would Janet lend him her little Honda? Like Shorter, he could switch tags, slow the search.

But Shorter was not at the shack. Nor was he walking along the highway in either direction. At first Joe floored the gas pedal in disgust, but gradually he found himself thinking about ramming poles through the mud to flush out gators. Gow was right: whatever you used for a prod was expendable. If he could get Cindy out of the line of fire, it wouldn't matter who else got hurt.

He found he had decided unequivocally that Easter had killed Amy Wells. Not on the evidence; on gut hatred. All he wanted now was to stop Cindy from learning what Amy Wells had, learning it the hard way, in the ultimate degradation of her quick true foolish soul to rotting scraps of flesh on the forest floor.

From the restaurant he dialed the number Janet had given Gow. It was long distance, but not Homestead. A receptionist answered, and left him waiting long minutes, soaking the sweat off his face with his shirt sleeve, before Janet came to the phone.

"Oh, Joe." He knew instantly something was very wrong. "I have to see you. Please come."

"Janet, where are you?"

"Working. I'm subbing for a friend, up on Kendall Drive in west Miami. So you won't have to go all the way to Homestead."

"Tell me what's the matter?"

"Oh, I can't. Not on the phone."

He should not have been surprised to find that Janet's strength, her calm, had been but a thin shell around a raw core of grief. Nor should he have been surprised, or dismayed, that he was the one she turned to when the shell cracked. But to have to soothe her now, with so little time, so few desperate hours left him, so much to find out. . . .

Yet, he thought, if Gow was right, then getting hold of her car might well buy him more time than he would lose by humoring her. He disciplined the impatience out of his voice. "Tell me where to come."

He didn't see the Honda in the parking lot of the small orthopedic clinic just off Kendall, but all the spaces warned that they were for patient parking only, so she might have parked in the back. He zipped the Nissan under a trashy row of white-barked melaleucas, thinking about what Gow had said about them. Joe had always heard the trees called punk trees. Their characteristic mess of seed pods and brittle, downed branches crunched under his feet as he climbed out.

Janet must have been watching. Suddenly, from across the lot, she rushed blindly into his grasp. She stopped on the brink of kissing him. "Thank God you came."

He pushed her away gently so he could see her. The prim white uniform, the stiff white cap riding neatly on her crisp brown hair, should have set off her habitual neatness. But the emotional disarray in her face, in the reckless way she held him, had somehow spilled onto her spotless facade. In some intangible way he had never sensed before she looked disheveled. Her skin was so dead and waxen he could have peeled it off her as he might have stripped the papery bark from one of the punk trees.

She wasn't crying. She was too distressed to cry. "Have they found out anything about Kevin yet?" she begged.

"I don't know. I don't think so. They're trying."

"You *must* know. You *do* know."

He gripped her cold hands but she didn't stop shaking. "I *don't* know. Please. I'm here now. It's all right."

"They won't tell me. Why won't they tell me?"

"It isn't personal. They can't compromise the investigation, that's all."

She ducked her head, burrowing close to him again, and her voice when she spoke was so muffled he felt her words through his heart more than he heard them. "I know who killed him," she said.

He made her look up. Her frightened eyes, searching his, had nothing to tell him, but much to ask.

"He tried to warn me." She talked fast, as if he might stop her. "He was . . . he had gotten mixed up with this man. They stole money."

"Kevin?" Plain, unassuming, white-bread Landry?

"It was the only thing like that he had ever done. He was miserable. He hinted to me. . . . I wasn't sure. He said he was going to turn them both in."

"What was this man's name?"

But she shook her head. "He didn't tell me. I think he was going to tell you. I think that was why he had to see you. Since you knew about the law. To ask you what he should do."

"But why didn't you tell Gow, Janet?" he asked, bewildered. "Why keep all this from us?"

"Oh, Joe. Turn in Kevin? Even after he was. . . . I

couldn't. But I can't live with it. Only I don't want the sheriff. I want you to find out."

He drew in a breath. It was one of his and Gow's unlikely scenarios—a totally unrelated event catching up to Landry just when logic made it seem the attack ought to have been aimed at Joe. And a stroke of luck for the killer, striking Landry so neatly at such great odds. "This is just something Landry told you?" he persisted. "Isn't there any evidence? any proof?"

She was silent a moment. Then she blurted, "There was a letter."

"Signed? With a name?"

"No! No, it wasn't signed. But it threatened Kevin."

"Where is it?"

"I burned it."

"Oh, Janet." He sighed. The tears had started flowing now. He folded her in his arms, feeling her break against him in unexpected places. She was feverish, shuddering.

"I don't want the sheriff," she whispered. "I want you."

"I have to tell Gow."

"No. No. I want you."

"Janet." He hushed her with a squeeze. "It's not that simple. I have a personal . . . situation . . . I have to take care of first."

She shifted against his chest to look up at him, blanched with a new worry. "But you're the only one who can do it. What if he gets away? You have to go do it now."

"Gow's perfectly capable. For that matter, so is Akins."

"No, please. You."

Her need was immeasurable and compelling, strengthened with his own guilt over the last time she had asked him to be generous and he had closed his ears. It was as if they had gone back in time, and she was still clutching, and he was still shaking off, the small shredding threads of their unravelling love.

"All right, me," he lied. "But I've got a problem and I need your help."

"Mine? But how?"

"I want to borrow your car."

She surprised him, pushing away stiffly with a flutter of confusion. "Oh, but I can't, I. . . . It's not here."

"Where is it?"

"Hunter has it. He borrowed it. This morning."

"Maybe I can find him. Where is he?"

She looked up, and beneath her candor was an unexpected, furtive evasion. She shook her head defiantly, not at him, he thought, but to shore up her own resolution. "I don't know."

It didn't ring true. Not coupled with that look of incongruous preyed-upon panic, as if she had sensed a broad-winged shadow drifting over her, and had retreated deep in her soul to hide.

"He didn't borrow it, did he?" Joe asserted suddenly. "He took it."

"No, he didn't. Why should he?"

"Because he wanted to go up to Orren's and pick up Cindy Cruse, that's why."

He had expected either denial or confession. But what she did was step free of him and then sway so ominously he had to leap forward and catch her. She put both hands to her mouth. Her eyes against her drained skin, blue-centered and unbelieving, unexpectedly made him think of the glazed realization on Amy Wells's face as she died.

"Her!" she whispered.

"He took the car, didn't he?"

"Yes, yes. But—" She shook her head slowly, her whole body rocking in his grip at the motion. "I never thought of her."

What she had guessed of Joe's own relationship with Cindy he wasn't certain. Who would have told her? He had thought that what she was hiding from him was Hunter's entanglement in Cindy's rebellion. But if she hadn't known? "Maybe I'm wrong. Maybe he's not with her."

"No," she contradicted, focusing ahead of her, as if staring down some mystic revelation, "you're right. I should have guessed it. I knew when he met her—"

She broke off hopelessly. Yes, Janet would have sensed the threat in Cindy. "It's okay." He tried unconvincingly to soothe her. "Hunter's a smart kid. He'll be all right."

"No," she said again, just as adamantly. "She's wild. She's crazy. She's kept him out all night once already, and he wouldn't tell me what happened." She collapsed her shoulders, sobbing. "Oh, Joe, she's going to get him in awful trouble. Oh, why couldn't she leave him alone?"

A tendril of hair had escaped from beneath the cardboard-stiff cap. He stroked the dark strand off her damp temple. "Don't worry," he promised. "If they're together, I'll find them. I won't let them get hurt."

But instead of accepting his reassurance, she disengaged her hands. Her trembling didn't stop, but it became less visible, moving inward, so that he could see the slate veins in her throat jump. She blinked back tears. "You will find them, won't you?"

"Of course I will. They're probably perfectly all right. Probably just running around wasting—"

"Nobody but you *could* find them, Joe."

It sounded like an intimation of disaster. Confused, he touched her hair again. "Janet, what's wrong?"

She looked away from him, into the past, but not into a past he remembered. What she saw he couldn't envision, where she traveled, he couldn't go. Overhead, the punk trees rustled dryly, rattling their rotten bones.

"Ever since Hunter was born I've had a nightmare. Ever since . . . I wake up at night and go into his room and he's gone. Someone's taken him away."

"That's normal. You worry about him."

"I've known ever since Kevin died something else was

going to happen. Something terrible's going to happen, Joe."

"That's your nerves. Imagination."

"No. There's something horrible happening. And there's nothing I can do."

"There's something *I* can do." He gripped her arms, hard enough to hurt her. She focused on him, and for the first time in long moments he knew she saw him. "I can get the hell out there after them. Except now I'm worried about you."

"It's all right now," she said softly. "I know you're going to find them. I couldn't have found them. I've done all I can." She shook her head again, still oblivious. "There's nothing I can do."

If she had gone on staring past him in that cold trance, he could not have left her. He would have come back to find her ice-rigid, frozen, or broken into a million pieces. But then a tear broke loose, and in that simple human admission of her grief, he read her struggle, and he breathed again. Now she came to him as he had hoped she would, catching his shirt and twisting it. "Oh, Joe, I know you think I'm silly. Or crazy. But I've just been so afraid. I've been so alone."

"When this is all straightened out," he promised, rocking her, "I want us to spend some time together. I want to understand. I want to know what makes you afraid."

"Are you sure, Joe?"

"Would you like it?"

"Oh, yes."

He was close to kissing her. He felt her realize it, and he felt her still her breathing and wait. But the last person he had kissed was Cindy—a truth he couldn't bear to tell her, but one she would have to know. He hugged her wordlessly instead.

"It's okay," she murmured. "I know you have to find them. I'm all right."

"You don't think you should go home?"

"I'm better off here, busy."

"I will find them. You don't worry."

"No," she said. "I won't worry now. There's nothing I can do."

He stopped at the big Indian reservation headquarters building to use the phone. Meek Kevin Landry an embezzler? Okay, tentatively he would buy it. The change of conscience, at least, was in character. Joe wasn't quite so sanguine about the mysterious letter. She had made that up to convince him. But her efforts to live with her guilty knowledge explained the intensity of her emotional crash.

But Landry would have to be Akins's and Gow's worry. He had more urgent business. It was beginning to be clear that it would soon rain. The northern sky boiled toward him: a foamy line of white, below it that blue-silted shadow, and overhead a fan of encroaching haze. The sun was working steadily westward. Chasing Cindy and Hunter around was going to be that much harder on slick roads in a downpour. The young fools.

He thought he understood what had happened. Janet had indeed guessed where Hunter had gone but hadn't wanted to admit the danger he might be in, even to herself. Joe had made her face the horror squarely, and it had stunned her. She might well sway in Joe's arms and retreat into shock: Hunter was all she had now. Losing him might destroy once and for all the peace and stability she had fought so hard to win.

Punching in Gow's number and his credit card number, Joe found himself wrestling once more with the irrational vision that had climbed up inside him the instant he suspected what Hunter was up to. He had no business being jealous of Hunter. Wasn't Hunter just a mixed-up kid, with a legitimate chance at what Joe had renounced?

Stop it, he told himself. But what he could not stop

was the sudden abject despair he was feeling, something that jealousy had nothing to do with. He had tried telling himself to be glad Cindy had Hunter with her. But he knew Hunter couldn't protect Cindy. Easter would flick him aside like an insect and do what he damn well pleased.

Once more he reached Gow easily. "I just got back from talking to Janet," he said.

"I know what you're gonna tell me," said Gow. "Cindy Cruse and your ex-wife's son, Hunter, are loose out in the Cypress somewhere."

"How did you know?"

"Cruse radioed me she'd run off again just after I left off talking to you. I sent out a description, and one of my deputies called back he'd seen a girl he thought was her riding north in a dark-blue Honda on Birdleg Lane about half an hour before. There was a young fella with her, he said. We made the car."

"Where's Birdleg Lane?"

"It's the turn you take up to Jimmy's."

"How long ago was all this?"

"About an hour and a half. I sent a man out there to look for her, but he didn't turn up her or the car or Jimmy, either."

"There's a thousand places they could have ditched the car."

"Well, I don't have time to beat the bushes for her."

"That's not all Janet told me," Joe continued. Quickly he outlined Janet's assertion about Landry.

"Well, I'll be damned," Gow said.

"It's not impossible."

"Right now nothing's impossible. I'll get Akins right on it. And I got more news for you."

"About Cindy?"

"No, about our case. We had a white Ford turn up stolen. That screwball Portman happened to be cruising the Trail looking for you and he spotted it. I reckon you can guess who had taken it."

"Shorter."

"Portman decided to follow him instead of calling in." Gow did not quite chuckle. "That's what I like best about working with you state boys—the way you cooperate."

"Let me guess. He led Portman to the Meachams'."

"Yep, straight to the shop. The place was closed up, so he started rummaging around. Portman finally got around to requesting backup, and about the time my men got there, Shorter had broke into a shed at the back of the property. Now you get another guess."

"He found a lock of Amy Wells's hair. A lock of that girl Cherry's hair." Something clicked. "Photographic equipment. Chemicals."

"Not bad for a beginner. Developer, fixer, all the stuff to go with it, hidden at the bottom of a trash barrel. There was even a red bulb."

Joe breathed out in guarded relief.

"So Portman decided he had cause, and looked around some more," Gow went on. "He let my men have Shorter, and he took a turn through the trailer the two boys share. In a drawer by Wesley's bed he found a picture."

"One of the set I found at Kang's?"

"One taken that night, but not one of the ones on the contact sheet. It showed Wesley. Plain as day." Gow paused. "Going at it."

After a minute Joe said, "There was someone else there, then. Holding the camera."

"Lee."

"Lee said it was Easter."

"Oh, shit, Hope. To get the heat off him and his brother."

"I just don't have your motives for protecting Easter."

"I told you I wouldn't protect Easter. Not for this."

"Nothing you've said completely eliminates him."

"Say Easter was in on it with Lee and Wesley, like Lee told you," Gow protested. "We pick him up, he immediately turns state's evidence against his partners, the Meachams. What has Lee gained? So the fact Lee named him is a point on his side."

Joe wasn't convinced. "I didn't tell you everything about how I got that bullet."

"I thought maybe you hadn't."

"Shorter had kidnapped Wesley. Wesley got scared, and he was the one who named Easter. That was what brought Lee running. He must have known Wesley wouldn't keep his mouth shut. He didn't want Easter picked up because he knew Easter would implicate them, but the best he could do was try to shift the burden of proof, discredit Easter, in a hurry. He hoped the story behind that bullet would work."

Gow ruminated. "I admit you could make your theory work. I just like mine better. For one thing, even if Jimmy is a crazed killer, I can't see him and those redneck boys holding hands."

"Unless, when and if you do come down on him, he conveniently produces ironclad evidence to condemn the Meachams."

"I see," said Gow thoughtfully.

"If Amy had something on him—"

"Which we don't know."

"But which isn't impossible, then he might have killed her to shut her up, at the same time he framed Wesley and Lee."

"I still like mine better. It's simpler."

Joe shrugged to himself. "All right. It's simpler. Where are Lee and Wesley now?"

"We don't know. Believe me, we're looking."

"Does Easter know you're after them?"

"He might if he's listening to his radio. Look, Hope, don't let whatever it is you've got against Easter run away with you."

"I haven't got anything against him."

Gow let it ride. "I guess it's too much to hope you'll come in?"

"I promised Janet I'd find her boy. And I have to find Cindy."

"My men will find them."

"You should have taken me into custody this morning."

"You're right," agreed Gow wryly. "I should have."

It was after five. "Look," said Joe impatiently, "you find Cindy and Hunter before I do, or else find the Meachams and get a full confession that lets out Easter. Then I'll know Cindy's safe and I'll come in."

"So you're still bound and determined to do it single-handed?"

"If I have to."

Gow chuckled quietly. "I won't waste breath telling you to be careful. Cruse is right, you're crazy, but Lordamighty, you keep things jumping, Hope."

The shelf of clouds had come hunting down from the north and west, engulfing the sun and the high summer sky. Standing in an ominous gust of wind outside the reservation building, he cross-examined his imagination. Because his imagination had created Easter, clapping him into shape out of swamp mud, pasting on sticks and spiderwebs for hair, bird droppings for eyes. The sane and logical answer seemed surely to pick up the lifeline Gow had offered. The case was breaking. Orren and Gow had the men, the information. Turn himself in, take his punishment, cut his losses. They would save her, and that was what mattered. They would get it solved.

Yet he could not shake the terrifying certainty that it was Gow's vision that was clouded, not his. He could see, as clearly as if he had written it, Easter winding Wesley up by the stem of his weakness and setting him to perform a retribution they both wanted, then trusting to Wesley's guilt to keep their secret. Gow seemed to doubt that Easter would have left himself open to a defense that had turned out so fragile. Yet for how long had Easter staked his life on Gow's tongue?

And there were things here beyond reason, beyond logic. Lee said Easter had already killed once, horribly. What if he had killed again, more horribly yet? And again? What if he found himself needing less and less reason, less and less logic? What if all the killings piling up on each other had become at last a bloody dance whose beat he could not stop?

He looked up at the sky. There was no sun at all now, no light, just a residual leakage from the ground and road upward. On the horizon the sky plunged from slate to blue-black, and peering up for yet more omens, he saw flights of white birds materializing above the tree-tops, beating feebly ahead of the darkness in directionless alarm.

He stopped well out of sight of the cabin, concealing the Sentra in the brush. The pines under the brewing storm shelf hung absolutely motionless. From all around came muted tickings, like the slow hearts of hidden watchers. Doubling low so that no one watching from the cabin porch would see him, he slipped up the narrow lane of palmettos. His own footfalls struck the sand and pine needles with a muffled resonance he felt must carry for a dangerously long distance, but he did not know how to be quieter. He had felt certain he would come upon Janet's car, but he didn't. He edged around the corner of the trail with palmetto fronds shielding him and saw the quiet cabin, apparently empty. There was no sign of the swamp buggy; the airboat was still in its shed. He paused, gun ready, hoping that something would stir on the shadowy porch.

But when confirmation came, it came as he had known it would, from behind him, silently, disdainfully: he saw its motion late, out of the corner of his eye, and barely had time to draw and wheel to his left, toward the narrowing trail into the tangle of forest into which he had pursued Kang yesterday; it was only because he wanted to be sure of his aim that he didn't fire, and then he realized he had no need to. The huge brindled dog just glanced at him once with an intense, unexpected intelligence and then veered toward the cabin, nose working, disappearing around the back of the building as serenely and noiselessly as it had appeared. Its tongue was snaking in and out, its broad, mottled dewlaps and multicolored forehead smeared with an unmistakable, rose-colored residue of blood.

So he had not, after all, wanted this revelation. He had not, after all, wanted to be right. But now that he was sure he was right, he grew more certain than ever this was his duty, his problem. He was the one on the right track. No one else believed him. Only he could save whatever was left to save.

The gun still in his hand, he turned away from the cabin and down the path where Kang had driven his Jeep yesterday. Moving slowly, nerves bared, he suddenly made out automobile tracks in the bare sand before him. Not Kang's Jeep tires: the tread was too fine and too shallow. Suddenly, right overhead, came a very loud clap of thunder, and he sucked in his breath as if the sound had been a blow. Still the trees didn't stir. The trail wound left. He saw the movement in time to drop to a crouch and slither up under the brush at the side of the path, and so he could watch Easter as unseen as he had watched Kang yesterday. The car sat hidden in a shaded gap in the palmettos, and Easter was shutting the door very softly with one hand, balancing his big M16 with the other. Then he stepped back and stood there, turning his head from side to side by infinite degrees. He was not languid now; he was stretched into a metallic rigor as unwavering as that of the deadly gun itself.

Joe knew he was listening, and he tried not to breathe, though he knew ordinary human breath was not the sort of thing Easter counted on hearing. In fact, Easter turned and looked directly through the fronds toward him. He was wearing a camouflage suit whose organic greens and browns seemed to have knitted over his swamp-water coloring like matted algae. Joe could not be sure their eyes met, but something—a connection, a sharing of intent—passed between them. Then Easter smiled and turned and in a few steps disappeared.

And in that smile had been a dose of the pointed malevolence Joe had sensed from the start, the pathological gloating of a killer, an ugly glee that underscored the certainty Joe had felt in the cabin clearing. It would all be played out now, between the two of them. Suddenly his own life did not matter. Bringing Easter down for his sins was all that did.

Ordinarily he would not have dreamed of outstalking the Indian. But as he sprang up after him, the impending culmination made him feel carried, protected, inspired. His feet seemed to find quiet places of their own accord, and the foul thickets gave way. As he drew alongside, he glanced at the car briefly, took in the bare seats, saw no blood, didn't stop in his pursuit to look closer. Wherever Cindy was, whatever had happened to her, was now part of his business with Easter. It would all come together out there, somewhere, unheralded and at once.

Whatever the reason, keeping up with Easter was absurdly easy. He moved slowly, sometimes stopping altogether. At first it seemed to Joe that the Indian was deliberately waiting for him, but then he realized that most often he stopped to listen, as he had by the car.

The forest, as he had known it would, led downward. The thunder seemed to have drawn off a little, but the shadows had thickened. The mud-choked trees began to twist and writhe, and ferns sprang up, with narrow, root-strewn avenues among them. Nor had the swamp done with tormenting him. He was making his way awkwardly over slick jumbled logs when the curtain of clouds dropped another foot, and instantly a thousand screeching voices exploded all around him, accusing and harsh. From impossibly near came a guttural, hollow, almost feline complaining that started on one side of him and echoed on the other and drew sweat on every plane of his body before it resolved itself into the caterwauling of invisible arguing owls.

He shook himself, realizing with dismay that in that moment of distracting him the swamp had betrayed him, and once more Easter had disappeared.

But Easter, he thought, would not make the mistake Kang had; he would not reappear unless he wanted to. Joe inched forward. He saw with relief that the Indian had left footprints in the softening muck. Ahead, through the warped trees, the pond itself, the heart of the slough, came into view. The little trail, the mucky footprints, led right to the edge of the water.

Ah, no. But he made his way doggedly forward, against his will, against the deepening going, against the exposure of the light.

At the edge of the pond, planted in Easter's footprints, he stopped. He had only two choices: go on and confront whatever was waiting, or turn around and run.

He started forward. The water was cold, the mud thick and sucking. On the second step, he found there was no bottom; he sank to his knees.

Could this possibly be right? Could Easter have come this way safely, silently, quickly? But there had been no tracks leading off along either shore, and to his left, fallen trees thrust out bare branches in an impassable tangle. Would the going toward the right be smoother? But a single floundering step told him the water there was even deeper. Directly ahead, halfway to the far bank, lay yet another deadfall, a jumble of stark roots long ago swept to the pond's center and stranded. He set his sights on it grimly. At each step he held his breath until he stopped sinking. Thunder came again, nearer. It seemed to send a shock wave through the water. He moved slowly, hating the wet, cold, seductive drag.

Now he could see the jumble of footprints emerging from the water, the trail breaching the darkness ahead. So he had chosen right. He had almost reached the deadfall; a sunken log, part of the jumble, blocked his crossing. To lift a foot over it, he clutched at a rotten branch near his head for balance. Only as an afterthought, at the last moment, did he glance up before he settled his hand.

This time the snake was not half a room away from him. This time it had let him get close, and now here it came, a twist of brown and amber peeling off the branch at him, launching itself head first. He flung himself sideways and backward, sprawling hard, the water spraying up and around him, and like the most potent of his nightmares, the thin hard ribbon of snake wound up between his legs. He raised the gun out of the water, and only some innate scrap of self-preservation stopped him from blowing his own balls off. By the time he had the gun leveled, the snake was gone. Something big splashed behind him; water lapped over him. He rolled, up to his chin in ooze. Easter was wading smoothly toward him, the rifle slung on his back. The Indian bent down and straightened, the snake looping out of his fingers. Joe pushed up on his knees, jerking the gun out of the muck where he had dropped it, aiming it straight through the snake's narrow gut right at Easter's heart.

"I wouldn't fire that," said Easter calmly. "Like as not it'll take your hand off. Barrel's packed full of mud."

EASTER MADE NO ATTEMPT TO MOVE. HE
let the long twist of snake's tail wind through his hands.
Joe straightened slowly, dumping the silt-laden scum
from the barrel of the .38.

"Kill it," he said.

"What for? It won't hurt nothing."

"It came at me."

"It was trying to jump in the water. Brown water
snakes do that. It's moccasins that stand their ground."
Carefully he pivoted and flung the snake away from
them into the water. With a twirled shiver it disappeared
beneath a knot of floating leaves. Easter turned back.
"How'd you know the girl was here?"

"Guessed."

"Yeah, I heard you're good at guessing."

"What did she say to you this morning?"

"That's my business."

"Is she dead?"

"I don't know yet."

Joe jerked the gun. "Let's go find out."

But Easter shook his head. "First put away that cannon. You wouldn't shoot me on purpose, but you just might trip."

"Don't be so sure I won't shoot," Joe answered shortly.

"Bullshit. You can't follow these tracks, and I can."

"Your tracks?"

"I don't leave tracks. Hers. And a man's with her."

"An eighteen-year-old kid she talked into coming up here."

Easter's lips curled in his habitual half smile, but his eyes had gone blank.

"Unless you've already killed both of them," Joe said.

Easter looked over his shoulder, then past Joe, to the woods beyond. "For the last couple of months somebody's been breaking into my cabin, leaving these same tracks. I tried locks, but then they started cutting screens and breaking windows. I been thinking it was Lee Meacham."

Joe kept the gun aimed. "If they're Meacham's tracks, where are Hunter's? It doesn't add up."

Easter just turned his palms over. "Time's what's adding up," he said.

As if in agreement the thunder rumbled, muffled but still near. Joe gestured with the barrel. "You come on past."

Easter just shifted the big rifle higher on his shoulder. Slogging past Joe, he turned left suddenly, toward the wall of brush at the end of the pool. To Joe's surprise the water barely came to his knees. On the far shore he turned back, smirking. "You walked into the deepest hole."

Joe fitted the .38 back into its holster. "I didn't see any signposts."

"I reckon not."

Joe, too, skirted the edge of the opaque water. He stopped several feet short of Easter, his fingers still curled around the butt of the revolver. Just by the edge of the pond there was enough light for the Indian to point out the slurred gouges. "What size shoe this kid wear?" he asked.

"I haven't the faintest idea."

"Too bad," said Easter. "That's the kind of thing that would help."

He set off, as if not in the least worried about Joe behind him. The ground rose, and in the firmer humus they found fewer prints. The woods were pitch now, the close air trembling, and suddenly there came a blast of white light that penetrated deep between the slits in the overhanging branches. Immediately the crack followed, abrupt and brittle, trailing off into a booming rumble that seemed to go on and on.

"What if it rains?" Joe called to Easter.

"What do you mean, what if?"

"Then you won't be able to track them, will you?"

"I don't know."

The thunder gave out and again there was silence. "But I think I know where they're headed," said Easter.

"Where?"

"You'll see."

The trees, he realized, were thinning out, slender cypress taking the place of the gnarled and nameless hulks bent by the grip of the strand. But as they emerged from beneath the thick canopy, he saw that the cypress trees were not dark against the clouds but light vertical scratches on an utterly kohl canvas, the whole world a negative, the sudden stretch of grass, the dark lines of the other strands, all suffused by an unreal blue glow. Easter stopped, looking south across the open prairie. Joe stopped, too, ten feet away. Easter barely glanced at him. "The one thing I ain't wild about is lightning," he said.

"So go back."

Easter shifted his rifle again but didn't unsling it. Just ahead of them, so close Joe could have thrown a rock past it, a thin electric finger skittered down and then vanished. The thunder came right on its heels, dry and harsh. Joe's skin tightened. "Squall line's a ways off yet," Easter judged. "Come on."

He moved quickly. Joe had no choice but to follow. Ahead of them the leading edge of clouds hung so low they could have touched its dirty tatters. Another strobe of light pierced downward, ephemeral and deadly. Behind this stab there seemed to be no thunder. That was how the blow would come, Joe thought, silent and unseen.

And all the while Easter's back was a clear target before him. He could have killed him easily, and maybe, for a second, wondering if the Indian had lured him out here beyond the reach of help on purpose, he considered it. But he knew he was not going to. Not unless he had to. Not unless he found out for certain that Cindy was dead.

"How far is it from here to the Meachams' camp?" he called abruptly.

Easter flicked a glance over his shoulder. "Good ways. Couple of prairies and a big strand."

Above the trees the black curtain of sky had come alive, parting, thickening, rifting, unveiling behind it a blue and blacklit luminosity through which the intermittent lightning descended, writhed, dissolved. Wind crackled through the limber treetops. The lightning came down like tongues, seeking human heat and motion. Even Easter, it seemed to him, started at the unpredictable flashes, stooping as he ran.

At last the faint trail they seemed to be following led them back into shelter. Easter stopped. Joe hung back warily. The Indian jerked a brusque shoulder. "Keep quiet. Come on."

The black ground softened, and there the footprints began again, not as deep but still distinct. Joe kept up determinedly. This time when Easter stopped, Joe knew he was going to. Just ahead the light changed, turning silver. He prayed they would not have to do any more wading. But this time it was not a pond cutting a gap in the forest. It was the long metal cigar shape of a crashed plane, once painted white but long ago overwhelmed by the damp. Its body cavity had been raked open, the twisted aluminum edges of the wound still glistening; they could see through to a row of windows that looked out on the wall of verdure that was slowly eating it up. It all looked deserted. Suddenly and decisively Easter stood.

Joe followed him across the rotting logs the plane had severed, stepping up into the torn fuselage itself. It contained no seats, no compartments; instead it was as bare as a scraped-out bone. An old carpet, littered with trash blown in from the trees, covered the raw metal floor.

Forward, a rotting curtain shielded a narrow passage to what remained of the cockpit. Just to the left of the passage a hatch had been torn open, a network of vines worming in. Joe crossed, keeping an eye on Easter, and looked out. Below him among the weeds and ferns glittered the shattered remains of dozens and dozens of whiskey bottles and the more durable cylinders of beer cans, like the spit-out shells of an enormous weapon. Easter edged past Joe with a knowing tilt of his thin lips, thrust back the rotten curtain, and disappeared beyond.

Joe took out his gun and cautiously followed. There in the dim light from the shattered windows dangled the desiccated remains of two human beings. They had been hung by the neck, their clothes rotted to dingy gauze, their skin flaking from the tobacco-colored bones. They were long past the point of stinking. Someone had propped the pilot's seat against the wall of the cockpit below the effigies, and before it, on the battered console, sat a single burned-down candle stuck to a plastic plate and a pint bourbon bottle, a finger of liquid still in it. Easter had settled into the chair, at last shifting the heavy gun from his shoulder and bracing it, muzzle up, between his thighs. He eyed the .38. Joe stuck it loosely in his belt. "Did you shoot them?" Joe asked.

"Hell, no. I found them like that."

"And you didn't call the sheriff to come get them?"

"What for? They were just a couple of Colombians."

"And you stripped the plane?"

"No, somebody had already seen to it." He picked up the bourbon bottle, uncapping it.

"Your brand?" Joe asked.

"I never touch it."

"Then whose?"

"Poachers, hunters, kids from Miami wanting a private place to party."

"You thought Cindy might be here."

"Her tracks led here."

"Well, she's not here. Not alive, anyway."

Easter set the bottle down lazily, shrugging.

"So let's get going."

But Easter tilted his head back. "Listen."

On the roof of the plane Joe could hear a sudden, hard, staccato spattering. Then it stopped.

"You won't be able to see two feet in front of you," Easter said.

"I can't sit here."

"I don't want to," said Easter, "but I guess I can."

The spattering came again, harder, threatening and abrupt. The rising wind carried the faintly burnt smell of rain with it. The light dimmed yet another notch, so that the skeletons were just laddered silhouettes against the plane's slit eyes. Joe let the curtain drop, leaving Easter enthroned at their feet.

He thought about making a run for it, fighting his way back across the prairie and through the strand and finding Hube and Orren. Easter suddenly reappeared through the curtain, balancing the gun in his bent arm. If Easter shot him now, Joe thought, no one would ever find his body. But all Easter did was plant the gun against the wall beside him and dig a rolled joint and a Bic lighter from his shirt pocket. "You smoke dope?"

"No."

Easter lit the joint calmly. The bittersweet aroma

overwhelmed the rain scent. "Lee Meacham's been telling tales on me, hasn't he?"

"I wouldn't know."

"Sure you would. Half a dozen people saw your friend
from Tampa pumping booze into his brother last night.
Knowing what I do about you, I know you made hay out
of the situation."

"So what? I thought you were above the law."

Easter sucked in smoke. "The law's not what I'm worried about."

At the back of the plane was a closed door leading into
a compartment, probably what had been the head. A
sliver of pale daylight from the gouge in the plane's side
leaked under the door. Joe tried it, but it resisted.

"Tell me about the little Cruse girl," Easter said.

"You tell me about Amy Wells."

Easter was holding smoke in his lungs. He let it out
slowly. "So we can compare notes?"

"So you did fuck her?"

"Once or twice," said Easter casually. "I would just
hate for Dave to know about it. He feels bad enough already." He pinched the joint out with his fingers, dropping it back in his pocket. "Amy told him she thought
someone was after her, probably Lee, but he told her she
was imagining things."

Joe could feel the stuck door giving. The line of daylight widened. "Where did your dog get that blood on his
face?"

Easter stiffened. "What blood?"

"I saw him at your cabin. His face was smeared with
it."

"Maybe he caught himself an armadillo."

Joe turned back to face him. "Or maybe he found
some fresh meat."

They stood meeting each other's eyes. Easter let his
arms drop to his sides. "Get this straight. I didn't kill her
back at the cabin. I didn't kill her at all."

"So where is she?"

Almost indifferently, Easter hoisted the gun again, cradling it. "Out here somewhere. Or don't you believe her tracks either?"

"I didn't see *her* tracks. I just listened to you telling me you did."

"You know what I think?" said Easter, suddenly vehement. "I think you're a fucking liar. You don't give a shit about catching no murderer. You want to hang me because you think I might make a move on Cindy. Well, you better get on with it, because I will, and bro, she'll beg for more."

Sanity, logic, all the virtues he had been pursuing, told him he should not react. But suddenly, out here, so far from reason, the chance he had been waiting for seemed to have caught up with him. One side of his soul preached caution; another side of him knew, screamed at him, that the answers were here, and only the most visceral resolve would deliver them. From the start, Easter's spirit had been like a ghost, trailing and taunting him, certain he would run. But now he had an unassailable mission, and a duty, and he was goddamn through giving ground.

So—not without thinking but without thinking in words, thinking only in the clench of his muscles and heart—he put a hand on the barrel of the rifle and shoved it upward, striking at Easter's jaw with a full angry sweep of his arm.

Rage was not quite enough. He missed as the Indian ducked, coming up under Joe's fist into his belly. Joe dodged, still holding off the M16. To his surprise Easter suddenly let go of it, and with the resistance he had been fighting gone, Joe stumbled forward. Before he could recover, Easter straightened and stepped around him, locking his hands together into a mallet he aimed at Joe's kidney. Again Joe rolled clear, getting a grip on the rifle as Easter bent for it. He didn't let go when Easter pulled up on it. Easter hauled him across the plane and lifted a foot and kicked him loose, knocking his head against the jammed door of the compartment; then he straddled him, and Joe found himself looking straight up the gun into the black funnels of Easter's eyes.

"You heard me," said Easter, breathless. "She'll like it."

"Like Amy Wells liked it?" Joe gasped. "Like Walter Cantrell liked it? You ass-fuck him before you shot him, too?"

Easter's lips curled back. Joe didn't hear what he answered. A wind blew through the plane, cold and rain-laden. From over Joe's head, on the compartment door, came a solid thump. Then another. With a growl Easter stood back, drew up, and kicked the door back on its hinges. Light flooded in. Easter's face changed. He plunged forward. Joe rolled onto his belly, grappling for his own gun. But Easter had turned. Behind him was the big hole in the plane's side, gray daylight pouring in. In his arms was a bulky shape. He threw it at Joe. "Fuck that, Romeo." Then he turned, rifle pointed skyward, and jumped.

The thing in Joe's arms was wet and cold and sticky. He hurled it away with a stifled cry. It was not her. But it was her clothes, her flamingo shirt, her jeans, stuffed with the wadded-up remains of an old foam pillow, smeared, drenched, sprayed, with still-viscous blood.

He pushed up, stumbled into the compartment, tee-tering on the lacerated floor. The thing had been hanging from an overhead strut, bound there by a strip of rag. He plucked at it. It came loose in his hands. It was an Ocean Pacific T-shirt, a man's, roughly Hunter's size. From the neckline down, covering the logo, ran a gummy triangle of blood.

He clambered through the hole into the clearing. He saw no sign of Easter. Once more the rain rattled off the plane roof and the quaking vegetation, big hard clear drops that left Joe's face stinging. This time the pummel-ing didn't stop, but thickened to a numbing assault. There was a crack that might have come from the breaking up of a volcano, and a flash beyond the trees, atomic and chilling. He felt his hair rise, his nerves tingle. Ahead reared a green clump of elephant ears the size of dinosaur scales, the stiff leaves quivering. Joe pushed through them. Here it was nearly pitch, the rain deflected, knifing in sporadically. Before him, Easter was kneeling on the black forest floor. The Indian straightened, turning with the blade of his stiffened fingers between them. The tips of his fingers were red, peppered with the black organic dirt.

Without a word he wheeled and set off through the darkness, nose down, hunched. The flash came again, so white-hot this time the rain itself seemed to sizzle, and the crack sounded right on top of it, on top of Joe, so that he ducked and gasped. When he could see again, all that was left of Easter was a trodden place in the ferns and brambles, a trail working its way faintly upward. He plunged forward, the rain coming harder; the trees began to thin again, their crowns suddenly wrenched toward him by the wind.

He emerged from the woods into a slate fog, and looked around him for the cypress prairie, but as he faltered there it suddenly began to rain, to *really* rain, so hard he could see nothing, so hard that even with his hand to his forehead all he could make out was a liquid opacity in which he detected tremors but no bearings, no known shapes. His clothes grew soaked in seconds; his hair streamed.

Then from the heart of the icy torrent came a burst so nerve-searing he was sure he must have been hit, though when he heard the thunder he knew he had lived. And in that moment so long and yet so fleeting, he saw, like a surreal etching, the limber writhing spikes of the cypress stretching on and on around him, and among them, above the grass and palmetto, a moving form that might have been Easter, might have been anyone; then it was gone. He had lost all sense of where he was; he began struggling forward because the grass and rain seemed to give way in that direction, and as he hurried, in this seascape where there was no chance of thinking or planning, he heard, or thought he heard, a human shriek, shrill, lung deep, possibly female, and he thought what it cried was his name: *"Jo-oe-e!"*

He couldn't tell where the cry had come from. The wind rose and rushed him, and suddenly he found himself fighting a suffocating wave of air and water, so cold, so forceful, so solid, he toppled backward, stumbling in the bowing grass. The rain came at him in huge wheeling blades. "Where are you? Cindy? I'm here!"

Then, not twenty yards away, he saw rise, like a great licking tongue, a huge white rope of light. It seemed to issue from the throat of a single bare tree, which just for that second, in its monumental effort, gave off its life energy by the hundred thousand volts. Something exploded, spinning out shrapnel in monochrome arcs; then it all went out, leaving a black streak on his retina, and the air stank and he felt the shock wave behind the wind like a heart attack. Close on that assault came another blast, broader, enlightening, and he saw the bent-double trees, the tracks of the hissing rain.

He had seen something else, too; he blinked, but there was so much water in his eyes he couldn't clear them; he stood fighting the buffeting wind and waited, and sure enough the light came again, the strobing on-off-on that froze shapes out of the void. And there it was, a glimpse subliminal, ephemeral, as soon as he saw it the image already fading to memory or illusion: the figure, bare to the waist, running toward him, one arm flung out, the mouth open and screeching, the wind twisting the sound as it carried it, this time clearly Hunter's voice: "Help me! He's killing me! Jo-o-e!" And beyond, the ghostly shape of Easter, the raised rifle, aimed unmistakably at the two of them, at him through Hunter's naked back.

The thunder burst simultaneously, and before it died came another strobe, this one so bright the shapes themselves were white torches, photons sucked up in a vortex of radiation, and then he heard or did not hear, knew or did not know, the gun's disturbed reptilian popping. Something caught him; he seemed to soar up high, as if a wave had swept under him, and the impact of landing he somehow missed, didn't remember. All he knew was that he was drowning, that he couldn't breathe, couldn't feel. An immense shadow passed over him before he could shrink from it, and it was the water on his face, its incessant heavy-footed dancing, that told him that the shadow had not taken any of him with it, that he was all there, hurt but whole. He struggled at last onto his belly; beneath him flowed a clear, hasty river into which were dropping big dollops of his blood.

He put his hand to his forehead, and it came away scarlet; then his eyes filled, his vision fogged; he felt the pain for the first time, felt sick and faint. Then Hunter was here somewhere. Perhaps dying. But if he wasn't dead already, he would know where she was.

But Easter was back there, too, possibly seeing him move and even now aiming. He didn't know what to do, nothing was right, to rise was to die, to sink to let them die, nothing answered. Crawling forward, he saw, in the cutting torrents, a hint of motion, something flesh-colored disappearing—Hunter? He had a fleeting intimation the shape was slighter, female. But the intimation could have been wishful thinking, desperation, the way his stricken vision faded in and out. Still, it could be Cindy, escaping Easter, escaping the deadly prairie. He could not be sure of anything. In his confusion, all he could think was that if he could catch up to that shape as it fled from him, he would know.

Dazed, he pushed up and stumbled forward. His head weighed tons, and it was all he could do to keep his legs under it. He came to trees he could hold on to, bounce off of, and sometimes, like a surly friend, the lightning granted glimpses, though knowing what lay ahead didn't help.

So he ran back into the swamp, under the shield of the trees. He had no idea where he was going, whether he was tracking the figure or taking the trail back to the plane or plunging deeper into the forest; he just pushed through where he could, in a fog of pain and rage. He didn't think until he had struggled a long way to open his mouth and shout their names, first Cindy's, then Hunter's. Now everywhere he put his feet he found rising black water; he knew that he was lost, and getting more lost by the minute, and he was hurt and losing all chance of saving his own life, let alone hers.

So he stopped. He stood still. He put his hand to the gash in his forehead and found his blood thickening. Under the trees the leaves slowed the rainfall, and the thunder bursts were beginning to pace themselves, the lightning flashes to seem less dry and electric and deadly. He turned around and around in place. The options rushed him. Find Hunter. Go back. Find Cindy. But how? Reason, damn it. Where was Easter? Coming after him?

He stopped spinning, sick and dizzy. Something knocked against his foot, and instead of jerking away, he looked down into the shadowy water and found that it was only a branch, caught in the steady downward current. Yes, there was a current, all that water rushing to the lowest point, even when common sense told him the ground had to be level. And where was that lowest point likely to be? A pond.

So, between throbbing bursts of pain, he began to follow the slope, using the gathering water to guide him. By the time he saw the glow that marked the clearing ahead of him, he was inching along knee deep, hanging onto branches against the rapid flow. When he emerged from the trees the pond itself had grown so wide and turbulent, so mottled with the still-pummeling rain, he was not even sure it was the same one. But he made himself take stock and saw the deadfalls along the bank, now on his right, and the lone deadfall at the center where the snake had jumped out at him. He felt relief settle over him. His head stilled a little. Now he knew where he was.

But what next? His first instinct was to turn and plunge back into the forest, as if he had one chance in ten of finding his way back out onto the prairie, of finding Cindy in all that expanse if he did get there, if she even was there, in the still-raging storm. Where was Hunter? Lying dead in some bramble-choked eddy? Or had he already struggled back to the cabin, and was he even now frantically driving off after help?

He was putting together a sickening guess at what had happened. Only one thing made sense. Easter had cached Hunter and Cindy out on the prairie, planning to lead Joe to them and then murder them all together. Somehow the Indian's victims had gotten free; certainly Hunter had, anyway. Joe had seen Easter try to kill the boy; he had tried to kill Joe as well. And now, having failed, he'd be after them, ready to finish what he'd begun.

But where was Cindy? Still out on the prairie? Floundering around in the forest? Driving off with Hunter? He just didn't know.

Swiping with his soaked sleeve at the graze wound in his hairline, he made up his mind: he would go back to the cabin. If the Honda was there but Hunter and Cindy weren't, he would come back out here and look for them, however dismal the prospect of finding them. If the car was gone, Joe would go, too, and get to a phone.

Wading around the shallow end of the pond was treacherous. Once he lost his balance and toppled, roiling the water even more. There was a sudden splash among the dead branches and a dark sleek shadow disappeared in the flood. He started, but it had been an otter. He had caught just one glimpse of its huge black eyes.

By contrast the trail back seemed easy to follow. The ground rose, the vegetation changed, the soil was soft but not swamped. He saw the parked car through the trees before he reached it and judged, almost before he stepped out of the woods and approached it, that Hunter had not been near it. He almost paid it no attention; he almost turned and headed back out into the woods without looking inside. Then it occurred to him, perhaps as an artifact of his slowly-clearing disorientation, that if Hunter had left the keys in the ignition, he should somehow take charge of them. So without really thinking what he was doing, he edged out of the brush and bent groggily to the driver's door, looking in.

The driver's seat belt had been pulled under the front seat back before being locked into its catch.

HE STRAIGHTENED, TRYING TO SUCK IN
air that had turned to slush. He backed away from the
car.

Easter did this, he thought wildly. Easter did this just
like he did everything else. Easter set this up.

Beyond the car there was movement. The dog had
come back. It stood staring at him soundlessly, its coat
ruffled. Then it lowered its head and rooted forward, licking at a rain puddle that had collected under the car's
left rear wheel. When it raised its head to look at him
once more, a fresh red wash smeared the peppery
freckles on its flat nose.

He started forward. The dog met his stare with cold,
translucent eyes. Its upper lip rose, the yellow spikes of
its canines gleaming. Its growl rose up into Joe's body
through the ground. Abruptly the dog leapt, a hard
twisting pack of muscle. Joe jerked out his gun and shot
it twice through the skull.

It fell, mortal after all. He veered around it as if it bled
venom, kneeling by the car. A thin fluid was plunking
slowly from the chassis into the shallow puddle. He put
his hand up under the frame. When he withdrew it, the

drops stippling his palm were watered-down splotches of blood.

He rose, circled quickly, ducked into the front seat, bent to look under the dash, on the floor, snatched open the glove compartment. He found no keys.

He circled back to the trunk, hoisting the .38. The first shot scratched the edge of the lock but ricocheted. He aimed straighter. But if she was in there, if, by one chance in a million, she was still breathing. . . . He hesitated, his gun hand suddenly limp.

But as he raised the gun to aim again, from behind him came a whoosh like the earth inhaling. He wheeled. Over the tree tops, in the direction of Easter's cabin, flames and black smoke were boiling skyward. The shock wave followed, rattling the windows on the car. On the tail of the blast came a shriek like the shriek he had heard on the prairie, a violated cry for mercy, too high, too wild, to be male or female, and to his ears once more calling his name.

He wheeled and ran. The cabin burned with a roaring force that made the light rain sizzle. He ran through standing pools of water turned fiery beneath the shafts of fire and smoke. He rounded the corner and fell back. Flames romped out of the doors and windows, and before his eyes the fronds on the banana trees blackened and withered. From within, firecracker bursts rat-a-tatted with the vengeance of executions. A lemon tree beside the porch went up like a scented torch.

"Cindy!" he howled. "Hunter!" No one answered. He pocketed his gun and battled forward, arms up, squinting. The porch roof crashed in on itself in a wave of heat. He bolted back out into the trail, and knew when he saw the tracks in the wet sand he had once more let himself be baited. When he reached the spot where the car had been, the dog lay with its guts splashed out where a tire had flattened it, and the car was gone.

Somebody else. Somebody he had overlooked com-

pletely. A welter of motives he had put utterly out of his mind. . . .

Thinking did no good, took too long. He ran back down the palmetto trail, past the flaming cabin. The cut in his head throbbed, making him dizzy. The Nissan was where he had left it, out of sight in the brush.

He was wrestling the keys from his pocket when he heard the shot behind him and spun, fumbling his gun out. Easter stood in the track, the M16 pointed skyward. Joe drew a long breath. His gun hand steadied. But then Easter ran straight up to him, into spitting range of Joe's .38. If he had moved one bit slower Joe would have shot him. Their eyes met and for a moment Joe saw what he himself must look like: dripping, dirt-smeared, and panting. "Goddamn fucking cocksucker," Easter gasped.

"Where is Cindy?"

"I don't know, man. I couldn't find her."

"Did you see the car go?"

"Yeah. I couldn't catch up to it."

"Who was driving?"

"One person. I think it was him. I couldn't see good."

"There was blood dripping out of the car trunk," said Joe, not lowering the .38.

Easter put his free hand, fingers spread, on his flat belly. For a moment he just stood there and breathed.

"Could he have fucking carried her back here?" he asked.

Joe made a decision. He turned.

"Where are you going?" said Easter.

Joe didn't answer. Easter caught him from behind. Joe wheeled, the gun up.

"So shoot me," said Easter. "I'm coming with you."

"The hell you are."

"He's got a .38, too," said Easter. "I saw it. He'll kill you."

"And you can stop him?"

"Yeah," said Easter simply. "I can."

Joe looked at the M16, as if it could tell him something the Indian's living gaze couldn't. He no longer knew what to believe. Easter sensed his challenge. "You think I'd burn my own damn cabin? You're nuts."

There was still that one chance that Cindy was not in the car, that she was out on the plain or in the woods somewhere. Did he want to leave Easter here with her?

"I'll be motherfucking right behind you, anyway," Easter persisted.

Joe jerked the car door open. "All right, come on."

Neither of them spoke until they had plowed wildly back through the forest to the shell road. There was no sign of the Honda. Joe turned south by instinct, while Easter sat watching him mutely, his gun upended between his knees. Joe was thinking about the pictures, about the thing he had found in his motel room, trying to piece the fractured days together. Nothing said that either of the Meachams or for that matter Easter couldn't have found out from Gow where Joe was staying. But Hunter had been there. Hunter knew.

And he was seeing, too, the rusty square stain by the bed in the motel room. The knapsack Hunter had brought with him to Tampa had been exactly the right size.

Easter, studying his frown, seemed to pick up on his speculations. "You know this kid, huh?" the Indian asked.

Joe glanced at him, at the deadly weapon. "Do you?"

"Don't you ever answer a goddamn question?"

"Not unless I'm the one with the answers. What happened out there?"

The storm had cut moonscape arroyos in the road shoulder, and Easter grabbed the dash as the car plunged down and up again with a jolt that made Joe's head scream. "The blood trail led out on the prairie," said Easter.

"You claim he laid that to get us out there?"

"Yeah," said the Indian with barely controlled anger. "That's what I claim."

"You saw him before the storm hit?"

"I just made it out in the open before the rain started. All of a sudden I heard someone call behind me. I thought it was you, but when I turned around it was him." The sinews in his brown jaws locked at the memory. "I started for him. He was covered with blood and I thought he was hurt. I thought Meacham must have dragged him out there and cut him."

"Why Meacham?"

"Who else was there?"

"Meacham wasn't anywhere out there."

Easter shrugged brusquely. "When I got close to the kid I saw he had that goddamn .38 in his hand."

"Why didn't you shoot him?"

"He had the jump on me. I ducked down into the grass. Then the rain hit. I heard a scream, and I was dodging around under cover, trying to figure out where it came from. Then there were a couple of close lightning strikes, and I saw the kid running away from me, running toward you. If I'd fired at him, I'd have killed both of you. So I fired up in the air. When I could see again, you were both gone."

"So he shot me?"

"Well, I sure as hell didn't," said the Indian, half wheeling at his tone.

"They've got evidence tying Amy Wells to the Meachams."

"I figured that when I heard they were looking to pick them up."

They were coming up on the highway. Easter leaned forward, pointing. Tracks in the wet shell veered ahead of them, unmistakably eastward.

"He's my ex-wife's son," Joe said abruptly.

"Then you're his stepfather?"

"No. We were already divorced when he was born."

"Then what has he got against you?" Easter asked.

Joe had nosed the car onto the asphalt. There was a gap in traffic but he didn't start forward.

"We'll fucking lose him," said Easter.

Joe put his hand to his forehead. The blood had dried. "Let's get this straight," he said. "We still don't know who killed who or what happened. We take my wife's son alive. You don't blow his head off just because you happen to feel like it."

Easter didn't smile. He just shifted the big gun as if to make it more comfortable. "I got a feeling he'll make the rules, not us."

For the first long, constricted stretch of the straight highway, the soaked road stretched ahead of them, glistening, wide open. If the Honda was indeed ahead of them, mirages and rising mist cloaked it. To the east the mean clouds were jostling each other seaward. Joe was certain Hunter would turn south, toward Homestead, and he prayed they would catch him first. They flew past the little town of Monroe Station, then Oasis, then through cypress strands and past scrub prairie, into a troubled black night. The Nissan sailed at ninety, shimmying. The sun plunged behind them, an incandescent quarry shot down and snared on trees. From time to time they picked up trucks and campers and tourist cars.

The road swung southeastward. Suddenly Easter sat forward. "There he is," he said.

Joe could not be sure. The car Easter pointed out was just a dark blur caught behind a riff of bogged-down traffic. But as they gained on it, he could make out the pale rectangle of Janet's nursing sticker. "We run up behind him and spook him, he'll take a chance and kill half a dozen people," Easter warned.

Joe thought about it. He let the Nissan slow a little.

"He's passing," Easter said.

Sure enough, the Honda had pulled out, accelerating

boldly; they saw its taillights flash as it dodged back into line.

"We're coming up on Forty Mile Bend," said Easter. "Where the Loop Road comes back in. Once we pass that, there's not a hell of a lot of places he can turn."

They were both right: the Honda pressed straight on, just ahead of them, until they reached 997, where it did indeed veer south toward Homestead, just as Joe had guessed. Traffic on the straight road on the outskirts of Miami inched along bumper-to-bumper, a circus of headlights chasing back the encroaching dark. Joe stopped at a 7-Eleven with a phone and gave the male department dispatcher his name and his fragmented message: "My ex-wife's kid—he may be the one who's been killing all these people. I think he's headed for my ex-wife's place in Homestead—"

The cool voice that interrupted him had gone wary. "Where could Agent Cruse reach you?"

"Nowhere. We need some goddamn backup."

"Sir, I'd stay calm if I were—"

Joe broke in impatiently. "Tell Orren I'll be waiting for him. Tell him to hurry up."

Easter patted the M16 reverently as Joe whipped back into traffic. Joe was still disoriented, still thinking. He still found it hard to believe. He kept trying to picture Hunter. An ordinary kid—right? With the deep heat of youth, of impressionable emotion and insecurity moving him, sometimes very close to harm. But a killer? It was so much easier to believe that the killer of all these people would show it, that you would be able to look into his eyes and sense the ferocious abandon of all that was normal, of all sets of rules.

He glanced at Easter. "You know," he said, braking for a light, "even if we're right, and Hunter did shoot at me, and did kill Landry, and even if he did kill Cindy . . . that still doesn't prove he had anything to do with Amy Wells."

"No, it just makes it damn likely."

"But somebody else could have killed her, and Hunter could have latched onto her story to lure me down here so he could get his crack at me."

Easter turned to him, his eyes perfectly adapted to shadow, nocturnal. "Are you opening it all the fuck back up again?"

"The Meachams had those pictures."

"So did I," said Easter. "That what you mean?"

Joe said nothing.

"Look, for the last time, if it was me," said Easter, "why the fuck haven't I killed you? Why didn't I kill you back at the fucking plane, when I had you on your back?"

"Maybe you think Hunter has some evidence and you want me to help you shut him up."

They sat looking at each other. But Easter just spread his palms on his wiry thighs. "You've got a hell of an imagination," he said coldly. "But I guess you'll find out before it's over. In the meantime, believe what you motherfucking want."

Now it was really dark. Inch by inch they waffled along, rushing lights, changing lanes. Joe kept spinning alternatives. What if Easter had beaten him back to the cabin, rigged that seat belt, set off the explosion? Up ahead of them Hunter could be driving stunned, in a panic, going for help. Joe fought to maintain his resolve, resist the agony that was wearing on him: headache, stomach cramps, breath hurting. Sometimes he thought he could smell Easter, the way you can suddenly smell a wild animal when you get too close to it. He hoped he would not have to dive between anyone and Easter's big gun.

They passed Kendall Drive. Was Janet still there working? Waiting for reassurance he wouldn't be able to give . . . ?

Janet. Janet, who knew Hunter had stolen her car

and had raced off into the swamp on some irrational errand. Who had not wanted Joe to know that. And who had then fed him a story about a nebulous plot, for which the only evidence was her own memory, and which, had he not been caught up in saving Cindy, would have drawn him away from the Wells killing, from the Big Cypress, and from her son.

There was a gap in the traffic coming toward him. He hit the brakes and spun the car around.

"What the hell is the matter with you?" yelped Easter, rubbing his head where he had smacked it on the window.

Joe didn't answer. The car's turning radius wasn't quite tight enough, and he had to bounce up on the shoulder and wait out the teeming traffic for a chance to worm back in. If Janet had suspected Hunter of killing Amy, of killing Kevin, then she must have known that when her son and Joe finally faced each other, the confrontation would end in blood. When she heard Cindy was with Hunter, she knew Joe would be bound, for Orren's sake if nothing else, not to give up until he found them. All her lies, her efforts, to keep him away from Hunter had done no good.

He whipped down Kendall. Now the refrain made sense: nothing she could do. And if Hunter knew she suspected him? How much time had they lost stopping at the 7-Eleven? Too damn much: He didn't recognize the car coming at him by its headlights, but he knew it as it raced past him. He saw Hunter's profile. And saw another figure against the far window. Grimly he hung another U in a gas station, while Easter braced against the doorframe. "That was him, wasn't it?" Easter said.

"Yes. He's got his mother with him."

"What does he want with her?"

"I don't know yet."

"Then where's he going?"

"I don't know that either." He forced his way in and out of the other stacked-up drivers, until he found himself only two cars behind the Honda. A light ahead of them turned red. Joe started to brake.

"He's going to run it," said Easter keenly. "You're clear on my side. Go."

It was not strength but inertia, the suck that had been after him all along, that carried him through the red light and whipped him around the intervening traffic so that he fell in one car behind the Honda. "I don't think he saw you," Easter said.

But without warning the Honda turned left. This time Easter didn't ask where it was going. He just sat forward, nursing his gun.

And all maps, all memories, said the same: There was nowhere out there it could be going. All the clean red lines of civilization died out there, in green variegation. Emptiness. Disappointment. A termination—because from that point it all went on forever, always the same.

Still, they followed, Easter straining forward like a starved cat, alert and poised. They left residential outposts behind quickly. Abruptly all around them spread the black interminable flatness of sown fields, over which the distant lightning now flashed in sheets. Only here and there white lights sparkled like snagged bits of sanity left when the tide went out. Then pungent weedy walls cut off their view of the lightning and they could smell stagnant water. The Nissan bounced off onto sand and gravel. They could still see the Honda's red taillights; it drew away a little. Beside him, Easter seemed to lock in more fixedly, his concentration growing even stiller and more closely honed. Suddenly Easter hissed, and Joe hit the brakes. The Honda's lights had disappeared.

"Think he turned?"

"No. He just stopped."

Joe let the car inch forward. Easter let his window down. The unpaved road was damp, and in the mud, frogs were bawling. The Nissan's high beams picked up a red glitter: the rear end of the Honda, against shadow, a good way ahead. Easter was right. It was not moving. Joe stopped the car.

Easter reached up and clicked the dome light. It came on, and he snapped it to the opposite setting, so it wouldn't come on at all. Then he put his hand on the handle of his door.

Joe turned toward him, the .38 in his hand. "Leave the gun here."

"You're crazy."

"If I'm not, I'm getting there."

"You still don't think it's him?"

"I don't know."

"You got to go with it, man. You're setting him up to kill us."

"You said I could believe what I wanted to believe," said Joe quietly, "and that's what I want to believe, that you should leave the gun here."

He couldn't tell if Easter's face changed or not. It was just too dark. Sight was not the sense he needed. But whatever he needed failed him. He just couldn't tell.

But then Easter said, "I'll trade you. I'll take your gun, you take mine."

The Indian cartwheeled the rifle and extended the butt toward Joe. And at last Joe reversed the .38, offered it, and made contact with the rifle. It was hard and heavy and cold; it had not even absorbed the warmth of life where Easter had been gripping it. "Reload the cylinder," Joe said, nodding toward the revolver. "Shells in the glove compartment." Working by feel, Easter obeyed grimly. Then he opened the car door. For a moment he was a presence in the darkness. Then he was nothing, invisible, gone.

Joe got out of the car. He left the headlights on, skirting the fan they cut in the shadows. The big gun was strangely light, buoyant in his grip. He kept his finger off the trigger. He couldn't see the sky, except as a vague, paler wedge over the brush and trees. Except for the continuous, urgent bleating of the frogs, everything was still.

As he drew closer to the car, he grew certain no one was in it. No one alive, at least. The closed trunk looked innocent. He stepped down off the shoulder a little, hugging the shadows. He raised the rifle, though he still didn't touch the trigger. He drew even with the door of the car.

"Hunter," he said.

No one answered. He took a turn, seeing nothing.

"Hunter. Come out and talk to me. What's going on?"

Then something in front of the car, off to his left, shifted, pale in the pale shell. He wheeled. She was lying on her stomach, white nurse's dress rucked up, dark hair flaring messily around her. He dropped to his knees beside her. She was crying. He listened for the sound of the footsteps he was tempting, and put a hand on her shoulder. She struggled for a second to stop him from turning her, then yielded. Her eyes at first were unseeing. A big bruise was spreading across her cheekbone and temple. Knowledge came back into her face and she threw her hands over it, writhing away from him. He looked around, but still there was no sign of Hunter. Nor of Easter. The rifle in his right hand, he gathered her to him with his left. "Janet. Janet. Stop."

She let him lift her, a dead weight. Then she started shaking, so hard he wondered she didn't shatter. He held her awkwardly, stroking the dust and shell fragments from her body.

"*Joe,*" she said.

"Where is he?"

"Don't do it."

"I don't want to. Where is he?"

"Don't hurt him."

"Did he hit you?"

"He didn't do anything. Please."

"Come back to the other car. Hurry."

"He didn't do anything," she repeated, more fiercely. "I know he didn't. Come on."

She hooked a hand in the front of his shirt. "I did." "You did what?"

"Killed Kevin. Tried to kill you."

It did no good to tell her not to make up more stories. "Fine. Fine. Then it can't hurt him if you come with me."

"You think I'm hysterical," she went on. "But I knew you had come down here to get him. I knew you were after him. You must listen. Don't hurt him. It's not his fault."

"You tried to stop me from going after him this afternoon, didn't you?" he asked her gently. "All that crap about Landry?"

"I knew you would try to kill him. Please don't kill him," she begged.

He managed to turn her. Down the narrow road the Nissan's lights were bright and distinct and blinding. But then she cried out, a broken bird noise. Her hands flew up to her face. Hunter had risen from the ditch, maybe twenty yards away, waiting for them just out of the wedge of light. The shirt he wore now hung open, his long muscular arms dangled. His face was in shadow, his boyish haircut ruffled. The shape of his right hand muddled the silhouette of his dark gun.

Joe could hear them all breathing. Such a small sound in the immense discordance of the swamp. Such a small disturbance in all that inert matter and breeding gas. Yet for that moment, the frail energy that moved them defining a tiny triangle of horror, a concentration of feeling that briefly but surely gave meaning to that hurt-bounded space to which they had all come.

"What has she been telling you about me?"

The ache was there, the plea, the denial. Joe had heard it from the start, the child's cry, had known what he was hearing, but had not known what to do about it. The headlights cast the boy's face in nightmarish relief, making the web of his tears glitter. Certainly it was the face Joe remembered: full of aching rancor, of fear born of vulnerability. But by the light of his own fear he saw, too, a stifling desperation, and knew he had sensed it before, had seen it, but had wanted no part of it. Had closed his heart and ears.

There was a prayer in his own voice: for Hunter to let go of this horror he had in his power. "She hasn't been telling me anything about you," he said.

"Don't lie," said Hunter. He turned very slightly, so that she was the one he singled out. "Bitch. Murderer." He spoke the words so plaintively they might have been endearments. "What have you said?"

"Put the gun down, Hunter," she whispered. "Please, darling. He won't hurt you. He knows."

Hunter looked down at the gun, tilting his face. Again an edge of light caught it. He looked bewildered, lost, surprised. "It's not loaded." He raised it over his head. Click. Click. Heavily he lowered it to his side again.

"I told him," she said again, forcing the words as if she couldn't find the air for them. "I told him. It's all right."

"Did you tell him then?" the boy said, suddenly savage. "Did you, Mother? Did you?"

"Hunter, please. . . ."

"Did you tell him about trying to kill me? Did you tell him that?"

"I didn't mean to."

"You did mean to."

"I didn't."

Hunter turned on Joe, moving closer. "She hates me because of you, because she says you made her have me. She tried to kill all of us. When she killed Kevin instead of you, that was all right, because she had to kill him anyway. She didn't hate him." He made a sneering face. "She *loved* him. But he knew."

Joe pulled Janet closer. She had gone still and cold under his hand. It seemed he could stop it, change it, if he could force sense from the boy's troubled logic. "What did he know, Hunter? Are you telling me she also killed Amy Wells?"

"Fuck Amy Wells."

Janet gasped each time Hunter spoke, as if his denials cut her. Joe felt his way, his own gun hand unsteady. "And where is Cindy? What have you done with her?"

"The Indian," said Hunter wildly. "The Indian got her. Ask *him* about that Amy Wells."

"He's telling the truth," said Janet. "Oh, Joe, he's telling the truth."

"I want to go back with you," said Hunter fiercely.

"Go back where?"

"I want you to take me away from her."

"So put the gun down," Joe urged softly, "and come to me."

But Hunter only shook his head. "I told you it was empty," he countered. *"You* put your gun down. *You* come to me."

Maybe, though he didn't know it, that was when he made the fatal decision: when he didn't put Easter's gun down but instead moved it infinitesimally, and said, "Open the trunk of the car."

Hunter's head tilted. He seemed to frown, perplexed.

"Now," Joe ordered.

Hunter took a step backward. "I don't have the keys. She took them."

"Open the trunk," Joe said.

Hunter edged sideways, toward the car. The big revolver, with its swollen chamber, shook in his uncertain hand. He stopped a few feet from the car, staring down at it. Then he moved the gun, as if he had forgotten it was empty, bringing it up to the level of the trunk lock. But he didn't fire. He moved again, the gun hand coming up, his face a black oval with the two moving chips of his eyes sorting light into hard digital flashes. Suddenly Janet flinched again. Hunter whirled. Easter stood there in the headlight swath, feet apart, the short-barreled .38 almost swamped in his dark fist. "Drop the gun," he said.

"It's empty." The boy's voice cracked. "Didn't you hear me? It's empty. Didn't you hear it click?"

"Empty chambers will click," said Easter coldly. "If it's useless, do what Hope said. Put it on the ground."

"You took her. You killed her. I saw you."

"Put the gun on the ground."

Hunter turned to Joe. "He's a killer. He's killed lots of people. I can prove it."

Easter said nothing.

"I can show you," said Hunter. "I know where people he killed are buried. I can take you there."

"Who told you that, kid?" Easter's voice had a sting to it. "Lee tell you? Or maybe Amy, the night you murdered her? She knew."

"*I* murdered her?" Hunter's cry took on a fervent incredulity. "I didn't murder anybody."

"So none of us did," said Easter. "Put the gun down."

Joe was never sure about the seconds that followed; he did not think anyone else ever knew just what happened, either. He thought he saw Hunter's .38 bounce upward, saw Easter point his gun. He saw the white flurry of Janet's body between Easter and Hunter; he knew there was an explosion, muffled by flesh but still too loud. Then Easter was sinking, trying to let Janet's limp form down slowly, trying to back out from under her, get his own gun hand free. Hunter, still aiming, stumbled back and wheeled to cover them, keeping them both at bay.

"Murderer!" he shrieked, face contorted, body wrenching.

"She's not dead," said Easter from where he crouched over Janet. He had worked the revolver clear, but kept it out of sight, letting it dangle. "It got her in the shoulder. Put the gun down."

But Hunter wasn't listening. "You took her away from

me! Just like you took the others." It was to Joe he turned, and he was sobbing. *"He* killed her. Don't you believe me? I tried to stop him. He killed her and he fucked her. I saw him. He fucked her and fucked her and fucked her until she died."

Joe heard Easter's breath catch. Hunter spun back to face the Indian. He flung the gun up between them.

"You lying bastard," breathed Easter.

"Fucked her and fucked her and fucked her." Slowly Hunter drew the hammer back.

"Hope," said Easter, in a monotone so cautious the words were almost indistinguishable, "somebody's going to die now. If you still got doubts about who ought to, don't take more than a second to make up your mind."

For just one instant, Joe stood motionless. He thought ever afterward that he saw Hunter's fingers clench around the trigger, in the infinitesimal second before the big rifle in his own arms fired.

The worst of it was that Hunter did not fall right away. Until long after the rattle ended, he seemed to frolic insanely in the headlights, pattering his feet and spinning, head snapping back and forth, euphoric and possessed. Enough lifetimes passed for all three of them before he went down with soft sounds leaking out of him, like an overwrought child consenting finally to sleep.

Slowly, drawing a dark hand across his mouth, the Indian hiked himself the rest of the way to his feet. Hunter's gun had fallen a few inches from his outstretched fingers. Easter kicked it, so that it scuttled through the shell. It came to rest not far from Janet, where she still lay inert.

Easter knelt, putting an arm around her shoulders, and at his touch she whimpered. He helped her sit up. Her face was as blanched as her uniform; on her shoulder spread a big dark bloom of blood. Joe saw her see Hunter lying there. She patted the shell dully, reaching for him, making pointless sounds. Easter steadied her and eased away from her, crossing to bend over Hunter.

Joe stumbled past them toward the car, thinking absurdly that Cindy's body must be there, it had to be there. Easter looked up, his eyes, like Hunter's, brittle trinkets in the flat planes of his dimly lit face.

"He would have made you kill him sooner or later," Easter said. "It was what he wanted."

"It wasn't what I wanted."

"It's done now. No use—" The young man's body stiffened. "Watch out."

Joe turned. Janet's searching hand had fallen on Hunter's gun. She picked it up and sat with both feet spread before her, her uniform a filthy tangle around her, pointing it at them.

"He was right," she said, in a slow voice so muted it might have been her own mind talking to itself. She moved the gun from one of them to the other. "I did try to kill him. Over and over. It never worked."

Joe felt Easter trying to make himself smaller. He could not.

"But I killed the wrong person, too," she said.

The gun flared pure red, lighting her face.

For just that second it seemed something had burned through and then burned out, leaving only the scar of its passing. And a long, long time later, he found that he was still standing there, a breeze lapping his sweat. He heard Easter walk away from him, crunching softly. Another spitting gun burst punched through metal. The car trunk flew open without Easter's having to touch it. The new smell emerged, just ripening. A piece of moon had come out. It shone down on the white discarded tangle and the dark one, the two thrown away lives so near him. Easter was lifting something bruise-blue and heavy from the trunk. When he spoke, for the first time he sounded beaten. "Deer parts. Wrapped in plastic. Fucking bloody cut-up deer parts," he said.

HE AND EASTER DID NOT SPEAK TO EACH
other; the time for accusations and denials was gone.
They got in the Nissan together. Easter directed him on
back roads through the raw fields so that for the most
part they could stay off 997. They stopped once, for Joe
to call the department. The same man answered. Joe
could not tell if the man believed anything he was saying,
but he told him anyway. He also bought them puny
flashlights and batteries, ignoring the way the cashier
stared at the blood crusting in the grooves of his forehead and his filthy clothes. Easter stuck his light in his
belt. "If they came to the fire," he said, "they'll have the
cabin staked off."

"Is there another way out to that prairie?"

"We can come in the backside of it, if you don't mind
getting wet."

Once inside Collier County, it was not long before the
Indian gestured. "Turn here." Then, much later, they
stopped at a dead end where the track nosed under a
silver, percolating expanse of water spiked with dwarf
cypress. They got out of the car. "See that black line?"
said Easter. "That's the tree line, the strand the plane's

in." He looped the rifle strap over his shoulder, pointing to the hollow-gutted moon, which had trailed them. "Keep it at your back. If you get lost, walk toward it. You'll hit this trail."

The flashlights were useless. The moon shrank as it rose, like a disk of chalk dissolving, dripping its milky contamination at their feet. But Joe moved through the treacherous footing with an unstoppable fury. She was not dead. He had not failed her. Later, off in the distance, he saw lights, heard far-off shouts, and the roars of motors bouncing off the dark westward tree line. So they had believed him; he was not alone in searching. But he was alone with that desperate avowal: She was not dead. He had not killed her. And if anyone was going to find her, he would. He shuddered at a bitter memory: oh yes, he was the cop with ESP.

But the dark and futile night wore on. The lights ahead began to move with the coherent rhythms of walking people, sorting themselves into clumps and small armies. He began to be able to hear words. Sometimes Easter's rail-thin shadow faded in and out of the moonlight near him; other times it vanished. Joe began to realize that his time was growing shorter: Once he reached the rafts of bobbing lights, someone he knew would catch up with him, and his part in the search would be over. In a listless corner of his tired mind he wondered if it mattered. How many people were searching? Fifty? A hundred? Barely enough to cover a tiny sector of the tremendous pinwheel of darkness. How could he help?

Yet he couldn't quite give himself up. He had no destiny out here, but he did have a duty. Deliberately he veered northward so he wouldn't intersect the other searchers, picking his way across the plain. He couldn't see Easter any longer; he half expected to meet the Indian coming back, the body in his arms.

. . .

So perhaps he had given up; perhaps he searched out of habit, a leftover reflex of conscience. He only knew that when, after the passage of an indeterminate lifetime of anguish, the shape evolved out of the darkness before him, it took him a long, unsteady moment to realize it was not Easter's craggy scarecrow form.

He turned on the flashlight for the first time since he had left the car. She blinked, cried out, putting her hands to her face. She was wrapped in something opaque and shapeless. He said, "Cindy. Cindy. It's me. Joe."

He could feel her trembling before he reached her. She wasn't crying. She was swaying, almost flinching from him, unbelieving.

"Jesus," she said. "Joe."

He held her up as she started to topple. The thing wrapped around her was a sheet of soaked, stinking canvas, stolen, perhaps, from a camp somewhere. "Joe," she whispered. She began shaking her head dully against him. "I'm so tired."

He wound his arms around her. He couldn't talk, didn't want to know.

"He was going to kill me," she stuttered. "Kill me . . . I got away. In the storm. I've been walking. . . ."

He forced his question between them. "Did he hurt you? Did he—"

She may not have known what he was asking. "He tied me up. He left me. I found some rocks, I cut—"

But there was one more thing he must finally be sure of. A moment when he must let doubt near him. "Cindy. Who?"

"Hunter," she said.

He kissed her grit-smeared forehead, feeling the strength beginning to ebb out of her.

"I'm sorry," she murmured.

"It's all right. He won't kill you now."

A shadow like a dark worry coalesced out of the

moonlight: Easter, working his way to them. He stopped, hands dangling, ten feet away.

"It's over," Joe told her, looking past her to Easter, though they couldn't see each other's faces.

She was trying to withdraw from him, find her balance, stand on her own. He wasn't sure she had seen Easter. She looked up at Joe. The moonlight touched her young girl's face, making it shimmer. So she was crying. He wished he could have said, *I love you.* Before he could decide what else to say, she sagged against him. He wasn't sure if she fainted or just lost the power to stand.

He had to kneel to get under her. Suddenly Easter was there, too, helping to catch her, contending with him for the right. But the Indian was not strong enough to take her away except at gunpoint. For just an instant, Joe thought he might try it. But then he let his hands once more droop to his sides. Slowly Joe lifted her, winding the stiff canvas sheet around her. "She *is* breathing?" Easter asked.

"Yes."

Joe could not read his face. The darkness had claimed it. Finally the young Indian turned. "Cabin's this way," he said.

They didn't reach the cabin. They had walked, Joe staggering in the rough going under his burden, what seemed like much too long, when yet another shape appeared against the moonlit plain. A light seared Joe's eyes. "Thank God in Heaven." Gow.

Easter pulled up, facing the sheriff. Still aiming the light, Gow stepped up to Joe. But something in the way Joe held her must have stopped him. He clicked the light out. "She all right?" he asked.

"I think so. I think she's sleeping now."

"Did he rape her?"

"I don't know."

Gow swung the light on Easter briefly, then turned it

off. "Let's get moving," he ordered. "Ambulance waiting."
He started ahead of them across the prairie, surefooted
in shin-high rubber boots. The moving lights had drawn
closer. Again voices materialized. "Listen to me, both of
you," Gow snapped in low tones over his shoulder as
they walked. "Who killed those people down there?"

Neither Joe nor Easter spoke.

"Don't play games," said Gow tersely. "We're about to
meet up with a search party. I need to know."

"I killed Hunter," said Joe. "She killed herself."

"You killed him with Jimmy's gun, then?"

"We had traded."

"You'll swear to this?"

"Of course."

He heard Gow sigh above the splash of their feet in
the water. "Goddamn rattler," said Gow suddenly.
"Watch out." But Joe couldn't see any snake and didn't
change course. Approaching lights began to flicker before them like a platoon of fireflies. Gow signaled with his
own light. Shouts on their left were picked up by shouts
on the far side of them. "We've got her!" called Gow.
"She's all right!"

The lights became electric lanterns, the patterns of
their movement walking rhythms. "Radio ahead," said
Gow to a man in a Park Service uniform who came up to
him. "Let the paramedics know where to meet us. Call
the others in."

The man set off into the darkness at a noisy jog. Suddenly Gow stopped. "You don't come with us," he said to
Easter. He ordered Joe, "He's still out on the prairie
somewhere. We didn't see him."

"What difference does that make now?" Joe demanded.

"I don't want a lot of pictures of him."

Easter said nothing.

"You better let me take her," Gow told Joe.

But Joe made no move to surrender her. They stood
in a silent triangle. Once more battalions of lights were

converging. Gow sighed. He chopped the light at Easter. "You do what I said. Go on."

Joe shifted the warm weight in his arms and started walking again. Gow caught up. If Easter was still pacing them, Joe could not see him. "So you shot the kid," said Gow gruffly, talking as he walked.

"Yes."

"He make any sort of confession?"

"He said Easter was there with them when Amy Wells died."

Gow looked around sharply. "You believed him?"

"By that time all I believed was that I had to kill somebody."

"So what made you decide you were killing the right man?"

Gow's voice was not mean. If anything, it was pitying. But Joe did not know now why he had chosen to turn the gun on Hunter, and he had not known then, either. Finally he answered. "I just did the best I could."

"Well, let me relieve your mind," Gow assured him.

"You found something."

"After your second call, we sent men into your ex-wife's place. Tore it apart. Found more pictures. And some kind of writing. A diary, I guess you'd say."

"So he did confess?"

"The diary wasn't conclusive," said Gow grimly. "But the pictures are."

"And Easter?"

"Easter was after them. They were getting a bang out of playing mind games with him. One of them—your wife's kid, probably—came up with the idea of saying Easter was in on it if he ever caught up."

"What does Lee say?"

"*Lee* don't know nothing."

"Then why did he give me that bullet?"

"He says he barely knew the kid, except that he was bad news. Claims they had worked on his car some, that was all. Claims he had a bad feeling and tried and tried to warn his brother, but he couldn't get his brother to level with him. *He* denies ever trying to accuse Easter—"

"Bullshit."

"*He* says he was just trying to shift attention where he thought some of it ought to lie."

"But now he's backed off Easter?"

"Well," said Gow, smug for the first time, "since his brother's alibi's obviously no good, his don't look so healthy either. Even if you aren't guilty, it costs money to fight an accessory charge."

"But how can you keep Easter out of it when Shorter knows Wesley named him?"

"Shorter also thought from the start Wesley was lying. He signed that into a statement and now we've got evidence to back it up."

"Easter will have to testify."

"We can cover him. He went along with you because he was in love with the girl and wanted to save her."

"He is in love with her."

"Don't remind me."

"Cantrell and the undercover business, is that it?"

Gow nodded, pausing again to look back at him. They could not see each other's eyes, so the pact was not between men but between shadows. There was no sign of Easter. Joe said, "All right."

The stench of the burned cabin drifted toward them over the muck smell long before they reached the tree line. Gow led a growing procession of called-in searchers off the plain onto high ground under the rustling pines.

He and Joe had said no more. For Joe there was nothing to say. It *was* over. He was willing to admit he had done something foolish, even evil, but it hadn't felt evil. Over and over it had seemed to have a chance of leading somewhere beautiful and fine. With the death of that faith, something else had died, too, a whole universe of possibilities. He held her tightly because he knew when they took her away part of him would go along.

And the time when he would have to submit to that mutilation came quickly. Long before they reached the clearing, they found that the paramedics, alerted, had backed their ambulance down one of the buggy lanes; he and Gow came up on it before they ever saw where the cabin had stood. Joe was tired; he couldn't make out faces, details, in the milling, excited crowd that suddenly began to throng toward him. The paramedics dragged their stretcher forward. Cindy was awake then, if dazed, clinging to him. Gow stopped short, turning to face him; behind the sheriff materialized a pair of his indomitable deputies, their solid faces set. The paramedics, bland-faced strangers, came forward; impersonally, as if lopping off a tree branch, they removed her from his arms and took her away.

Gow was watching him worriedly. "Am I under arrest?" Joe asked.

"I don't know. You're not my responsibility."

"Then I guess I'm Orren's."

"I reckon so," conceded Gow, as if he wasn't any happier about it than Joe was. "We'll see soon enough." He jerked his chin brusquely. "He's right there."

Joe turned. Sure enough, Orren was approaching, lumbering his authoritative way down the trail from the prairie. He was leading a pack of figures, two of which, at least, Joe recognized. None of them had seen him. He would rather have waited, maybe forever, but putting it off was pointless. He started forward.

"Wait a minute, Hope," said Gow suddenly, reaching for his arm.

But Joe was thinking about what he would say to Orren, what he would defend, what he would confess. He felt Gow grab him, but, almost absently, shook the sheriff's hand off. The last thing he remembered was hearing Gow say, "Don't—"

All the rest of it, people told him about later. People

told him, as if it had happened to someone else, how he had walked blindly up to Orren, how he stopped dead in front of him, how Orren's jaw dropped and he blurted, "Joe!" He thought later he remembered that moment, seeing Orren's face. He knew later he did see Cindy's father, a thin replica of Orren, shoving forward past the bulwark of Orren's body. He knew he had seen him because he dreamed about his face, vehement and savage, as Orren said again, "Christ! Joe!"

Cindy's father stepped forward and hit him. People told him later it was Orren who pulled his brother off him. He did not know because that first blow sent him reeling; others followed it. Something roared and sprang up and swallowed him, and then the jaws closed, and he was gone.

40

HUBE LIKED FANCY HOTELS, AND SINCE
the department was paying for it, he picked one where,
when they moved in about four A.M. Friday morning, the
covers on the double beds in the big inner room had
been turned down and Godiva truffles, not mints, had
been placed reverently on the enormous pillows. They
had an outer parlor, with a kitchenette and overstuffed
chairs and a sofa that unfolded into a sleeper. The inner
room gave onto a roomy bathroom with a big tub with
whirlpool outlets. There was a balcony as well, facing the
parking lot, but the room was six stories up, too high to
jump.

Again Kaplan had flown down, but this time Joe
hadn't seen him. Hube had taken Joe's statement. He
told the truth as best he remembered it, leaving out only
Lee Meacham's allegations about Easter and Cantrell. If
Gow wanted Easter more thoroughly covered, let him see
to it. That was one debt Joe could not manage, and one
he was not entirely sure he owed.

Afterward he lay wide awake on his back, in pain, on
one of the beds in the inner room, while Hube and
Portman lurked in the sitting room, both wearing their

guns. Orren had told them, in Joe's hearing, that if he tried to get away again they had permission to shoot him. He did not believe Orren meant it, or that even Portman had taken it seriously, but he hoped he would not have to put it to the test. About nine o'clock in the morning, with sunlight cat-footing over the balcony, Hube came into the bedroom, shutting the door behind him, a hand out as if Joe might try to spring off the bed at him. "Don't talk to me. Just don't talk."

"What are you afraid I'll do? Ask you to understand it?"

"Just don't."

Hube fled into the bathroom. When he came out he shoved both hands at Joe, in one a plastic cup of water, and in the other a small red pill. "Take this."

"I don't want it."

"The doctor said it's for the bruises."

"They don't hurt."

"I'm going out," said Hube, less patiently, "and I'm leaving Portman here."

"And you don't trust him to stand guard over me unless you knock me out?"

Hube advanced, his sad gray eyes narrowed. Menace was not his calling. "Goddamn it, Joe," he sputtered. "What would you do with her? Fly off to—to Bora-Bora and live in a grass hut with her?"

"Hube, in the first place, it's not that simple."

"Of course it's that simple," said Hube, unashamedly bitter. "Assault. Kidnapping. Homicide. There is an edge, and you are damned near it. You are over it." He slapped the pill and glass down on the bureau. "Ten minutes. Then I'll be back . . . and I'll bring Portman in here with me to help hold you down."

"I want to see my friend Zack," Joe said. "At the *Herald.*"

Hube glanced at the closed door. "I don't know."

"Decide, then."

"I'll come back in ten minutes."

"You'll do it?"

"Will I get some peace out of it?"

"Yes, Hube. I promise."

Hube shut the door with uncharitable vigor. When he was alone Joe got stiffly off the bed. After he swallowed the pill, he let himself down again carefully. If Hube came back in again, he did not know it, because the pill, like a potent brother to forgiveness, instantly and effectively shut all knowledge out.

When he came to in the late afternoon, only Portman was on guard in the sitting room, reading the paper with sitcoms running. Joe found a saucepan in the kitchenette sink and a jar of instant coffee and Styrofoam cups on the counter. He was starting the water boiling when Portman flipped a section of the paper inside out assertively. "You know what's going to happen, don't you?" Portman said. "The shrinks'll take you back in a strait jacket. You'll either go to the loony bin or to jail."

Joe just lifted his shoulders without speaking and took the coffee back into the main bedroom. Once again Hube had transplanted his belongings for him. His accumulation of clothes had been laundered. All his money, all his credit cards, his identification, were gone.

On the other bed sat Hube's overnight bag, unzipped, as if to convey to him that this time there was nothing of importance in it; beside it, rubber-banded into a cylinder, was a thick manilla folder Joe did not remember having seen before. He picked it up. It was Hube's working file on the sinkhole killings, a new set of suspects but still so much ancient history. He took it into the bathroom and stared at the various ragged notes and transcripts and computer printouts as he lay in a tub of hot water, but finally he set it aside indifferently. He realized that the reason his eyes were blurring was that tears were welling up in them. He decided he was still hung over from the pill. Getting out of the bath, getting into the clean clothes, was an enormous effort. He did not see how Hube could have meant these soft sweet-smelling garments for him.

He went back out and made himself as comfortable across the room from Portman as his body would let him, taking pieces of the paper as Portman discarded them. Whether by his presence he was tormenting Portman or himself, he could not tell.

The brief lead article carried Zack's byline:

Hunter S. Jameson, 18, of Homestead, who is believed to have been involved in the April rape-murder of National Park Service employee Amy Wells, was gunned down last night in a west Dade shootout with a Florida Department of Law Enforcement officer who had formerly been married to Jameson's mother. Officials allege that Janet Jameson, who had witnessed her son's death, then seized the revolver that had fallen from his hand and took her own life.

The shootout came after Jameson had abducted a seventeen-year-old Windwood woman and led agents on a high-speed chase across Dade and Collier counties, during which his pursuers believed he had the young woman's body in his trunk. Officials allege that he had, in fact, left the young woman bound but unharmed on a Big Cypress National Preserve prairie; she subsequently freed herself and walked to safety. Her name is being withheld.

A handwritten document and photographs discovered in a search of the Jamesons' home clearly tie young Jameson to the Wells killing, but police say it may be months before they can determine whether or not Jameson actually committed the dozen or so other unsolved murders throughout the Collier-Dade area for which he claimed credit. Said a Collier Sheriff's Department spokesperson, "Most of those people were prostitutes and drifters. He might have read about them in the paper and fantasized that he killed them."

Joe took special notice of a line at the top of the inside continuation:

Wesley Meacham of Sweetwater, who with his brother, Lee, was convicted through Amy Wells's testimony of killing an endangered Florida panther, has confessed to participating with Jameson in her murder, but police are uncertain Meacham will be declared competent to testify. His brother denies all knowledge of the killings, and police refuse to say whether or not they will press charges. Jameson had enlisted his brother, Lee Meacham suggested, because Wesley "couldn't think much for himself and would do whatever he was told."

Neither Dave Kang's name nor Easter's appeared. But Joe did not think Gow had counted on Zack. Zack would not be content with speculation and silence for long.

Joe had retreated once more into the inner bedroom, Hube's file on his stomach, open but unread. The light coming in from the balcony had gone dusky. He heard the knock, then arguing voices. When he went out, absently dangling the folder from his fingers, Zack was posed in the open doorway, chortling, with his arms stuck high overhead. "Go on," he was saying to Portman. "Strip-search me. One of us might as well have some fun."

Seeing Joe, Portman slammed the door savagely. "I didn't tell Habin I agreed with this."

"Tell you what," said Zack with needling condescension. "We'll sit right here on the couch, and you can listen. You can take notes, you can even record us."

"I'm watching television."

"Turn it up, then. We won't talk loud."

But Portman just slumped across from them with his arms folded. Joe backed up to the couch, dropping the file on the cushion beside him. Zack folded his short legs and tucked his feet under him. "Okay, Geronimo. What have you got?"

"You've got it backwards," said Joe. "You tell me."

"I wasn't there."

"But you've got that part already, from Gow, who got it from Easter, who was."

Zack made a face. "That close-mouthed kid with the

eyes like a snake's asshole? The one who looks like he uses baby bunnies for target practice? Sure." He slapped his pockets as if searching for a pack of cigarettes he didn't find. "By the way, somehow he got into the hospital to see her."

"To see her? To her room?"

"I'm not sure. But I saw her old man giving him the bum's rush from her hall."

"But what about her? Is she really okay?"

Zack was smiling, not ungently. "Oh, she's okay. Scareder than she lets on. She'll probably be a lot more careful about the kindness of strangers. Anyway, they're supposed to release her this afternoon." Idly he fingered the folder on the sofa between them. "How did that kid get hold of her? Was she friends with him, too?"

"Dave Kang was the friend she cared about," said Joe wearily. "She thought the sheriff was trying to pin the murders on him, and she thought she could help him if she could find some evidence against Jimmy Easter. She had met Hunter by chance at the police station, and he knew I liked her. So when she asked him to take her up to Easter's cabin—"

Zack nodded, adding two and two. "It must have seemed to him like things were dropping right into his hands."

Portman flapped his legs across each other querulously. They both looked at him. "Doesn't he ever write anything down?" he demanded. Neither of them answered. "I understand there was some sort of diary," Joe said.

"I wouldn't call it a diary. More like a cross between a porno novel and Ted Bundy's death-house confession."

"You've read it?"

"A pirated Xerox copy."

"You said in your article he claims he killed a lot of people."

Zack hunched over his spread knees, fitting his broad, dingy fingers together. "So far the cops think he just imagined killing them, and made up stories about it. Sort of a mental dress rehearsal until Wesley turned him onto Amy."

"So they're both nailed on Amy?"

"Tighter'n a do-gooder's ass." Zack spread his hands doubtfully. "Nobody seems to know whether Wesley knew what he was getting into, or whether he just got carried along."

Joe realized abruptly Portman had turned the TV off. The room had become uncomfortably quiet. "And Hunter blamed it all on his mother."

"And you."

Joe was thinking about watching Janet shoot herself. It was not something he had let himself do so far. This time he made it past seeing her pick up the gun.

"Joe," said Zack very gently, "did you know that after you broke up with her, she tried to kill herself twice?"

"Who told you that?"

"They've got her records."

"She didn't try to kill herself while I was married to her."

"I'm not accusing you of anything." Across the room Portman was visibly concentrating. "It seems they took Hunter away from her three times. He was almost six before they finally let her keep him. But the shrinks say he couldn't possibly remember half the stuff he claims he does."

"That she tried to kill him."

"How did you know that?"

"He said it. She said it."

"Well, whether she did or not, finally it must've seemed like it was all okay again. They were back home and she loved him. He was a good boy. He passed for normal. Until Kevin Landry came along."

"What did he write about that in the diary?"

Zack gave him a direct look. "Not a word."

Joe could not picture that scene, seeing Janet pull

the trigger, because every time he got near it, he got the scenes all mixed up; he saw himself killing her, too.

"They found a neighbor," said Zack. "Well, actually, I found her. She says that for all her law-and-order mentality Janet had a quirk about seat belts. Never wore them. When they passed that state law, right off she got a ticket. So she started doing that trick with the shoulder harness, hooking it under the front seat so anybody looking would think she was wearing it. Theories abound." He held up a finger. "One: She killed Landry, and did the seat belt that way out of habit. Or she could have been doing the same thing the shrinks think Hunter was doing, trying to call attention to herself, begging somebody to stop her." Another finger. "Two: The kid killed him, and rigged the getaway car like that to drag her into it, or to send her a message. As it turned out, the cops kept it out of the paper about the seat belt, so she never knew about it, unless someone at the department told her."

"Then she tried to claim credit in a last-ditch effort to save him?"

"Or out of misplaced guilt."

"You think it *was* Landry she—they—were after?"

"Or you?" Zack supplied for him. "Or both? I hear Orren and Kaplan and Gow all think she—he—was just shooting wild. Going psycho. It didn't matter who or what got hit."

"Janet couldn't have gotten the car out into the swamp. Hunter could have."

Zack shrugged. "When people's brains are that scrambled, there's no limit to what they can manage." He frowned, scratching futilely at a stain on his jacket. "It's not so off the wall that she had to kill Landry—if he had somehow found out about Hunter. And by the way, her neighbor says she could shoot. That thirty-eight was hers."

"Any evidence Landry was abusing her?"

"I haven't heard. For that matter, the kid could have been abusing her." He gave up on the stain. "My question," he went on innocently, "which no one will answer, is whether or not that old Indian—Kang?—was sleeping with Cindy or with Amy Wells?"

Joe shook his head. "Somebody else will have to answer. I've done enough to hurt Dave Kang. It isn't fun any more."

Zack's eyes narrowed. "And the Bambi-killer?"

"He's a hunting guide."

"But if he was Cindy Cruse's favorite suspect—you said that yourself—what did everybody else think?"

"All I know," said Joe doggedly, "is what Gow thinks."

"The Meachams hate him."

"The Meachams were jealous of him. Easter was making too much money. From the looks of it, Hunter and Wesley were making themselves at home at Easter's cabin, and Easter hadn't caught them at it. Gow thinks Wesley wasn't so dumb he didn't get a kick out of it. He might even have planted the pictures there himself."

"You sound like you like this Indian."

"Shouldn't I?"

Zack thumbed through the file again. "I hear you had his gun."

"Did he make a statement? What did he say?"

"He said you didn't trust him with it."

"By that time I didn't know who the hell to trust."

Zack was studying the file, not him. "You know, when he told me to come up here, Hube didn't warn me you'd find the truth this hard to come by. What am I paying, a charity call?"

"I don't know any truth," Joe said, rubbing his eyes.

"So give me some untruth. I'll manage."

"Fine." Joe was suddenly bitter. "How about a recurring nightmare? That I killed all of them. I certainly sicced Hunter onto Sapia and the Miller girl. I even killed Amy Wells."

Zack looked pained. "That way lies madness," he warned.

"Your article wasn't the first one about the sinkhole case that mentioned me. Maybe Hunter had seen one of them, and knew I was investigating that sort of murder. Maybe that was why he killed her, so he'd have a murder to point to he knew would draw me."

"That's pure speculation."

"Yeah, I've been doing a lot of it."

"Joe." Zack spoke so forcefully that Joe had to look around and confront him. "The boy was out of control. He was crazy. He was going to kill somebody—you, his mother, some girl he picked up at school." He dropped his voice so low only Joe could hear it. "You're a cop. You've seen it. You know."

"What are you doing with that report?" Portman suddenly demanded. They both looked up to find his thin features blackening with disapproval. He got up, advancing on them.

"I thought it was yours," Zack said meekly to Joe.

"It's Habin's," said Portman, snatching up the file and taking it back across the room with him. "We don't need your help solving it."

"Where do you find diapers big enough?" Zack asked Joe.

"Look here," Portman flumped down in the big chair with the file beside him. "*I* ran down that jerk Shorter and searched the Meacham place, which believe me was a big risk, but I took it. *I* got a confession out of that Wesley Meacham, without which the Jameson kid's statement would have been just so much demented rambling. So you go to hell."

Now Zack stood up. Short, shapeless in his ill-fitting clothes, he looked as lethally unpredictable as a home-made bomb. He ventured close to Portman, pulling up almost between the young agent's spread knees. He threw his head back, sniffing mightily. "I knew I was smelling something. It's an odor I get on my feet when I walk in shit piles," said Zack, "and in my business I walk in a lot of them."

"Fuck off," said Portman, grabbing a part of the paper Joe had already seen him read.

But Zack reached down and tapped him on the knee. "I think it's called the odor of sanctity," Zack said.

Portman wriggled up without touching him, and wrenched the door open, standing there imperiously. Zack turned back to Joe. "I still say you owe me."

"Get in line."

"I'd send my collection agency, but I know you've got a conscience."

"Don't hold your breath for that," Portman said.

41

PORTMAN PRETENDED TO READ THE FILE
for about twenty minutes before he lost interest. Later,
when he got up to adjust the color on the TV, Joe took
the file back into the bedroom, meaning to put it back
with Hube's things. But he did not think he would be
doing any sleeping, so he lay down on his own bed and
tried again to read the first page.

It was deathly boring, the kind of exercise in drudgery
he had always hated, the kind of duty he had come more
and more in recent years to wish on someone else. This
time the someone else had been Terry. He had interviewed two of the women who had responded to the call
for information, the two who seemed to be describing the
same man. But their descriptions were vague, barely
sufficient for a tenuous composite. Joe thumbed
through the printed transcripts. Terry had built profiles
of the women themselves, their jobs, friends, contacts,
looking for some minuscule common factor. He had
found nothing. Joe could imagine his weary disgust as
he sat up late at night at a keyboard, pounding all the
nonsense out.

But an insatiable restlessness was coursing through

him, and he kept reading. About nine, Hube walked into the room. He was carrying his jacket, and Joe could see the drying rings under his arms where he had sweated. He looked irritable. He glared at Joe holding the file but didn't speak.

Joe plopped the file heavily onto Hube's bed. Hube turned away from him and fiddled in his shaving kit, then went into the bathroom. After he came out, Joe got up and went into the bathroom himself, closing the door solidly. He didn't come out until he heard the bedroom door slam. He had expected to find the file shut up in Hube's bag, but it still lay on the bed where he had put it. That it was still there seemed like a gesture common sense told him not to interpret, but he did.

Hube was begging him to say it: Forgive me. I accept the punishment. I concede to the tedium of ordinary mortals. To the soul-stifling routine of slogging through a lifetime of boredom and tripe. Just let me back in the club.

So what price absolution? How many years of cleaning ashtrays and tearing the edges off computer paper? Whatever he ended up doing, it would not be that.

Around ten-thirty Portman opened the door and coughed. "There's a pizza out here if you want some." Joe, who was lying on the bed again, didn't stir right away, but he said, "Thanks."

It was a Domino's, still warm and quite good. Portman had pulled the mattress off the sofa bed and was making himself a pallet up against the door, where anyone coming in or out during the night would be sure to wake him. "Is Hube coming back soon?" Joe asked.

"I doubt it. He's probably trying to stack up points with Cruse in case Kaplan cans him."

"Why would Kaplan do that? Hube hasn't done anything."

Portman punched a pillow and tossed it down on the

bed. "He lost you yesterday. And believe me, I warned him."

"Kaplan couldn't fire Hube for that."

Portman straightened, hands on his hips. "So maybe he'll just request a transfer."

"He likes Tampa."

Portman pursed his lips and gave his prissy shrug. "Oh, well."

Joe threw down the unfinished slice of pizza and went back into the bedroom. He stood over Hube's bed looking down at the closed file for a long time. Then he picked up the sheaf drearily, carried it to the small table by the balcony, clicked on the floor lamp, and sat down, propping his jaws in his hands.

He was still reading two hours later when he heard yet another eruption from the outer room. This time, though he recognized the voice, he didn't get up. He waited. The bedroom door burst open and Orren barged in. Portman, working his shirttail into his trousers, was trying to squeeze in after him, but Orren slammed the door in his face. "She's gone."

"What?"

"That goddamn Indian. Goddamn it, Joe." He kicked a chair leg. "This has gone far enough."

Joe realized that his friend was not looking at him, or at least not focusing, and he was thankful. Although he had sat in this prison nearly twenty-four hours trying to argue himself into apathy, all the air had gone out of his chest at Orren's revelation. Orren would see it on his face if he looked for it. "I assume you mean Easter."

"It's goddamn kidnapping. We'll fucking hang him." He was pacing the width of the room, spitting expletives. "Right out of my house with all of us there! Who does he fucking think he is?"

Joe closed the folder and pushed it away from him. He sat a second, until he felt his breath cool. "So what are you and her father going to do with her when you catch her this time?" he said almost placidly. "Aren't convents a little out of date?"

Orren stopped moving. Joe had never seen him stand quite so still. "I thought you had learned something."

"Yeah, I did."

"That you can't stay a kid. Or go back to being one."

"No, that I'm a coward," Joe said.

Orren bent forward, bracing white-knuckled hands on the table, so violently it rocked. "At this rate she is going to get killed, isn't she? And you don't even care."

"Maybe *she* doesn't."

"She will when it happens." Orren's voice hardened. "So will we all."

Joe said nothing. Orren waited, his face flushed, the cores of his black eyes lit by the hot glitter around them. Then he brought a clenched fist down.

"*You* ran around with that Indian," he half shouted. "*You* know where he might have taken her. *You* saved her the first time, as much as anybody, by catching up to that kid before he could hurt her." His voice dropped, depleted. "I forgave you a lot for that." He leaned over Joe, his weight once more shifting the table. "But now it's started all over again. It's come back to you. You've got to save her. Or I'll fucking know why not."

Joe looked up at him, at the bristling eyebrows, the trembling black mustache, the rough but honest features that broadcast Orren's feelings like a clearly printed map. Orren raised a hand, and again Joe saw his fist clench. He managed not to move. "My brother didn't hit you hard enough," Orren said.

But he wheeled without striking, almost losing his balance. At the door he stopped. Despite his ferocity, the look he threw back hung between a threat and a plea.

Joe heard himself let his breath out. "Which direction do you think he took her?"

"He ditched his truck out on the Alley."

"Yeah, he'd be smart enough to do that."

"You like that fucker."

"Not exactly."

"Then you'll help."

Joe moved his hands. "I'm not sure what I can do. I didn't learn that much about him."

"Well, think what you did learn," ordered Orren. "Come up with something." He opened the door. Portman was hanging around just beyond it. Orren shut it again. "It's *your* only chance," he hissed. Then he snatched the door open. Joe saw Portman scramble out of his way as Orren barreled through.

Joe went to the glass door leading to the balcony, bracing on the metal frame. The door was shut against the summer night, but he could see out across the parking lot, across the lights of Miami. Out there somewhere was the sea, and the dark edge of reason, toward which others sailed bravely, in search of new worlds. No, he must not tell Orren what he felt or was thinking, that the tremor, the excitement building in him since the revelation, was no longer quite pain.

The night slowly clicked around to three A.M. Part of the time he spent reading. Part of it he spent thinking, drumming his fingers on the table, slowly at first, then with a growing frenzy. Part of it he spent with his eyes closed, listening to the blood churn through his veins, and wondering how you could tell when a person has finally gone insane.

A very few seconds, just before three, he spent listening in the open door between the two darkened rooms, realizing that Portman had made a small mistake when he decided to sleep on the mattress by the door: He had distanced himself from the phone. So all Joe had to do was slip over, unplug the phone from the jack, and carry it back with him, attaching it to a second jack he had found behind the night table. Nailing Zack was harder; all he got at his home number was his machine. He didn't leave a message. He made himself sit down on the bed, the open file beside him, and timed himself, allowing ten minutes. He would keep trying the apartment for an hour, then call the paper. But this time Zack answered drowsily. When he heard Joe's voice he woke up fast. "So you do have a conscience. I knew my man."

"Shut up and listen," said Joe curtly. "I've spent the last four hours reading that report of Hube's. I've read a hundred pages of interviews and another twenty-five of absolutely random facts and gossip."

"Good for you," Zack yawned. "Should I cheer?"

"You can break the sinkhole case."

"You're crazy."

"Try me."

There was a silence. "I'm listening."

"I want a deal."

"Gee. Next time try to surprise me."

Joe lowered his voice still more. "Easter's run off with Cindy."

"I know. Orren thought he was keeping it quiet, but with me around, that's a joke."

"Orren told me I could find her. I can't, not from here. But you can."

"Of course I can," bragged Zack blithely. "So? We turning her in?"

"I don't know yet. I just want to know where they've gone, and how close the cops are to finding them."

"And that's all?"

"For the moment."

"You better have something."

"Don't worry. Just don't waste time. I'll call you back at five. At the paper?"

"All right." Zack had regained his good humor. "And calm down. Piece of cake. I swear."

· · ·

He was true to his word, and picked up on his private line when Joe dialed it at five. "Like I said, piece of cake. Now pay up."

"Where are they?"

"What did I just say? Are you afflicted?"

"For a flash like this I expect to see some effort," Joe answered tersely. "Something that's not a piece of cake."

"You're pushing."

"No, I'm presuming on friendship. Portman could wake up any minute. Where?"

Zack sighed. But he loved showing off. "One of my airport contacts says that about an hour ago a man answering Easter's description came in and bought two tickets on Qantas for Rio. Called himself Tommy Cypress, since Easter can't really pretend he isn't Indian. First flight they could get was at eight, so they're holed up at the airport or somewhere near it, waiting. My friend thinks in another half hour, he'll know where." He paused a meaningful second. "And if you deliver, I might tell you."

Joe didn't return the banter. "What about the cops?"

"They started off concentrating on the preserve, out the Trail and the Alley, with all Easter's relatives. So they've lost time. But from the sound of the scanner, they're running out of the most obvious options. Someone'll tip them off to those tickets before too long."

Joe gathered himself. Now for the challenge. "Zack, how much do you really trust me?"

Of course Zack fell silent. Then he groaned.

"Or should I say," Joe persisted, "how much do you want this story?"

"You do *have* a story?"

Joe pushed on. "I want you to buy two tickets to Orlando. Preferably an earlier flight than theirs. Then I want you to come pick me up here."

"Joe . . . they haven't by any chance charged you with anything since my last information?"

"No."

"Then what about Portman?"

"Let me worry about Portman."

Zack made a choking noise. "You better be damn sure about this."

"I am," Joe lied.

"You wouldn't lie."

"No."

"I'm not sure how long it'll take."

"The sooner the better. Drive under the balcony window. I'll be watching."

"Hell of a friendship," said Zack, hanging up.

It was six-thirty, full daylight, before Zack pulled up to the curb in the lot below. When Joe walked into the outer room carrying his bag with the clean clothes in it, Portman was in the bathroom shaving, though he had left the door open. He ran out with lather dripping, brandishing his disposable razor. "That piece of plastic won't do it," Joe told him. "You need your gun." Then Portman had to run back into the bathroom after his gun, which he had apparently left hanging on a hook while he dressed. By the time he reemerged, Joe was halfway to the staircase. The hotel was one of those with the huge multistoried atrium lobbies surrounded by balconies dripping ivy; the staircase was public, exposed. At first Joe thought Portman might actually start shooting, but when he looked back, Portman was using both hands to button a shirt around him; his hair stood straight up and his feet were white and bare. "Stop that man!" he was shouting. "I'm a police officer!" But the few people eating breakfast in the open-air restaurant in the lobby only stared up at him and raised brows at each other as if wondering why they hadn't been told someone was filming a movie. One older man did head for the side entrance to intercept Joe, but Joe thought he looked relieved when he couldn't quite get there in time.

Zack had the Z at the curb with the engine running.

Joe climbed in, Zack let go a couple of backfires, and off they drove. Joe saw Portman burst out of the door behind them with the gun in his hand.

"Okay," said Zack sternly. "Talk."

"Did you find them?"

"Your meter's run out. Pay on account."

He unzipped the bag and took out the sinkhole file, while Zack goaded the Z up to sixty, changing lanes. "Two women," he began briskly, "who reported being approached in rest areas gave a description that might have been of the same guy."

"I know that. Every reporter and every cop, on both sides of the state, knows that."

"Neither of them came up with so much as a tag number, but he's the one the department's been concentrating on. They've done everything up to and including hypnosis to help these women remember the guy." He flipped pages while Zack drove with one hand and fiddled with the outside mirror with the other. "One was at the Gainesville rest area, the other one was at the next one up, closer to Lake City. But listen. The one who was approached in Gainesville—remember what she said?"

Zack did not have to think long. "She said just when she started getting worried, some people drove up and the guy backed off."

"Right. And she happened to look after him, and she saw him getting into a car she said was 'some kind of cheap Ford with dents all over it,' and even though it was hard to be sure under those lights, she thought it was light blue."

"Okay," said Zack guardedly.

"Later there was another report. Remember? From the one who claimed she'd been approached by a woman?"

"Sure," said Zack, "but that was—" He didn't finish.

"Yeah, they discounted her. I don't think anybody's even read this transcript. The edges of the pages haven't even been thumbed. But listen." He read. " 'She wanted me to get in her car for her and try the ignition while she did something under the hood. But the car she wanted me to get in—' this was in the Gainesville stop, remember? '—was all the way down the hill by itself in the dark and I had just been to the bank and I had a lot of cash in my purse and something told me not to go down there. So I lied and told her my husband was in the men's room and if she'd wait I'd go call him. I went back and got in my car and locked the door. When I looked for her again I couldn't see her. When I drove by the car on my way out, I thought I saw somebody sit up in the backseat when I passed. I couldn't be sure, but I didn't think it was the woman, I thought it was a man.' "

"But that's not—" Zack stopped again.

"She says, 'I noticed the license number because the whole thing made me feel funny. It was a silver or gray Mercury. It was pretty beat up.' "

"Joe, that's—"

"Quit interrupting."

"I haven't been interrupting. I've been trying to intersperse logic."

"They made the number. This woman's lived four places in the last twelve months. The next to the next to the last place she lived was in something called the Bivens Arm Apartments."

Zack was silent for a long minute. "It would be more to the point," he said at last, rushing up to tailgate a cab that had cut in front of him, "if she had given her apartment number as eleven twenty-four."

"Her apartment number was C-eight. But it seems just barely possible to me that the Bivens Arm Apartments might have a street address."

Again Zack fell silent. Then he asked, "And this is all you've got?"

"It's enough."

"It is not."

"I want you to find Hube, Zack."

"Why don't I just call Tampa?"

"I would rather Hube had it."

Zack always had a tendency to swerve as he drove, and the tension of his grip exacerbated it. "I've broken the law for you. What if Hube won't listen? In fact, why should he listen?"

"Zack . . . aren't the state phone books on line in your office?"

Even though the car was still moving, Zack turned to him full face.

"Stop and call," Joe said.

"If you're wrong," said Zack, "I'm taking you back and turning you in."

"All right," Joe said.

At the airport planes were coming and going in all directions like mutant mosquitoes. Now Zack was excited. Joe could see that he was in a hurry to be rid of him. He said, "I don't like the idea of you doing this, Joe."

"It's my neck."

"Joe, I think you know what you're running from, but not what you're running toward."

"Then it's a good thing you're not coming with me."

"Don't be a son of a bitch. I'm helping you. But I'm worried. You think you're going to take her away from that Easter." He shook his unkempt head grimly. "But she doesn't love you. She doesn't love anybody. Even I can see that."

"Have you ever met her?"

"No, but—"

"Then shut up about her."

Zack drummed on the steering wheel impatiently, but did not pull off.

"Listen," said Joe. "I don't know what I'll do. I may not do anything."

"You'll have to kill that Indian," Zack said.

Joe did not confess that it was a possibility he had considered.

Zack gunned the rattling engine. "Well, you got more guts than I do. Or else you're crazier."

"Crazier," said Joe.

It was Saturday, so the airport could have been a lot busier than it was. Still, the ticketing area, before which Zack had dropped him, was crowded, people jostling in and out of the coffee shops and newsstands. A good three quarters of them were Hispanic. He wished he knew for sure that the image he carried of Cindy's father was not just a dream.

He had told Zack the truth. He did not know why he had done this, nor what he was about to do. That it was an escape he was certain, but as Zack had said, an escape to what? Maybe he had only partly believed what he had told Orren, that the only one who could ever judge a choice was the one who dared to live it. Fear was part of the price.

Zack's informant had indeed found them, sitting in a car, either borrowed or stolen, in the parking garage. The contact had not stood guard over them, but had unobtrusively checked on them twice. But the informant had called back on Zack's car phone a second time with more news—Orren's office had picked up on the tickets. Orren and his brother were on their way.

"Got the troops with them?" Zack had demanded. The answer was no. They didn't want a commotion; they would rely on airport security. But Zack was smirking as he hung up. Joe had a feeling that sooner or later Orren would get a commotion whether he wanted it or not.

Now, pushing through the crowd, Joe did not know if the two brothers were ahead of him or behind him. But he saw no sign of them as he stashed his bag in a locker. If things got desperate, he might have to leave it, but there was nothing in it he wanted to be carrying when he and Easter met.

That, at least, he knew he must make happen. Orren,

Hube, Zack, would have told him it was asinine thinking he had to prove himself as much a man as Easter. But whatever he chose to do, fight for her or surrender, he had to know why.

He still thought, too, though he could only just admit it, that when he saw her something decisive would happen. A voice in him kept arguing that she had gone with Easter simply because he had offered her freedom, because he was the one who had managed to get to her first. The conviction grew as he made his way to the parking garage elevators: He would see her, and be sure.

No one got in the elevator with him. Good, he found himself thinking, no witnesses. The door slid shut. Looking out the narrowing crack, he caught his breath. That was when he knew the face he remembered had not been a dream. Orren's brother, so much like him, had turned from a magazine stand and seemed to be looking right at him.

The elevator began its smooth climb upward. Cruse's glance had been brief, accidental. How well had he seen Joe Thursday night in the dark? Joe had no way of knowing. Had the elevator door closed in time?

Oddly, the panic that should have followed his dismay did not come. He felt instead a fatalistic, stomach-churning surge of elation, like the first terrific drop of a long downward plunge on a roller coaster. For the first time, clearly, consciously, he thought back to the moment when he had pulled the trigger on Easter's rifle. When he had taken a chance the way he used to, and had taken the possibility of being wrong along with it. Had he not done so, Hunter would have killed them all.

And for the first time, the courage he had found in that moment seemed really part of him. For the first time he was sure that whatever he had to do, he would have no trouble seeing it through.

. . .

The fourth level of the parking lot, as he had hoped, was cool and quiet, empty except for the shining rows of cars. Follow the ramp up to the first turn, Zack's stooge had told them. Look for an old green station wagon, an old Chevrolet.

The top of the ramp was poorly lit and shadowy, but his urgency sharpened his senses: He stood there a moment blinking, and then made out the car with its owlish taillights, pulled in next to the concrete columns supporting the turn to the next level. As he approached quietly, he could make out the blur of someone sitting in it, though he couldn't quite distinguish figures or silhouettes.

He spared a sardonic moment to hope they weren't doing anything they wouldn't want interrupted. After all, it was less than an hour until their flight. Less than half an hour until his, until the flight for which he had two tickets in his pocket. That flight would soon be boarding. He let his footsteps clatter as he drew closer. The hell with it if they heard.

Would Easter have a gun? Probably. Would he use it? Quite possibly. And what would happen if he did was one of the things Joe had come to find out.

But when he drew even with the car, and the door opened, it wasn't Easter who got out to confront him. It was Cindy, alone.

She was wearing white, a pleated cotton dress that looked luminescent in the shadows, as if she had sucked up all the hope in that echoing place and it had made her shine. Her dark face, stark and beautiful, looked famished; her depthless eyes found his. They were wide, black-centered, more than a little frightened. But they told him nothing, not what she wanted or what she was frightened of.

"I guess I knew you would come," she said.

He had thought the sight of her would move him to affection or tenderness, but it hadn't. Maybe those things had never been what either of them wanted after all. In any case he knew now it wasn't a gesture of love his imprisonment and escape had prepared him to carry out. He looked around, down the ramp, then up, past the column to the hairpin turn to the next level. "Where is he?" he asked.

"He's gone to see if the flight is on time." She spoke matter-of-factly. She couldn't help knowing how tautly he was strung, but she didn't flinch.

"Your father and uncle are in the airport," he told her. "By now they've probably nailed him."

She shook her head, perfectly serious. "He won't let them," she said.

He kicked the Chevrolet's bald tire harshly. "Where did he steal it?"

"He didn't. It's his brother's."

"Is that what he told you?"

"Oh, what does it matter, Joe?"

His nerves began to quicken. He began to listen for approaching cars, people looking for parking places, interfering. He began to be sure her father had recognized him, was even now searching the other garage levels, summoning security guards. He had come to deliver a blow, not an explanation. He pivoted away from her, then back again, this time startling her a little, because she took a step away from him. "You can't go with him."

"Of course I can."

"You don't love him. He was just lucky." She didn't react at all, just let her gaze drift, as if she barely heard him speaking. "Listen to me, goddamn it. What would you have done if I had offered this to you first?"

But now she actively dodged him, hiding. "I don't know."

"You *do* know," he said.

She looked up, too squarely, as if she sensed how well he could read her, and had given up hope of keeping him out.

"All right," she said plainly. "Yes, I do."

It wasn't that he had never expected to hear it. It was

just that he had never expected to believe it, without question, on her word alone.

"I just don't think you could do it," she whispered. "You would always be asking . . . if you should have. I couldn't bear that."

If she had just met him with the violence and defiance he had come to expect of her, he might have been ready for her. Instead she had turned him aside with a new and fatal dignity. She was not the same person who had made him so angry on Thursday. Now she was the person who had walked into the storm and paid the price and then walked out of it again. He, and her uncle, and her father, might say she was foolish, but none of them could ever say again that she did not know or understand.

Once more he wheeled away, and then back. She seemed to cast around in the silence, as if looking for words to supply him. Finally she shrugged, simply and expressively. "You'll be happier. You would never be able to trust me."

"Can *he* trust you?"

She smiled then, as if at a secret. "I'm not sure he cares."

From around the turn to the next level came a scrape, leather on cement, and Joe looked up. Easter stood there, watching. He wore his black T-shirt and down-at-the-heels cowboy boots, and slouched with his thumbs hooked in the pockets of his stovepipe jeans.

"Get the hell out of here," he said to Joe almost serenely. Whatever camaraderie had ever grown up between them had faded. "Leave us the fuck alone."

This was the moment Joe had come primed for. Easter's disdain was so absolute and his own helplessness so taken-for-granted. Suddenly it all seemed absurdly simple.

"They know where you're going," said Joe, "and they're waiting. Show your face at that gate, and they'll grab you." He turned to Cindy. "I've got tickets on another flight they don't know about. You can still get away. With me."

For a moment no one spoke. Cindy touched a hand to her face, as if even she was not certain what her features were saying. Easter opened the car door on the driver's side, tilting his chin imperiously. "The hell with you."

"They'll put you in prison," Joe said brutally. "They'll charge you with Cantrell's murder. They'll send you to the chair."

Easter never moved. But something seemed to jerk the hide of his face tight against his angular bones.

Suddenly Cindy plunged forward, slashing with her nails, pummeling with her fists. What she meant to do he wasn't sure. Rip the tickets from him? He caught her wrist and spun her around, dragging her to his chest.

Easter started forward. Joe wrapped an arm around Cindy's windpipe. He could have broken her neck with a snap and he saw Easter think it. But before either of them could act there was a metallic whine below them. The elevator door had opened and Cindy's father had emerged. For a moment he didn't see them in the shadows above him. He stood with his feet spread, glancing left and right.

Joe felt Cindy's pulse jump at the sight of him. There was a second, an instant of decision, in which time seemed to wind down like a voice on a ruined record, in which Cindy drew in breath to scream but didn't, in which Easter seemed frozen and Cruse seemed caught in the motion of turning his head. And Joe's heart hissed like the heart of a stranger, *just one step. One step out of sight behind the column. Cruse will grab Easter, they'll stop each other. You can make her go with you. By the time her father gets past Easter, you'll be gone.*

She would have no choice then but him. For that second he saw unreel before him the scene between them— how he would make her love him, force his victory on her, mind and body, when he got her alone. He felt himself take that first step, dragging her with him. She began to struggle, daring him to hurt her. *You goddamned little bitch,* he heard his heart hiss.

In the next instant he had hurled her at Easter, renouncing not her but the part of him that would have gladly pulled them both to their deaths.

Easter caught her; she staggered, recovered. Suddenly the place echoed with Cruse's bellow. "Cindy! Let her go! Goddamn you! Stop!"

What did it matter? They weren't going anywhere, either. Wherever he ended up, they would end up someplace worse. Easter would go to the chair.

And that moment passed so fast he was not even aware of it until much later, the moment when he realized that even if he had no stomach for the plunge, it lay in his power to take away their one slim chance of making it, or to give that chance to them, sadly, but as a gift.

He pulled out his tickets. His watch said seven-thirty. "Take them," he said to Easter. "It leaves in ten minutes. It'll be boarding. Go."

Cruse had bounded toward them. His footsteps on the concrete boomed.

"For God's sake, hurry," Joe pleaded. "Go."

Easter took the tickets. He said no word of thanks. Cindy looked back once at Joe, once at her father. Joe thought her mouth moved, but if she spoke he couldn't hear it. Then Easter was hurrying her, rushing her away.

"Cindy!" screamed Cruse. "Listen to me, I'm your father! Stop!"

But they were gone then, scampering around the end of the ramp and up the other side. Cruse came rushing toward him, dodging, but Joe stepped in front of him. Blocked, Orren's brother faltered. "You bastard," he gasped.

There was not much Joe could answer. He shrugged.

"Out of my way," her father ordered hotly, shouldering forward.

"I think I owe you something," Joe said calmly.

And welcomed the hard, raw pain as bone met bone.

Epilogue

HE PUSHED OPEN THE THICK BLANK door slowly. The blinds in Kaplan's office were closed, so the room was dim. The shade made it seem cooler than it really was. He had known pretty much what to expect, so he was not surprised that it was not Kaplan sitting at the big desk with his back to the drawn blinds, but Hube. And as he had expected, Hube was finding it hard to meet his gaze disinterestedly, though he made himself. "Take a seat, Joe."

Joe obeyed. He used up some time fiddling with his tie. The badge in its leather folder sat on the desk in front of Hube's clasped hands.

"So they haven't got your name on the door yet?" Joe asked.

"No." Hube shrugged with his characteristic calm resignation. "It was misspelled the first time. They'll get it done soon."

Joe fiddled some more. After a moment, Hube pulled a thick black binder out of a drawer and let it drop onto the desk.

"The sinkhole case file?" Joe asked.

"Yeah, the last part of it. Thought you might like to

read the Waller woman's deposition. And about when Juan and Terry picked this guy Phillips up."

He slid the binder to Joe, who flipped open the cover, shut it again, and left the binder on the desk.

"Sad case," said Hube. "She claimed it was the only time she helped him, but Terry thinks that's garbage. He thinks she'd have done anything for Phillips, even though he'd dumped her. The funny thing is, she's not dumb. She's really pretty bright."

He was shaking his gray head. He always felt people's personal tragedies. It had sometimes made police work hard for him, but it would make him a good SAS.

"So how many did Phillips kill?" Joe asked.

"Don't know yet. Maybe dozens. They're still verifying. He showed us one of the places where he dumped their clothes and stuff. Solution hole up on the edge of Payne's Prairie, south of Gainesville. So far they've tied him definitely to twenty-one . . . countrywide."

"Yeah, I read Zack's article."

"Zack." Hube shook his head again, more gently. "That bird never lets up."

But the article had been interesting. It had pointed out the irony, that the man whose crimes had first come to light because of a collapsing sinkhole had lived near, and used as a disposal site, one of the largest sinkholes in the world. A series of collapses over eons, Zack had written, limestone ceilings caving in, turning an upland into a long, deep, flat depression where, in the 1890s, steamboats had plied a lake. Then, in the course of a week, without warning, something had lurched deep in the ground and all the water had run out, down into possibly endless caverns, leaving the steamboats sitting. Bivens Arm, on the bluff within Gainesville, site of a little urban park, was one of the last places there was any water standing. Hube was shifting some litter on his desk, shoving to one corner a paperweight, an empty picture frame, Joe recognized as Kaplan's. "Kaplan send you a postcard from Tallahassee?" Joe asked.

"No postcards," grumbled Hube. "Memos." He pulled open another drawer, this one empty. "You can see I haven't hung onto any of them. I hope they give him something else to do up there real fast."

"They will."

Hube shut the drawer with finality. He looked up again. His gaze was miserable. "I guess there's no point in putting it off any longer, huh?"

"Let's just consider as much as possible said already."

"No," insisted Hube. "I'm going to say thank you. Thank you."

"You're welcome."

"I'm sure Kaplan would thank you, too, for his promotion, if he had to."

"Well, he won't."

"So," Hube went on, more cheerfully. "Going to take up with those environmental crackpots? Run around down there in the swamp like a wild Indian?"

"That's not quite how the job description put it."

"Sounds great, though, doesn't it? No laws. Nobody breathing down your neck. Nobody telling you what to do."

"I doubt it would be that simple."

"But you'd probably like it," said Hube.

He didn't quite manage to make it sound as if he didn't mean it. He toyed with the badge, flipping it open to Joe's picture and shutting it again. Joe put his hands in his pockets and said nothing. "Whereas, of course, we would have some conditions," said Hube.

"I know."

"Not that you'd be hobbled forever. Just a little closer supervision."

"Yes, I know."

"I can't run renegades out of here, Joe."

"Maybe you should just say what you mean," Joe gently urged.

"I just don't think I'll ever quite forgive you," Hube

said bluntly. "And I'll never get it out of my mind something like it could happen again."

"Yeah," said Joe, drawing his feet under him and straightening. "I guess it could."

"It's a lot harder for guys like you than for guys like me," said Hube, for the first time letting the weeks of stored resentment edge into his tone. "I know what I am. So did Kaplan. Being reminded of it every day just isn't that tough for us. But for some people it's hard. They always think there's got to be more to it, somewhere else."

Joe stood up. Hube took his hands off the badge and folded them over his stomach.

"Yeah, it would be easier for both of us if I took that job, wouldn't it?" Joe said.

"You'll probably like it down there."

"Thanks for being honest."

Hube seemed as uncomfortable with Joe's thanks as Joe had been with his. He didn't stand up, but slumped in his chair a little, chin ducked. Joe went to the door. He stopped with his hand on the knob and rubbed his neck. Then Hube sat forward and looked across at him, fingers building a little chapel on the desk before him. He didn't flinch but he did seem to shudder as Joe walked back across and picked the badge up.

"You're sure?" Hube asked him.

"No."

Hube made a little gesture of defeat and turned away. Joe went out, putting the badge in his pocket, wishing he could reassure him. But it was hard, when he didn't know himself whether he had just been a coward, or very brave.